PENGUIN BOOKS

The Whisper Man

Alex North was born in Leeds, where he now lives with his wife and son. He studied Philosophy at Leeds University, and prior to becoming a writer he worked there in their sociology department.

D1512911

The Whisper Man

ALEX NORTH

PENGUIN BOOKS

PENGUIN BOOKS

UK | USA | Canada | Ireland | Australia
India | New Zealand | South Africa

Penguin Books is part of the Penguin Random House group of companies
whose addresses can be found at global.penguinrandomhouse.com.

First published by Michael Joseph 2019
This edition published by Penguin Books 2019

002

Set in 12.02/14.33 pt Garamond MT Std
Typeset by Jouve (UK), Milton Keynes
Printed and bound in Great Britain by Clays Ltd, Elcograf S.p.A.

A CIP catalogue record for this book is available from the British Library

ISBN: 978-1-40594-708-4

www.greenpenguin.co.uk

Penguin Random House is committed to a
sustainable future for our business, our readers
and our planet. This book is made from Forest
Stewardship Council® certified paper.

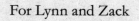
For Lynn and Zack

Jake.

There is so much I want to tell you, but we've always found it hard to talk to each other, haven't we?

So I'll have to write to you instead.

I remember when Rebecca and I first brought you home from hospital. It was dark and it was snowing, and I'd never driven so carefully in my life. You were two days old and strapped in a carrier in the back seat, Rebecca dozing beside you, and every now and then I'd look in the rear-view mirror to check you were safe.

Because you know what? I was *absolutely fucking terrified*. I grew up as an only child, completely unused to babies, and yet there I was – responsible for one of my own. You were so impossibly small and vulnerable, and me so unprepared, that it seemed ludicrous they'd allowed you out of the hospital with me. From the very beginning, we didn't fit, you and I. Rebecca held you easily and naturally, as though she'd been born to you rather than the other way around, whereas I always felt awkward, scared of this fragile weight in my arms and unable to tell what you wanted when you cried. I didn't understand you at all.

That never changed.

When you were a little older, Rebecca told me it was because you and I were so alike, but I don't know if that's true. I hope it isn't. I'd always have wanted better for you than that.

But regardless, we can't talk to each other, which means

I'll have to try to write all this down instead. The truth about everything that happened in Featherbank.

Mister Night. The boy in the floor. The butterflies. The little girl with the strange dress.

And the Whisper Man of course.

It's not going to be easy, and I need to start with an apology. Over the years, I told you so many times that there was nothing to be afraid of. That there was no such thing as monsters.

I'm sorry that I lied.

PART ONE
July

One

The abduction of a child by a stranger is every parent's worst nightmare. But statistically, it is a highly unusual event. Children are actually most at risk of harm and abuse from a family member behind closed doors, and while the outside world might seem threatening, the truth is that most strangers are decent people, whereas the home is often the most dangerous place of all.

The man stalking six-year-old Neil Spencer across the waste ground understood that only too well.

Moving quietly, parallel to Neil behind a line of bushes, he kept a constant watch on the boy. Neil was walking slowly, unaware of the danger he was in. Occasionally, he kicked at the dusty ground, throwing up chalky white mist around his trainers. The man, treading far more carefully, could hear the *scuff* each time. And he made no sound at all.

It was a warm evening. The sun had been beating down hard and unrestrained for most of the day, but it was six o'clock now and the sky was hazier. The temperature had dropped and the air had a golden hue to it. It was the sort of evening where you might sit out on the patio, perhaps sipping cold white wine and watching the sun set, without thinking about fetching a coat until it was dark and too late to bother.

Even the waste ground was beautiful, bathed in the amber light. It was a patch of shrub land, edging the village of Featherbank on one side, with an old disused quarry on the other. The undulating ground was mostly parched and dead, although bushes grew in tough thickets here and there, lending the area a maze-like quality. The village children played here sometimes, although it was not particularly safe. Over the years, many of them had been tempted to clamber down into the quarry, where the steep sides were prone to crumble away. The council put up fences and signs, but the local consensus was that they should do more. Children found ways over fences, after all.

They had a habit of ignoring warning signs.

The man knew a lot about Neil Spencer. He had studied the boy and his family carefully, like a project. The boy performed poorly at school, both academically and socially, and was well behind his peers in reading, writing and maths. His clothes were mostly hand-me-downs. In his manner, he seemed a little too grown-up for his age – already displaying anger and resentment towards the world. In a few years, he would be perceived as a bully and a troublemaker, but for now he was still young enough for people to forgive his more disruptive behaviour. 'He doesn't mean it,' they would say. 'It's not his fault.' It had not yet reached the point where Neil was considered solely responsible for his actions, and so people were forced instead to look elsewhere.

The man had looked. It wasn't hard to see.

Neil had spent today at his father's house. His mother and father were separated, which the man considered a good thing. Both parents were alcoholics, functioning to wavering degrees. Both found life considerably easier when their son was at the other's house, and both struggled to entertain him when he was with them. In general, Neil was left to occupy and fend for himself, which obviously went some way to explaining the hardness the man had seen developing in the boy. Neil was an afterthought in his parents' lives. Certainly, he was not loved.

Not for the first time, Neil's father had been too drunk that evening to drive him back to his mother's house, and apparently also too lazy to walk with him. The boy was nearly seven, his father probably reasoned, and had been fine alone all day. And so Neil was walking home by himself.

He had no idea yet that he would be going to a very different home. The man thought about the room he had prepared and tried to suppress the excitement he felt.

Halfway across the waste ground, Neil stopped.

The man stopped close by, then peered through the brambles to see what had caught the boy's attention.

An old television had been dumped against one of the bushes, its grey screen bulging but intact. The man watched as Neil gave it an exploratory nudge with his foot, but it was too heavy to move. The thing must have looked like something out of another age to the boy, with grilles and buttons down the side of the screen and a back the size of a drum. There were some rocks on the other side of the path. The man watched, fascinated, as Neil walked over, selected one, and then threw it at the glass with all his strength.

Pock.

A loud noise in this otherwise silent place. The glass didn't shatter, but the stone went through, leaving a hole starred at the edges like a gunshot. Neil picked up a second rock and repeated the action, missing this time, then tried again. Another hole appeared in the screen.

He appeared to like this game.

And the man could understand why. This casual destruction was much like the increasing aggression the boy showed in school. It was an attempt to make an impact on a world that seemed so oblivious to his existence. It stemmed from a desire to be seen. To be noticed. To be loved.

That was all any child wanted, deep down.

The man's heart, beating more quickly now, ached at the thought of that. He stepped silently out from the bushes behind the boy, and then whispered his name.

Two

Neil. Neil. Neil.

DI Pete Willis moved carefully over the waste ground, listening as the officers around him called the missing boy's name at prearranged intervals. In between, there was absolute silence. Pete looked up, imagining the words fluttering into the blackness up there, disappearing into the night sky as completely as Neil Spencer had vanished from the Earth below it.

He swept the beam of his torch over the dusty ground in a conical pattern, checking his footing as well as looking for any sign of the boy. Blue tracksuit bottoms and underpants, Minecraft T-shirt, black trainers, army-style bag, water bottle. The alert had come through just as he'd been sitting down to eat the dinner he'd laboured over, and the thought of the plate there on his table right now, untouched and growing cold, made his stomach grumble.

But a little boy was missing and needed to be found.

The other officers were invisible in the dark, but he could see their torches as they fanned out across the area. Pete checked his watch: 8.53 p.m. The day was almost done, and although it had been hot this afternoon, the temperature had dropped over the last couple of hours, and the cold air was making him shiver. In his rush to leave, he'd forgotten his coat, and the shirt he was wearing offered scant protection against the elements. Old bones too – he was fifty-six, after all – but no night for young ones to be out either. Especially lost and alone. Hurt, most likely.

Neil. Neil. Neil.

He added his own voice: 'Neil!'

Nothing.

The first forty-eight hours following a disappearance are the most crucial. The boy had been reported missing at 7.39 p.m. that evening, roughly an hour and a half after he had left his father's house. He should have been home by 6.20 p.m., but there had been little coordination between the parents as to the exact time of his return, so it wasn't until Neil's mother had finally phoned her ex-husband that their son's absence was discovered. By the time the police arrived on the scene at 7.51 p.m., the shadows were lengthening and approaching two of those forty-eight hours had already been lost. Now it was closer to three.

In the vast majority of cases, Pete knew, a missing child is found quickly and safely and returned to their family. Cases were divided into five distinct categories: throwaway; runaway; accident or misadventure; family abduction; non-family abduction. The law of probability was telling Pete right now that the disappearance of Neil Spencer would turn out to be an accident of some kind, and that the boy was going to be found soon. And yet, the further he walked, the more his gut instinct was telling him differently. There was an uncomfortable feeling curling around his heart. But then, a child going missing always made him feel like this. It didn't mean anything. It was just the bad memories of twenty years ago surfacing, bringing bad feelings along with them.

The beam of his torch passed over something grey.

Pete stopped immediately, then played it back to where it had been. There was an old television set lodged at the base of one of the bushes, its screen broken in several places, as though someone had used it for target practice. He stared at it for a moment.

'Anything?'

An anonymous voice calling from one side.

'No,' he shouted back.

He reached the far side of the waste ground at the same time as the other officers, the search having turned up nothing. After the relative darkness behind him, Pete found the bleached brightness of the street lights here oddly queasy. There was a quiet hum of life in the air that had been absent in the silence of the waste ground.

A few moments later, stuck for anything better to do right now, he turned around and walked back the way he'd come.

He wasn't really sure where he was going, but he found himself heading off to the side, in the direction of the old quarry that ran along one edge. It was dangerous ground in the dark, so he headed towards the cluster of torchlights where the quarry search team were about to start work. While other officers were working their way along the edge, shining their beams down the steep sides and calling Neil's name, the ones here were consulting maps and preparing to descend the rough path that led into the area below. A couple of them looked up as he reached them.

'Sir?' One of them recognized him. 'I didn't know you were on duty tonight.'

'I'm not.' Pete bent the wire of the fence up, and ducked under to join them, even more careful of his footing now. 'I live locally.'

'Yes, sir.' The officer sounded dubious.

It was unusual for a DI to turn up for what was ostensibly grunt work like this. DI Amanda Beck was coordinating the burgeoning investigation from back at the department, and the search team here was comprised mainly of rank and file. Pete figured he had more years on the clock than any of them, but tonight he was just part of the crowd. A child was missing, which meant that a child needed to be found. The officer was maybe too young to remember what had happened with Frank Carter two decades earlier, and to understand why it was no surprise to find Pete Willis out in circumstances like this.

'Watch yourself, sir. The ground's a bit shaky here.'

'I'm fine.'

Young enough to discount him as some old man as well, apparently. Presumably he'd never seen Pete in the department's gym, which he visited every morning before heading up to work. Despite the disparity in their ages, Pete would have bet he could outlift the younger man on every machine. He was watching the ground all right. Watching everything – including himself – was second nature to him.

'Okay, sir, well, we're about to head down. Just coordinating.'

'I'm not in charge here.' Pete pointed his torch down the path, scanning the rough terrain. The beam of light only penetrated a short distance. The bed of the quarry below was nothing but an enormous black hole. 'You report to DI Beck, not to me.'

'Yes, sir.'

Pete continued staring down, thinking about Neil Spencer. The most likely routes the boy would have taken had been identified. The streets had been searched. Most of his friends had already been contacted, all to no avail. And the waste ground was clear. If the boy's disappearance really was the result of an accident or misadventure then the quarry was the only remaining place that made sense for him to be found.

And yet the black world below felt entirely empty.

He couldn't know for sure – not through reason. But his instinct was telling him that Neil Spencer wasn't going to be found here.

That maybe he wasn't going to be found at all.

Three

'Do you remember what I told you?' the little girl said.

He did, but right now Jake was doing his best to ignore her. All the other children in the 567 Club were outside, playing in the sun. He could hear the shouting and the sound of the football skittering over the tarmac, and every now and then it would thud against the side of the building. Whereas he was sitting inside, working on his drawing. He would much rather have been left alone to finish it.

It wasn't that he didn't like playing with the little girl. Of course he did. Most of the time, she was the only one who *wanted* to play with him, and normally he was more than happy to see her. But she wasn't acting particularly playful this afternoon. In fact, she was being all serious, and he didn't like that one bit.

'Do you remember?'

'I guess.'

'*Say* it then.'

He sighed, put the pencil down, and looked at her. As always, she was wearing a blue-and-white checked dress, and he could see the hash of a graze on her right knee that never seemed to heal. While the other girls here had neat hair, cut level at the shoulders or tied back in a tight ponytail, the little girl's was spread out messily to one side and looked like she hadn't brushed it in a long time.

From the expression on her face now, it was obvious she wasn't going to give up, so he repeated what she'd told him.

'If you leave a door half open . . .'

It should have been surprising that he did remember it all, really, because he hadn't made any special effort to make the words stick. But for some reason, they had. It was something about the rhythm. Sometimes he'd hear a song on CBBC and it would end up going round and round in his brain for hours. Daddy had called it an *earworm*, which had made Jake imagine the sounds burrowing into the side of his head and squirming around in his mind.

When he was finished, the little girl nodded to herself, satisfied. Jake picked up his pencil again.

'What does it mean anyway?' he said.

'It's a warning.' She wrinkled her nose. 'Well – kind of anyway. Children used to say it when I was little.'

'Yes, but what does it *mean*?'

'It's just good advice,' she said. 'There are a lot of bad people in the world, after all. A lot of bad things. So it's good to remember.'

Jake frowned, and then started drawing again. Bad people. There was a slightly older boy called Carl here at the 567 Club who Jake thought was bad. Last week, Carl had cornered him while he was building a Lego fortress, and then stood too close, looming over him like a big shadow.

'Why's it always your dad who picks you up?' Carl had demanded, even though he already knew the answer. 'Is it because your mum's dead?'

Jake hadn't answered.

'What did she look like when you found her?'

Again, he hadn't answered. Apart from in nightmares, he didn't think about what it had been like to find Mummy that day. It made his breath go funny and not work properly. But one thing he couldn't escape from was the knowledge that she wasn't here any more.

It reminded him of a time long gone when he had peered

round the kitchen door and seen her chopping a big red pepper in half and pulling out the middle.

'Hey, gorgeous boy.'

That was what she'd said when she'd seen him. She always called him that. The feeling inside when he remembered she was dead had the kind of sound the pepper made, like something ripping with a *pock* and leaving a hollow.

'I really like seeing you cry like a baby,' Carl had declared, and then walked away like Jake didn't even exist.

It wasn't nice to imagine the world was full of people like that, and Jake didn't want to believe it. He drew circles on the sheet of paper now. Force fields around the little stick figures battling there.

'Are you all right, Jake?'

He looked up. It was Sharon, one of the grown-ups who worked at the 567 Club. She had been washing up at the far side of the room, but had come over now, and was leaning down with her hands between her knees.

'Yes,' he said.

'That's a nice picture.'

'It's not finished yet.'

'What is it going to be?'

He thought about how to explain the battle he was drawing – all the different sides fighting it out, with the lines between them and the scribbles over the ones who had lost – but it was too difficult.

'Just a battle.'

'Are you sure you don't want to go outside and play with the other children? It's such a lovely day.'

'No, thank you.'

'We've got some spare suncream.' She looked around. 'There's probably a hat somewhere too.'

'I need to finish my drawing.'

Sharon stood back up again, sighing quietly to herself, but with a kind expression on her face. She was worried about him, and while she didn't need to be, he supposed that was still kind of nice. Jake could always tell when people were concerned about him. Daddy often was, except for those times when he lost his patience. Sometimes he shouted, and said things like, 'It's just because I want you to talk to me, I want to know what you're thinking and feeling,' and it was scary when that happened, because Jake felt like he was disappointing Daddy and making him sad. But he didn't know how to be different from how he was.

Round and round – another force field, the lines overlapping. Or maybe it was a portal instead? So that the little figure inside could disappear from the battle and go away, somewhere better. Jake turned the pencil around and began carefully erasing the person from the page.

There.

You're safe now, wherever you are.

One time, after Daddy lost his temper, Jake found a note on his bed. There was what he had to admit was a very good picture of the two of them smiling, and underneath that Daddy had written:

I'm sorry. I want you to remember that even when we argue we still love each other very much. Xxx.

Jake had put the note into his Packet of Special Things, along with all the other important things he needed to keep.

He checked now. The Packet was on the table in front of him, right beside the drawing.

'You're going to be moving to the new house soon,' the little girl said.

'Am I?'

'Your daddy went to the bank today.'

'I know. But he says he's not sure it's going to happen. They might not give him the thing he needs.'

'The *mortgage*,' the little girl said patiently. 'But they will.'

'How do you know?'

'He's a famous writer, isn't he? He's good at making things up.' She looked at the picture he was drawing and smiled to herself. 'Just like you.'

Jake wondered about the smile. It was a strange one, as though she was happy but also sad about something. Come to think of it, that was how he felt about moving too. He didn't like it in the house any more, and he knew it was making Daddy miserable too, but moving still felt like something they maybe shouldn't do, even though *he* was the one who'd spotted the new house on Daddy's iPad when they were looking together.

'I'll see you after I move, won't I?' he said.

'Of course you will. You *know* that you will.' But then the little girl leaned forward, speaking more urgently. 'Whatever happens, though, remember what I told you. It's important. You have to promise me, Jake.'

'I promise. What does it *mean*, though?'

For a moment, he thought she might be about to explain it some more, but then the buzzer went on the far side of the room.

'Too late,' she whispered. 'Your daddy's here.'

Four

Most of the children seemed to be playing outside the 567 Club when I arrived. I could hear the mingled laughter as I parked up. They all looked so happy – so *normal* – and for a moment my gaze moved between them, searching for Jake, hoping to see him amongst them.

But of course, my son wasn't there.

Instead, I found him inside, sitting with his back to me, hunched over a drawing. My heart broke a little at the sight of him. Jake was small for his age, and his posture right then made him seem tinier and more vulnerable than ever. As though he was trying to disappear into the picture in front of him.

Who could blame him? He hated it here, I knew, even if he never objected to coming or complained about it afterwards. But it felt like I had no choice. There had been so many unbearable occasions since Rebecca's death: the first haircut I had to take him to; ordering his school clothes; fumbling the wrapping of his Christmas presents because I couldn't see properly through the tears. An endless list. But for some reason, the school holidays had been the hardest. As much as I loved Jake, I found it impossible to spend all day, every day with him. It didn't feel like there was enough left of *me* to fill all those hours, and while I despised myself for failing to be the father he needed, the truth was that sometimes I needed time to myself. To forget about the gulf between us. To ignore my growing inability to cope. To be able to collapse and cry for a while, knowing he wouldn't walk in and find me.

'Hey, mate.'

I put my hand on his shoulder. He didn't look up.

'Hi, Daddy.'

'What have you been up to?'

'Nothing much.'

There was an almost imperceptible shrug under my hand. His body seemed barely there, somehow even lighter and softer than the fabric of the T-shirt he was wearing.

'Playing with someone a bit.'

'Someone?' I said.

'A girl.'

'That's nice.' I leaned over and looked at the sheet of paper. 'And drawing too, I see.'

'Do you like it?'

'Of course. I love it.'

I actually had no idea what it was meant to be – a battle of some kind, although it was impossible to work out which side was which, or what was going on. Jake very rarely drew anything static. His pictures came to life, an animation unfolding on the page, so that the end result was like a film where you could see all the scenes at once, superimposed on top of each other.

He was creative, though, and I liked that. It was one of the ways in which he was like me: a connection we had. Although the truth was that I'd barely written a word in the ten months since Rebecca died.

'Are we going to move to the new house, Daddy?'

'Yes.'

'So the person at the bank listened to you?'

'Let's just say that I was convincingly creative about the parlous state of my finances.'

'What does "parlous" mean?'

It was almost a surprise that he didn't know. A long time

ago, Rebecca and I had agreed to talk to Jake like an adult, and when he didn't know a word we'd explain it to him. He absorbed it all, and often came out with strange things as a result. But this wasn't a word I wanted to explain to him right now.

'It means it's something for me and the person at the bank to worry about,' I said. 'Not you.'

'When are we going?'

'As soon as possible.'

'How will we take everything?'

'We'll hire a van.' I thought about money, and fought down a hint of panic. 'Or maybe we'll just use the car – really pack it up and do a few trips. We might not be able to take *everything* with us, but we can sort through your toys and see what you want to keep.'

'I want to keep all of them.'

'Let's see, eh? I won't make you get rid of anything you don't want to, but a lot of them are very young for you now. Maybe another little boy would like them more.'

Jake didn't reply. The toys might have been too young for him to play with, but each of them had a memory attached. Rebecca had always been better at everything with Jake, including playing with him, and I could still picture her, kneeling down on the floor, moving figures around. Endlessly, beautifully patient with him in all the ways I found it so hard to be. His toys were things she'd touched. The older they were, the more of her fingerprints would be on them. An invisible accumulation of her presence in his life.

'Like I said, I won't make you get rid of anything you don't want to.'

Which reminded me of his Packet of Special Things. It was there on the table beside the drawing, a worn leather pouch, about the size of a hardback book, which zipped shut around three of the sides. I had no idea what it had been in a previous life. It looked like a large Filofax without the pages, although God knew why Rebecca would have had one of those.

A few months after she died, I went through some of her things. My wife had been a lifelong hoarder, but a practical one, and many of her older possessions were stored in boxes, stacked in the garage. One day, I'd brought some in and started to look through them. There were things going back to her childhood in there, entirely unconnected to our life together. It felt like that should have made the experience easier, but it didn't. Childhood is – or should be – a happy time, and yet I knew these hopeful, carefree artefacts had an unhappy ending. I began crying. Jake had come and put his hand on my shoulder, and when I hadn't immediately responded, he'd wrapped his small arms around me. After that, we'd looked through some of the things together, and he'd found what was to become the Packet and asked me if he could have it. Of course he could, I said. He could have anything he wanted.

The Packet was empty at that point, but he began to fill it. Some of the things inside had been sifted from Rebecca's possessions. There were letters and photographs and tiny trinkets. Drawings he'd done, or items of importance to him. Like some kind of witch's familiar, the Packet rarely left his side and, except for a few things, I didn't know what was in there. I wouldn't have looked even if I'd been able to. They were *his* Special Things, after all, and he was entitled to them.

'Come on, mate,' I said. 'Let's get your things and get out of here.'

He folded up the drawing and handed it to me to carry. Whatever the picture was meant to be, it clearly wasn't important enough to go into the Packet. He picked that up himself and carried it across the room to the door, where his water bottle was hanging on a hook. I pressed the green button to release the door, then glanced back. Sharon was busying herself with the washing-up.

'Do you want to say goodbye?' I asked Jake.

He turned around in the doorway, and looked sad for a moment. I was expecting him to say goodbye to Sharon, but instead, he waved at the empty table he'd been sitting at when I arrived.

'Bye,' he called over. 'I promise I won't forget.'

And before I could say anything, he ducked out under my arm.

Five

On the day Rebecca died, I had picked Jake up by myself.

That afternoon was supposed to have been one of my writing days, and when Rebecca had asked if I could pick Jake up instead of her, my first reaction had been one of annoyance. The deadline for my next book was a handful of months away, and I'd spent most of the day failing miserably to write, at that point counting on a final half-hour of work to deliver a miracle. But Rebecca had looked pale and shaky, and so I had gone.

On the drive back, I had done my best to question Jake about his day, to absolutely no avail. That was standard. Either he couldn't remember, or he didn't want to talk. As usual, it had felt like he would have responded to Rebecca, which, coupled with the ongoing failure of the book, had made me feel more anxious and insecure than ever. Back home, he had been out of the car like a flash. Could he go and see Mummy? Yes, I had told him. I was sure she'd like that. But she wasn't feeling well, so be gentle with her – and remember to take your shoes off, because you know Mummy hates mess.

And then I had dawdled at the car a little, taking my time, feeling bad about what an abject failure I was. I'd trailed in slowly, putting stuff down in the kitchen – and noting that my son's shoes had *not* been taken off and left there as I'd requested. Because, of course, he never listened to me. The house was silent. I presumed that Rebecca was lying down upstairs, and that Jake had gone up to see her, and that everyone was fine.

Apart from me.

It was only when I finally went into the living room that I saw Jake was standing at the far end, by the door that led to the stairs, staring down at something on the floor that I couldn't see. He was completely still, hypnotized by whatever he was looking at. As I walked slowly across to him, I noticed he was not motionless at all, but shaking. And then I saw Rebecca, lying at the bottom of the stairs.

Everything was blank after that. I know I moved Jake away. I know I phoned for an ambulance. I know I did all the correct things. But I can't remember doing them.

The worst thing was that, although he would never talk to me about it, I was sure Jake remembered everything.

Ten months later, we walked in together through a kitchen where the surfaces were all but covered with plates and cups, the little visible counter space dirty with smears and crumbs. In the front room, the toys spread over the bare floorboards looked scattered and forgotten. For all my talk of sorting toys before we moved, it looked like we'd already gone through all our possessions, taken what we needed, and left the rest dotted around like rubbish. There had been a constant shadow over the place for months now, always growing darker, like a day gradually drawing to an end. It felt like our home had started falling apart when Rebecca died. But then, she had always been the heart of it.

'Can I have my picture, Daddy?'

Jake was already on his knees on the floor, gathering his coloured pens together from wherever they'd rolled this morning.

'Magic word?'

'Please.'

'Yes, of course you can.' I put it down beside him. 'Ham sandwich?'

'Can I have a treat instead?'

'Afterwards.'

'All right.'

I cleared some space in the kitchen and buttered two slices of bread, then layered three slices of ham into the sandwich and sliced it into quarters. Trying to fight through the depression. One foot in front of the other. Keep moving.

I couldn't help thinking about what had happened at the 567 Club: Jake waving goodbye to an empty table. For as long as I could remember, my son had had imaginary friends of some kind. He'd always been a solitary child; there was something so closed off and introspective about him that it seemed to push other children away. On good days, I could pretend that it was because he was self-contained and happy in his own head, and tell myself that was fine. Most of the time, I just worried.

Why couldn't Jake be more like the other children?

More *normal*?

It was an ugly thought, I knew, but it was only because I wanted to protect him. The world can be brutal when you're as quiet and solitary as he was, and I didn't want him to go through what I had at his age.

Regardless, until now the imaginary friends had manifested themselves subtly – more like little conversations he'd sometimes have with himself – and I wasn't sure I liked this new development. I had no doubt the little girl he told me he'd been talking to all day had existed only in his head. This was the first time he'd acknowledged something like that out loud, talking to someone in front of other people, and that scared me slightly.

Of course, Rebecca had never been concerned. 'He's fine – just let him be him.' And since she knew better than me about most things, I'd always done my best to abide by that. But now? Now, I wondered if maybe he needed real help.

Or maybe he was just being him.

It was one more overwhelming thing that I should have been able to deal with, but didn't know how. I didn't know what the right thing to do was, or how to be a good father to him. God, I wished that Rebecca was still here.

I miss you . . .

But that thought would make the tears come, so I cut it dead and picked up the plate. As I did so, I heard Jake speaking quietly in the front room.

'Yes.' And then, in answer to something I couldn't hear, 'Yes, I *know*.'

A shiver ran through me.

I walked quietly over to the doorway, but didn't step through it yet – just stood there listening. I couldn't see Jake, but the sunlight through the window at the far end of the room was casting his shadow across the side of the settee: an amorphous shape, not recognizably human but moving gently, as though he was rocking back and forth on his knees.

'I remember.'

There were a few seconds of silence then, in which the only sound was my own heartbeat. I realized I was holding my breath. When he spoke next, it was much louder, and he sounded upset.

'I don't want to say them!'

And at that, I stepped through the doorway.

For a moment, I wasn't sure what I was going to see. But Jake was crouched down on the floor exactly where I'd left him, except that now he was staring off to one side, his drawing abandoned. I followed his gaze. There was nobody there, of course, but he seemed so intent on the empty space that it was easy to imagine a presence in the air.

'Jake?' I said quietly.

He didn't look at me.

'Who were you talking to?'

'Nobody.'

'I *heard* you talking.'

'Nobody.'

And then he turned slightly, picked his pen back up and started drawing again. I took another step forward.

'Can you put that down and answer me, please?'

'Why?'

'Because it's important.'

'I wasn't talking to anybody.'

'Then how about putting the pen down because I said so?'

But he kept drawing, his hand moving more fervently now, the pen making desperate circles around the little figures there.

My frustration curdled into anger. So often, Jake seemed like a problem I couldn't solve, and I hated myself for being so useless and ineffective. At the same time, I also resented him for never offering me so much as a clue. Never meeting me halfway. I wanted to *help* him; I wanted to make sure he was okay. And it didn't feel like I could do that by myself.

I realized I was gripping the plate too tightly.

'Your sandwich is ready.'

I put it down on the settee, not waiting to see if he stopped drawing or not. Instead, I went straight back through to the kitchen, leaned on the counter there and closed my eyes. For some reason, my heart was pounding.

I miss you so much, I thought to Rebecca. *I wish you were here. For so many reasons, but right now because I don't think I can do this.*

I started to cry. It didn't matter. Jake would either be drawing or eating his tea for a while, and he wasn't going to come through. Why would he, when there was only me through here to see? So it was fine. My son could talk quietly to people who didn't exist for a while. As long as I was equally quiet, so could I.

I miss you.

That night, as always, I carried Jake up to bed. It had been that way ever since Rebecca's death. He refused to look at the place where he had seen her body, clinging to me instead, with his breath held and his face buried in my shoulder. Every morning, every night, every time he needed the bathroom. I understood why, but he was beginning to grow too heavy for me, in more ways than one.

Hopefully that would change soon.

After he was asleep, I went back downstairs and sat on the settee with a glass of wine and my iPad, loading up the details of our new house. Looking at the photograph on the website made me uneasy on a different level.

It was safe to say it was Jake who had chosen this house. I hadn't been able to see the appeal at first. It was a small, detached property – old, two storeys, with the ramshackle feel of a cottage. But there was something a little strange about it. The windows seemed oddly placed, so that it was hard to imagine the layout inside, and the angle of the roof was slightly off, so that the face of the building appeared to be tilted inquisitively, perhaps even angrily. But there was also a more general sensation – a tickling at the back of the skull. At first glance, the house had unnerved me.

And yet, from the moment Jake had seen it, he had been set on it. Something about the house had utterly entranced him, to the point that he refused to look at any others.

When he'd accompanied me to the first viewing, he had seemed almost hypnotized by the place. I had still not been convinced. The interior was a good size, but also grimy. There were dusty cabinets and chairs, bundles of old newspapers, cardboard boxes, a mattress in the spare room downstairs. The owner, an elderly woman called Mrs Shearing, had been apologetic; this all belonged to a tenant she had been renting to, she explained, and would be gone by the time it was sold.

But Jake had been adamant, and so I'd organized a second viewing, this time by myself. That was when I had started to see the place with different eyes. Yes, it was odd-looking, but that gave it a sort of mongrel charm. And what had initially felt like an angry look now seemed more like wariness, as though the property had been hurt in the past and you'd have to work to earn its trust.

Character, I supposed.

Even so, the thought of moving terrified me. In fact, there had been a part of me that afternoon that had hoped the bank manager would see through the half-truths I'd told about my financial situation and just turn down the mortgage application outright. I was relieved now, though. Looking around the front room at the dusty, discarded remnants of the life we'd once had, it was obvious that the two of us couldn't continue as we were. Whatever difficulties lay ahead, we had to get out of this place. And however hard it was going to be for me over the coming months, my son needed this. We both did.

We had to make a fresh start. Somewhere he wouldn't need to be carried up and down the stairs. Where he could find friends that existed outside his head. Where I didn't see ghosts of my own in every corner.

Looking at the house again now, I thought that, in a

strange way, it suited Jake and me. That, like us, it was an outsider that found it hard to fit in. That we would go together well. Even the name of the village was warm and comforting.

Featherbank.

It sounded like a place where we would be safe.

Six

Like Pete Willis, DI Amanda Beck knew very well the importance of the first forty-eight hours. She had her team spend the next twelve of them continuing to search the various routes that Neil Spencer might have taken, along with interviewing family members and beginning to build a profile of the missing boy. Photos were acquired. Histories were probed. And then at 9.00 a.m. the next morning, a press conference was held and a description of Neil and his clothing was released to the media.

Neil's parents sat mutely on either side of Amanda while she made the requisite appeals and encouraged witnesses to come forward. Cameras flashed intermittently across the three of them. Amanda did her best to ignore them, but she could sense Neil's parents registering each one, flinching a little as though the photographers were jabbing at them.

'We encourage people to check any garages and sheds on their property,' she told the room.

It was all kept as calm and low-key as possible. Her main aim right now, besides locating Neil Spencer, was to assuage people's fears, and while she could hardly claim outright that Neil had absolutely *not* been abducted, she could at least make it clear where the focus of the investigation rested for the moment.

'The most likely explanation is that Neil has had an accident of some kind,' she said. 'While he has been missing for fifteen hours, we are holding out every hope of finding him safe and well, and soon.'

Privately, she was not so confident.

*

One of Amanda's first actions back in the operations room, after the press conference had finished, was to arrange for the handful of known sex offenders in the area to be brought in quietly, and then questioned more loudly.

Over the course of the day, the search area was expanded. Sections of the canal – an unlikely proposition – were dredged, and extensive door-to-door enquiries were begun. CCTV footage was analysed. She studied the latter herself; it showed the beginning of Neil's journey but lost him before he reached the waste ground, and failed to pick him up again afterwards. Somewhere between those two points, the little boy had vanished.

Exhausted, she tried to rub some life into her face.

Officers went over the waste ground again, this time in daylight, and the exploration of the quarry continued.

There was still no sign of Neil Spencer.

The boy did make an appearance of sorts, though, and increasingly so as the day wore on: photographs were circulated on the news, particularly the one of Neil smiling shyly in a football shirt – one of the few pictures his parents had of him looking happy. Reports showed simple maps with key locations marked by red circles, and possible routes dotted in yellow.

Footage of the press conference was also aired. Amanda watched it on her tablet in bed at home that evening, and thought that Neil's parents seemed even more beaten down on camera than it had felt at the time. They looked *guilty*. And if they weren't feeling guilty yet, they would soon; they would be made to. At the briefing that afternoon, she had cautioned her officers, many of whom were parents themselves, that while the circumstances surrounding Neil Spencer's disappearance might be controversial, his mother and father were to be treated with sensitivity. It went without saying that they were hardly model parents, but Amanda didn't suspect them of any direct involvement. The father had some minor offences on his record – drunk and disorderlies, and a caution for fighting – but nothing that raised any warning flags. The mother's record was clean. More to the point, they both appeared genuinely devastated by events. There hadn't even been any recriminations between the two of them, as hard as that was to imagine.

They both just wanted their boy home.

Amanda slept badly and was back at the department early. With over thirty-six hours behind her, only a bare handful of them spent resting, she sat in her office, thinking about the five categories of child disappearance, forced increasingly towards an uncomfortable conclusion. She did not believe that Neil had been abandoned or disposed of by his parents. If he had suffered an accident on his route home, he would have been found by now. Abduction by a different family member seemed unlikely. And while it was not impossible that he'd run away, she refused to believe that she'd been outwitted for this long by a six-year-old boy with no money or supplies.

She gazed at the photo of Neil Spencer on the wall, considering the nightmare scenario.

Non-family abduction.

The public at large might generally think of it as *stranger* abduction, but precision was important. Children in this category were rarely abducted by people who were completely unknown to them. More often, they were befriended – groomed by people on the periphery of their lives. So the focus of the investigation now shifted, with the strands that had formed a more subtle part of the last day and a half being brought front and centre. Friends of the family. Families of friends. An even closer look at known offenders. Internet activity in the home. Amanda loaded up the available CCTV footage again and began examining it from different mental angles, concentrating less on the prey now than on potential predators in the background.

Neil's parents were interviewed again.

'Did your son express any concerns about unwanted attention from other adults?' Amanda said. 'Did he mention being approached by anyone?'

'No.' Neil's father looked affronted by the very idea of it. 'I'd have fucking well done something about that, wouldn't I? And for fuck's sake, don't you think I'd have mentioned it before now?'

Amanda smiled politely.

'No,' Neil's mother said.

But less firmly.

When Amanda pressed her, the woman said that actually she *did* recall something. It hadn't occurred to her to report it at the time, or even when Neil went missing, because it had been so strange, so stupid – and anyway, she'd been half asleep at the time, so she hardly even remembered it.

Amanda smiled politely again, while also resisting the urge to rip the woman's head off.

Ten minutes later, she was in the upstairs office of her superior, DCI Colin Lyons. Whether from tiredness or nerves, she was having to stop her leg from jittering slightly. Lyons himself just looked pained. He had been closely involved in the investigation and understood as fully as Amanda did the situation they were now likely to be facing. Even so, this recent development was not one he'd wanted to hear.

'This doesn't go to the media,' Lyons said quietly.

'No, sir.'

'And the mother?' He looked at her suddenly, alarmed. 'You've told her not to mention this in public? At all?'

'Yes, sir.'

Of fucking course, sir. Although Amanda doubted it had been necessary. The tone of some of the press coverage was already judgemental and accusatory, and Neil's parents had enough culpability to deal with already without deliberately copping to more.

'Good,' Lyons said. 'Because Jesus Christ —'

'I know, sir.'

He leaned back in his chair and closed his eyes for a few seconds, breathing deeply. 'Do you know the case?'

Amanda shrugged. Everybody knew the case. That wasn't the same thing as *knowing* it.

'Not everything,' she said.

Lyons opened his eyes and sat there staring at the ceiling. 'Then we're going to need some help,' he said.

Amanda's heart sank a little at that. For one thing, she'd worked herself to the brink of exhaustion these last two days, and she didn't relish the thought of having to share any spoils of the case now. For another, there was also the spectre that was being acknowledged here.

Frank Carter.

The Whisper Man.

Assuaging fear amongst the public was going to get harder now. Impossible, even, if this new detail got out. They would have to be very careful indeed.

'Yes, sir.'

Lyons picked up the phone on his desk.

Which was how, as the time since Neil Spencer's disappearance ticked close to the end of that crucial forty-eight-hour period, DI Pete Willis became involved in the investigation again.

Seven

Not that he wanted to be involved.

Pete's philosophy was a relatively simple one, ingrained in him over so many years that it was now more implicit than consciously considered: a blueprint on which his life was built.

The Devil finds work for idle hands.

Bad thoughts find empty heads.

So he kept his hands busy and his mind occupied. Discipline and structure were important to him, and after the non-result at the waste ground he had spent most of the last forty-odd hours doing exactly what he always did.

Early that morning had found him in the department's gym: overhead presses; side laterals; rear deltoids. He worked on a different body part each day. It wasn't a matter of vanity or health, more that he found the solitude and concentration involved in physical exercise a comforting distraction. After three-quarters of an hour, he was often surprised to discover his mind had been mercifully empty for most of it.

That morning, he had managed not to think about Neil Spencer at all.

He had then spent most of the day upstairs in his office, where the multitude of minor cases piled on his desk provided ample distraction. As a younger, more impetuous man, he would probably have yearned for greater excitement than the trivial crimes he was dealing with, but today he appreciated the calm to be found in boring minutiae. Excitement was not only rare in police work, it was a bad thing; usually it meant someone's life had been damaged. Wishing for excitement was wishing for hurt, and Pete had had more than enough of both. There was comfort to be had in the car thefts, the shoplifting, the court appearances for endless banal offences. They spoke of a city ticking quietly along, never quite perfect, perhaps, but never falling apart either.

But while he'd had no direct involvement with the Neil Spencer investigation, it was impossible to avoid it entirely. A small boy, when missing, casts a large shadow, and it had rapidly become the most prominent case in the department. He heard officers talking about it in the corridors: where Neil might be; what might have happened to him; and the parents, of course. The latter was quieter speculation, and had been officially discouraged, but he kept hearing it anyway – the irresponsibility of letting a little boy walk home alone. He remembered similar talk from twenty years ago, and walked on quickly, no more disposed to entertain it now than he had been back then.

Just before five o'clock that evening, he was sitting quietly at his desk, already considering what he would do that evening. He lived alone and socialized rarely, so his habit was to work his way through cookery books, often making elaborate meals before eating them alone at the dinner table. Afterwards, he would watch a film or read a book.

And the ritual, of course.

The bottle and the photograph.

And yet, as he gathered his things together, almost ready to leave, he realized his pulse was racing. Last night, the nightmare had returned for the first time in months: Jane Carter whispering 'You have to hurry' down the phone to him. Despite himself, it had been impossible to escape from Neil Spencer completely, which meant the darker thoughts and memories were a little closer to the surface than he preferred to keep them. And so, as he pulled his jacket on, he was not entirely surprised when the phone on his desk began ringing. There was no way of knowing for sure, and yet somehow he already did.

His hand trembled a little as he picked it up.

'Pete,' DCI Colin Lyons said down the line. 'Glad to catch you. I was hoping I could have a quick word upstairs.'

His suspicions were confirmed as soon as he entered the DCI's office. Lyons had revealed nothing in the call, but DI Amanda Beck was there too, sitting with her back to him at the desk nearest the door. There was only one investigation she was working on right now, which meant there was only one reason his presence could have been requested.

He tried to keep calm as he closed the door. Tried – especially – not to think about the scene that had awaited him when he finally gained access to Frank Carter's extension twenty years ago.

Lyons smiled broadly. He had a smile that could power a room.

'Good of you to come up. Have a seat.'

'Thanks.' Pete sat down beside Beck. 'Amanda.'

Beck nodded a greeting, and gave him the flicker of a smile – an exceedingly low-wattage equivalent of the DCI's beam that barely even powered her face. Pete didn't know her well. She was twenty years younger than him, but right now looked much older than her years. Blatantly exhausted – and nervous too, he thought. Maybe she was worried her authority was being undermined and that the case was about to be taken away from her; he'd heard she was ambitious. He could have set her mind at rest on that score. While Lyons was probably ruthless enough to remove her from the investigation if it suited him, he was never going to pass it on to Pete instead.

They were relative contemporaries, he and Lyons, but despite the disparity in their ranks Pete had actually joined the department a year earlier, and in many ways his career had been the more decorated. In a different world, the two of them would have been sitting on opposite sides of the desk right now, and perhaps even *should* have been. But Lyons had always been ambitious, whereas Pete, aware that promotion brought conflict and drama of its own, had little desire to climb the professional ladder any further than he already had. That had always rankled with Lyons, Pete knew. When you go after something as hard as he had, there were few things as irritating as someone who could have had it more easily but never seemed to want it.

'You're aware of the investigation into the disappearance of Neil Spencer?' Lyons said.

'Yes. I was involved in the search of the waste ground on the first evening.'

Lyons stared at him for a moment, perhaps evaluating that as a criticism.

'I live close to there,' Pete added.

But then, Lyons lived in the area as well, and he hadn't been out there trawling the streets that night. A second later, though, the DCI nodded to himself. He knew that Pete had his own reasons to be interested in any cases of missing children.

'You're aware of developments since?'

I'm aware of the lack of them. But that would come across as a rebuke to Beck, and she didn't deserve that. From the little he'd seen, she'd handled the investigation well and done everything she could. More to the point, she'd been the one to direct her officers not to criticize the parents, and he liked that.

'I'm aware that Neil hasn't been found,' he said. 'Despite extensive searches and enquiries.'

'What would your theory be?'

'I haven't followed the investigation closely enough to have one.'

'You haven't?' Lyons looked surprised at that. 'I thought you said that you were out searching on the first night?'

'That was when I thought he'd be found.'

'So you don't think he will be now?'

'I don't know. I hope he is.'

'I'd have thought you would have followed the case, given your history?'

The first mention there. The first hint.

'Maybe my history gives me a reason not to.'

'Yes, I can understand that. It was a difficult time for all of us.'

Lyons sounded sympathetic, but Pete knew this was another source of resentment between them. Pete was the one who'd closed the area's biggest case in the last fifty years, and yet Lyons was the one who'd ended up in charge. In different ways, the investigation they were circling was uncomfortable for both of them.

Lyons was the one to bring that spiral to its point.

'I also understand you're the only one Frank Carter will ever talk to?'

And there it was.

It had been a while since Pete had heard the name out loud, and so perhaps it should have delivered a jolt. But all it did was bring the crawling sensation inside him to the surface. Frank Carter. The man who had kidnapped and murdered five young boys in Featherbank twenty years ago. The man whom Pete had eventually caught. The name alone conjured up such horror for him that it always felt like it should never be spoken out loud – as though it was some kind of curse that would summon a monster behind you.

Worse still was what the papers had called him. *The Whisper Man.* That was based on the idea that Carter had befriended his victims – vulnerable and neglected children – before taking them away. He would talk quietly to them at night outside their windows. It was a nickname that Pete had never allowed himself to use.

He had to fight down the urge to leave the room.

You're the only one he'll ever talk to.

'Yes.'

'Why do you think that is?' Lyons said.

'He enjoys taunting me.'

'About what?'

'The things he did back then. The things I never found out.'

'But he never tells you?'

'No.'

'Why bother speaking to him then?'

Pete hesitated. It was a question he had asked himself numerous times over the years. He dreaded the encounters, and always had to suppress the shivers he felt as he sat in the private interview room at the prison, anticipating Carter's approach. He would feel broken afterwards, sometimes for weeks. There would be days when he would shake uncontrollably, and evenings when the bottle would be harder to resist. At night, Carter found him in dreams – a hulking, malevolent shadow that would bring him screaming out of sleep. Every meeting with the man damaged Pete a little more.

And yet still he went.

'I suppose I'm hoping that one day he'll slip up,' he answered carefully. 'That maybe he'll reveal something important by accident.'

'Something about where he dumped the Smith boy?'

'Yes.'

'And about his accomplice?'

Pete didn't reply.

Because again, there it was.

Twenty years ago, the remains of four of the missing boys had been found in Frank Carter's house, but the body of his final victim, Tony Smith, had never been recovered. There was no doubt in anyone's mind that Carter was responsible for all five murders, and he himself had never denied it. But it was also true that there were certain inconsistencies within the case. Nothing that could have exonerated the man: just little strands that left the investigation frayed and untidy. One of the abductions was estimated to have occurred within a certain time period, but Carter had an alibi for most of it, which didn't make it impossible for him to have taken the boy, just stretched the likelihood somewhat. There were witness accounts that, while not definitive, described a different individual at certain scenes. The forensic evidence in Carter's house was overwhelming, and they had witness statements that were far more concrete and reliable, but a doubt had always remained as to whether Carter had acted alone.

Pete wasn't sure whether he shared that doubt or not, and most of the time he did his best to ignore the possibility. But that was clearly why he was here. And like any horror that had to be faced, it was preferable to drag it out into the light and get it over with. So he decided to ignore the DCI's question and get to the point.

'Can I ask what this is about, sir?'

Lyons hesitated.

'What we're going to discuss goes no further than the four walls of this office right now. Is that clear?'

'Of course.'

'The CCTV we have suggests Neil Spencer did walk in the direction of the waste ground but, somewhere in the vicinity, he vanished. The search has drawn a blank so far. All the locations he's likely to have wandered into by accident have been cleared. He's not with friends or other family members. Naturally, we're forced to consider other possibilities. DI Beck?'

Beside Pete, Amanda Beck came to life. When she spoke, she sounded a little defensive.

'Obviously, we considered those other possibilities from the beginning. We've done the door-to-doors. Interviewed all the usual candidates. That's got us nowhere yet.'

There has to be more to it than that, Pete thought. 'But?'

Beck took a deep breath. 'But I interviewed the parents again an hour ago. Looking for anything that might have been missed. Any kind of lead. And his mother told me something. She hadn't mentioned it before because she thought it was stupid.'

'What was it?'

But even as he asked the question, he knew the answer. Perhaps not the exact form it would take, but close enough. Over the course of the meeting, the pieces of a new nightmare had been steadily coming together into a single picture.

A little boy missing.

Frank Carter.

An accomplice.

Beck added the final piece now.

'A few weeks ago, Neil woke his mother in the middle of the night. He said that he'd seen a monster outside his window. The curtains were open, like he really had been looking out, but there was nothing there . . .'

She paused.

'He said it had been whispering things to him.'

43

PART TWO
September

Eight

Jake was excited when we collected the keys from the estate agent in Featherbank, whereas I just felt anxious as we drove to our new home. What if the house wasn't how I remembered it from the viewings? What if I got inside and hated the place now – or worse, Jake did?

All of this would have been for nothing.

'Stop kicking the passenger seat, Jake.'

The drumming of his feet from behind me stopped, but then started up again almost immediately. I sighed to myself as I turned a corner. But then, he was excited, which was a rare enough occurrence in itself, so I decided to ignore it. At least one of us was happy.

It was a lovely day, though. And my nerves aside, it was impossible to deny that Featherbank was beautiful in the late-summer sun. It was a suburb, and while it was only five miles away from a heaving city centre, it felt more like the countryside here. Down by the river, on the southern edge of the village, there were cobbled roads and cottages. Further north, away from a single row of shops, there were steep streets of pretty sandstone houses, and most of the pavements were lined with trees, the leaves thick and green overhead. With the window rolled down, the air outside smelled of cut grass, and I could hear music and children playing. It felt peaceful and tranquil here – as slow and warm as a lazy morning.

We reached our new street, which was a quiet residential

road with a large field on one side. There were more trees around the edges, the sun cutting through the leaves and dappling the grass with light, and I tried to imagine Jake out there, running around just across from our own house, his T-shirt bright in the sun. Still as happy as he was now.

Our house.

We had arrived.

I pulled into the driveway. The house still looked the same, of course, but the building seemed to have different ways of staring out at the world. The first time I'd seen it, it had seemed forbidding and frightening – almost dangerous – and then the second, I'd thought it had character. Now, just for a moment, the odd arrangement of windows reminded me of a beaten face, with an eye pushed up over a badly bruised cheek, the skull injured and lopsided. I shook my head and the image disappeared. But an ominous feeling remained.

'Come on, then,' I said quietly.

Outside the car, the day was still and quiet. With no breeze to move the warm air, we were in a capsule of silence. But the world was humming softly as we approached the house, and it felt to me as though the windows were watching us, or perhaps something just out of sight behind the glass. I turned the key in the lock and opened the door, and stale air wafted out. For a second, it smelled as though the house had been sealed up for far longer than it had been, perhaps even with something left out in the sun, but then all I could detect was the bleachy scent of cleaning products.

Jake and I walked through the house, opening doors and cupboards, turning lights on and off, drawing and closing curtains. Our footsteps echoed; otherwise, the silence was absolute now. But as we worked our way through each room, I couldn't shake the sensation that we were not alone. That someone else was here, hiding just out of sight, and that if I turned at the right moment, I'd see a face peering around a door frame. It was a stupid, irrational feeling, but it was there. And it wasn't helped by Jake. He was excited, moving quickly from room to room, but every now and then I'd catch a slightly puzzled look on his face, as though he had been expecting to find something that wasn't here.

'Is this my room, Daddy?'

What was going to be his bedroom was on the first floor, raised up from the landing outside, so that his window was smaller than the rest: the eye staring out across the field from above the swollen cheek.

'Yes.' I ruffled his hair. 'Do you like it?'

He didn't reply, and I stared down at him nervously. He was gazing around, lost in thought.

'Jake?' I said.

He looked up at me.

'Is this really *ours*?'

'Yes,' I said. 'It is.'

And then he hugged my legs — so suddenly that it almost knocked me off-balance. It was as though I'd shown him the best present he'd ever seen and he'd been worried he might not be able to keep it. I crouched down so we could embrace properly. The relief I felt was palpable, and suddenly that was all that mattered. My son was happy to be here, and I'd done something good for him, and nothing else was important. I stared over his shoulder at the open door and the landing beyond. If it still felt like something was just around the corner there, I knew it was only my imagination.

We were going to be safe here.

We were going to be happy.

And for the first week, we were.

*

At the time, I was stood looking at a newly assembled bookcase, marvelling at my industry. DIY had never been a strong point of mine, but I knew this was something Rebecca would have wanted me to do, and I imagined her pressed up behind me now, with the side of her face against my back and her arms around my chest. Smiling to herself. 'You see? You can do this.' And while it was only a small taste of success, even that was an unusual feeling recently, and I liked it.

Except, of course, I was still alone.

I began filling the shelves.

Because that was another of the things Rebecca would have done, and even though this new house was about Jake and me moving on, I still wanted to honour that. 'You always put out the books,' she told me once. 'It's like buttering a cat's paws.' She had never been happier than when reading. There had been so many warm, contented evenings, with the two of us curled up at different ends of the settee, me writing as best I could on my laptop, her lost in novel after novel. Over the years, we had accumulated hundreds of books, and I set to work unpacking them now, sliding each one carefully into place.

And then it came to my own. The shelves beside my computer desk were reserved for copies of my four novels, along with the various foreign translations. It felt ostentatious to have them on display, but Rebecca had been proud of me and had always insisted on it. So this was another gesture to her – as was the empty space I left on the shelves, ready for the ones that hadn't been written yet, but would be.

I glanced warily at the computer. Beyond turning it on to check the new WiFi worked, I hadn't really done much with it this last week. I hadn't written a thing for a year. That was another thing that was going to change. New start, new –

Creak.

A noise from above me, the sound of a single footstep. I looked up. It was Jake's room directly overhead, but I'd left him in the front room playing while I did the assembling and unpacking.

I moved to the doorway and looked up the stairs. There was nobody on the landing. In fact, the whole house suddenly felt still and quiet, as though there was no movement at all. The silence rang in my ears.

'Jake?' I shouted upstairs.

Silence.

'Jake?'

'Daddy?'

I almost jumped. His voice had come from the front room, directly beside me. Keeping one eye on the landing, I took a step towards the front room and peered in. My son was crouched on the floor with his back to me, drawing something.

'Are you all right?' I said.

'Yes. Why?'

'I was just checking.'

I stepped back, then stared up at the landing again for a few seconds. It was still quiet up there, but the space had a strange sense of potential to it now, once again as though there was somebody standing just out of sight. Which was ridiculous, of course, because nobody could have come in through the front door without me knowing. Houses creaked. It took a while to get used to their noises, that was all.

But even so.

I walked upstairs slowly and cautiously, stepping quietly, with my left hand raised, ready to deflect anything that leapt out at me from that side. I reached the top – and of course, the landing was empty. When I stepped into Jake's room, that was empty too. A wedge of afternoon sunlight was coming through the window, and I could see tiny curls of dust hanging in the air, undisturbed.

Just an old house creaking.

I went downstairs more confidently, feeling silly but also more relieved than I'd have liked to admit. At the bottom, I had to edge past the piles of post on the last two steps. There had been a lot so far: the usual documents that inevitably come with moving into a new house, along with innumerable local takeaway flyers and other junk mail. But there had also been three proper letters, addressed to someone called Dominic Barnett. All three were printed with either *Private* or *Addressee Only*.

I remembered that the previous owner, Mrs Shearing, had rented the house out for years, and on a whim, I ripped one of the letters open now. Inside, I found an itemized account from a debt collection company. My heart sank. Whoever Dominic Barnett was, he owed the company just over a thousand pounds in arrears on a mobile phone contract. I opened the others, and they were the same: notices for unpaid debts. I scanned the details, frowning to myself. The amounts weren't large, but the tone of the letters was threatening. I told myself it wasn't an insurmountable problem – that a few phone calls would sort it out – but this move was meant to be a new start for Jake and me. I hadn't expected it to deliver a fresh set of obstacles for me to overcome.

'Daddy?'

Jake had appeared in the front-room doorway beside me. He was holding his Packet of Special Things in one hand and a piece of paper in the other.

'Is it all right if I play upstairs?'

I thought of the *creak* I'd heard, and for a second I wanted to say no. But again, that was absurd. There was nobody up there, and it was his bedroom; he had every right to play in it. At the same time, we hadn't seen much of each other that day, and it felt isolating for him to disappear upstairs now.

'I guess,' I said. 'Can I see your drawing first?'

He hesitated. 'Why?'

'Because I'm interested. Because I'd like to.'

Because I'm trying here, Jake.

'It's private.'

Which was fair enough, and a part of me wanted to respect that, but I didn't like the idea of him keeping secrets from me. The Packet was one thing, but it felt like if he wouldn't even show me his pictures now, then the distance between us must be increasing.

'Jake –' I started to say.

'Oh, fine.'

He thrust the sheet out at me. Now that it was being offered, I was reluctant to take it.

But I did.

Jake had never been good at drawing straightforward, realistic scenes before, preferring his convoluted, unfolding battles instead, but he'd attempted one here. The picture was rough, but it was obviously an approximation of our house from the outside, reminiscent of the original photograph that had caught his attention online. He had captured the odd look of the place well. The curved, childlike lines stretched the house into a strange shape, elongating the windows, and making it look more like a face than ever. The front door appeared to be moaning.

But it was the upstairs that drew my attention. In the right-hand window, he'd drawn me, standing by myself in my bedroom. On the left, there he was in his own room, the window large enough here to include his whole body. There was a smile on his face, and the jeans and T-shirt he was wearing right now were shaded with crayon.

And beside him, he'd drawn another person in his bedroom. A little girl, her black hair splayed almost angrily out to one side. Her dress was coloured in with patches of blue, leaving the rest white.

Little scrapes of red on one of her knees.

A corkscrew smile on her face.

Nine

After Jake's bath that night, I sat down beside his bed so that we could read to each other. He was a good reader, and we were currently working our way through *Power of Three* by Diana Wynne Jones. It was a childhood favourite of mine, which I'd chosen without thinking. The horrible irony of the title had only occurred to me afterwards.

When we'd finished that night's chapter, I put the book down with all his others.

'Cuddle?' I said.

He slipped out of the covers without a word and sat sideways on my knees, wrapping his arms around me. I savoured the cuddle for as long as I could, and then he clambered back into bed.

'I love you, Jake.'

'Even when we argue?'

'Of course. *Especially* when we argue. That's when it matters the most.'

That reminded me of the picture I'd drawn for him, which I knew he'd kept. I glanced down at his Packet of Special Things, which was under the bed now, so that if he were to drape his small arm out in the night he'd be able to touch it. But that in turn made me think of the drawing he'd done that afternoon. He hadn't been pleased about showing it to me, and so I hadn't asked him about it at the time. But in the warm, soft light of his bedroom, it felt like maybe I could now.

'It was a good picture of our house today,' I said.

'Thank you, Daddy.'

'I'm curious about something, though. Who was the little girl in the window with you?'

He bit his lip and didn't answer.

'It's okay,' I said gently. 'You can tell me.'

But again, he didn't reply. It was obvious that, whoever it was meant to be, the little girl was the reason he hadn't wanted to show me the drawing today, and he didn't want to talk about her now either. But why not?

The answer occurred to me a second later.

'Is she the little girl from the 567 Club?'

He hesitated, then nodded.

I sat back on my heels, doing my best to hide the frustration I felt. The disappointment, even. For the last week, everything had seemed fine. We had been happy here, Jake had seemed to be adjusting well, and I had been cautiously optimistic. And yet apparently his imaginary friend had been following us all along. The thought made me shiver slightly – the idea that we had left her behind in the old house, and ever since she had been working her way slowly across the intervening miles to find us.

'Do you still talk to her?' I said.

Jake shook his head.

'She's not here.'

From his own disappointment, it was obvious that he wanted her to be, and once again, I felt uneasy. It was unhealthy for him to be fixated on someone who wasn't there. At the same time, he looked so dejected and lonely right now that I almost felt guilty about depriving him of his friend. And also hurt that, as always, I wasn't enough.

'Well,' I said carefully. 'You start school tomorrow. I'm sure you'll make lots of new friends there. And in the meantime, I'm here. *We're* here. New house, new start.'

'Is it safe here?'

'Safe?' Why was he asking that? 'Yes, of course it is.'

'Is the door locked?'

'Yes.'

The lie – a white one – came automatically. The door wasn't locked; I didn't think I'd even put the chain on. But Featherbank was a quiet village. And anyway, it was early evening and the lights were all on. Nobody was going to be that blatant.

But Jake looked so frightened that I was suddenly conscious of the distance between the two of us and the front door. The noise of running his bath. If someone had crept in while we were up here, would I have heard it?

'You don't need to worry about that.' I did my best to sound firm. 'I'd never let anything happen to you. Why are you so worried?'

'You have to close doors,' he said.

'What do you mean?'

'You have to keep them locked.'

'Jake –'

'If you leave a door half open, soon you'll hear the whispers spoken.'

A chill ran through me. Jake looked scared, and the phrase certainly wasn't the kind of thing he would have come up with by himself.

'What does that mean?' I said.

'I don't know.'

'Where did you hear it then?'

He didn't answer. But then, I realized, he didn't need to.

'The little girl?'

He nodded, and I shook my head, confused. Jake couldn't have heard the strange rhyme from someone who wasn't there. So perhaps I'd been wrong at the 567 Club and the little girl was real? Perhaps Jake had just called goodbye without realizing she had gone outside? Except he had been alone at the table when I'd arrived. It must have been one of the other children, then, trying to scare him. From the expression on his face right now, it had worked.

'You're completely safe, Jake. I promise you.'

'But I'm not in charge of the door!'

'No,' I said. 'I am. And so there is nothing for you to worry about. I don't care what somebody told you. You need to listen to *me* now. I'm not going to let anything happen to you. Ever.'

He was listening, at least, although I wasn't sure he was convinced.

'I promise you. And do you know why I won't let anything happen to you? Because I love you. Very much indeed. Even when we argue.'

That brought the slightest of smiles.

'Do you believe me?' I said.

He nodded, looking a little more reassured now.

'Good.' I ruffled his hair and stood up. 'Because it's true. Good night, sweetie.'

'Good night, Daddy.'

'I'll come up and check on you in five minutes.'

I turned the light off as I left the room, then padded downstairs as quietly as I could. But rather than collapsing on the settee as I wanted to, I stopped at the front door.

If you leave a door half open, soon you'll hear the whispers spoken.

Rubbish, of course, wherever he had heard it. But the words still bothered me. And just as the idea of the little girl trailing us across the country had disturbed me, now I couldn't shake the image of her sitting next to him, her hair swept out to one side and that strange smile on her face, whispering frightening things in his ear.

I put the chain on for the night.

Ten

DI Pete Willis had spent the weekend miles away from Feath-erbank, walking in the nearby countryside and trailing a stick through random tangles of undergrowth. He checked the hedges he passed. Occasionally, when the fields were empty, he hopped over stiles and trawled through the grass there.

Anyone watching might have mistaken him for a rambler, and to all intents and purposes he supposed that was what he was. These days, in fact, he deliberately thought of such expedi-tions as walks and outings – as just another way for an old man to fill his time. It had been twenty years now, after all. And yet a part of him remained focused. Rather than absorbing the beauty of the world around him, he was constantly searching the ground for bone fragments and snatches of old fabric.

Blue jogging bottoms. Little black polo shirt.

For some reason, it was always the clothes that stayed with him.

However much he tried not to think about it, Pete would never forget the day he'd viewed the horrors plastered inside Frank Carter's extension. Returning to the department after-wards, he had still been reeling from the experience. But as he had stepped through the sliding doors, there had at least been some sense of relief. Four little boys had been killed. But even though Carter remained at large for the moment, the monster finally had a name – a real one, not the one the papers had given him – and four victims would be all the bastard claimed.

In that moment, he had believed it was nearly over.

But then he had seen Miranda and Alan Smith sitting in

the reception. Even now, he could still picture them clearly. Alan had been wearing a suit and sitting bolt upright, staring into space, his hands forming a heart between his knees. Miranda's hands had been pressed between her thighs, and she had been leaning against her husband, resting her head on his shoulder with her long brown hair trailing down his chest. It had been late afternoon, but they had both looked exhausted, like long-distance travellers who were trying and failing to sleep where they sat.

Their son Tony was missing.

And twenty years on from that afternoon, he still was.

Frank Carter had managed a day and a half on the run before he was finally arrested, his van pulled over on a country road nearly a hundred miles from Featherbank. There was forensic evidence that Tony Smith had been held in the back of his van, but no sign of the boy's body. And while Carter had admitted killing Tony, he refused to reveal where he had discarded his remains.

The weeks that followed had seen extensive searches along the myriad possible routes Carter could have taken, all of them to no avail. Pete had attended several. The number of searchers had dwindled over time until, two decades later, he was the only one still out searching. Even Miranda and Alan Smith had moved on. They lived far away from Featherbank now. If Tony had been alive today, he would be twenty-seven years old. Pete knew that Miranda and Alan's daughter, Claire, born in the tumultuous years that followed, had just turned sixteen. He attached no blame to the Smiths for rebuilding their lives after the murder of their son, but the fact remained that he himself could not let it go.

A little boy was missing.

A little boy needed to be found and brought home.

*

As he drove back into Featherbank now, the homes he passed looked comfortable. Their windows were illuminated in the darkness, and he could imagine whispers of laughter and conversation drifting out from within.

People together, as people should be.

He felt a degree of loneliness at that, but you could find pleasure where you looked for it, even in as solitary a life as his. The road was lined with enormous trees, their leaves lost in the darkness except for where the street lights touched them, scattering the street with intricate yellow-green explosions that undulated in the soft breeze. It was so quiet and peaceful in Featherbank that it was almost impossible to believe it had once played host to atrocities as terrible as Frank Carter's.

A flyer was attached to the lamp post at the end of his street – one of the many MISSING posters that had been put up in the previous weeks by Neil Spencer's family. There was a photograph of the boy, details of his clothing, and an appeal for witnesses to come forward with information. Both the image and the text had faded under the incessant beating of the summer sun, so that driving past it now, it reminded him of wrinkled flowers left at the scene of an old accident. A little boy who had disappeared was beginning to disappear for a second time.

Nearly two months had passed since Neil Spencer went missing, and despite the resources, as well as the heart and soul, that had been poured into the investigation, the police knew little more now than they had on the evening he'd vanished. As far as Pete could tell, Amanda Beck had done everything right. It was a reflection on her efficiency, in fact, that even DCI Lyons, a man with a constant eye on his own reputation, had stood by her and left her in charge of the case. Although the last time Pete had passed Amanda in the corridor, she had looked so worn out that he had wondered if that wasn't its own kind of punishment.

He wished he could tell her that it would get easier.

After being summoned to the DCI's office, Pete had talked Amanda through the original investigation, but his involvement in the case had turned out to be cursory. There had been the familiar feeling of dread when he made the request to visit Frank Carter. He had imagined himself sitting across from the monster, being treated like a plaything. As always, he had wondered if he could do it – whether this encounter would be the one that finally proved too much for him. And yet his fear had been in vain. For the first time that he could remember, his request to talk to Carter had been met with refusal. The so-called Whisper Man, it seemed, had decided to stay silent.

Pete had visited him on several occasions, and he had been prepared to do so again, but still – it had been impossible to suppress his relief. That feeling had brought guilt and shame along with it, of course, but he had talked himself out of it. Sitting across from Frank Carter was an ordeal. It was bad for his health. And since the only connection was what Neil's mother claimed her son had seen and heard at his bedroom window, there was no reason to think it would help.

Relief was the correct response.

Back home, he tossed his keys on to the dining-room table, already planning the meal he would make and the programmes he would watch to fill the handful of hours before sleep. Tomorrow would bring the gym, the paperwork, the admin. Life as usual.

But before then, he performed the ritual.

He opened the kitchen cabinet and took out the bottle of vodka he kept in there, turning it around in his hands, weighing it, feeling how thick the glass was. There was a solid, protective layer between him and the silky liquid inside. It had been a long time since he'd opened a bottle like this, but he could still remember the comforting *click* he would hear if he turned the top and broke the seal.

He retrieved the photograph from a drawer.

And then he sat down at the dinner table, with the bottle and photograph before him, and asked himself the question.

Do I want to do this?

Over the years, the urge had come and gone, but to some extent it was always present. There were many obvious things that could jostle it awake, but there were also times when it seemed to stir at random, following its own oblique schedule. The bottle was often as dead and powerless as a mobile phone without charge, but sometimes there was a flicker there. Right now, the urge was stronger than he could recall. For the last two months, in fact, the bottle had been talking to him increasingly loudly.

You're only delaying the inevitable, it told him now.

Why make yourself suffer like this?

A full bottle — that was important. Pouring a drink from a half-finished bottle was less comforting than breaking the seal on a fresh one. The comfort lay in knowing you had enough.

He gently tested the seal now, tempting himself. A little more pressure and it would break, and the bottle would be open.

You might as well give in.

It will make you feel worthless, but we both know that's what you are.

The voice could be cruel as well as friendly. Play the minor chords as easily as the major.

You're worthless. You're useless.

So open the bottle.

As so often, the voice was his father's. The old man was

63

long dead but, even forty years on, Pete could picture him: fat and sprawled in a threadbare armchair in the dusty front room, a look of contempt on his face. Nothing Pete had done as a boy had ever been good enough for him. 'Worthless' and 'useless' were words he'd learned early and heard often.

Age had brought with it the understanding that his father had been a small man, disappointed with everything in his life, and that his son had just been a convenient punchbag to vent his many frustrations on. But that understanding had come too late. By then, the message had been absorbed and become part of his programming. Objectively, he knew it wasn't true that he was worthless and a failure. But it always *felt* true. The trick, explained, still convinced.

He picked up the photograph of Sally. It was many years old, and the colours had faded over time, as though the paper was attempting to erase the image imprinted upon it and return to its original blank state. The two of them looked so happy there, their faces pressed together. It had been taken on a summer's day. Sally appeared full of joy, grinning in the sun, while Pete was squinting against the light and smiling.

This is what you lose by drinking.

This is why it's not worth it.

He sat there for a few minutes, breathing slowly, then he put the bottle and the photograph away and began to make dinner. It was easy to understand why the urge had strengthened in these last few weeks, and that was why it was good his involvement had come to nothing. *Let the urge flare in the light of recent events*, he thought. *Let it have its moment.*

And then let it die.

Eleven

That night, as always, I found it difficult to fall asleep.

Once upon a time, when I had a new book out, I would go to events and even do the occasional signing tour. I generally went by myself, and I would lie awake afterwards in unfamiliar hotel rooms, missing my family. I always found it hard to sleep when Rebecca wasn't there beside me.

It was harder still, now that she never would be. Before, if I stretched my arm out across the cold side of a hotel bed, I could at least imagine she was doing the same back home – that we might feel the ghosts of each other. After she died, when I stretched my arm out in our own bed, I felt nothing but the cold emptiness of the flat sheets there. Perhaps a new house and bed should have changed that, but they hadn't. When I stretched my arm out in the old house, I had at least known that Rebecca had lain there once.

So I stayed awake for a long time, missing her. Even if moving here had been the right decision, I was aware of a greater distance between Rebecca and me than ever before. It was terrible to leave her behind. I kept imagining her spirit in the old house, staring out of the window, wondering where her family had gone.

Which reminded me of Jake's imaginary friend. The little girl he'd drawn. I did my best to empty my head of that picture, concentrating instead on how peaceful it was here in Featherbank. The world outside the curtains was quiet and still. The house around me was entirely silent now.

It allowed me to drift off, at least after a time.

Glass smashing.

My mother screaming.

A man shouting.

'Daddy.'

I jerked awake from the nightmare, disorientated, dimly aware that Jake was calling me and so I needed to do something.

'Hang on,' I shouted.

A shadow at the end of the bed moved, and my heart leapt. I sat up quickly.

Jesus Christ.

'Jake, is that you?'

The small shadow moved around from the foot of the bed to my side. For a moment I wasn't convinced it was him at all, but then he was close enough that I could recognize the shape of his hair. I couldn't see his face, though. It was occluded entirely by the darkness in the room.

'What are you doing, mate?' My heart was still racing, both from what was happening now and from the residue of the nightmare I had woken from. 'It's not time to get up yet. Absolutely nowhere near.'

'Can I sleep in here with you tonight?'

'What?'

He never had before. In fact, Rebecca and I had always held firm on the few occasions he'd suggested it, assuming that relenting even once would be the beginning of a slippery slope.

'We don't do that, Jake. You know that.'

'Please.'

I realized that his voice was deliberately quiet, as though

there was someone in another room – someone he didn't want to overhear us.

'What's the matter?' I said.

'I heard a noise.'

'A noise?'

'There's a monster outside my window.'

I sat there in silence, remembering the rhyme he'd told me at bedtime. But that had been about the door. And anyway, there was no way anybody could be outside his window. We were one floor up.

'You were dreaming, mate.'

He shook his head in the darkness. 'It woke me up. I went across to the window and it was louder there. I wanted to open the curtains but I was too scared.'

You would have seen the dark field across the road, I thought. *That's all.* But he sounded so serious that I couldn't say that to him.

'All right.' I slipped out of bed. 'Well, let's go and check then.'

'Don't, Daddy.'

'I'm not scared of monsters, Jake.'

He followed me into the hall, where I switched on the light at the top of the stars. Stepping up into his room, though, I left the light off, and then approached the window.

'What if there's something there?'

'There isn't,' I said.

'But what if?'

'Then I'll deal with it.'

'Will you punch it in the face?'

'Absolutely. But there's nothing there.'

And yet I didn't feel as confident as I sounded. The closed curtains seemed ominous. I listened for a moment, but there was nothing to hear. And it was impossible for there to be anybody out there.

I pulled the curtains open.

Nothing. Just an oblique angle of the path and garden, the empty road beyond, and then the dark, shadowy expanse of the field stretching away into the distance. A dim reflection of my face was staring back into the room. But there was nothing else out there. The whole world seemed to be sleeping peacefully in exactly the way that I wasn't.

'See?' I did my best to sound patient. 'Nobody there.'

'But there was.'

I closed the curtains and knelt down.

'Jake, sometimes dreams can seem very real. But they're not. How can anybody have been outside your window when we're all that way above the ground?'

'They could have climbed up the drainpipe.'

I started to answer, but then pictured the outside of the house. The drainpipe *was* just to the side of his window. A ridiculous idea occurred to me. If you lock and chain a door to keep a monster out, what choice does it have but to climb up and get in some other way?

Stupidity.

'There was nobody out there, Jake.'

'Can I sleep with you tonight, Daddy? Please?'

I sighed to myself. Obviously, he wasn't going to sleep alone in here now, and it was either too late or too early to argue. I couldn't decide which. It was easier right now just to give in.

'All right. But just for tonight. No fidgeting, though.'

'Thank you, Daddy.' He picked up his Packet of Special Things and followed me back through. 'I promise I won't fidget.'

'So you say. But what about *stealing all the covers*?'

'I won't do that either.'

I turned the hall light off and then we clambered into bed, Jake on what should have been Rebecca's side.

'Daddy?' he said. 'Were you having a nightmare before?'

Glass smashing.

My mother screaming.

A man shouting.

'Yes,' I said. 'I suppose so.'

'What was it about?'

The dream itself had faded a little now, but it had been a memory as much as a nightmare. Me as a child, walking towards the doorway to the small kitchen of the house I had grown up in. In the dream, it was late, and a noise from downstairs had woken me. I had stayed in bed with the covers pulled over my head and the dread thick in my heart, trying to pretend that everything was okay, even though I knew that it wasn't. Eventually, I had tiptoed quietly down the stairs, not wanting to see whatever was happening, but drawn to it all the same, feeling small and terrified and powerless.

I remembered approaching the bright kitchen along the dark hall, hearing the noises coming from in there. My mother's voice was angry but quiet, as though she thought I was still asleep and was trying to keep me safe from this, but the man's voice was loud and uncaring. All their words overlapped. I couldn't make out what either of them was saying, only that it was ugly, and that it was building towards a crescendo – accelerating towards something awful.

The kitchen doorway.

I reached it just in time to see the man's red face contorted in rage and hatred as he threw the glass at my mother as hard as he could. To see her flinch away, far too late, and to hear her scream.

The last time I'd ever seen my father.

It was such a long time ago now, but the memory still surfaced every now and then. Still clawed its way up out of the dirt.

'Grown-up stuff,' I told Jake. 'Maybe I'll tell you one

day, but it was just a dream. And it's fine. It all had a happy ending.'

'What happened in the end?'

'Well, *you* did, eventually.'

'Me?'

'Yeah.' I ruffled his hair. 'And then you went to sleep.'

I closed my eyes, and the two of us lay there in silence for so long that I assumed he'd dropped back off to sleep. At one point, I stretched my arm out to one side and rested my hand gently on top of the covers over him, as though to reassure myself he was still there. The two of us together. My small, wounded family.

'Whispering,' Jake said quietly.

'What?'

'Whispering.'

His voice sounded so far away that I thought he was already dreaming.

'It was whispering at my window.'

Twelve

'You have to hurry.'

In the dream, Jane Carter was whispering down the phone to Pete. Her voice was quiet and urgent, as though what she was saying was the most frightening thing in the world.

But she was doing it anyway. Finally.

Pete was sitting at his office desk, his heart thumping in his chest. He had spoken to Frank Carter's wife numerous times during the investigation. He had appeared outside her place of work, or found himself accidentally walking alongside her on busy pavements, always careful not to be seen with her somewhere her husband might hear of. It was as though he had been making covert attempts to turn a spy, which he supposed wasn't far from the truth.

Jane had provided alibis for her husband. She had defended him. But it had been obvious to Pete from his first encounter with her that she was terrified of Frank – he thought with good reason – and he had worked hard to convert her: to convince her it was safe to talk to him. To take back what she had said and tell the truth about her husband: 'Talk to me, Jane. I'll make sure that Frank can't hurt you and your son any more.'

And now it seemed like she was going to. Such fear had been beaten into Jane Carter over the years that even now, phoning him without the bastard in the house, she could still only bring herself to whisper. Courage is not the absence of fear, Pete knew. Courage requires fear. And so, even as the adrenaline hit – even as he felt the case beginning to close ahead of him – he also recognized the bravery of this call.

'I'll let you in,' she whispered, 'but you have to hurry. I've no idea how long he'll be.'

In reality, Frank Carter would never return to the house. Within an hour, it would be crawling with police and CSIs, and an alert would be out to locate Carter and the van he was driving. But at the time, Pete hurried. The journey to the house only took ten minutes, but they were the longest of his life. Even with backup on standby, he felt alone and scared when he arrived, like someone in a fairy tale where a monster was absent but might return at any moment.

Inside, he watched Jane Carter's trembling hands as she unlocked the door to the extension with the key she'd stolen. The whole house was silent, and he felt a shadow looming over them.

The lock came undone.

'Step back now, please, both of you.'

Jane Carter stood in the middle of the kitchen, her son hiding behind her legs, as Pete pushed open the door with one gloved hand.

No.

At once, there was the hot smell of rotting meat. He shone his torch inside – and then came the pictures, appearing to him one by one in swift succession, the sights and sensations illuminated as if by camera flashes.

No.

Not yet.

For the moment, he lifted his hand, moving the torchlight over the walls instead. They were painted white, but Carter had decorated them, drawing crude green blades of grass at the bases and childlike butterflies fluttering above. Close to the ceiling, there was the skewed yellow approximation of a sun. A face had been sketched on it, the dead black eyes staring down at the floor below.

Pete followed its gaze, finally lowering the beam.

It became difficult to breathe.

He had been searching for these children for three months, and while he had always anticipated an outcome like this, he had never entirely given up hope. But here they were, lying in this rank, warm darkness. The four bodies looked real and unreal at the same time. Lifelike dolls that had been broken and now lay still, their clothes intact except for their T-shirts, which had been pulled up to cover their faces.

Perhaps the worst thing about that particular nightmare was that it had become familiar enough over the years not to disturb his sleep. It was the alarm that woke him the next morning.

He lay there for a few seconds, trying to keep calm. Attempting to ignore the memory was like shoving at mist, but he reminded himself that it was only recent events that had roused these nightmares, and that they would fade in time. He turned off the alarm.

Gym, he thought. *Paperwork. Admin. Routine.*

He showered, dressed, packed the bag for his workout, and by the time he headed downstairs to make coffee and a light breakfast, the dream had receded and his thoughts were more under control. There had been a brief interruption to his life – that was all. It was completely understandable that turning the soil over had released some pungent ghosts from the earth, but they would fade soon. The urge to drink would weaken again. Life would return to normal.

It was only when he took his breakfast through to the front room that he saw the red light on his mobile blinking. He'd missed a call; there was voicemail to listen to.

He dialled the number and listened to the message, chewing the food slowly.

Forcing himself to swallow it. His throat was tight.

After two months, Frank Carter had agreed to see him.

Thirteen

'Just stand against the wall for me,' I said. 'A little to the right. No, *my* right. A little more. That's it. Now give me a smile.'

It was Jake's first day at his new school, and I was far more nervous about the prospect than he was. How many times could you check a drawer to make sure clothes were ready? Were there names on everything? Where had I put his book bag and water bottle? There was so much to consider, and I wanted everything to be perfect for him.

'Can I move yet, Dad?'

'Hang on.'

I held up my phone in front of me as Jake stood against the only blank wall in his bedroom, dressed in his new school uniform: grey trousers, white shirt and blue jumper – all of it fresh and clean, of course, with name tags on absolutely everything. His smile was shy and sweet. He looked so grown-up in his uniform, but also still so small and vulnerable.

I tapped the screen a couple of times. 'Done.'

'Can I see?'

'Of course you can.'

I knelt down and he leaned on my shoulder as I showed him the photographs I'd taken.

'I look okay.' He sounded surprised.

'You look the business,' I told him.

And he did. I tried to enjoy the moment, even though it was tinged with sadness, because Rebecca should have been here too. Like most parents, she and I had taken pictures on Jake's first day in a new year at school, but I'd changed my phone recently, and it was only earlier this week that I'd realized what that meant. All my photographs were gone – lost forever. To add insult to injury, I did have Rebecca's phone, but while the photos would be on there, I had no way of accessing them. I'd stared at her old handset in frustration for a full minute, facing down the hard truth of the situation. Rebecca was gone, which meant that those memories were gone as well.

I had tried to tell myself that it didn't matter. That it was just another harsh joke bereavement had played on me – and a minor one in the grand scheme of things. But it had hurt. It felt like another failing on my part.

We'll get so many more.

'Come on, mate.'

Before we left, I uploaded copies to the ether.

Rose Terrace Primary School was a low, sprawling building, secluded from the street behind iron railings. The main part was old and pretty: a single storey with numerous peaked roofs. BOYS and GIRLS were carved into the black stone above separate entrances, although much newer signs indicated that Victorian separation was now used to delineate different key stages instead. I'd been shown around before enrolling Jake. Inside, there was a hall with a polished wooden floor, which acted as a central hub for the surrounding classrooms. Between the doors, the walls were covered with small handprints in different-coloured paint, pressed there by a selection of former pupils, with the dates they'd attended written underneath.

Jake and I stood at the railings.

'What do you think?'

'I don't know,' he said.

It was hard to blame him for being doubtful. The playground beyond the railings was teeming with children, along with parents clustered together in groups. It was the first day of a new year, but everybody here – kids and parents alike – already knew each other from the previous two years, and Jake and I were going to be walking in as strangers to everyone except each other. His old school had been larger and more anonymous. Everyone here seemed so tightly knit that it was impossible to imagine we wouldn't always feel like outsiders. God, I hoped that he would fit in.

I gave his hand a light squeeze.

'Come on,' I said. 'Let's be brave.'

'I'm okay, Daddy.'

'I'm talking about me.'

A joke, but only half of one. There were five minutes before the doors were due to open, and I knew I should make an effort to talk to some of the other parents and begin to form bonds of my own. Instead, I leaned against the wall and waited.

Jake stood beside me, chewing his lip slightly. I watched the other children running around, and wished he'd go and make an effort to play.

Just let him be him, I told myself.

That should be good enough, shouldn't it?

Eventually, the door for Key Stage One opened, and Jake's new teacher stood outside smiling. The children began lining up, book bags swinging. Because it was the first day of term for everyone here, most of those bags would be empty for now, but Jake's wasn't. As usual, he'd insisted on bringing his Packet of Special Things with him.

I passed him the bag and his water bottle.

'You'll look after that, won't you?'

'Yes.'

God, I hoped so. The thought of it getting lost was probably as intolerable for me as it would be for him. But it was my son's equivalent of a comfort blanket, and there was no way he could have left home without it.

He was already moving over to the queue of children.

'I love you, Jake,' I said quietly.

'Love you too, Daddy.'

I stood there, watching until he was inside, hoping he'd turn back and wave. He didn't. It was a good sign, I supposed, that lack of clinging. It showed that he wasn't intimidated by the day ahead of him and didn't need the reassurance.

I wished I could say the same about myself.

Please, please, please be okay.

'New boy, eh?'

'Sorry?'

I turned to find a woman standing next to me. Even though the day was already warm, she was wearing a long dark coat with her hands pushed into the pockets, as though braced for a winter breeze. Her hair was dyed black, shoulder-length, and she had a slightly amused expression on her face.

New boy.

'Oh,' I said. 'You mean Jake? That's my son, yes.'

'Actually, I was meaning both of you. You look worried. Honestly, I'm sure he'll be fine.'

'Yes, I'm sure he will. He didn't even look back.'

'Mine stopped doing that a while ago. In fact, once we get to the playground on a morning, I might as well not exist. Heartbreaking at first, but you get used to it. It's a good thing really.' She shrugged. 'I'm Karen, by the way. My son's Adam.'

'Tom,' I said. 'Nice to meet you. Karen and Adam? I need to start learning all these new names.'

She smiled. 'It'll take a while. But I'm sure Jake won't have any problems. It's hard when you move somewhere new, but they're a good bunch of kids. Adam only started here the middle of last year. It's a good school.'

As she walked back towards the gate, I committed the names to memory. Karen. Adam. She'd seemed nice, and I needed to make some kind of effort here. Perhaps, despite all the evidence to the contrary, I really could become one of those normal adults who talked to other parents in the playground.

I took out my phone and put my headphones in for the short walk home, with something else to be nervous about now. I had been a third of the way into a new novel when Rebecca died, and while some writers might have thrown themselves into their work as a distraction, I hadn't looked at those words since. The idea I'd been working on felt empty to me now, and I suspected I was going to have to abandon the whole thing, and leave it decaying on my hard drive as some uncompleted folly.

In which case, what would I write?

Back home, I turned on the computer, opened up a blank document in Word, and then saved it under the file name *bad ideas*. I always did that to begin with. Acknowledging it was early days took some of the psychological pressure off. And then, since I'd always been of the mind that making coffee didn't count as procrastination, I went through to the kitchen and started the kettle boiling, then leaned against the counter and stared out of the window at the back garden.

A man was standing out there.

He had his back to me, and appeared to be rattling the padlock on my garage door.

What the fuck?

I tapped on the glass.

The man jumped and turned around quickly. He was in his fifties, short and portly, with a monk's ring of grey hair around his otherwise bald head. He was also dressed neatly in a suit, grey overcoat and scarf, and seemed about as far away from a potential burglar as I could imagine.

I made an actual *what the fuck* gesture at him with my hands and face. He stared back at me for a moment, a shocked expression still on his face, then turned and disappeared off in the direction of the driveway.

I hesitated for a moment, still thrown by what I'd just seen, then moved back through the house, determined to confront him and find out what he'd been doing.

As I reached the front door, the bell rang.

Fourteen

I opened the door too quickly, and found the man standing on the step outside, an apologetic look on his face. Up close, he was even shorter than he'd seemed through the window.

'I'm terribly sorry to bother you.' He spoke formally, in keeping with the old-fashioned suit he was dressed in. 'I wasn't sure if anybody would be home.'

One obvious way to check if someone is home, I thought, *would be to ring the fucking doorbell.*

'I see.' I folded my arms. 'What can I do for you?'

The man shuffled uncomfortably. 'Well, it's a slightly unusual request, I have to admit. But the thing is – this house. I actually grew up here, you see? Many years ago now, obviously, but I have such fond memories of the place . . .'

He trailed off.

'Okay,' I said.

And then I waited for him to continue. But he just stood there, looking expectant, as though he'd provided me with enough information already and it was awkward, or perhaps even rude, of me to make him say the rest.

A moment later, the penny dropped.

'You mean you want to come in and look around, or something?'

He nodded gratefully. 'It's a terrible imposition, I know, but I would appreciate being able to do so immensely. This house holds such special memories for me, you see.'

Again, his tone was so ostentatiously formal that I almost

laughed. But I didn't, because the idea of having this man in my house set my nerves on edge. He was dressed so properly, and his manner was so absurdly polite, that it all felt like some kind of disguise. Despite the apparent lack of physical threat, the man seemed dangerous. I could picture him stabbing someone with a sliver of a knife, looking into their eyes and licking his lips as he did so.

'That's not possible, I'm afraid.'

The prissy manner faded immediately, and a hint of annoyance crept on to his face. Whoever he was, he was clearly used to getting his own way.

'What a terrible shame,' he said. 'May I ask why?'

'For one thing, we've only just moved in. There are boxes everywhere.'

'I see.' He smiled thinly. 'Perhaps another time, then?'

'Well, no. Because I'm also not particularly inclined to let complete strangers into my house.'

'That is . . . disappointing.'

'Why were you trying to get into my garage?'

'I was doing no such thing.' He took a step back, looking affronted now. 'I was looking to see if I could find you.'

'What – inside a locked garage?'

'I don't know what you think you saw, but no.' He shook his head sadly. 'I see this has been a regrettable mistake. What a shame, indeed. Perhaps you'll change your mind.'

'I won't.'

'Then I'm sorry to have bothered you.'

He turned and began walking away up the path.

I followed him out, remembering the letters I'd received.

'Mr Barnett?'

He hesitated at that, then turned around and looked at me. I stopped where I was. His expression was entirely different now. His eyes had gone completely blank, and despite the difference in our sizes, I thought that if he took a step towards me right now, I would back away.

'I'm afraid not,' he said. 'Goodbye.'

And then he walked away, reaching the street then heading away without another word. I followed him again, then stood on the pavement, unsure whether to pursue him down the road or not. Despite the warmth of the sun, I was shivering slightly.

I'd been so preoccupied with the house that I hadn't got round to looking in the garage yet. Certainly, it was not the most desirable part of the property: two blue corrugated-metal doors that barely met in the middle; bobbled white walls with a cracked window on the side. Overgrown grass wavered at the base. The estate agent had told me there was asbestos in the roof and that I'd require specialist help if I decided to demolish it, but it looked as though it might fall down on its own at some point. It seemed to be squatting at the back of the house like an old drunk, unsteady on its feet and trying not to teeter over to one side.

The doors were secured by a padlock, but the estate agent had given me the key. The metal scraped and scratched against the tarmac as I unlocked it and pulled one door open, and then I ducked slightly and stepped inside.

I looked around in disbelief. It was full of junk.

I'd assumed that when Mrs Shearing had emptied the house after that first viewing, she'd hired a removal firm to empty out the old furniture. It was clear now that she'd saved herself that particular expense, and that it was all in here instead, smelling of mould and dust. There were piles of cardboard boxes in the centre, the ones at the bottom crumpling damply under the weight of the ones above, and old tables and chairs had been stacked and intermingled like wooden puzzles down one side. An old mattress was leaning against the back wall, the tea-coloured stains on the fabric so extensive that it resembled a landscape map of some foreign world. I could smell the blackened barbecue to one side of the door.

There were piles of crisp, brown leaves around the walls. I gingerly moved a paint pot in the corner with my foot, and found the largest spider I'd ever seen. The thing just bounced gently where it sat, apparently unperturbed by my presence.

Well, I thought, looking around. *Thank you very much, Mrs Shearing.*

There wasn't much room to move about, but I stepped forward to the piles of boxes and opened the one on top, the cardboard moist beneath my fingers. I peered in to find old Christmas decorations. Faded coils of tinsel, dull baubles, and what looked like jewels on the surface.

One of the jewels flew straight out into my face –

'Jesus Christ!'

I nearly lost my balance, one foot skidding on the leaves behind me, my arm waving at the air in front of my face. The thing fluttered up to the roof, then bounced down and whirled around, before hitting the grey window and smacking itself repetitively against it.

Tap, tap, tap. The gentlest of collisions.

A butterfly, I realized. Not one I recognized, although admittedly my knowledge extended about as far as cabbage whites and tortoiseshells.

I edged carefully over to the window, where the butterfly was still fluttering against the glass, and watched for a few seconds until it finally got the message and settled down on the grubby sill, its wings splayed flat. The thing was as large as the spider behind me, but where that had been an ugly shade of grey, the butterfly had astonishing colouring. Yellow and green swirls played across its wings, with hints of purple at the tips. It was beautiful.

Moving back over to the box, I looked in again and saw three more butterflies, resting on the surface of the tinsel. These weren't moving, so perhaps they were dead, but glancing down, I saw another one on the side of the lowest box in the pile, its wings moving as slowly and gently as breath.

I had no idea how long they had been in here, or what their life cycle might be, but there didn't seem to be much hope for them in here, except perhaps as meals for that spider. I felt an urge to disrupt that particular ecosystem. Tearing off a damp square of cardboard from the top box, I made an effort to waft one of the butterflies towards the door. The butterfly was having none of it, though. I tried the one by the window instead, but it was equally stubborn. And despite the size of them, they appeared very delicate close up, as though they might crumble to dust at the faintest touch. I didn't want to risk damaging them.

So that was that.

'Well, guys.' I threw the cardboard to one side and rubbed my hand against my jeans. 'I did my best.'

There didn't seem any point in staying in the garage any longer. It was what it was. Clearing it out could now be added to my long list of tasks, but at least it wasn't an urgent one.

What was it in here that had interested my visitor so much? It was obviously just junk. But now that the encounter had faded a little, I wondered if he might even have been telling the truth and I'd simply misunderstood what I had seen.

Outside, I clicked the padlock back in place, sealing the butterflies within. It seemed remarkable that they'd survived in there for so long in such fruitless and inhospitable conditions. But as I walked back up the drive to the front of the house, I thought about Jake and me, and I realized that was just what happened.

The butterflies didn't have a choice, after all.

That's what living things do. Even in the toughest of circumstances, they keep living.

Fifteen

The room was small, but because every surface was painted white it had the sensation of infinite space. A place without walls. Or perhaps somewhere out of space and time altogether. To anyone watching on CCTV, Pete always imagined it must look like a scene from a science-fiction film, with one person sitting in an endless, empty environment in which the virtual surroundings had yet to be built around them.

He ran his fingertip over the surface of a desk that completely divided the room. It squeaked slightly. Everything here was clean, polished, sterile.

And then the room was silent again.

He waited.

When there was something awful that had to be faced, it was better to face it immediately; as bad as the event might be, it would occur regardless, and at least that way you wouldn't have to endure the anticipation as well. Frank Carter understood that. Pete had visited him at least once a year since his incarceration, and the man always made him wait. There would be some petty delay back in the cell block – some manufactured incident. It was a statement of control, making it clear which of the two men was in charge of proceedings. The fact that Pete was the one who could leave afterwards should have been reassuring, but it never was. He had nothing to offer Carter but diversion and entertainment. Only one of them had anything the other wanted, and they both knew it.

So he waited, like a good boy.

A few minutes later, the door on the far side of the desk was unlocked, and two prison guards entered, moving to either side of it. The doorway itself remained empty. The monster, as always, was taking his time to arrive.

There was the usual sense of unease as the moment approached. The escalation of the pulse. He'd long stopped trying to prepare questions for these meetings, as the words inevitably scattered into a jumble in his mind, like birds startled from a tree. But he forced his face into a blank expression and tried to keep as calm as possible. His upper body ached from the gym session that morning.

Finally, Carter stepped into view.

He was dressed in pale blue overalls, and was manacled at the hands and feet. Still sporting the familiar shaved head and ginger goatee. As always, he ducked slightly as he shuffled in, even though he didn't need to. At six foot five and seventeen stone, Carter was an enormous man, but he never missed an opportunity to make himself seem bigger.

Two more guards followed him in, escorting him to the chair on the far side of the desk. Then the four departed, leaving Pete alone with Carter. The door closing at the back of the room seemed like one of the loudest sounds he had ever heard.

Carter stared at him, amused.

'Good morning, Peter.'

'Frank,' Pete said. 'You're looking well.'

'Living well.' Carter patted his stomach, the chains binding his wrists rattling softly. 'Living very well indeed.'

Pete nodded. Whenever he visited, it always surprised him how Carter seemed to be not only surviving his incarceration but thriving on it. Much of his time appeared to have been spent in the prison gym, and yet, while he remained as physically formidable as he had been at the time of his arrest, there was also no denying that the years in prison had softened him in some way. He looked *comfortable*. Sitting there now, with his legs splayed and one beefy arm resting on the chair arm, he might have been a king lounging on a throne, surveying a courtier. It was as though, outside these walls, Carter had been a dangerous animal, angry and at war with the world, but caged in here with his celebrity status and coterie of fawning fans, he'd finally found a niche in which he could relax.

'You're looking well too, Peter,' Carter said. 'Eating well. Keeping in good shape, I see. How's the family?'

'I don't know,' Pete said. 'How's yours?'

The sparkle went out of Carter's eyes at that. It was always a mistake to needle the man, but it was sometimes hard to resist, and Carter's wife and son provided an easy target. Pete still remembered the look on Carter's face as he listened to Jane Carter's testimony playing in the court via video link. The man must have imagined she was too scared and broken to turn against him, but in the end she had, letting Pete into the extension and retracting the alibis she'd given her husband in the months before. His expression that day was similar to the one he wore now. However comfortable Carter might be in here, the hate he felt for his family had never waned.

He leaned forward suddenly.

'Do you know,' he said, 'I had the most extraordinary dream last night.'

Pete forced a smile.

'Did you? Jesus, Frank. I'm not sure I want to know.'

'Oh no, you do.' Carter settled back, then laughed to himself. 'You really do. Because the boy was there, you see? The Smith boy. At first, as I'm dreaming, I'm not sure it's him, because all those little bastards are the same, aren't they? Any one of them will do. Plus his top is all pulled up over his face so I can't see it properly, which is the way I like it. But it's him. Because you see, I remember what he was wearing, right?'

Blue jogging bottoms. Little black polo shirt.

Pete didn't say anything.

'And someone's crying,' Carter said. 'But it isn't him. For one thing, he's long past the crying stage by now; that's all done with. And the sound's coming from off to one side anyway. So I turn my head, and I spot them both there – the mother and father. They've seen what I've done to their boy and they're sobbing – all their hopes and dreams, and look what I've gone and done.' He frowned. 'What are their names?'

Again, Pete didn't reply.

'Miranda and Alan.' Carter nodded to himself. 'I remember now. They were in court that time, weren't they? You sat with them.'

'Yes.'

'Right. So, Miranda and Alan are crying these big fat tears, and they're looking at me. *Tell us where he is.* They're begging me, you see? It's a bit pathetic, but all that does is remind me of you, and I think to myself, Peter wants to know that too, and he might come visit me again soon.' Carter smiled across the table. 'He's my friend, right? I should try and help him out. And so I look around more carefully, trying to work out where I am and where the boy is. Because I've never been able to remember that one, have I?'

'No.'

'And then the most amazing thing happens.'

'Does it?'

'Really amazing. Do you know what it is?'

'You wake up,' Pete said.

Carter tipped his head back and laughed, then clapped his hands together as best he could. The chains rattled as he applauded. When he finished and spoke again, his voice was back to its normal volume, and his eyes had regained that familiar sparkle.

'You know me too well, Peter. Yeah, I wake up. A shame, though, isn't it? Guess Miranda and Alan – and you – will have to keep crying for a while longer.'

Pete wasn't going to take the bait.

'Did you see anyone else in your dream?' he said.

'Anyone else? Like who?'

'I don't know. Anyone else there with you? Helping you maybe.'

It was too blunt an approach to get a direct answer but, as always, he watched Carter's reaction to the question carefully. On the matter of a potential accomplice, Carter had generally played it well: sometimes amused, sometimes bored, but never confirming or denying a second individual having been involved in the murders. This time, he smiled to himself, but the reaction was different from normal. Today, there was an extra edge to it.

He knows why I'm here.

'I wondered how long it would take you to come and see me,' Carter said. 'With that little boy going missing and all. I'm surprised it's taken you until now.'

'I asked before now. You said no.'

'What? Refuse to see my good friend Peter?' Carter feigned outrage. 'As if I'd do that. I'm guessing that maybe the requests didn't filter through to me. An administrative error. They're next to useless in here.'

Pete forced a shrug.

'That's okay, Frank. You're not actually a priority. You've

been in prison a while now, so it's safe to say that you're not a suspect with this one.'

The smile returned to the man's face.

'Not me, no. But for you, it always comes back to me, doesn't it? It always ends where it starts.'

'What does that mean?'

'It means what it means. So what is it you want to ask me?'

'Your dream, Frank, like I said. Was there anyone else there?'

'Maybe. You know what dreams are like, though. They fade quickly. Shame, isn't it?'

Pete stared at Carter for a moment, evaluating him. It would have been easy enough for him to have learned about Neil Spencer's disappearance; it had been all over the news. Did Carter know anything else, though? He was clearly enjoying giving the impression that he did, but that didn't mean anything in itself. It could easily be just another power play. Another way for him to make himself seem bigger and more important than he really was.

'Lots of things fade,' Pete said. 'Notoriety, for one.'

'Not in here.'

'In the outside world, though. People have forgotten all about you.'

'Oh, I'm certain that's not true.'

'You've not been in the papers for a while, you know. Yesterday's man. Barely even that actually – this little boy went missing a couple of months ago, like you say, and you know how many of the news reports mentioned you?'

'I don't know, Peter. Why don't you tell me?'

'None of them.'

'Huh. Maybe I should start granting the interviews all those academics and journalists keep asking for? I might do that.'

He smirked, and the futility of the situation hit Pete. He was putting himself through this for nothing; Carter didn't know anything. And it would end the same as it always did. He knew full well how he would be afterwards – the way that talking to Carter brought everything back. Later, the pull of the kitchen cabinet would be stronger than ever.

'Yes, maybe you should.' He stood up, turned his back on Carter and walked away. 'Goodbye, Frank.'

'They might be interested in the whispers.'

Pete stopped, one hand on the door. A shiver ran up his back, then spread down his arms.

The whispers.

Neil Spencer had told his mother about a monster whispering outside his window, but that aspect of the boy's disappearance had never been made public or found its way into the news. It could still be fishing, of course. Except that Carter had played it more triumphantly than that, like a trump card.

Pete turned around slowly.

Carter was still reclining nonchalantly in his chair, but there was a smug look on his face now. Just enough bait added to the hook to keep his fish from swimming off. And Pete was suddenly sure that the reference to whispers hadn't been guesswork at all.

Somehow, the bastard knew.

But how?

Right now, more than ever before, he had to remain calm. Carter would feed on any sense of need he detected in the man across from him, and he already had enough of that to play with.

They might be interested in the whispers.

'What do you mean by that, Frank?'

'Well, the little boy saw a monster at his window, didn't

he? One that was talking to him.' Carter leaned forward again. 'Talking. Very. Quietly.'

Pete tried to fight down the frustration, but it was beginning to whirl inside him. Carter knew something, and a little boy was missing. They needed to find him.

'How do you know about the whispers?' he said.

'Ah! That would be telling.'

'So tell me.'

Carter smiled. The expression of a man who had nothing to lose or gain beyond the pain and frustration of others.

'I'll tell you,' he said, 'but first you have to give me something I want.'

'And what would that be?'

Carter leaned back, the amusement suddenly gone from his face now. For a moment, his eyes were blank, but then the hate flared there, as visible as two pinpricks of fire.

'Bring my family to me,' he said.

'Your family?'

'That bitch and that little cunt. Bring them here and give me five minutes alone with them.'

Pete stared at Carter. For a second, he was overwhelmed by the anger and madness blazing across the table from the man. Then Carter threw back his head, rattled the chains at his wrists, and the silence in the room was broken as he laughed and laughed and laughed.

Sixteen

'Give him five minutes alone with his old family?' Amanda thought about it. 'Could we conceivably do that?'

But then she saw the look on Pete's face.

'I'm joking, by the way.'

'I'm aware of that.'

He slumped down in the chair on the other side of her desk and closed his eyes.

Amanda watched him for a moment. He looked drained and diminished compared to their first meeting. She didn't know him well, of course, and their interactions over the past two months had hardly been extensive, but he'd struck her as . . . well, what? A man in control of his emotions. In excellent shape for a guy his age, obviously. Calm and capable. He'd barely wasted a word talking her through the old case, and had even been implacable and detached when he was showing her the photographs taken inside Frank Carter's extension – scenes of horror that he'd witnessed first-hand. It had actually been quite intimidating. It had made her worry about how she was bearing up already, never mind how she'd cope if it came to the worst.

It won't.

The sensible coppers let it go. DCI Lyons was like that, she was sure, because that was the only way to climb – with as little weight holding you down as possible. Before Neil Spencer went missing, she'd imagined she would be the same, but she was no longer quite so sure. And if she'd initially thought Pete Willis was calm and detached, then looking at him now made her re-evaluate that first impression. He was just good at keeping the world at a distance, she thought, and Frank Carter was a man who could get closer to him than most.

Not so surprising, given the history they shared, and the fact that one of Carter's victims had never been found – a kid that had effectively gone missing on Pete's watch. She glanced at her computer screen and saw the familiar photo of Neil Spencer in his football shirt. Neil had vanished just over two months ago, and his absence was an actual physical *ache* inside her. No matter how much she tried not to think about it, the feeling of failure worsened every day. She couldn't imagine how bad it might feel after twenty years. She didn't want to end up like the man sitting across from her now.

It won't come to that.

'Talk me through the accomplice theory again,' she said.

'There's very little there, really.' Pete opened his eyes. 'There's a witness report of an older man with grey hair talking to Tony Smith, which doesn't match Carter's description. And then there are some overlaps on the abduction windows.'

'Pretty thin stuff.'

'I know. Sometimes people want things to be more complicated than they really are.'

'It's possible for him to have committed these crimes entirely alone. Occam's Razor states that –'

'I know what Occam's Razor states.' Pete ran his hand through his hair. '*Do not multiply assumptions unnecessarily.* The simplest solution that fits all the facts is the one you go with.'

'Exactly.'

'And that's what we do here, isn't it? We get our guy, and we prove he's done it, and that's enough for us. So we tie a bow round the investigation, stick it in the filing cabinet and move on. Case closed, job done. On to the next.'

She thought about Lyons again. About climbing.

'Because that's what we have to do,' she said.

'But sometimes it's not good enough.' Pete shook his head. 'Sometimes things that look simple turn out to be much more complicated, and the extra stuff ends up being missed.'

'And the extra stuff in this case,' she said, 'could include someone getting away with murder?'

'Who knows? I've tried not to think about it over the years.'

'I think that's wise.'

'But now we have Neil Spencer. We have the whispers and the monster. And we have Frank fucking Carter sitting there, knowing something about it.'

She waited.

'And I don't know what to do about it,' Pete said. 'Carter isn't going to tell us anything. And we've been over his known associates a hundred times. They're all clear.'

Amanda thought about it. 'Copycat?'

'Possibly. But Carter wasn't guessing back in that room. The whispers never made it to the press, and he knew about them. No visitors aside from me. The correspondence he receives is all vetted. So how does he *know*?'

His frustration was suddenly so palpable that she was surprised he didn't hit the table. Instead, he shook his head again and looked away to one side. At least it had brought him back to life a little, Amanda thought. That was a good thing. Fuck calm – she was a keen believer in the idea that rage was a good motivator, and God knew there were times when you needed something to keep you going. At the same time, she could tell that a great deal of Pete's anger was directed inwards: that he blamed himself for not having been able to get to the truth. And that was no good. She was an equally keen believer in the idea that guilt was about as unhelpful as emotions got. Once you let guilt get hold of you, the bastard never lets go.

'Carter was never going to help us,' she said. 'Not willingly.'

'No.'

'The dream about Tony Smith – ?'

He waved it away. 'That's just business as usual. I've heard all that before. I have no doubt he killed Tony, and that he knows exactly where he left him. But he's never going to say. Not when it's something to hold over us. Over *me*.'

It was clear to her now how much going to see Carter took out of Pete. And yet, as hard as it must be, he went regardless – still put himself through the ordeal – because finding Tony Smith meant that much to him. But Carter had found a new game to play now, and they had to focus on that. While she understood Pete's turmoil, the fact remained that Tony Smith had been dead for a long time, while Neil Spencer could still be alive.

Was still alive.

'Well, he's got another hold over us now,' Amanda said. 'But remember something. You said that you go to see him in case he gives information away by accident.'

'Yes.'

'Well, he has – he knows something, doesn't he? That can't have happened by magic. So we have to work out how.'

When he didn't reply, she thought about it herself.

No visitors. No correspondence.

'What about friends inside?' she said.

'He's got loads of those.'

'Which is surprising on one level. Child killer, and all.'

'There was never a sexual element to the murders, which helps him a bit. And physically, he's still an absolute monster. Plus, there's the celebrity of it all – all that Whisper Man rubbish. He has his own little kingdom in there.'

'Okay. So who's he closest to?'

'I've no idea.'

'But we can find out, right?' Amanda leaned forward. 'Maybe he's been passed the information second-hand? Someone visits one of his friends. Friend tells Carter. Carter talks to you.'

Pete considered that. A moment later, he looked annoyed with himself for not having thought of it himself.

She felt a flush of pride – not that she needed to impress him, of course. She just needed him motivated, or at least not walking so obviously wounded.

'Yes,' he said. 'That's a good idea.'

'So do it . . .' She hesitated. 'Not that's it my place to give you things to do. But that would be a way forward for us, wouldn't it? If you've got time.'

'I've got the time.'

But he paused at the door.

'There's another thing,' he said. 'You said Carter had given something away – that he knows about the whispers somehow.'

'Right.'

'But there's also the timing. For two months now, he's been refusing to see me. That's never happened before. And suddenly he changes his mind and wants to see me.'

'Meaning?'

'I don't know for sure. But we might need to prepare ourselves for there being a reason for that.'

It took a second for her to understand what he was implying, and then she looked back at the photo of Neil Spencer, not wanting to think about the possibility.

It won't come to that.

Except that Pete was right. There had been two months without a single development or break in the case. Perhaps Carter's decision to talk meant one was about to come.

Seventeen

At lunchtime, Jake sat by himself on a bench in the playground, watching the other children running around getting all hot and sweaty. It was very noisy and they all seemed oblivious to him. This was a new school year, but his class had all known each other for a long time, and it had become apparent that morning that they weren't much interested in knowing anyone else. Which was okay. Jake would have been happier sitting inside drawing, but you weren't allowed, so he had to sit out here next to some bushes instead, kicking his legs and waiting for the bell to ring.

You start school tomorrow. I'm sure you'll make lots of new friends there.

Quite often, Daddy didn't know how wrong he was. Although Jake wondered if perhaps he did, because the way he'd said it had sounded more hopeful than anything else, and maybe deep down they had both known it was never going to turn out that way. Mummy would have told him it didn't matter, and she would have made him believe it too. But Jake thought that it did matter to Daddy. Jake was aware that he could be very disappointing sometimes.

The morning had basically gone okay, at least. They had practised some simple times tables, which were all pretty easy, and that was good. The classroom had a traffic-light system on the wall for bad behaviour, and everybody's name was currently on the green area at the bottom. George, the classroom assistant, was nice, but Mrs Shelley, the class teacher, seemed very stern indeed, and Jake really didn't want to move up to amber on his first day. He couldn't make friends, but he could at least manage that. That was really your job at school – to do what you were told and fill in the answers to the blanks, and not cause any problems by thinking up too many questions of your own.

Crunch.

Jake flinched as a football crashed into the bushes beside him. He had already memorized the names of all the children in his class, and it was Owen who came sprinting over to retrieve it. He was coming for the ball but glaring at Jake the whole time, which made Jake think it might have been deliberate. Unless Owen was just really bad at football.

'Sorry about that.'

'It's okay.'

'Yeah. I know it's okay.'

Owen pulled the ball roughly out of the branches, still glaring at Jake as though it was all his fault, and then stalked away. Which didn't make sense. Perhaps Owen was just really stupid. Even so, it might be better to move.

'Hello, Jake.'

He looked to one side, and saw the little girl kneeling in the bushes. His heart leapt with relief, and he started to get up.

'Shhh.' She put a finger to her lips. 'Don't.'

He sat down again. But it was hard. He wanted to bounce on the bench! She looked exactly the same as she always did, wearing the same blue and white dress, with that graze on her knee and her hair swept oddly out to one side.

'Just sit as you were,' she said. 'I don't want the other children to see you talking to me.'

'Why not?'

'Because I shouldn't be here.'

'Yes, you're not wearing the right uniform for one thing.'

'That is one thing, yes.' She thought about it. 'It's good to see you again, Jake. I've missed you. Have you missed me?'

He nodded vigorously, but then forced himself to calm down. The other children were there, and the football was still thudding around. He didn't want to give the little girl away. But it was so good to see her! The truth was that he'd been very lonely in the new house. Daddy had tried to play with him a few times, but you could tell his heart wasn't really in it. He'd play for ten minutes and then get up and say his legs needed a rest, even though it was obvious he really just wanted to do something else instead. Whereas the little girl would always play with him for as long as he wanted her to. He'd been expecting to see her *all the time* after moving to the new house, but she hadn't been there at all.

Until now.

'Have you made any new friends yet?' she said.

'Not really. Adam, Josh and Hassan seem okay. Owen isn't very nice.'

'Owen is a little shit,' she said.

Jake stared at her.

'But a lot of people are, aren't they?' she said quickly. 'And not everybody who acts like your friend really is.'

'But you are?'

'Of course I am.'

'Will you come and play with me again?'

'I'd like to. But it's not as simple as that, is it?'

Jake's heart sank, because no, he knew that it wasn't. He wanted to see her all the time but Daddy didn't want him talking to her. 'I'm here. *We're* here. New house, new start,' he'd said.

Or at least, Jake wanted to see her all the time when she wasn't looking as serious as she was right now.

'Tell me,' she said. 'Tell me the rhyme.'

'I don't want to.'

'Say it.'

'If you leave a door half open, soon you'll hear the whispers spoken.'

'And the rest.'

Jake closed his eyes.

'If you play outside alone, soon you won't be going home.'

'Keep going.'

She sounded barely there now.

'If your window's left unlatched, you'll hear him tapping at the glass.'

'And?'

The word was so quiet that it might have been nothing more than air. Jake swallowed. He didn't want to say it, but he forced himself to, speaking as quietly as the little girl just had.

'If you're lonely, sad and blue, the Whisper Man will come for you.'

The bell rang.

Jake opened his eyes to see the children in the playground in front of him. Owen was there with a couple of older boys Jake didn't recognize. They were watching him. George was there too, a concerned expression on his face. After a second, the children started laughing, and then headed away towards the main doors, glancing over their shoulders at him.

Jake looked to his side.

The little girl was gone again.

'Who were you talking to at lunchtime?'

Jake wanted to ignore Owen. They were supposed to be writing joined-up letters in their lined books, and he wanted to concentrate on that, because it was what they'd been told to do. Obviously, Owen didn't care; he was leaning over the table and staring at Jake. It was clear to Jake that Owen was one of those boys who didn't care about being told off. He also knew that telling Owen about the little girl would be a very bad idea. Daddy didn't like him talking to her, but Jake didn't think he would ever make fun of him for doing so. He was pretty sure that Owen would.

So he shrugged. 'Nobody.'

'Somebody.'

'I didn't see anybody there. Did you?'

Owen considered the matter, then leaned back.

'*That*,' he said, 'was Neil's chair.'

'What was?'

'Your chair, idiot. It was Neil's.'

Owen seemed angry about this, although once again, Jake wasn't sure what he was supposed to have done wrong. Mrs Shelley had told them all where to sit that morning. It wasn't like he'd stolen this Neil person's chair on purpose.

'Who's Neil?'

'He was here last year,' Owen said. 'He's not here any more, because someone took him away. And now you've got his chair.'

There was an obvious error in Owen's thinking.

'You were in the Year One classroom last year,' Jake said. 'So this was never Neil's chair.'

'It would have been, if he hadn't been taken away.'

'Where did he move to?'

'He didn't move anywhere. Someone took him.'

Jake didn't know what to think about that, as it didn't make sense. Neil's parents had taken him somewhere but he hadn't moved? Jake looked at Owen, and the boy's angry eyes were clearly full of dark knowledge that he was desperate to pass on.

'A bad man took him,' Owen said.

'Took him where?'

'Nobody knows. But he's dead now, and you're sitting in his chair.'

A girl called Tabby was also sitting at the table.

'That's horrible,' she told Owen. 'You don't know Neil's dead. And when I asked my mummy, she said it wasn't nice to talk about anyway.'

'He *is* dead.' Owen turned back to Jake and gestured at the chair. 'That means you'll be next.'

That didn't make sense either, Jake decided. Owen really hadn't thought this through at all. For one thing, whatever had happened to Neil, he'd never sat in this particular chair, so it wasn't like it was cursed or anything.

And also, there was a much more likely possibility. It was one he knew he shouldn't say, and he remained silent for a second. But then he remembered what the little girl had told him outside, and how alone he felt, and he decided that if Owen could treat him like this then why couldn't he treat Owen the same right back?

'Maybe it means I'll be *last*,' he said.

Owen narrowed his eyes.

'What's that supposed to mean?'

'Maybe the bad man will take the class one by one, and they'll all be replaced by new boys and girls. So that means the Whisper Man will take you all before me.'

Tabby gasped in shock, then burst into tears.

'You've made Tabby cry,' Owen said matter-of-factly. The teacher was making her way over to the table. 'Mrs Shelley, Jake told Tabby the Whisper Man was going to kill her like he did Neil, and she got upset.'

Which was how Jake went up to amber on his first day.

Daddy was going to be very disappointed.

Eighteen

The day had gone better than I expected.

Eight hundred words might have been a relatively meagre tally, but after not writing anything for months, at least it was a start.

I read it through again now.

Rebecca.

At the moment, it was about her. Not a story in itself, or even the beginning of one as things stood, but the beginning of a letter to her, and one that was difficult to read. There were so many happy memories to draw on, and I knew they would surface as I continued, but while I loved and missed her more than I could say, I also couldn't deny the ugly kernel of resentment I felt, the frustration at being left alone with Jake, the loneliness of that empty bed. The sense of being *abandoned* to deal with things I felt I couldn't cope with. None of that was her fault, of course, but grief is a stew with a thousand ingredients, and not all of them are palatable. What I'd written was an honest expression of a small part of how I felt.

Groundwork, basically. I had an idea now of what I could write about. A man, a little like me, who had lost a woman, a little like her. And as painful as it would be to explore, I could do that, moving from the ugliness to the beauty, and hopefully some final sense of resolution and acceptance. Sometimes writing can help to heal you. I didn't know if that would be the case here, but it was something to aim for.

I saved the file, and then went to pick up Jake.

When I arrived at the school, all the other parents were lined up against the wall, waiting. There was probably strict but unspoken etiquette about where to stand, but it had been a long day and I decided I didn't care. Instead, I spotted Karen standing by herself near the gate and just went over to her. The afternoon was even warmer than the morning, but she was still dressed as though prepared for snow.

'Hello again,' she said. 'Do you think he survived?'

'I'm pretty sure they'd have phoned by now if not.'

'I imagine so. How was your day? Well, I call it a day. How were your six hours of freedom?'

'Interesting,' I said. 'I finally looked in our new garage and discovered that the previous owner decided to empty out all the junk by hiding it in there.'

'Ah. How annoying. But also how *cunning*.'

I laughed, but only slightly. The writing had taken away some of the unease from the man calling round, but it returned to me now.

'I also had some random guy snooping about.'

'Okay, that sounds less good.'

'Yeah. He said he grew up in the house and wanted to look around. Not sure I believed him.'

'You didn't let him in, right?'

'God, no.'

'Whereabouts have you moved?'

'Garholt Street.'

'Just around the corner from us.' She nodded. 'The scary house, by any chance?'

The scary house. My heart sank a little.

'Probably. Although I prefer to think of it as having character.'

'Oh, it does.' She nodded again. 'I saw it was up for sale over the summer. It's not really scary at all, obviously, but Adam used to say it looked strange.'

'Totally the right place for me and Jake, then.'

'I'm sure that's not true.' She smiled, then leaned away from the wall as the school door opened. 'Here we go. The beasts are loose.'

Jake's class teacher came out and stood by the door, looking over the parents and then calling over her shoulder for individual children. They came scurrying out one by one, their book bags and water bottles swinging at their sides. Mrs Shelley, I remembered. She looked somewhat unforgiving. I was sure her gaze landed on me a few times, but it moved on before I could tell her I was Jake's dad. A boy I presumed was Adam joined us and Karen ruffled his hair.

'Good day, kid?'

'Yes, Mum.'

'Come on, then.' She turned to me. 'See you tomorrow.'

'You will.'

After they headed off, I waited some more, until it seemed I was the only parent still standing there. Finally, Mrs Shelley beckoned me over. I walked across, effectively summoned.

'You're Jake's dad?'

'Yes.'

Jake stepped out towards me, staring down at the ground, looking small and subdued. *Oh God*, I thought. *Something has happened.*

That was why we'd been left until last.

'Is there a problem?'

'Nothing major,' Mrs Shelley said. 'But I still wanted a word. Do you want to tell your father what happened, Jake?'

'I got put on the amber square, Dad.'

'The what?'

'We have a traffic-light system on the wall,' Mrs Shelley explained. 'For naughtiness. As a result of his behaviour today, Jake's the first of our children to move up to amber. So not an ideal first day.'

'What did he do?'

'I told Tabby she was going to die,' Jake said.

'And Owen too,' Mrs Shelley added.

'And Owen too.'

'Well,' I said. And then, because I couldn't think of anything more sensible to add, 'We *are* all going to die.'

Mrs Shelley was not impressed.

'That is not funny, Mr Kennedy.'

'I know.'

'There was a boy here last year,' Mrs Shelley said. 'Neil Spencer? You might have seen about him on the news.'

The name rang the vaguest of bells.

'He went missing,' she said.

'Oh yes.'

I remembered now. Something about the parents letting him walk home on his own.

'It's all been very unpleasant . . .' Mrs Shelley looked at Jake and hesitated. 'It's not something we like to talk about. Jake suggested that these other children might be next.'

'Right. And so he's . . . on amber?'

'For the next week. If he moves up to red, he'll have to go to see the headmistress.'

I looked down at Jake, who appeared utterly miserable. I didn't much like the idea of him being publicly shamed on a wall, but at the same time, I was frustrated with him. It seemed such an awful thing for him to have said. Why would he have done that?

'Right,' I said. 'Well, I'm disappointed to hear about this behaviour, Jake. Very disappointed.'

His head sank lower.

'We'll talk about it on the way home.' I turned to Mrs Shelley. 'And it won't happen again, I promise.'

'Let's make sure it doesn't. There's something else too.' She stepped closer to me and spoke more quietly, even though it was obvious Jake would still be able to hear. 'Our teaching assistant saw him at lunchtime, and was a little concerned. He said that Jake was talking to himself?'

I closed my eyes, my heart properly falling now. God, not that as well. Not in front of everyone.

Why couldn't things be simple?

Why couldn't we just fit in here?

'I'll talk to him,' I said again.

Except that Jake refused to talk to me.

I tried to coax the information out of him on the way home, gently at first, but after being met by repeated stony silences, I lost my temper a little. I knew it was wrong even as I did, because the truth was that I wasn't really angry with *him*. It was just the situation. Irritation that things hadn't gone as well as I'd hoped. Disappointment that his imaginary friend had returned. Concern about what the other children would think and how they would treat him. Eventually I fell into a silence of my own, and we walked alongside each other like strangers.

Back home, I went through his book bag. His Packet of Special Things was still there, at least. There was also some reading to do, which I thought looked a little basic for him.

'I mess everything up, don't I?' Jake said quietly.

I put the papers down. He was standing by the settee, head bowed, looking smaller than ever.

'No,' I said. 'Of course you don't.'

'That's what you think.'

'I don't think that, Jake. I'm actually very proud of you.'

'I'm not. I hate myself.'

Hearing him say that was like being stabbed.

'Don't say that,' I said quickly, then knelt down and tried to hug him. But he was completely unresponsive. 'You mustn't ever say that.'

'Can I do some drawing?' he asked blankly.

I took a deep breath, moving away slightly. I was desperate to get through to him, but it was obvious that wasn't going to happen right now. We could talk about it later, though. We *would* do.

'All right.'

I went through to my office, and touched the trackpad so that I could look back over the day's work. *I hate myself.* I'd told him off for saying that, but if I was honest, they were words I'd thought about myself quite a lot over the last year. I felt them again now. Why was I such a failure? How could I be so incapable of saying and doing the right thing? Rebecca had always told me that Jake and I were very much alike, and so perhaps the same thoughts were going through his head right now. While it might be true that we still loved each other when we argued, it didn't mean that we loved ourselves.

Why had he said such an awful thing at school? He'd been talking to himself – but of course, that wasn't really the case. I had no doubt at all that it was the little girl he'd been speaking with – that she'd finally found us – and I had no idea what to do about that. If he couldn't make real friends, he would always have to rely on imaginary ones. And if they caused him to behave the way he had today, surely that meant he needed help?

'Play with me.'

I looked up from the screen.

A moment of silence followed in which my heart began beating harder.

The voice had come from the living room, but it hadn't sounded like Jake at all. It had been croaky and vile.

'I don't want to.'

That was Jake.

I stepped closer to the doorway, listening intently.

'Play with me, I said.'

'No.'

Although both voices had to belong to my son, they seemed so distinct that it was easy to believe there really was another child through there with him. Except it didn't sound like a child at all. The voice was too old and throaty for that. I glanced at the front door beside me. I hadn't locked it when we got back home and the chain wasn't on. Was it possible someone else had come in? No – I had only been in the next room. I would have heard them, if so.

'Yes. You're going to play with me.'

The voice sounded like it was relishing the prospect.

'You're scaring me,' Jake said.

'I want to scare you.'

And at that, I finally moved into the front room, walking quickly. Jake was kneeling on the floor next to his drawings, staring at me with wide, frightened eyes.

He was totally alone, but that did nothing for my heart rate. As had happened before in the house, there was a sense of a lingering presence in the room, as though someone or something had darted out of sight just before I arrived.

'Jake?' I said quietly.

He swallowed hard, looking like he was going to cry.

'Jake, who were you talking to?'

'Nobody.'

'I heard you talking. You were pretending to be someone else. Someone who wanted to play with you.'

'No, I wasn't!' Suddenly, he seemed less frightened than angry, as though I'd let him down somehow. 'You always say that, and it isn't fair!'

I blinked in surprise, and then stood there helplessly as he began stuffing papers into his Packet of Special Things. I didn't always say that, did I? He must have known I didn't like him talking to himself – that it bothered me – but it wasn't as though I'd ever actually told him off for it.

I walked across and sat down on the settee near him.

'Jake –'

'I'm going to my room!'

'Please don't. I'm worried about you.'

'No, you're not. You don't care about me at all.'

'That's *not* true.'

But he was already past me and heading for the living-room door. My instinct told me to let him go for now – to allow things to cool down, and then talk later – but I also wanted to reassure him. I struggled for the right words.

'I thought you liked the little girl,' I said. 'I thought you wanted to see her again.'

'It wasn't her!'

'Who was it then?'

'It was the boy in the floor.'

And then he was out of sight in the hallway.

I sat there for a moment, unable to think of what to say. The boy in the floor. I remembered the raspy voice that Jake had been talking to himself with. And of course, that was the only explanation for what I'd heard. But even so, I felt a chill run through me. It hadn't sounded like him at all.

I want to scare you.

And then I looked down. While Jake had gathered most

of his things together, a single sheet of paper remained there, a few crayons lying abandoned around it. Yellow, green and purple.

I stared at the picture. Jake had been drawing butterflies. They were childishly imprecise, but still clearly recognizable as the ones I'd seen in the garage this morning. But that was impossible, because he'd never been in the garage. I was about to pick the sheet up and examine it more closely when I heard him burst into tears.

I stood up and ran out into the hallway, just as he emerged, sobbing from my office, pushing past me and running up the stairs.

'Jake –'

'Leave me alone! *I hate you!*'

I watched him go, feeling helpless, unable to keep up with what was happening, not understanding.

His bedroom door slammed.

I walked numbly into my office.

And then I saw the awful things I'd written to Rebecca there on the screen. Words about how hard everything was without her, and how a part of me blamed her for leaving me to deal with all this. Words my son must have just read. And I closed my eyes as I understood only too well.

Nineteen

Pete was sitting at his dinner table when the call came through. He should have been cooking or watching television, but the kitchen behind him remained dark and cold, and the living room was silent. Instead, he was staring at the bottle and the photograph.

He had been staring at them for a long time.

The day had taken a heavy toll on him. Seeing Carter always did, but this was much worse than usual. Despite waving away Amanda's question, the killer's description of his dream about Tony Smith had got to Pete – it was anything but 'business as usual'. Last night, he had been determined to forget about Neil Spencer, but that wasn't possible now. The cases were connected. He was involved.

But what use was he? An afternoon spent investigating visitors to friends of Carter inside had proved fruitless – so far, at least. There were still several to look at. The sad truth was that the bastard had more friends in prison than Pete had outside of it.

So drink then.

You're worthless. You're useless. Just do it.

The urge was stronger than ever, but he could survive this. After all, he had resisted the voice in the past. And yet the idea of returning the bottle unopened to the kitchen cabinet brought a sense of despair. It felt like there was an inevitability to him drinking.

He pressed his hand to his chin, slowly rubbing the skin

around his mouth, and looked at the photograph of him and Sally.

Many years ago, in an effort to combat the self-hatred that plagued him, Sally had encouraged him to make a list: two columns, one for his positive attributes, one for negative, so that he could see for himself how well they balanced out. It hadn't helped. The feeling of failure was too ingrained to be dispelled with mathematics. She had tried so hard to help him, but in the end it had always been the drink he'd turned to instead.

And he could see that in the photograph. Although they both looked happy, the signs were there. The way Sally's eyes were wide open to the sun, her skin luminescent, whereas he seemed unsure, as though a part of him was reluctant to allow the light in. He had loved her as deeply as she loved him, but the gift and receipt of love was a language with foreign grammar to him. And because he believed he was undeserving of such love, he had slowly drunk himself into becoming a man who was. As with his father, distance had helped him understand all that. Battles often make more sense when viewed from the sky.

Too late.

It had been so many years now, but he wondered where Sally was and what she was doing. The only consolation was that he knew she must be happy somewhere, and that their separation had saved her from a life with him. The idea that she was out there, living the life she had always deserved, sustained him.

This is what you lose by drinking.
This is why it's not worth it.

But of course, the voice had an answer to that, just as it had an answer to everything. If he'd already lost the most amazing thing he'd ever have in his life, why put himself through this torment?

What did it matter?

He stared at the bottle. And then he felt his phone vibrating against his hip.

For you, it always comes back to me, doesn't it?

It always ends where it starts.

Frank Carter's words returned to him as he swept the beam of his torch over the waste ground, walking slowly and carefully into its pitch-black heart. The sense of sickness and foreboding in his chest was matched only by the feeling of failure. The certainty of it. Carter's words had seemed casual and throwaway at the time, but he should have known better. Nothing Carter said or did was meaningless. He should have recognized the subtle deployment of a message, one deliberately intended to be understood only in hindsight.

He saw the tent and floodlights up ahead of him, with the silhouettes of officers moving cautiously around. The sickness intensified, and he almost stumbled. *One foot in front of the other.* Two months earlier, he had been here searching for a little boy who had gone missing. Tonight, he was here because a little boy had been found.

He remembered how, that night in July, he'd left a dinner going cold on the dining-room table. Tonight, the bottle was there. If he found what he was expecting to here, he would be opening it when he got home.

He reached the canopy and clicked off his torch. The beam was redundant under the strength of the floodlights positioned around it. Seeing what was lying in the centre, in fact, there was altogether too much light. He wasn't ready for that yet. Glancing away, he spotted DCI Lyons standing at the side of the tent, staring back at him, the man's expression blank. For a moment, Pete imagined he saw a flash of contempt there – *you should have stopped this* – and he looked away again quickly, his gaze falling on the television with the pock-marked screen. It was a moment before he realized Amanda was standing beside him.

'This is where he was taken from,' Pete said.

'We can't know that for sure.'

'I'm sure of it,' he said.

She looked away into the darkness. The brightness and intensity of activity in front of them only emphasized the blackness of the waste ground surrounding them.

'It always ends where it starts,' Amanda said. 'That's what Carter told you, right?'

'Yes. I should have picked up on that.'

'Or I should. It's not your fault.'

'Then it's not yours either.'

'Maybe.' She smiled sadly. 'But you look like you need to hear it more than I do.'

He could tell that wasn't true. She looked pale and sick. Over the past couple of months, he'd noticed how efficient and capable she was, and he'd suspected she was ambitious too – that she'd imagined a case like this might help her career without fully understanding what else it might do. He felt a strange kind of kinship with her now. Finding the dead boys in Carter's house had broken him for a time. He knew that Amanda had worked – and hoped – just as hard as he had twenty years ago, and that right now, whatever her expectations, she must be feeling like an open wound.

But it wasn't a kinship that could be spoken of out loud. You walked the road alone. You got through it or you didn't.

Amanda breathed out slowly.

'The fucker *knew*,' she said. 'Didn't he?'

'Yes.'

'So the question then is *how* did he know?'

'I'm not sure yet. I've got nothing on that angle so far. But there's still a long list of friends inside to look at.'

She hesitated.

'Do you want to see the body?'

You can have a drink when you get home.

I'll let you.

'Yes,' he said.

Together, they moved under the canopy, to where the boy was lying spread-eagled close to the old television. His army-fatigue rucksack was on the ground beside him. Pete did his best to take in the details as dispassionately as possible. The clothes, obviously: the blue tracksuit bottoms; the white T-shirt that had been pulled up over the boy's face, turning the design on the front inside out.

'That was never made public,' he said.

Another connection to Carter.

'No real blood.' He peered around the body. 'Not enough, anyway – not for those injuries. He was killed elsewhere.'

'Looks that way.'

'That's a difference between our new man and Carter. Carter killed those children where I found them, and he kept them in his house. He never made any attempt to dump the remains.'

'Apart from Tony Smith.'

'That was down to circumstances. And also, this is public.' He gestured around. 'Whoever did this, they wanted the body to be found. And not just anywhere either. Back where it started, just like Carter told me.'

You can have a drink when you get home.

'The clothes are the ones he went missing in. The injuries aside, it looks like he's been reasonably well cared for. Not obviously emaciated.'

'Another difference from Carter,' Amanda said.

'Yes.'

Pete closed his eyes, trying to think this through. Neil Spencer had been held somewhere for two months before he was killed. He had been looked after. And then something had changed. Afterwards, he had been returned to the place he'd been abducted from.

Like a present, he thought.

A present someone had been given that they decided they didn't want any more.

'The rucksack.' He opened his eyes. 'Is the water bottle in there?'

'Yes. I'll show you.'

He followed her closer still, edging around the boy's body. She used a gloved hand to open the top, and he looked inside. There was the bottle, half full of water. Something else. A blue rabbit – a bedtime toy. That had never been on the list.

'Did he have that with him?'

'We're trying to find out from the parents,' Amanda said. 'But yes. I think he had that with him as well, and they just didn't know.'

Pete nodded slowly. He knew all about Neil Spencer by now. The boy had been disruptive at school. Aggressive. Already old and toughened beyond his years, the way people get when life bruises them.

But underneath all that, still just six years old.

He forced himself to look at the boy's body, not caring about the feelings it evoked or the memories it stirred. He could have a drink when he got home.

We're going to get the person who did this to you.

And then he turned around and stepped away, flicking his torch back on as he entered the darkness beyond the floodlights.

'I'm going to need you on this, Pete,' Amanda called after him.

'I know.' But he was thinking about that bottle on the dining-room table and trying not to break into a run. 'And you're going to have me.'

Twenty

The man stood shivering in the darkness.

Above him, the blue-black sky was clear and speckled with stars, the night a stark, cold contrast to the heat of the day behind him. But it was not the temperature that was making him tremble. Even though he refused to think directly about what he had done that afternoon, the impact of his actions remained with him, just out of sight, buried beneath his skin.

He had never killed before today.

Beforehand, he had imagined he was prepared to do so, and the rage and hatred he had felt in the moment had carried him through. But the act had left him off-kilter afterwards, unsure what he was feeling. He had laughed this evening, and he had cried. He had shaken with shame and self-hatred, but also rocked on the bathroom floor in confused elation. It was impossible to describe. Which made sense, he supposed. He had opened a door that could never be closed, and experienced something few others on the planet ever had or would. There was no preparation or guidebook for the journey he had embarked on. No map showing the course through it. The act of killing had left him adrift on an entirely uncharted sea of emotions.

He breathed the cool night air in slowly now, his body still singing. It was so quiet here that all he could hear was the rush of the air, as though the world was murmuring secrets in its sleep. The street lights in the distance shone brightly, but he was so far from the light here, and standing so motionless, that someone could walk past metres away without seeing him. He would see them, though – or sense them, at least. He felt attuned to the world. And right now, in the early hours of the morning, he could tell that he was totally alone out here.

Waiting.

Full of shivers.

It was difficult now to remember how angry he had been this afternoon. At the time, the rage had simply consumed him, flaring within his chest until his whole body was twisting with the force of it, like a puppet wrenched about on its strings. His head had been so full of blinding light that perhaps he wouldn't be able to recall what he'd done even if he tried. It felt like he had stepped outside himself for a time, and in doing so had allowed something else to emerge. If he had been a religious man, it would have been easy to imagine himself possessed by some external force. But he was not, and he knew that whatever had taken him over in those terrible minutes had come from inside.

It was gone now – or at least it had slunk back down into its cave. What had felt right at the time now brought little more than a sense of guilt and failure. In Neil Spencer, he had found a troubled child who needed to be rescued and cared for, and he had believed that he was the one to do so. He would help and nurture Neil. House him. Care for him.

It had never been his intention to hurt him.

And for two months, it had worked. The man had felt such peace. The boy's presence and apparent contentment had been a balm to him. For the first time he could remember, his world had felt not only possible but *right*, as though some long-standing infection inside him had finally begun to heal.

But of course, it had all been an illusion.

Neil had been lying to him all along, biding his time and only ever pretending to be happy. And finally, the man had been forced to accept that the spark of goodness he'd imagined in the boy's eyes had never been real, just trickery and deceit. From the beginning, he had been too naive and trusting. Neil Spencer had only ever been a snake dressed up in a little boy suit, and the truth was that he had deserved exactly what happened to him today.

The man's heart was beating too hard.

He shook his head, then forced himself to calm down, breathing steadily again and putting such thoughts out of his mind. What had happened today was abhorrent. If, amongst all the other emotions, it also brought its own strange sense of harmony and satisfaction, that was horrible and wrong and had to be fought against. He had to cling instead to the tranquillity of the weeks beforehand, however false it had turned out to be. He had chosen badly, that was all. Neil had been a mistake, and that wouldn't happen again.

The next little boy would be perfect.

Twenty-one

It was harder than ever to get to sleep that night.

I hadn't managed to resolve anything with Jake after our argument. While I could justify what I'd written about Rebecca to myself, it was impossible to make a seven-year-old boy understand. To him, they were just words attacking his mother. He wouldn't talk back to me, and it wasn't clear whether he was even listening. At bedtime, he refused a story, and I stood there helplessly again for a moment, torn between frustration and self-hatred and the desperate need to make him understand. In the end, I just kissed the side of his head gently, told him I loved him, and said goodnight, hoping things might be better in the morning. As if it ever works like that. Tomorrow is always a new day, but there's never any reason to think it will be a better one.

Later, I lay in my own bedroom, shifting from side to side, trying to settle. I couldn't bear the distance that was growing between us. Even worse was the fact that I had no idea how to stop it increasing, never mind close it. And lying there in the dark, I also kept remembering the rasping voice Jake had put on, and shivering each time I did.

I want to scare you.

The boy in the floor.

But as unnerving as that had been, for some reason it was his drawing of the butterflies that bothered me more. The garage was padlocked. There was no way Jake could have been in there without my knowledge. And yet I'd looked at the picture over and over, and there was no mistaking them. Somehow, he'd seen them. But how and where?

It was a coincidence, of course; it had to be. Maybe they were more common than I realized – the ones in the garage must have arrived from somewhere, after all. Obviously, I had tried to talk to Jake about them too. Equally obviously, he had refused to answer me. And so, as I tossed and turned, trying to sleep, I realized the mystery of the butterflies came down to the same thing as the argument itself. I'd just have to hope it would be better in the morning.

Glass smashing.

My mother screaming.

A man shouting.

Wake up, Tom.

Wake up now.

Someone shook my foot.

I jerked awake, soaked with sweat, my heart hammering in my chest. The bedroom was pitch black and quiet – still the middle of the night. Jake was standing at the bottom of the bed again, a black silhouette against the darkness behind him. I rubbed my face.

'Jake?' I said quietly.

No reply. I couldn't see his face, but his upper body was moving gently from side to side, swaying on his feet like a metronome. I frowned.

'Are you awake?'

Again, there was no answer. I sat up in bed, wondering what was the best thing to do. If he was sleepwalking, should I wake him gently, or try to steer him, still asleep, back to his room? But then my eyes adapted a little better to the darkness, and the silhouette grew clearer. His hair was wrong. It was much longer than it should have been, and it seemed to be splayed out to one side.

And . . .

Someone was whispering.

But the figure at the end of the bed, still swaying ever so slowly from side to side, was entirely silent. The sound I could hear was coming from somewhere else in the house.

I looked to my left. The open bedroom door gave me a view of the dark hallway. It was empty, but I thought the whispering was coming from somewhere out there.

'Jake –'

But when I looked back, the silhouette at the end of my bed had disappeared and the room was empty.

I rubbed the sleep from my face, then slid across the cold side of the bed and padded quietly out into the hall. The whispering was a little louder out here. While I couldn't make out any words, it was obvious now that I was hearing two voices: a hushed conversation, with one participant slightly gruffer than the other. Jake was talking to himself again. I moved instinctively towards his room, but then glanced down the stairs and froze where I stood.

My son was at the bottom, sitting by the front door. A soft wedge of street light was curling round the edge of the curtains in my office, off to the side, staining his tousled hair orange. His legs were curled up underneath him, and his head was against the door, with one hand pressed against the frame beside it. In the other, resting against his leg, were the spare keys I kept on the desk in the office.

I listened.

'I'm not sure,' Jake whispered.

The reply was the gruffer voice I'd heard.

'I'll look after you, I promise.'

'I'm not sure.'

'Let me in, Jake.'

My son moved his hand over the door towards the letter

box. That was when I noticed that it was being pushed open from the outside. There were fingers there. My heart leapt at the sight of them. Four thin, pale fingers, poking through amongst the spidery black bristles, holding the letter box open.

'Let me in.'

Jake rested the side of his small hand against one of the fingers, and it curled round to stroke him.

Just let me in.

He reached up for the chain.

'Don't move!' I shouted.

It came out without me thinking, from my heart as much as my mouth. The fingers retreated immediately and the letter box snapped shut behind them. Jake turned to look up at me as I thudded down the stairs towards him, my heart hammering in my chest. At the bottom, I snatched the keys out of his hand.

Sitting like that, he was blocking the door.

'Move,' I shouted. *'Move.'*

He scrabbled out of the way, crawling on his hands and knees into my office. I scraped the chain out of the lock, then tried the door handle, which turned easily – Jake had already unlocked the fucking thing with the keys. Pulling the door open, I stepped quickly on to the front path and stared out into the night.

As far as I could tell, there was nobody up or down the street. The amber haze beneath the street lights was misty, the pavements empty. But looking across the road, I thought I could see a figure running swiftly across the field. A vague shape, legs pummelling away through the darkness.

Already too far away for me to catch.

My instinct took me down the front path anyway, but I stopped halfway to the street, my breath visible in the cold night air. What the hell was I doing? I couldn't leave the house open behind me and go chasing someone across a field. I couldn't leave Jake in there by himself, alone and abandoned.

So I stood there for a few seconds, staring into the darkness of the field. The figure – if it had ever been there at all – had disappeared now.

It *had* been there.

I stood there for a moment longer. And then I went back inside, locked the door, and phoned the police.

PART THREE

Twenty-two

Credit where it's due, two police officers arrived on my doorstep within ten minutes of my phone call. After that, things began to go downhill.

I had to take some responsibility for what happened. It was half past four in the morning, and I was exhausted, frightened and not thinking straight, and the account I had to give was light on detail anyway. But there was no getting away from Jake's role in what unfolded.

When I'd come back inside to make the call, I'd found him at the bottom of the stairs, hugging his knees and with his face buried in them. I had eventually calmed down enough to be able to calm him down too, and then I'd carried him into the front room, where he'd curled up at one end of the settee. And then refused to talk to me.

I had done my best to hide the frustration and panic I was feeling. I probably hadn't succeeded.

Even when the police officers joined us in the front room, Jake remained in that same position. I sat down awkwardly beside him. Even then, I was aware of the distance between us, and I was sure it was also very obvious to the police. The two of them – a man and a woman – were both polite and made the requisite concerned and understanding faces, but the woman kept glancing curiously at Jake, and I got the impression the worry on her face was not wholly because of what I was telling them.

Afterwards, the male officer referred to the notes he'd made.

'Has Jake sleepwalked before?'

'A little,' I said. 'But not often, and only ever to my room. He's never gone downstairs like that.'

That was if he even *had* been sleepwalking, of course. While it made me feel better to think he hadn't been about to open that door out of choice, I realized I couldn't be sure of it. And Jesus, if that was true, what did it say about how much my son hated me?

The officer made another note.

'And you can't describe the individual you saw?'

'No. He was quite far away across the field by then, running fast. It was dark, and I couldn't see him properly.'

'Build? Clothes?'

I shook my head. 'No, sorry.'

'Are you sure it was a man?'

'Yes. It was a man's voice I heard at the door.'

'Could that have been Jake?' The officer looked at my son.

Jake was still curled up next to me, staring off into space as though he was the only person in the entire world.

'Sometimes children talk to themselves.'

Not something I wanted to get into.

'No,' I said. 'There was definitely somebody there. I saw this man's fingers holding the letter box open. I heard him. The voice was older. He was trying to persuade Jake to open the door – and he was going to as well. God knows what would have happened if I hadn't woken up in time.'

The reality of the situation crashed down on me then. In my mind's eye, I saw the scene again, and realized what a close call it had been. If I hadn't been there, Jake would be gone now. I imagined him missing, with the police seated across from me for a different reason, and felt helpless. Despite my frustration at his behaviour, I wanted to wrap my arms around him – to protect him and hold him close. But I knew that I couldn't. That he wouldn't let me, or even want me to right now.

'How did Jake get the keys?'

'I left them in my office across the hall.' I shook my head. 'That's not a mistake I'll be making again.'

'That's probably wise.'

'And what about you, Jake?' The female officer leaned forward, smiling kindly. 'Can you tell us anything at all about what happened?'

Jake shook his head.

'You can't? Why were you at the door, sweetheart?'

He shrugged almost imperceptibly, and then seemed to move a little further away from me. The woman leaned back, still looking at Jake, her head tilted slightly to one side. Evaluating him.

'There was another man,' I said quickly. 'He came by the house yesterday. He was hanging around the garage, acting strangely. When I confronted him, he said he'd grown up here and wanted to look around.'

The male officer looked interested by that.

'How did you confront him?'

'He came to the door.'

'Oh, I see.' He made a note on his pad. 'Can you describe him?'

I did, and he scribbled away. But it was clear that the man actively knocking on the door had made the development significantly less interesting to him. Plus, it was difficult to convey how uneasy the man had made me feel. There had been nothing physically threatening about him, and yet he had still seemed dangerous on some level.

'Neil Spencer,' I remembered.

The male officer stopped writing.

'I'm sorry?'

'I think that was his name. We've only just moved here. But another little boy went missing, didn't he? Earlier this summer?'

The two officers exchanged a glance.

'What do you know about Neil Spencer?' the man asked me.

'Nothing. Jake's teacher just mentioned him. I was going to look it up online, but it was a . . . busy night.' And again, I didn't want to go into the argument Jake and I had had. 'I was working.'

But of course, that was the wrong thing to say as well, because work was writing, and Jake had read what I'd done. I felt him shrink slightly beside me.

Frustration got the better of me.

'It's just that I'd have thought this would be more worrying to you than it seems to be,' I said.

'Mr Kennedy —'

'It feels like you don't believe me.'

The man smiled. But it was a careful smile.

'It's not a case of not believing you, Mr Kennedy. But we can only work with what we have.' He looked at me for a moment, considering me in much the same way his partner was still evaluating my son. 'We take everything seriously. We'll log a record of this, but based on what you've told us, there's not a vast amount we can do right now. As I said, I recommend you keep your keys out of your son's way. Observe basic home security. Keep an eye out. And don't hesitate to get in touch with us if you see anyone else around your property who shouldn't be here.'

I shook my head. Given what had happened — given that *someone had tried to take my son* — this response wasn't remotely good enough. I was angry at myself, and I couldn't help being angry at Jake as well. I was trying to help him! And in a minute, the police would be gone, and it would just be me and him again. Alone. Neither of us up to the job of living with the other.

'Mr Kennedy?' the female officer said gently. 'Is it just you and Jake here? Does his mother live elsewhere?'

'His mother is dead.'

I said it too bluntly, a trace of the anger I was feeling escaping. She seemed taken aback by it.

'Oh. I'm very sorry to hear that.'

'I'm just . . . it's hard. And what just happened tonight, it scared me.'

And that was the point when Jake came back to life, perhaps animated by anger of his own. What I'd written. The fact I'd just said his mother was dead so brazenly. He uncurled and slowly sat up straight, finally looking at me, his face expressionless. When he spoke, it was with a raspy, unearthly voice that sounded far too old for his years.

'*I want to scare you,*' he said.

Twenty-three

When the alarm went off, Pete lay very still for a moment, letting it ring on the bedside table. Something was wrong and he needed to prepare himself. Then there was a burst of panic as he remembered the events of yesterday evening. The sight of Neil Spencer's body on the waste ground. The almost frantic race to get home afterwards. And the reassuring weight of the bottle in his hand.

The *clicks* as he'd broken the seal.

And then . . .

Finally, he opened his eyes. The early-morning sun was already strong, streaming through the thin blue curtains and falling in a wedge over the covers bunched up over his knees. Sometime in the night, sweating with heat, he must have thrown them off his upper body, and the tangle of material felt ridiculously heavy now, wrapped tightly round his knees.

He turned his head and looked at the bedside table.

The bottle was there. The seal was broken.

But the contents remained untouched, full to the top.

He remembered how long he'd deliberated last night, battling the urge again and again as it came back at him from different angles, both he and the voice refusing to relent or retreat. He'd even brought the bottle and a tumbler up here to bed with him. Still fighting, even then.

And in the end, he had won.

Relief rushed through him. He glanced at the tumbler now. Before going to sleep, he had put the photograph of Sally on top of it. Even after everything that had happened – the horrors of the evening – that photograph and those memories had still been enough to keep him clean.

He tried not to think about the day ahead of him or the evenings to come.

Enough for now.

He showered and ate breakfast. Even without drinking, he felt so worn down that he contemplated not going to the gym. A briefing had been scheduled for first thing, and he needed to be prepared for it, to be filled with the case. But he already felt soaked to the skin by it. As dispassionate as he'd tried to be when viewing Neil Spencer's body, it was like pointing a camera without looking through the viewfinder; your mind took the photograph regardless. If anything, if he was going to be competent and professional in a couple of hours, he needed to empty some of that horror out.

He went to the gym.

Afterwards, feeling calmer, he went upstairs. He called into his office, and for a moment he stared at the blissful piles of safe, innocuous paperwork. Then he found the old, malignant bundle of notes he was going to need and headed to the operations room, one floor above.

His calm faded slightly as he opened the door. It was still ten minutes before the briefing was due to begin, but the room was already heaving with officers. Nobody was talking; every face he could see looked sombre. Most of these men and women would have worked this case from the beginning and, whatever the odds, each of them would have clung on to hope. By now, they all knew what had been found last night.

Before today, a child had been missing.

Now, a child was dead.

He leaned against a wall at the back of the room, aware as

he did so that gazes were directed at him. It was understandable. While his initial involvement in the case had come to nothing, all of them must know that his presence here now was not a coincidence. He spotted DCI Lyons sitting near the front, looking back at him. Pete met his eyes for a moment, trying to read the expression on the man's face. Like last night at the waste ground, it had been blank, which only left Pete free to imagine. Was the man feeling an odd sense of triumph? It seemed unfair to contemplate such an idea, but it was certainly possible. Despite the disparity in their career trajectories since, Pete knew that Lyons had always resented him on some level for being the one to catch Frank Carter. This recent development meant the case had never really been closed. And now here was Lyons, presiding over what might turn out to be the end game, with Pete reduced to the status of a pawn.

He folded his arms, stared at the floor and waited.

Amanda arrived a minute later, stalking quickly through the assembled throng towards the front of the room. Even from the brief side view he got of her, it was obvious she was harried and tired. Same clothes as last night, he noticed. She'd slept in one of the overnight suites or, more likely, hadn't slept at all. As she took to the small stage, there was a subdued, defeated look about her.

'Right, everyone,' she said. 'You've all heard the news. Yesterday evening, we had a report that a child's body had been found on the waste ground off Gair Lane. Officers attended and secured the scene. The identity of the victim has yet to be confirmed, but we believe this to be Neil Spencer.'

They had all known it already, but still: Pete watched the slump travel around the room. The emotional temperature of the room dropped. The silence among the assembled officers, already absolute, somehow seemed to intensify.

'We also believe it to be a case of third-party involvement. There are significant injuries to the body.'

Amanda's voice almost broke at that and he saw her wince slightly. Too hard on herself. Under different circumstances, it might have been perceived as weakness, but Pete didn't think it would be in this room right now. He watched as she gathered herself.

'Details of which are obviously not going to be released to the press at this time. We have a cordon in place, but the media know we've found a body. That is all they are going to know until we get a handle on what's happening here.'

A woman by the wall was nodding to herself. Pete recognized it as the kind of action he had made in the deepest throes of his addiction, pining for a drink and riding out the pain.

'The body has been removed from the scene and a post-mortem will take place this morning. We have an estimated time of death somewhere between three and five p.m. yesterday afternoon. Assuming this is Neil Spencer, he was found in roughly the same place he went missing, which may be significant. We also believe Neil was killed at a different location, presumably wherever he had been held. Fingers crossed that forensics will give us some clue as to where that might be. In the meantime, we'll be going over all the CCTV in the area. We'll be knocking on every door in the vicinity. Because I am simply not having this monster wandering around this village undetected. I'm not having it.'

She looked up. Despite the obvious tiredness and upset, there was fire in her eyes now.

'All of us here, we've all worked on this investigation. And even if we'd steeled ourselves, this is not the result any of us were hoping for. So let me be absolutely clear. It will not be allowed to stand. Do we agree?'

Pete glanced around again. A few nods here and there; the room coming back to life. He admired the sentiment and acknowledged the need for it right now, but he also remembered giving equally angry speeches twenty years ago, and while he had believed them at the time, he knew now that things not only stood, whether you wanted them to or not, but that sometimes they followed you forever.

'We did everything we could,' Amanda told the room. 'We didn't find Neil Spencer in time. But make no mistake, we are going to find the person that did this to him.'

And Pete could tell that she believed what she was saying just as passionately as he had all those years ago. Because you had to. Something awful had happened on your watch, and the only way to ease the pain was to do everything you could to put it right. To catch whoever was responsible before they hurt anybody else. Or at least try.

We are going to find the person that did this.

He hoped that was true.

Twenty-four

It was astonishing how quickly life could revert to normal when it had to.

After the police left, I decided there was no point in either Jake or me trying to go back to sleep, and as a result, by half past eight, I felt half dead on my feet. I went through the motions of preparing him breakfast and getting him ready for school. After what had happened, it seemed ridiculous, but I had no excuse for keeping him home. In fact, given his performance in front of the officers earlier on, a horrible part of me wanted not to be around him right now.

While he ate cereal, still refusing to speak to me, I stood in the kitchen, poured myself a glass of water and downed it in one. I didn't really know what to do or how to feel. With just a handful of hours' perspective, the events of the night seemed distant and surreal. Could I be sure I'd seen what I'd seen? Perhaps it had been my imagination. But no, I *had* seen it. A better father – an average one, even – would have convinced the police to take him seriously. A better father would have a son who talked to him, not undermined him. Who could see that I was just scared for him and trying to protect him.

My hand tightened round the glass.

You're not your father, Tom.

Rebecca's quiet voice in my head.

Never forget that.

I looked down at the empty glass in my hand. My grip was too tight on it. That awful memory came back to me – shattering glass; my mother screaming – and I put it down on the side quickly, before I could start to fail in an altogether worse way.

At quarter to nine, Jake and I walked to school together, him trailing along to the side of me, still resisting any attempts at conversation. It was only when we reached the gates that he finally spoke to me.

'Who's Neil Spencer, Daddy?'

'I don't know.' Despite the subject matter, I was relieved that he was talking to me. 'A boy from Featherbank. I think he went missing earlier this year; I remember reading something about it. Nobody knows what happened to him.'

'Owen said he was dead.'

'Owen sounds like a charming little boy.'

It was clear that Jake was thinking about adding something to that, but then he changed his mind.

'He said I was sitting in Neil's chair.'

'That's stupid. You didn't get a place in the school because this Neil kid went missing. Someone else moved house like we did.' I frowned. 'And anyway, they'd have all been in a different classroom last year, wouldn't they?'

Jake looked at me curiously.

'Twenty-eight,' he said.

'Twenty-eight what?'

'Twenty-eight children,' he said. 'Plus me is twenty-nine.'

'Exactly.' I had no idea if that was true, but I went with it. 'They have classes of thirty here. So wherever Neil is, his chair is waiting for him.'

'Do you think he *will* come home?'

We stepped into the playground.

'I don't know, mate.'

'Can I have a hug, Daddy?'

I looked down at him. From the expression on his face

now, last night and this morning might as well not have happened at all. But then, he was seven. Arguments were always resolved in his time and on his terms. In this instance, I was too tired not to accept that.

'Of course you can.'

'Because even when we argue –'

'We still love each other. Very much.'

I knelt down, and the tight embrace felt like it was powering me back up a little. That a hug like this, every so often, would keep me running. And then he ambled inside past Mrs Shelley without giving me even a backward glance. I walked back out through the gate, hoping he didn't get into any more trouble today.

But if he did . . .

Well, he did.

Just let him be him.

'Hello there.'

I turned to find Karen slightly behind me, walking just fast enough to catch up.

'Hey,' I said. 'How are you?'

'Looking forward to a few hours' peace and quiet.'

She fell into step beside me. 'How did Jake do yesterday?'

'He went up to amber,' I said.

'I have no idea what that means.'

I explained the traffic-light system. The gravity and supposed seriousness of it seemed so meaningless after the events of the night that I almost laughed at the end.

'That sounds fucking abominable,' she said.

'That's what I thought.'

I wondered if there was some nominal moment when playground parents decided to drop a certain level of pretence and swear like normal people. If there was, I was glad to have passed it.

'In some ways it's a badge of honour, though,' she said. 'He'll be the envy of his classmates. Adam said they didn't have much of a chance to play together.'

'Jake said Adam was nice,' I lied.

'He also said Jake talked to himself a bit.'

'Yes, he does do that sometimes. Imaginary friends.'

'Right,' Karen said. 'I sympathize with him completely. Some of my best friends are imaginary. I'm joking, obviously. But Adam went through that, and I'm sure I did too when I was a kid. You probably did as well.'

I frowned. A memory suddenly came back to me.

'Mister Night,' I said.

'Sorry?'

'God, I haven't thought about that in years.' I ran my hand through my hair. How had I forgotten about it? 'Yeah, I did have an imaginary friend. When I was younger, I used to tell my mother that someone came into my room at night and hugged me. *Mister Night*. That's what I called him.'

'Yeah . . . that's pretty creepy. But then, kids say scary stuff all the time. There are whole websites devoted to it. You should write that down and submit it.'

'Maybe I will.' But it reminded me of something else. 'Jake's been saying other weird things recently. "If you leave a door half open, soon you'll hear the whispers spoken." Have you ever heard that?'

'Hmmm.' Karen thought about it. 'It does ring a bell; I'm sure I've heard it somewhere before. It's one of those rhymes kids say in the playground, I think.'

'Right. Maybe that's where he heard it then.'

Except not in *this* playground, of course, because Jake had said it the night before his first day at his new school. Maybe it was some common kids' chant that I didn't know about – something from one of those television programmes I put on for him and then zoned out without paying them any attention.

I sighed. 'I just hope he has a better day. I worry about him.'

'That's natural. What does your wife say?'

'She died last year,' I said. 'I'm not sure how well he's coping with that. Understandably, I suppose.'

Karen was silent for a moment.

'I'm very sorry to hear that.'

'Thanks. I'm not sure how well I'm coping either, to be honest. I'm never sure whether I'm being a good father or not. Whether I'm doing the best I can for him.'

'That's also natural. I'm sure you are.'

'Maybe it's whether my best is good enough that's the real question.'

'And again, I'm sure it is.'

She stopped and put her hands in her pockets. We'd come to a junction, and it was obvious from our mutual body language that she was heading straight on while I was turning right.

'But whatever,' she said, 'it sounds like both of you have had a rough time of it. So I think – not that you asked for my opinion, I realize, but fuck it – that maybe you should stop being so hard on yourself?'

'Maybe.'

'Just a little, at least?'

'Maybe.'

'Easier said than done, I know.' She gathered herself together, her whole body suddenly like a sigh. 'Anyway. Catch you later on. Have a good one.'

'You too.'

I thought about that the rest of the way home. *Maybe you should stop being so hard on yourself.* There was probably some truth in that because, after all, I was just fumbling through life the same as everyone else, wasn't I? Trying to do my best.

But back home, I still paced around the downstairs of the house, unsure what to do with myself. Earlier on, I'd been thinking it would be good to have some time without Jake. Now, with the house empty and silent around me, I felt an urge to have him as close as possible.

Because I needed to keep him safe.

And I *hadn't* imagined what had happened in the night.

That brought on a flash of panic. If the police weren't going to help us, that meant that I had to. Walking through the empty rooms, I felt a sense of desperation – an urgent need to do something, even though I had no idea what. I ended up in my office. The laptop had been left on standby overnight. I nudged the trackpad and the screen came to life, revealing the words there.

Rebecca . . .

She would know what to do right now; she always had. I pictured her sitting cross-legged on the floor with Jake, play-ing enthusiastically with whatever toys were between them. And curled up on our old settee, reading to him, his head underneath her chin and their two bodies so close that they looked like a single person. Whenever he'd called out in the night, Rebecca would already be padding through to him as I was still waking up. And it had always been his mother he called for.

I deleted the words I'd written yesterday and then typed three new sentences.

I miss you.

I feel like I'm failing our son and I don't know what to do.

I'm sorry.

I stared at the screen for a moment.

Enough.

Enough wallowing. As difficult as everything might be, it was my job to look after my son, and if my best wasn't sufficient, then I'd have to get better.

I walked back to the front door. It had a lock and a chain, but that clearly wasn't good enough. So I would install sash jammers as well, too high for Jake to reach on his own. Motion detectors at the bottom of the stairs. It could all be done. None of this was insurmountable, whatever my self-doubt was telling me.

But there was something else I could do first, and so I turned my attention to the pile of post on the stairs behind me. There had been another two letters for Dominic Barnett, both of them debt collection notices. I took them through to my office, closed down Word on the laptop and opened the web browser instead.

Let's see who you are, Dominic Barnett.

I wasn't sure what I was expecting to discover about him online. A Facebook page, perhaps – something with a photo that would tell me whether he was the man who'd called round yesterday – or if not that, maybe a forwarding address of some kind that I could follow up in the real world. Anything that might help me to protect Jake and work out what the hell was going on with my house.

I found a photograph on the very first search. Dominic Barnett was not my mysterious visitor. He was younger, with a full head of jet-black hair. But the picture wasn't on a social media site.

Instead, it was beside a news item at the top of the search page: POLICE TREAT DEATH OF LOCAL MAN AS MURDER.

The room receded around me. I stared at the words until

they began to lose their meaning. The house had gone silent, and all I could hear was the thud of my heartbeat.

And then —

Creak.

I glanced at the ceiling. That noise again, the same as before, as though someone had taken a single step in Jake's bedroom. My skin tingled as I remembered what had happened in the night — the figure I'd imagined standing at the base of my bed, its hair splayed out like the little girl that Jake had drawn. The sensation of my foot being shaken.

Wake up, Tom.

But unlike the man at the door, that had been my imagination. I'd been half asleep, after all. It had been nothing more than a remnant of a nightmare from the past, shaped by fears from the present.

There was nothing in my house.

Determined to take my mind off the noise, I forced myself to click on the article.

POLICE TREAT DEATH OF LOCAL MAN AS MURDER

Police have revealed that they are treating the death of Dominic Barnett, whose body was found in woodland on Tuesday, as murder.

Barnett, 42, of Garholt Street, Featherbank, was discovered at the edge of a stream by children playing in Hollingbeck Wood. Today, DCI Lyons revealed to the press that Barnett had died as a result of 'significant' head injuries. A number of possible motives for the attack were being explored, but items recovered at the scene suggested that robbery was not among them.

'I would like to take this opportunity to reassure the public at large,' Lyons said. 'Mr Barnett was known to officers, and we believe this to be an isolated incident. However, we have increased patrols in the area, and we encourage anyone with any information to come forward immediately.'

I read it through again, the panic inside me intensifying. From the address, there was no doubt that this was the right Dominic Barnett. He had lived in this house. Maybe sat exactly where I was right now, or slept in what had become Jake's bedroom.

And he had been murdered in April this year.

Trying to keep calm, I clicked back and searched for more articles. The facts, such as they were, emerged piecemeal, and many of them from between the lines. *Mr Barnett was known to officers*. Careful phrasing, but the implication appeared to be that he'd been involved with drugs in some way, and that this was presumed to be the motive for his murder. Hollingbeck Wood was south of Featherbank, on the other side of the river. Why Barnett had been there was unclear. A murder weapon was recovered a week later, and then the reports tailed off shortly afterwards. From what I could find online, his killer had never been caught.

Which meant that they were still out there.

The realization brought an awful crawling sensation with it. I didn't know what to do. Call the police again? What I'd discovered didn't seem to add much to what I'd already told them. I would call them, I decided, because I had to do *something*. But I needed more information first.

After some deliberation, and with my hands shaking, I searched through the paperwork I'd kept on the house purchase, found the address I needed, then picked up my keys. The extra security would have to wait for the moment. There was one person who would be able to tell me more about Dominic Barnett, and I figured it was time to talk to her.

Twenty-five

It always ends where it starts, Amanda thought.

She was looking through the CCTV footage that had been retrieved from the area around the waste ground, and couldn't help remembering that, two months ago, she'd been examining images of these exact same streets. Back then, it had been in the hope of seeing someone taking Neil Spencer away. Now, she was searching for someone returning the boy's body. But so far the result was the same.

Nothing.

Early days, she told herself – but that thought was like ash in her head. It was actually far too fucking late, not least for Neil Spencer himself. Her mind kept flashing back to the sight of his body, even though dwelling on the horrors she'd seen last night – on her failure to find Neil in time – wasn't going to help. What she needed to do instead was concentrate on the work. One foot in front of the other. One detail at a time. That was the way they'd eventually get the bastard who'd done those things to that little boy.

Another flash.

She shook her head, then looked towards the back of the room, where Pete Willis was working quietly at the desk he'd been allocated. After she'd had the chance to sit down, she'd found herself keeping a surreptitious eye on him. Occasionally, he picked up the phone and made a call; the rest of the time, his attention was totally focused on the photographs and paperwork before him. Frank Carter knew something, and Pete was working through the visits received by the man's friends and associates in the prison, trying to figure out if one of them might be responsible for passing Carter information from the outside world. But it was Pete himself who fascinated her now.

How could he be so *calm*?

Except that she knew that he was suffering too, below the surface. She remembered how he'd been yesterday, after visiting Frank Carter, and then at the waste ground last night. If he seemed detached now, it was only because he was distracting himself in the exact same way that she was trying to. And if he was succeeding, it was simply because he'd had so much more practice at doing it.

Amanda wanted to ask him the secret.

Instead, she forced her attention back to the footage, already knowing deep down that it would yield nothing, just like two months ago, when her team had slowly identified and eliminated the individuals caught on the village's meagre selection of cameras. It was frustrating work. The more you accomplished, the worse it felt like you were doing. But it was necessary.

She picked her way through the fuzzy images. Freeze-frames of men, women and children. All of them would have to be interviewed, even though none of them would have witnessed anything significant. The man they were looking for was too careful for that. And it would be the same with the vehicles. Her conviction during the briefing had been real, and a part of her was still cultivating that now, but she knew deep down they were all impotent. The fact remained that it wasn't difficult to drive around Featherbank and avoid the CCTV cameras. Not if you knew what you were doing.

On the pad beside her, she jotted that thought down.

Knowledge of camera positions?

But again, she'd made the same note two months earlier. History repeating itself.

It always ends where it starts.

She threw the pen down in frustration, then stood up and walked over to where Pete was working, so engrossed that he didn't even notice her. The printer on his desk was releasing a steady stream of photographs – CCTV stills of visitors to the prison. Pete was cross-referencing them with details on the screen and writing notes on the back. There was also an old newspaper printout on the desk. She tilted her head to read the headline.

'"Prison Marriage for Coxton Cannibal"?' she said.

Pete jumped. 'What?'

'The news article.' She read it out again. 'The world never stops surprising me. Generally in terrible ways.'

'Oh. Yes.' Pete gestured at the photographs he was accumulating. 'And these are all his visitors. His real name's Victor Tyler. Twenty-five years ago, he abducted a little girl. Mary Fisher?'

'I remember her,' Amanda said.

They had been roughly the same age. While Amanda couldn't picture the girl's face, her mind immediately associated the name with scary stories and grainy images in old newspapers. Twenty-five years. Hard to believe it had been that long, and how quickly people faded away into the past and were forgotten by the world.

'She'd probably have been married herself by now,' Amanda said. 'Doesn't seem right, does it?'

'No.' Pete took another photograph from the printer and peered at the screen for a second. 'Tyler got married fifteen years ago. Louise Dixon. Unbelievably, they're still together. They've never spent a night together, of course. But you know how it can be sometimes. The allure men like this can have.'

Amanda nodded to herself. Criminals, even the worst of

them, often weren't short of correspondents in the outside world. For a certain type of woman, they were like catnip. *He didn't do it*, they'd convince themselves. Or else he'd changed – or if not, they'd be the one to redeem him. Maybe some of them even liked the danger. It had never made the slightest bit of sense to her, but it was true.

Pete wrote on the back of the photo, then put it to one side and reached for another.

'And Carter is friends with this guy?' she said.

'Carter was best man.'

'Well, that must have been quite a lovely ceremony. Who married them? Satan himself?'

But Pete didn't answer. Rather than looking at the screen, he was focused entirely on the photograph he'd just picked up. Another of Tyler's visitors, she assumed, except this one had caught his attention completely.

'Who's that?'

'Norman Collins.' Pete looked up at her. 'I know him.'

'Tell me.'

Pete ran through the basics. Norman Collins was a local man who had been questioned during the investigation twenty years ago, not because of any concrete evidence against him, but because of his behaviour. From Pete's description, he sounded like one of those creepy fuckers that sometimes insinuated themselves into ongoing investigations. You were trained to watch out for them. The ones who hung around at the back of press conferences and funerals. The ones who seemed to be eavesdropping or asking too many questions. The ones who appeared too interested or just felt off, in some way. Because while it could simply be sick or ghoulish behaviour, it was also the way that killers sometimes acted.

But not Collins apparently.

'We had nothing on him,' Pete said. 'Less than nothing, in fact. He had solid alibis for all the abductions. No connection to the kids or the families. No sheet to him at all. In the end, he was just a footnote in the case.'

'And yet you remember him.'

Pete stared at the photograph again.

'I never liked him,' he said.

It was likely nothing, and Amanda didn't want to get her hopes up any more than they already were, but while you had to be methodical and sensible, there was also something to be said for gut instinct. If Pete remembered this man, there must have been something to prompt that.

'And now he turns up again,' she said. 'Got an address?'

Pete tapped on his keyboard.

'Yeah. He still lives in the same place as before.'

'Okay. Go and have the conversation. It's probably nothing, but let's find out why he was visiting Victor Tyler.'

Pete stared at the screen for a moment longer, then nodded and stood up.

Amanda walked back across the room. DS Stephanie Johnson caught her before she could reach her own desk.

'Ma'am?'

'Please don't call me that, Steph. It makes me sound like someone's grandmother. Anything from the door-to-doors yet?'

'Nothing so far. But you wanted to know if anything had come in from concerned parents? Reports of prowlers – things like that?'

Amanda nodded. Neil's mother had missed that at first, and Amanda didn't want them to repeat the mistake.

'We had one come in, early hours this morning,' Steph said. 'A man called us saying somebody had been outside the house, talking to his son.'

Amanda reached across Steph's desk and turned the screen around so that she could read the details. The boy in question was seven. Rose Terrace school. A man outside the front door, supposedly speaking to him. But the report also mentioned the boy had been behaving strangely, and reading between the lines it was clear the attending officers hadn't been sure the account was genuine.

She might have words with them about that.

Amanda leaned away, then walked across the room, glancing around angrily. She spotted DS John Dyson. He would do – the lazy bastard was sitting behind a pile of paperwork and messing around on his mobile. When she walked over and clicked her fingers in front of his face, he actually dropped it into his lap.

'Come with me,' she told him.

Twenty-six

It was a ten-minute drive to the house of Mrs Shearing, the woman who had sold me our new home.

I parked up outside a detached two-storey property with a peaked roof and a large paved driveway, gated off from the pavement by metal railings with a black letter box on a post outside. This was a much more prestigious area of Featherbank than the one where Jake and I now lived, in the house that Mrs Shearing had owned and rented out for years.

Most recently, presumably, to Dominic Barnett.

I reached through the railings of the gate and undid the clasp there. As I pushed it open, a dog began barking furiously inside the house, and the noise intensified as I reached the front door, pressed the buzzer and waited. Mrs Shearing opened it on the second ring, but kept the chain on, peering out through the gap. The dog was behind her: a small Yorkshire terrier yapping angrily at me. Its fur was tipped with grey and it looked almost as old and fragile as she did.

'Yes?'

'Hello,' I said. 'I don't know if you remember me, Mrs Shearing. My name's Tom Kennedy. I bought your house off you a few weeks ago? We met a couple of times when I came to view it. My son and I.'

'Oh yes. Of course. Shoo, Morris. Get back.' The latter was to the dog. She brushed down her dress and turned back to me. 'I'm sorry, he's very excitable. What can I do for you?'

'It's about the house. I was wondering if I could talk to you about one of the previous tenants?'

'I see.'

She looked a little awkward at that, as though she had a good inkling of which one I meant and would rather not. I decided to wait her out. After a few seconds of silence, civility got the better of any reservations she had, and she undid the chain.

'I see,' she said again. 'Then you'd better come in.'

Inside, she seemed flustered, fussing at her clothes and hair, and apologizing for the state of the place. For the latter, there was certainly no need; the house was palatial and immaculate, the reception area alone the size of my front room, with a broad wooden staircase winding up to the floor above. I followed Mrs Shearing into a cosy sitting room, with Morris cantering more enthusiastically around my ankles. Two settees and a chair were arranged around an open fire, the grate empty and spotless, and there were cabinets along one wall, with carefully spaced crystalware visible behind the glass panels. Paintings on the walls showed countryside and hunting scenes. The window at the front of the house was covered with plush red curtains, closed against the street.

'You have a lovely house,' I said.

'Thank you. It's too big for me, really, especially after the children moved out and Derek passed, bless him. But I'm too old to move now. A girl comes in every few days to clean it. An awful luxury, but what else can I do? Please, have a seat.'

'Thank you.'

'Can I get you some tea? Coffee?'

'No, I'm fine.'

I sat down. The settee was rigid and hard.

'How are you settling in?' she asked.

'We're doing okay.'

'That's wonderful to know.' She smiled fondly. 'I grew up in that house, you know, and I always wanted it to go to someone nice in the end. A decent family. Your son – Jake, if I remember correctly? How is he?'

'He's just started school.'

'Rose Terrace?'

'Yes.'

That smile again. 'It's a very good school. I went there when I was a child.'

'Are your handprints on the wall?'

'They are.' She nodded proudly. 'One red, one blue.'

'That's nice. You said you grew up on Garholt Street?'

'Yes. After my parents died, Derek and I kept it on as an investment. It was my husband's idea, but I didn't take much persuading. I've always been fond of it. Such memories there, you see?'

'Of course.' I thought of the man who had called round, attempting to do the maths. He had been considerably younger than Mrs Shearing, but it wasn't impossible. 'Did you have a younger brother, at all?'

'No, I was an only child. Perhaps that's why I've always had such affection for the house. It was mine, you see? All mine. I loved it.' She pulled a face. 'When I was growing up, my friends were a little scared by it.'

'Why scared?'

'Oh, it's just that kind of house, I think. It looks a little strange, doesn't it?'

'I suppose so.' Karen had said much the same to me yesterday. I repeated what I'd said to her, even though, frankly, it was beginning to sound hollow. 'It has character.'

'Exactly!' Mrs Shearing seemed pleased. 'That's exactly what I always thought too. And that's why I'm glad it's in safe hands again now.'

I swallowed that down, because the house didn't feel remotely safe to me. But as I'd suspected, whoever the man was who'd called round, he had been lying about growing up there. I was also struck by her phrasing. Safe hands again *now*. She had wanted it to go to someone nice *in the end*.

'Was it not in safe hands before?'

She looked uncomfortable again.

'Not especially, no. Let's just say that I haven't been blessed with the best of tenants in the past. But then, it's so hard to tell, isn't it? People can seem perfectly pleasant when you meet them. And I never had any real reason to complain. They paid their rent on time. They looked after the property well enough . . .'

She trailed off, as though she didn't know how to explain what the real problems had been, and would rather leave it. While she had that luxury, I didn't.

'But?'

'Oh, I don't know. I never had anything concrete I could use against them, or else I wouldn't have hesitated. Just suspicions. That perhaps there were other people staying there from time to time.'

'That they were renting out rooms?'

'Yes. And that unsavoury things might sometimes be going on.' She pulled a face. 'The house often smelled funny when I called round – but of course, you're not allowed to do that these days without an appointment. Can you believe that? An appointment to enter your own property. Advance warning, more like it. The only time I ever turned up unannounced, he wouldn't let me in.'

'This would be Dominic Barnett?'

She hesitated.

'Yes. Him. Although the one before was no better. I think I've just had a run of very bad luck with that house.'

Which you've passed on to me.

'You do know what happened to Dominic Barnett?' I said.

'Yes, of course.'

She looked down at her hands, resting neatly and delicately in her lap, and was silent for a moment.

'Which was terrible, obviously. Not a fate I would wish on anyone. But from what I heard afterwards, he did move in those kinds of circles.'

'Drugs,' I said bluntly.

Another moment of silence. Then she sighed, as though we were talking about aspects of the world that were wholly alien to her.

'There was never any evidence he was selling them from my property. But yes. It was a very sad business. And I suppose I could have searched for another tenant after he died, but I'm old now, and I decided not to. I thought it was time to sell the house and draw a line. That way, I could give my old home a new chance with someone else. Someone who would make a better go of it than I had recently.'

'Jake and me.'

'Yes!' She brightened at the thought. 'You and your lovely little boy! I had better offers, but money doesn't matter to me these days, and the two of you seemed right. I liked to think of my old house going to a young family, so that there'd be another small child playing there again. I wanted to feel it might end up full of light and love again. Full of colour, like it was when I was a little girl. I'm so pleased to hear that both of you are happy there.'

I leaned back.

Jake and I *weren't* happy there, of course, and a part of me was very angry with Mrs Shearing. It felt like the history of the house was something she should really have told me at the time. But she also seemed genuinely pleased, as though she thought she really had done a good thing, and I could understand her motivation for choosing me and Jake to sell the property to, instead of . . .

And then I frowned.

'You said you had better offers on the house?'

'Oh yes – very much so, actually. One man was prepared to pay far more than the asking price.' She wrinkled her nose and shook her head. 'But I didn't like him at all. He reminded me a little of the others. He was very persistent, as well, which put me off even more. I dislike being pestered.'

I leaned forward again.

Someone had been prepared to offer way over the asking price for the house, and Mrs Shearing had refused him. He had been persistent and pushy. There had been something off about him.

'This man,' I said carefully. 'What did he look like? Was he quite short? Bald on top, with grey hair round here?'

I gestured to my head, but she was already nodding.

'That's him, yes. Always impeccably dressed.'

And she pulled another face, as though she had been no more fooled by that veneer of respectability than I had.

'Mr Collins,' she said. 'Norman Collins.'

Twenty-seven

Back home, I parked up and stared down the driveway.

I was thinking — or trying to, at least. It felt like facts and ideas and explanations were all whirling around in my head like birds, slow enough to glimpse but too swift to catch.

The man who had been snooping round here was called Norman Collins. Despite his claims, he had not grown up in this house, and yet for some reason he had been prepared to pay well over the asking price to purchase it. The property obviously meant something to him.

But what?

I stared down the driveway at the garage.

That was where Collins had been skulking when I first spotted him. The garage, filled with the detritus removed from the house before I moved in, some of which had presumably belonged to Dominic Barnett. Had it been Collins at the door last night, trying to persuade Jake to open it? If so, maybe it wasn't that Jake himself had been in danger, just that Collins had wanted something.

The key to the garage, perhaps.

But thinking could only take me so far. I got out of the car and headed down to the garage, unlocking it, and then pulling one of the doors open and wedging it in place with an old can of paint.

I stepped inside.

All the junk remained, of course: the old furniture; the dirty mattress; the haphazard piles of damp cardboard boxes in the centre. Looking down to my right, the spider was still spinning its thick web, surrounded now by a few more remnants than before. Butterflies, presumably, chewed into small, pale knots of string.

I glanced around. One of the butterflies remained perched delicately on the window. Another was resting on the side of the box of Christmas decoration, its wings lifting and lowering gently. They reminded me of Jake's picture – along with the fact that he couldn't possibly have seen them in here. But that was a mystery I couldn't solve for now.

What about you, Norman?
What were you looking for in here?

I scraped some dry leaves away with my foot to clear a space, then took the box of decorations down and began sifting through it.

It took half an hour to work my way through all the cardboard boxes, emptying each one in turn and spreading the contents around. Kneeling down amongst it all, the stone floor of the garage felt cold, as though the knees of my jeans were gathering ovals of damp.

The garage door rattled behind me, and I turned around quickly, startled by the noise. But the driveway was sunlit and empty. Just the warm breeze, knocking the door against the tin of paint.

I turned back to what I'd found.

Which was nothing. The boxes all contained the kind of random debris you had no immediate use for but were still unwilling to throw away. There were the decorations, of course; ropes of tinsel were strewn around me now, their colours dulled and lifeless with age. There were magazines and newspapers, with nothing obvious to unite the dates and editions. Clothes that had been folded and stored away and smelled of mould. Dusty old extension cables. None of it looked to have been deliberately hidden so much as casually packed away and forgotten about.

I fought down the frustration. There were no answers here.

My investigation had disturbed several more of the butterflies, though. Five or six of them were crawling over the debris I'd unpacked, their antennae twitching, while another two were fluttering against the window. I watched as one on the tinsel lifted up into the air, then flickered past me, heading for the open door, before the stupid thing looped back in again and landed on the floor in front of me, on one of the bricks there.

I watched it for a moment, once again admiring the rich, distinctive colours on its wings. It crawled steadily across the surface of the bricks, and then disappeared down into a crack between them.

I stared at the ground.

A large section of the garage floor in front of me was made up of haphazardly arranged house bricks, and it took me a second to recognize what I must be looking at. An old mechanic's pit, where someone could lie down underneath a car to work on it. It had been filled in with bricks to approximate a flat surface.

Tentatively, I lifted up the one the butterfly had been on. The brick came out of the floor covered in dust and old webbing, the butterfly clinging obstinately to one side.

In the hole the brick had left, I could see the top of what appeared to be another cardboard box below.

The garage door banged again behind me.

Jesus.

This time I stood up and walked back out on to the driveway to check. There was nobody in sight, but in the last few minutes the sun had disappeared behind a cloud and the world felt darker and colder. The breeze had picked up.

Looking down, I saw that I was still holding the brick, and that my hand was trembling slightly.

Back in the garage, I put the brick to one side, and then began to remove more from the pit, gradually revealing the box hidden underneath. It was the same size as the others, but had been sealed across the top with parcel tape. I took out my keys and selected the one with the sharpest tip, my heart humming.

Is this what you were looking for, Norman?

I drew the point across the centre of the tape, then dug my fingers in to pull the seams apart. They came away with a *crack* at each end. Then I peered inside.

Immediately, I sat back on my heels, either unable or unwilling to comprehend what I had seen. My thoughts went back to what Jake had said last night after he'd been talking to himself in the front room. *I want to scare you.* That was when I'd assumed the imaginary little girl had come back into our lives.

A car door slammed. I glanced behind me and saw that a vehicle was parked at the end of my driveway, and that a man and a woman were walking down towards me.

It wasn't her, my son had told me.

It was the boy in the floor.

'Mr Kennedy?' the woman called.

Instead of answering her, I turned my attention back to the box in front of me.

To the bones inside.

To the small skull that was staring up at me.

And to the beautifully-coloured butterfly that had landed and rested there, its wings moving gently, like the heartbeat of a sleeping child.

Twenty-eight

Back in the day, Pete had encountered Norman Collins on several occasions, but he had never had cause to visit the man's home. He knew of it, though: a semi-detached house that had once belonged to Collins' parents, and which Collins had never moved out of. Following his father's death, he had lived there alone with his mother for a number of years, and then continued to do so after she died.

There was nothing untoward about that, of course, but the idea still made Pete feel a little queasy. Children were supposed to grow up, move out and fashion their own lives; to do otherwise suggested some kind of unhealthy dependency or deficiency. Perhaps it was simply because Pete had met Collins. He remembered him as soft and doughy, and always sweating, as though there was something rotten inside him that was constantly seeping out. He was the kind of man who it was easy to imagine might have kept his mother's bedroom carefully preserved over the years, or taken to sleeping in her bed.

And yet, as much as he'd raised Pete's hackles, Norman Collins had not been Frank Carter's accomplice.

There was some consolation to be had there. Whatever Collins' involvement right now, Pete hadn't missed him at the time. While the man had never officially been a suspect, he had been very much suspected. His alibis had checked out, though. If someone really had been helping Carter, it was physically impossible for it to have been Norman Collins.

So what had he been doing at the prison?

Maybe nothing. And yet Carter had to have received communication from the outside world somehow, and as Pete parked up outside Collins' house, he felt a small thrill inside him. Better not to hope too much, of course. But he still had the sense that they were on the right track here, even if it wasn't clear as yet where it was leading.

He approached the house. The small front garden was untended and overgrown, filled with sweeping whorls of grass that had collapsed down upon themselves. A bush close to the house was so thick that he had to turn sideways and scrape past to reach the front door. He knocked. The wood beneath his knuckles felt weak and flimsy, half eaten away. The front of the house had been painted white at some point, but so much had flaked away since that it reminded Pete of an old lady's face plastered with cracked make-up.

He was about to knock again when he heard movement on the other side of the door. It opened, but only to the limit of a chain. There had been no sound of it being applied, which meant Collins liked to keep his property nice and secure, even when he was home.

'Yes?'

Norman Collins didn't recognize Pete, but Pete remembered him well enough. Twenty years had barely changed him, beyond his monk's hair having faded to grey. The top of his head was mottled and red, like something angry that needed to be burst. And even though he was presumably relaxing at home, he was dressed almost absurdly formally, in a dapper little suit and waistcoat.

Pete held out his identification.

'Hello, Mr Collins. My name's DI Peter Willis. You might not remember me, but we met a few times years ago?'

Collins' gaze flicked from the identification to Pete's face, and then his expression became tight and tense. He remembered, all right.

'Oh, yes. Of course.'

Pete put the ID away.

'Can I come in for a chat? I'll try not to take up too much of your time.'

Collins hesitated, glancing behind him into the shadowy depths of the house. Pete could already see beads of sweat appearing on the man's forehead.

'It's not the most convenient time. What is it regarding?'

'I'd prefer to talk inside, Mr Collins.'

He waited. Collins was a stuffy little man, and Pete was confident he wouldn't want the silence to become awkward. After a few seconds, Collins relented.

'Very well.'

The door closed, and then opened fully this time. Pete stepped into a drab square of hallway, with stairs leading straight up ahead to a misty landing. The air smelled old and musty, but with a trace of something sweet to it. It reminded him of the ancient school desks from his childhood, where you'd open the top and smell wood and old bubblegum.

'How can I help you, DI Willis?'

They were still standing at the bottom of the stairs, far too cramped for Pete's liking. This close, he could smell Collins, sweating beneath his suit. He gestured to the open door to what was obviously the living room.

'Perhaps we can go through there?'

Again, Collins hesitated.

Pete frowned.

What are you hiding, Norman?

'Of course,' Collins said. 'This way, please.'

He led Pete into the living room. Pete was expecting to be met with squalor, but the room appeared tidy and clean, and the furniture was newer and less old-fashioned than he would have imagined. There was a large plasma screen attached to one wall, while the others were covered with framed artwork and small glass display cases.

Collins stopped in the middle of the room, and then stood rigid, with his hands clasped in front of him like a butler. Something about his oddly formal manner made the hairs on the back of Pete's neck stand up.

'Are you . . . all right, Mr Collins?'

'Oh, yes.' Collins nodded curtly. 'May I ask again what this is regarding?'

'A little over two months ago, you went to see an inmate named Victor Tyler in HMP Whitrow.'

'That I did.'

'And what was the purpose of that visit?'

'To talk to him. The same purpose as my other visits.'

'You've visited him before?'

'Indeed. Several times.'

Collins was still standing motionless, as if he'd been posed. Still smiling politely.

'Can I ask what you discussed with Victor Tyler?'

'Well, his crime, of course.'

'The little girl he killed?'

Collins nodded. 'Mary Fisher.'

'Yes, I know her name.'

A ghoul. That was what Collins had always struck Pete as – a strange little man, obsessed with the kind of darkness that others instinctively shied away from. Collins was still standing there smiling, as though waiting patiently for this business to be concluded and for Pete to leave, but the smile was all wrong. Collins was nervous, Pete thought. Hiding something. And he was aware that he had grown still himself – that there was an uncomfortable lack of movement

169

in the room – so he walked over to one wall, idly examining some of the pictures and items that Collins had framed and mounted there.

The drawings were strange. Up close, it became apparent how childlike many of them were. His gaze moved here and there, over stick figures, amateurish watercolours, and then his attention was drawn to something more unusual. A red plastic devil mask. It was the kind of item you'd find in a cheap fancy-dress shop, but for some reason Collins had encased it in a thin rectangle of glass and hung it on his wall.

'A collector's item, that.'

Collins was suddenly beside him. Pete resisted the urge to shout, but couldn't stop himself taking a step away.

'A collector's item?'

'Indeed.' Collins nodded. 'It was worn by a fairly notorious murderer during the crimes he committed. It cost a small fortune to acquire, but it's a handsome piece, and the source and paperwork are impeccable.' Collins turned quickly to look at Pete. 'All completely legal and above board, I assure you. Was there anything else I could help you with?'

Pete shook his head, trying to make sense of what Collins had just said. Then he looked at some of the other items on the wall. It wasn't just pictures, he realized. Several of the frames contained notes and letters. Some were clearly official documents and reports, while others were handwritten, scrawled on cheap notepaper.

He gestured at the wall, feeling slightly helpless.

'And . . . these?'

'Correspondence,' Collins said happily. 'Some personal, some acquired. Forms and paperwork from cases, as well.'

Pete stepped away again, this time moving all the way back to the middle of the room. And then he turned, looking this way and that. As he understood what he was seeing, the feeling of unease deepened, folding over inside him, drawing the heat away from his skin.

Drawings, mementos, correspondence.

Artefacts of death and murder.

He had been aware before now that there were people in the world who were driven to acquire such macabre things, and that there were even thriving online marketplaces dedicated to the activity. But he had never before stood in the heart of such a collection. The room around him seemed to be throbbing with menace, not least because this was clearly not simply a collection, but a celebration. There was reverence in the way these things had been put on display.

He looked at Norman Collins, who remained standing by the wall. The smile had disappeared from the man's face now, his expression replaced by something altogether more alien and reptilian. Collins had not wanted to let Pete in, and he had clearly hoped to conclude the conversation without Pete noticing his pictures and ornaments. But there was a sneer of pride on his face now – a look that said he knew how abhorrent Pete must find his collection, and that a part of him relished it. That he was even above him, in some way.

All completely legal and above board, I assure you.

And so Pete simply stood there for a moment, not knowing what to do, unsure if there was even anything he could do. Then his mobile rang, jolting him. He took it out and then turned away, speaking quietly as he pressed the phone hard to his ear.

'Willis here.'

It was Amanda.

'Pete? Where are you?'

'I'm where I said I would be.' He noticed the urgency in her voice. 'Where are you?'

'I'm at a house on Garholt Street. We've got a second body.'

'A second?'

'Yes. But these remains are much older – it looks like they've been hidden for a long time.'

Pete tried to take in what he was hearing.

'The house here was sold recently.' Amanda sounded a little breathless herself, as though she was still trying to process all this too. 'The new owner found the body in a box in the garage. He also made a report that someone might have attempted to abduct his son last night. And your man, Norman Collins – it looks like he's been creeping around at the property. Owner puts him at the scene. I think Collins knew the body was there.'

Pete turned around quickly then – suddenly aware of a presence. Collins had magicked himself closer once again. He was standing right next to Pete now, his face near enough to see the pores of his skin and the blankness in his eyes. The air was singing with menace.

'Is there anything else, DI Willis?' Collins whispered.

Pete took a step away, his heart beating hard.

'Bring him in,' Amanda said.

Twenty-nine

I parked one street away from Jake's school, thinking that it should have been reassuring to have a policeman in the car with me.

I'd been frustrated that the officers who called round that morning hadn't taken my night-time visitor and the attempted abduction of my son as seriously as they should. That had certainly changed now, but there was nothing remotely comforting about it. It meant all this was actually happening. It meant that the danger to Jake was real.

DS Dyson looked up.

'We're here?'

'It's just round the corner.'

He slipped his mobile into his suit trouser pocket. Dyson was in his fifties, but had spent the journey from the police station silently absorbed by something on his phone, like some kind of teenager.

'Okay,' he said. 'I want you to behave exactly as you usually would. Pick your son up. Chat to the other parents, or whatever it is you normally do. Take your time. I'll have you in sight throughout, and I'll just be keeping an eye on the other people present.'

I tapped the steering wheel. 'DI Beck told me you'd already arrested the man responsible.'

'Sure.' Dyson shrugged, and from his manner, it was clear that he was simply following an order and going through the motions. 'It's just a precaution.'

A precaution.

That was the same word DI Amanda Beck had used at the police station. Things had moved quickly after the police arrived at my house and I'd shown them what I'd found. In the intervening time, Norman Collins had been arrested, which brought home to me all too clearly what could have happened to Jake last night. But with Collins in custody, my son should have been safe.

So why the escort?

Just a precaution.

It hadn't reassured me at the police station, and it didn't now. The police were a capable, powerful resource to have behind me, and yet it still felt that Jake wouldn't be safe until he was right next to me. Somewhere *I* could look after him.

Dyson melted away behind me as I walked to the school, and it was surreal to think I was being covertly shadowed by a police officer. But then, the whole day had been off-kilter and unworldly. With events moving so swiftly, I still hadn't processed the fact that I'd found human remains, most likely those of a child, on my property. The reality of that hadn't hit me yet. I'd given my statement at the police station dispassionately, and it would be typed up and waiting for me to sign when I'd picked up Jake. I still had no idea what was going to happen after that.

Just behave normally, Dyson had told me, which was a completely impossible instruction in the circumstances. But when I reached the playground, I saw Karen leaning against the railings, hands stuffed into the pockets of her big coat, and figured that talking to her was about as normal as anything else. I walked in and leaned against the railings beside her.

'Hello there,' she said. 'How's tricks?'

'Tricky.'

'Ha, ha.' Then she looked at me properly. 'Although that's not actually a joke, is it, by the look of things. Bad day?'

I breathed out slowly. The police hadn't explicitly told me I couldn't talk to anyone about the day's events, but I suspected it would be wise not to yet. Aside from anything else, I had absolutely no idea where to begin.

'You could say that. It's been a very complicated twenty-four hours. I'll tell you about it properly some time.'

'Well, I'll look forward to that. I hope you're okay, though. No offence, but you look like shit.' She thought about it. 'Although that probably is quite offensive, isn't it? Sorry. I always say the wrong thing. Bad habit.'

'It's fine. I just didn't get much sleep last night.'

'Your son's imaginary friends keeping you up?'

I actually laughed.

'That's closer to the truth than you know.'

The boy in the floor.

I thought of the rusty-looking bones, and the hollow-eyed skull with its crest of jagged cracks. The beautiful colours of the butterflies Jake couldn't have seen, but had somehow drawn. And as much as I wanted him out here right now, I was also slightly unnerved by the prospect. Unnerved by *him*. My sensitive son, with his sleepwalking and his imaginary friends, and the way he talked to people who weren't there, who told him frightening rhymes and tried to scare him.

They scared me too.

The door opened. Mrs Shelley appeared and then began looking at the parents and calling children's names back over her shoulder. Her gaze drifted across Karen and me.

'Adam,' she said, and then moved immediately on to a different boy.

'Uh-oh,' Karen said. 'Looks like you're on the naughty step again.'

'The day I've had, that really wouldn't surprise me.'

'It can feel like you're a child again yourself, can't it? The way they talk to you sometimes.'

I nodded. Although I wasn't sure I was in the mood to put up with it today.

'Anyway, take care of yourself,' Karen said, as Adam reached us.

'I will.'

I watched them go, then waited while the rest of the children were released. At least Dyson was getting a good chance to take *precautions*, I supposed – and the thought made me scan the faces in the playground myself. Except what was the point? I recognized a few of the parents already, but I hadn't been here long enough to know more than a handful. To them, I probably looked like a suspicious character myself.

When there was only Jake left, Mrs Shelley beckoned me over. Jake emerged at the side of her, once again staring down at the ground. He looked so vulnerable that I wanted to rescue him – just scoop him up and take him somewhere safe. I felt a burst of love for him. Maybe he was too fragile to be ordinary, to fit in and be accepted. But after everything that had happened, so fucking what?

'Trouble again?' I said.

'I'm afraid so.' Mrs Shelley smiled sadly. 'Jake was put on red today. He had to go to see Miss Wallace, didn't you, Jake?'

Jake nodded miserably.

'What happened?' I said.

'He hit another boy in the class.'

'Oh.'

'Owen started it.' Jake sounded as though he was about to cry. 'He was trying to take my Packet of Special Things. I didn't mean to hit him.'

'Yes, well.' Mrs Shelley folded her arms and looked at me pointedly. 'I'm not entirely sure that's an appropriate thing for a child your age to be bringing into school in the first place.'

I had no idea what to say. Social convention dictated that I side with the grown-up here, which meant that I should tell Jake that hitting was bad, and that maybe his teacher was right about the Packet. But I couldn't. The whole situation suddenly seemed so laughably trivial. The stupid fucking traffic-light system. The terror of Miss Wallace. And most of all, the idea of telling Jake off because some little shit had messed with him and, most likely, got exactly what he deserved.

I looked at my son, standing there so timidly, probably expecting me to tell him off, when what I actually wanted to say to him was: *Well done. I never had the courage to do that at your age. I hope you hit him hard.*

And yet social convention won out.

'I'll talk to him,' I said.

'Good. Because it's not been a fantastic start, has it, Jake?' Mrs Shelley ruffled his hair, and social convention lost.

'Don't touch my son,' I said.

'I'm sorry?'

She moved her hand away, as though Jake was electric. There was some satisfaction in that, even though my words had come out without thinking and I wasn't remotely sure what I was going to say next.

'Just that,' I said. 'You can't put him on your traffic-light system and then pretend to be nice. To be honest, I think it's a pretty terrible thing to do to any child, never mind one who's obviously having problems right now.'

'What problems?' She was flustered. 'If there are problems, then we can talk about them.'

I knew it was stupid to be so confrontational, but I still felt a small degree of pleasure in standing up for my son. I looked at Jake again, who was staring at me curiously now, as though he wasn't sure what to make of me. I smiled at him. I was glad he'd stood up for himself. Glad that he'd made an impact on the world.

I looked back at Mrs Shelley.

'I will talk to him,' I said. 'Because hitting is wrong. So he and I will have a long discussion about better ways to stand up to bullies.'

'Well . . . that's good to hear.'

'Fine. Got everything, mate?'

Jake nodded.

'Good,' I said. 'Because I don't think we can go home tonight.'

'Why not?'

Because of the boy in the floor.

But I didn't say that. The strangest thing was, I thought he knew the answer to his own question already.

'Come on,' I said gently.

Thirty

They've found him, Pete thought.

After all this time.

They've found Tony.

Sitting in his car, he watched the CSI officers entering Norman Collins' property. For the moment, it was the only activity on the street. Despite the gathering police presence, the media had yet to arrive, and whatever neighbours were home were staying out of view for the moment. One of the CSI team stood on the front step, put his hands in the small of his back and stretched.

Cuffed and ensconced in the back seat, Collins was watching the activity too.

'You have no authority to do this,' Collins said blankly.

'Be quiet, Norman.'

In the confines of the car, Pete couldn't avoid smelling the man, but he had no intention of talking to him. As the situation was still developing, he had arrested Collins on suspicion of receipt of stolen goods for the moment, simply because – given the nature of some of the items in the man's collection – it was a charge they could likely make stick, and also one that gave them authority to search the man's home. But of course, they wanted him for more than that. And no matter how many questions he had, Pete wasn't about to jeopardize the investigation by interviewing Collins here and now. It had to be done at the department. Recorded and watertight.

'They won't find anything,' Collins said.

Pete ignored him. Because, of course, they already had, and Collins appeared to be implicated in that. A second, older set of remains had been discovered. Collins had always been obsessed with Carter and his crimes; he had visited Frank Carter's friend in prison; he had been stalking the house where the second body had been found. Collins *had* known the body was there – Pete was certain of it. But more importantly, while official identification would come in time, he was also sure that the remains belonged to Tony Smith.

After twenty years, you've been found.

All else aside, the development should have brought a sense of relief and closure, because he had been searching for the boy for so long. But it didn't. He couldn't stop thinking of all those weekend searches, combing through hedgerows and woodland many miles from here, when the whole time Tony had been lying far closer to home than anyone imagined.

Which meant there must have been something he had missed twenty years ago.

He looked down at the tablet on his lap.

God, he wanted a drink right now – and wasn't it strange how that worked? People often thought of alcohol as a buffer against the horrors of the world. But Tony Smith's body had been found, and it was more than possible that the man responsible for Neil Spencer's murder was in custody, sitting behind him right now, and yet the urge to drink was stronger than ever. There were always so many reasons to drink, though. Only ever one real reason not to.

You can drink later. As much as you want.

He accepted that he would. Whatever works – it was that simple. In a war, you used any weapon to hand to win an individual battle, and then you regrouped and fought the next one. And the next. And all the ones that followed.

Whatever works.

'I've done nothing wrong,' Collins insisted.

'Shut up.'

Pete clicked on the tablet. There was no avoiding this: he needed to figure out what he had missed all those years ago and why, and the house on Garholt Street where Tony's remains had been found was the place to start.

He scanned through the details. Until recently, the house had been owned by a woman named Anne Shearing. She had inherited it from her parents, but hadn't lived in it for decades, instead renting it out over the years to numerous individuals.

There was a long list of those on record, but Pete presumed he could discount occupants from before 1997, when Frank Carter had committed his murders. The tenant at that time had been a man named Julian Simpson. Simpson had been renting the property for four years beforehand, and his residency continued until 2008. Opening a new tab on screen, Pete ran a search and discovered Simpson had died of cancer that year, at the age of seventy. He clicked back. The house's next tenant was a man named Dominic Barnett, who had occupied the house until earlier this year.

Dominic Barnett.

Pete frowned. The name rang a bell. Running another search, the details came back to him, even though he hadn't worked the case himself. Barnett had been a minor underworld figure involved in drugs and extortion, known to police but considered small fry in the grand scheme of things. There were no convictions on file for the last ten years – but of course, that didn't mean he'd gone straight, and nobody had been remotely surprised when he turned up dead. The murder weapon – a hammer – had been recovered with partial prints, but there had been no match on the database.

Subsequent enquiries had failed to turn up a credible suspect. But the public, at least, had been reassured. Despite the lack of an arrest, the police believed it to be an isolated, targeted incident, and anybody reading between the lines of that could probably have intuited what lay behind it.

Live by the sword, die by the sword.

To the extent that Pete had paid the case any attention, he had assumed the same. But he wondered about it now. Drugs remained the most likely motive for the murder, but Barnett had lived in a house where human remains had been kept hidden, and it seemed impossible that he would have been unaware of it. Did that suggest a different motive?

He looked up and watched Norman Collins in the rear-view mirror for a moment. Collins was staring blankly out of the window at his house.

There were three men to think about: Julian Simpson and Dominic Barnett, who had both lived in the property, and Norman, who seemed to be aware of what had been stored there. What was the connection between the three? What had happened twenty years ago, and in the time since?

Pete loaded up a map of Featherbank.

Garholt Street was on a natural route between the scene of Tony Smith's abduction and the direction in which Frank Carter had fled. At the time, forensic evidence established that Tony had been in Carter's vehicle – but if Carter had somehow been tipped off that his house was being searched, he could have dropped the boy's body at Garholt Street before going on the run. Julian Simpson had been living there then.

Pete didn't need to consult the case file to know that Simpson hadn't come up in the investigation at the time. All of Carter's known acquaintances had been investigated carefully. Simpson's name had not been among them.

And yet.

Simpson would have been around fifty at the time of the abductions, meaning his age matched the conflicting description given in one of the witness statements. Perhaps he had been Carter's accomplice. If so, there must have been some connection between the two men, however oblique, which Pete hadn't discovered.

The sense of failure hit hard.

You should have found him sooner.

Whatever he had or hadn't done, it would still be his fault. He knew he would find a way to twist it round so that the blame rested with him. But the feeling remained.

Worthless.

Useless.

You can drink later.

His phone rang – Amanda again.

'Willis,' he answered. 'I'm still at Collins' house. I'll be on my way back in a minute.'

'How's the search going?'

'It's going.'

He glanced at the house, knowing that was where his focus needed to be. The priority right now was nailing Collins for his involvement, not working out what Pete himself had and hadn't missed twenty years ago. That dissection could come later.

'Okay,' Amanda told him. 'I've got the homeowner and his son here, and I need someone to help me with them. Sort out accommodation for them for the night. That kind of thing.'

Pete frowned to himself. That was grunt work at best, and he knew the implications: Amanda would be the one handling the interview with Norman Collins. But perhaps that was better. Cleaner. They didn't want to risk his past history with the man colouring the investigation now. The answers to his questions would come in time, but he didn't need to be the one who asked them. He started the engine.

'On my way.'

'The guy's called Tom Kennedy,' Amanda said. 'His son is Jake. Book Collins in first, and then they're in one of the comfort suites.'

For a moment, Pete didn't respond. His free hand was on the steering wheel. He stared at it, and noticed it begin to tremble.

'Pete?' Amanda said. 'You there?'

'Yes. I'm on my way.'

He hung up and tossed the phone on to the passenger seat. But rather than driving away, he turned the engine off and picked up the tablet again. He'd been too lost in the past to think about the present. He hadn't even considered the man who owned the property now.

Failing, as always.

He clicked through to the report, wondering if he'd misheard what Amanda had said. But there it was.

Tom Kennedy.

Finally. A name he recognized.

Thirty-one

'Did they find him, Daddy?' Jake said.

I had been pacing back and forth across the room in the police station, waiting for DI Amanda Beck to bring the statement for me to sign, but my son's words brought me to a halt.

He was sitting on a chair that was far too big for him, kicking his legs slightly, an untouched orange Fruit Shoot on the table beside him. The latter had been a gift from DS Dyson after we'd arrived. Allegedly, there was coffee on its way for me, but we'd been here for twenty minutes now, and it showed about as much sign of imminent arrival as Beck did. Jake and I hadn't really spoken the whole time. I didn't know what to say to him right now, and my pacing had been as much about filling the silence in the room as the space.

Did they find him, Daddy?

I walked over now and knelt down in front of him.

'Yes. They found the man who came to our house.'

'That's not who I meant.'

The boy in the floor.

I stared at my son for a second, but he looked back at me without any apparent fear or concern. It was astounding that he could take everything that was happening in his stride, as though it was all perfectly normal – as though we were talking about a boy who had been playing hide and seek, not human remains that had been in the floor of our garage for God knew how many years, and which it was impossible for him to have known about.

It was something we shouldn't be talking about. Not here. My statement to the police had been honest but incomplete. I hadn't mentioned the drawings of the butterflies or told them about Jake talking to the boy in the floor. I wasn't sure why, beyond the fact that I couldn't make any sense of it myself, and because I wanted to protect my son. That all this was a grown-up's burden to shoulder, not a seven-year-old's.

'Yes, Jake,' I said. 'That *is* who you meant. Okay? This is serious.'

He thought about it.

'Okay.'

'We'll talk about the other thing later.' I stood up, realizing that what I'd said wasn't quite enough, and that he deserved to know more. 'But yes, they found him.'

I found him.

'That's good,' Jake said. 'He was scaring me a little.'

'I know.'

'Although I don't think he was meaning to.' Jake frowned. 'I think he was just hurt and lonely, and that was making him a little bit mean. But they've found him, and so he won't be lonely now, will he? He can go home. So he won't be mean any more.'

'It was just your imagination, Jake.'

'It wasn't.'

'We'll talk about it later. Okay?'

I gave him the serious look I always attempted when I wanted to draw a line under a conversation. It usually had no authority whatsoever, and a minute later one or the other of us would end up shouting, but today he nodded. Then he swivelled on his chair, picked up the Fruit Shoot and began drinking it without a care in the world.

The door opened behind me, and I turned to see DS Dyson entering, carrying two cups of coffee. He held the door open with his back for DI Beck who marched in past him. She was brandishing papers and looked as tired as I felt: a woman with a million things to do, determined to do each one of them herself.

'Mr Kennedy,' she said. 'I'm really sorry about your wait. Ah . . . and this must be Jake.'

Still distracted by the Fruit Shoot, my son ignored her.

'Jake?' I prompted. 'Can you say hello, please?'

'Hi.'

I turned back to Beck. 'It's been a long day.'

'I completely understand. This must be very strange for him indeed.' She leaned down towards him, pressing her hands against her knees a little awkwardly, as though unsure how to talk to a child. 'Have you ever been in a police station before, Jake?'

He shook his head but didn't answer.

'Well.' She gave an awkward laugh, then stood up. 'First and last time, hopefully. Anyway, Mr Kennedy. I have your statement here. If you could just read through it, make sure you're happy with the contents, and then sign it. And your drink is here too.'

'Thanks.'

Dyson passed me the coffee, and I sipped it while I scanned the statement on the table. I'd explained about Norman Collins, what Mrs Shearing had told me about him and Dominic Barnett, and the man who'd been at the door whispering to Jake last night. All of which had led me to investigate the garage, wondering what Collins might have been looking for. That was why and how I'd found the remains in there.

I glanced at Jake, who was now sucking at the end of his Fruit Shoot, the juice rattling at the bottom, and then signed on the final page.

'I'm afraid you won't be able to go home tonight,' DI Beck said.

'Okay.'

'Possibly tomorrow night as well. Of course, we're happy to arrange alternative accommodation for both of you over that period. We have a safe house nearby.'

My pen hovered over my signature.

'Why would we need a safe house?'

'You don't,' she said quickly. 'It's just property we have available for use. But I'll leave my colleague, DI Pete Willis, to talk you through all that. He should be here any moment, and I can leave you in peace. In fact, here he is now.'

The door opened again, a new man coming in.

'Pete,' Beck said. 'This is Tom and Jake Kennedy.'

I stared at the man, and everything else in the world seemed to disappear. It had been such a long time, and the years had been kind to him, but while he was much leaner and healthier than I remembered, adults changed far less than children do, and I still recognized him. A jolt of recognition in my heart, followed by a hundred buried memories bursting forth and blooming in my head.

And he knew me too. Of course he did. By now, he would have learned my name and had time to prepare himself for this. As he approached me, professional and formal, I imagined nobody else would have noticed the sick expression on his face.

Glass smashing.

My mother screaming.

'Mr Kennedy,' my father said.

Thirty-two

It had been a *very* confusing day, Jake thought.

He was extremely tired for one thing – that was the fault of the thing that had happened in the night, but he couldn't remember much about that. He'd been half asleep at the time. But then he'd still been very angry at Daddy for what he'd written, and when the police were there, and Daddy had said Mummy was dead as though it was nothing, he'd lost his temper. That wasn't good, but he hadn't been able to help himself.

The anger had faded through the day, though, and that was confusing in itself. But then, sometimes arguments disappeared like mist did when it was there first thing in the morning. In the classroom, though, he'd felt lonely and had wanted to hug Daddy a lot more and tell him he was sorry, and to hear Daddy tell him that, actually, he was too.

It had felt like things might be better then.

And then Owen had done what he'd done, and so had Jake, and there had been Miss Wallace's office to face as a result. That actually hadn't been so bad in itself, except for two big reasons. One was that the Packet of Special Things was back in the classroom, which meant it may very well be at the mercy of the evil Owen, which was an unbearable thought.

'Can you look at me, please?' Miss Wallace had needed to say it twice, because Jake couldn't take his eyes off the closed office door.

And reason number two: he knew Daddy was going to be

disappointed and angry with him for getting in trouble again, which meant that things weren't going to get better for a long time. Or maybe ever, at this rate.

Perhaps Daddy might even write horrible words down about *him* too.

Jake suspected that he wanted to.

But then, when he got back to the classroom, the Packet appeared to have been left untouched, and the possibility had occurred to him that maybe he should hit people more often. And at pick-up time, Daddy hadn't seemed angry with him at all. He'd actually argued with Mrs Shelley! Which was certainly brave, Jake thought. But! More importantly, Daddy had been on his side. Even if he hadn't said it outright, Jake could tell that he was. Even though he hadn't got a hug, that actually made things seem as good as if he had.

And now they were in a police station.

That had been fine at first because it was really quite interesting, especially as everybody had been very nice to him, but he quite wanted to leave now. And then the next thing had happened – the new policeman coming in – and everything was even more confusing now, because of how Daddy was behaving. He'd been fine with the other police people, but he looked pale and scared now – as though this was a classroom for him, and the new policeman was someone like Mrs Shelley.

Come to think of it, the new policeman looked uncomfortable too. When the woman police officer left, carrying the statement Daddy had signed, the door closed behind her, and then the air in the room had felt very strange indeed. It was like there was some kind of glue that was holding everybody in place.

Then the new policeman walked slowly over and looked down at him.

'You must be Jake?' he said.

'Yes.' This was safely true. 'I am Jake.'

The man smiled, but it was an odd one. He had a face that looked like it could be very kind indeed, but the smile right now was troubled. A moment later, he reached out his hand, and so Jake shook it, which was the polite thing to do. The hand was big and warm, and the grip was very gentle.

'I'm pleased to meet you, Jake. You can call me Pete.'

'Hello, Pete,' Jake said. 'It's nice to meet you too. Why can't we go home? One of the other policemen told my daddy that we couldn't.'

Pete frowned and knelt down in front of him, then peered into his face as though there might be some kind of secret there. Jake stared back at him to let him know he wasn't hiding anything. No secrets here, mister.

'It's very complicated,' Pete said. 'We have to do some investigation work at your house.'

'Because of the boy in the floor?'

'Yes.'

But then Pete looked across at Daddy, and Jake remembered that he wasn't supposed to have mentioned that. But honestly, the atmosphere in the room was so funny that it was easy to forget things like that.

'I told him what I found,' Daddy said.

'How did you know that it's a boy, though?'

Daddy was just standing there, but he looked caught somehow, as though he wanted to move forward or backward but had forgotten how his body worked. Jake had the uncomfortable feeling that if Daddy did remember how to move properly, it would be forward – and quite aggressively too.

'I didn't,' Daddy said. 'I said *body*. He must have misheard me.'

'That's true,' Jake added quickly. He didn't want Daddy to

hit anybody, especially not a policeman, because right now it really looked like he might.

Pete stood up slowly.

'Okay. Well, let's deal with some practicalities. Is it just the two of you?'

'Yes,' Daddy said.

'Jake's mother . . . ?'

Daddy still looked angry. 'My wife died last year.'

'I'm sorry. That must have been very hard for you.'

'We're fine.'

'I can see that.'

So confusing! Jake wanted to shake his head. Now Pete didn't seem able to look at Daddy. But Pete was a policeman, and that meant he was in charge, didn't it?

'We can arrange accommodation for you, but you might not want that. Do you have any family you'd prefer to stay with?'

'No,' Daddy said. 'Both of my parents are dead.'

Pete hesitated.

'Right. I'm very sorry to hear that as well.'

'It's okay.'

And then Daddy took a step forward.

Jake held his breath.

But now it seemed like Daddy only *wanted* to hit someone, rather than actually doing it.

'It happened a very long time ago.'

'Right.' Pete took a deep breath, but still didn't look at Daddy. He was just staring at the wall, and Jake thought he suddenly looked a lot older than he had when he'd first come into the room. 'In that case, we can arrange somewhere for you to stay in the meantime.'

'That would be good, yes.'

'And I'm sure you'll need some things. I can come back

with you to your house if you like, and you can get some things you both might need. Spare clothes and things.'

'You need to be there?'

'Yes. I'm sorry. It's a crime scene. I need to make a note of anything that's removed.'

'Okay. That's not ideal, is it?'

'I know.' Pete finally looked back at Daddy. 'I'm sorry.'

Daddy shrugged, his eyes still glittering.

'It is what it is. So let's get it over with, shall we? Jake, you'll need to have a think about what toys you might want, okay?'

'Okay.'

But Jake looked between the two of them – Daddy and Pete – and still nobody was moving, or seeming like they knew what on earth to do next, and Jake decided that if he didn't do something then nobody would. So he put the empty Fruit Shoot bottle down on the table with a loud, decisive thud.

'My drawing things, Daddy,' he said. 'That's all I want.'

Thirty-three

Small triumphs on terrible days. You had to cling to them, Amanda thought, as she sat back down in the interview room across from Norman Collins. After the horrors she had seen last night, and the failure she felt at not finding Neil Spencer in time, she was ready for a little blood. And often the small victories were as much as you ever got.

'Sorry about the interruption, Norman,' she said. 'Let's continue.'

'Indeed. Let's bring this to a swift conclusion, shall we?'

'Absolutely.' She smiled politely. 'Let's do just that.'

Collins folded his arms, smirking a little. Which didn't surprise her. She'd understood from the moment she set eyes on him exactly what Pete had meant about there being something off about the man. He was the sort of person you instinctively crossed the street to avoid. The exaggerated formality of his attire struck her as being a kind of disguise – an attempt at respectability that failed to hide the unpleasantness beneath. And it was clear from his manner that he felt removed from other people. Superior to them, even.

Twenty minutes into the interview, with an answer to every question she had offered, he'd still had every reason to feel superior to her. But then Steph had knocked and leaned into the room, and Amanda had signalled a break. Now she reached over, turned the recording equipment back on, and ran through the preliminaries.

Across from her, Collins sighed theatrically to himself.

She looked down now at the sheet of paper she'd brought

back in with her. It was going to be a pleasure to wipe the smirk off the creepy fucker's face.

First things first, though.

'Mr Collins,' she said. 'For clarity, let's quickly go back over some of the ground we've already covered. In July of this year, you visited Victor Tyler in Whitrow prison. What was the purpose of that visit?'

'I have an interest in crime. In certain circles, I am considered an expert. I was interested in talking to Mr Tyler about his actions. In much the same way, I'm sure, as the police have talked to him over the years.'

Probably not quite the same, Amanda thought.

'Did your conversation touch on Frank Carter?'

'It did not.'

'Were you aware that Tyler is friends with Carter?'

'I was not.'

'That seems strange. What with you being such an expert and all.'

'One can't be expected to know everything.' Collins smiled.

Amanda was sure he was lying, but the conversation between Collins and Tyler had not been recorded, and she had no way to prove it.

'All right,' she said. 'Your whereabouts on the afternoon and evening of Sunday the 30th of July this year, the evening Neil Spencer was abducted?'

'I've already told you. I was at home for much of the afternoon. Later on, I walked to Town Street and dined in the restaurant there.'

'It's good that you recall so clearly.'

Collins shrugged. 'I am a creature of habit. It was a Sunday. When my mother was alive, we went together. Now, I eat alone.'

Amanda nodded to herself. The owner of the restaurant had verified this, which meant that Collins appeared to have a solid alibi for the period of time in which Neil Spencer had been abducted. And while the search of his house was ongoing, officers had so far found nothing to suggest Neil had ever been held there. Collins, she was sure, was up to his neck in whatever was going on here somehow, but right now he seemed to be in the clear for the actual abduction of Neil Spencer.

'Number 13 Garholt Street,' she said.

'Yes?'

'You attempted to purchase the property.'

'Indeed. It was for sale. I have no idea why that's considered a crime.'

'I didn't say it was.'

'The house was on the market. I've lived where I do for a long time now, and it felt like time to spread my wings a little. Branch out on my own, so to speak.'

'And then, when your acquisition was refused, you stalked the property anyway.'

Collins shook his head. 'Absolutely not.'

'Mr Kennedy claims you tried to break into his garage.'

'He is simply incorrect.'

'A garage where the remains of a child have been discovered.'

And Amanda had to give Collins credit then. While she had no doubt he was well aware of what had been found, he remembered to at least feign surprise. It wasn't remotely convincing, but it was there.

'That's . . . shocking,' he said.

'I'm not sure I believe you, Norman.'

'I knew nothing about that.' He frowned. 'Have you spoken to the seller? Perhaps you should.'

'Right now, I'm more interested in why *you* were so interested in the property.'

'And I've told you: I wasn't. This Mr . . . Kennedy, was it? He is mistaken. I've been nowhere near his house.'

Amanda stared at him, and Collins stared implacably back. One person's word against another. Even if they could arrange a line-up, and Kennedy identified Collins, she wasn't sure that in itself would be enough to justify charges. The fact was that, right now, they couldn't prove he knew about the remains in the garage. And he appeared to be in the clear for the abduction of Neil Spencer. Given some of the items in his collection, they might have him on a charge of handling stolen goods, but perhaps not even that.

And the smug fucker knew it.

Or thought he did.

Amanda looked down again at the sheet of paper Steph had given her – the results of the search on the fingerprints taken from Norman Collins upon his arrival. And even though she was no closer to pinning Neil Spencer on him, she felt a thrill nonetheless. She lived for moments like this. She wished Pete was here to savour it with her. God knew, he deserved to feel it too.

'Mr Collins,' she said. 'Could you tell me where you were on the evening of Tuesday the 4th of April this year?'

Collins hesitated.

'I'm sorry?'

Amanda waited, still looking at the sheet of paper. That had got his attention at least. Presumably, he'd been anticipating more questions about his activity on the day of Neil Spencer's abduction, which he thought was safe ground to go over. But Amanda knew now that this new date was an enormous black pit beneath his feet.

'I'm not sure I recall,' Collins said carefully.

'Let me help you then. Were you in the vicinity of Hollingbeck Wood?'

'I wouldn't have thought so.'

'Well, your fingers were. Was the rest of you?'

'I don't —'

'Your prints were found on the hammer that was used to murder Dominic Barnett there that night.'

Amanda looked up, enjoying noticing the sweat that was forming on Collins' forehead. A fussy, superior man — but one easily thrown off course when it came to it. It was interesting to watch him going through his options, searching for a way out, and slowly realizing that he was in much more trouble than he'd thought.

'No comment,' he said.

Amanda shook her head. It was his right, of course, but the phrase had always rankled with her. You *don't* have the right to remain silent, she always wanted to tell people. And right now, she wanted Collins to take ownership of what he'd done rather than hiding away. Because there were other lives at stake.

'It's in your interests right now to tell me everything you know, Norman.' She rested her forearms on the table and tried to sound more sympathetic than she felt. 'And not just *your* interests, either. You say you had no involvement in the abduction of Neil Spencer. If you're telling the truth, that means there's a killer still out there right now.'

'No comment.'

'And unless we find him, that person is going to kill more children. I think you know a lot more about this person than you're telling me.'

Collins stared at her, his face completely pale. Amanda didn't think she'd ever seen a man melt so fast or collapse from smug self-confidence into a puddle of self-pitying misery with such speed.

'No comment,' he whispered.

'Norman –'

'I want a lawyer.'

'Well, we can certainly arrange that.' She stood up quickly, not bothering to hide the anger she felt. The disgust. 'Maybe then you'll realize how much trouble you're really in, and that cooperating with us is the best chance you've got.'

'No comment.'

'Yeah, I heard you the first time.'

Small victories.

But as she formally arrested Norman Collins for the murder of Dominic Barnett, Amanda thought about everything she'd said. If he was telling the truth about not killing Neil Spencer, then a child killer was still out there – which meant another little boy might die on her watch.

Her mind flashed back to the sight of Neil Spencer on the waste ground last night, and any of the elation she might normally feel vanished entirely.

A small victory wasn't good enough.

Thirty-four

The police presence at the house had intensified in my absence. We arrived to find two cars and a van parked outside, with officers and crime-scene investigators working in the taped-off driveway. The focus of the activity appeared to be the garage, but two police officers were stationed on the pavement to secure the whole property. My front door was open too – an incongruous sight to return home to, and one that felt invasive and wrong.

I pulled up after the other vehicles. My father's car drove past, then parked up in front of me.

Not my father, I reminded myself.

DI Pete Willis.

There was no need to acknowledge him as anything else, was there? And with the exception of the way he'd knelt down and looked at Jake, there was no sign he wanted to acknowledge it either. That was a situation I was more than happy to go along with.

The shock had subsided a little now, but only in the way I imagined there might be a few beats of silence after an earthquake hit before the screaming started. I could still remember what it had felt like at the police station, my father standing there, looking back at me, *seeing* me. My mind had immediately leapt back to the long-ago time when I'd last seen him, and I'd felt small and powerless. I had been transported. The fear and anxiety. The desire to diminish myself so that he might not notice me. But then the anger had come. He had no fucking right to talk to my son. And then the resentment. The fact that he got to be involved in my life – in a position of power over me, even – seemed so deeply unfair that I almost couldn't bear it.

'Are you all right, Daddy?'

'I'm fine, mate.'

I was staring at the car in front of me. At the man in the driver's seat.

His name is DI Pete Willis, I reminded myself, *and he means nothing to you.*

Nothing at all.

Not if I didn't let him.

'Right,' I said. 'Let's get this over with.'

He met us at the cordon, showed his identification to the officers there, and then led us into the house without saying anything. The resentment flowered again. I needed his permission to enter my own fucking home. It felt humiliating to follow him inside like a boy who had to do what he was told. And it was made worse by the fact that he seemed so indifferent to it all.

He had a clipboard and pen.

'I need to know what's yours, and what was here when you moved in that you haven't touched.'

'Everything is mine,' I said. 'And Mrs Shearing had cleaned all the rooms anyway.'

'We'll check with her, don't worry.'

'I'm not worried.'

We went from room to room, gathering some basic things together. Toiletries. Clothes for Jake and me. A few toys from his room. It burned me so hard that I had to ask my father each time, but he just nodded and noted the items down, and in the end I stopped asking. If he cared, he didn't mention it. He barely looked at me at all, in fact. I wondered what he might be thinking or feeling. But then I fought that down, because it didn't matter.

We finished in my office downstairs.

'I need my laptop –' I started to say, but Jake interrupted me.

'Who did Daddy find in the garage? Was it Neil Spencer?'

My father looked awkward.

'No. Those remains were much older.'

'Who are they of?'

'Well, between you and me, I think they might be from another little boy. One who disappeared a long time ago.'

'How long ago?'

'Twenty years.'

'Wow.' Jake paused to take in such an expanse of time.

'Yes. And I hope they are, because I've been searching for him ever since.'

Jake looked amazed by that, like it was some kind of accomplishment, and I didn't like that. I didn't want him interested in this man at all, never mind impressed by him.

'I'd have given up by now.'

My father smiled sadly.

'It's always been important to me. Everybody should get to go home, don't you think?'

'Can I take this, DI Willis?' I started unplugging my laptop, wanting to bring the conversation to an end. 'I need it for work.'

'Yes.' He turned away from both of us. 'Of course you can.'

The 'safe house' was just a flat above a newsagent's at one end of Town Street. It didn't look like much from the street, and it looked like even less when Willis took us inside.

A staircase led up from the front door to a landing with

four doors leading off it. There was a sitting room, bathroom, kitchen and a room with two single beds, all of it minimally furnished. The only signs that it was used by the police, rather than being simply rented out dirt cheap, were the security camera positioned subtly on the wall outside, the panic buttons within, and the proliferation of bolts on the inside of the front door.

'I'm sorry you'll have to share.'

Willis walked into the bedroom carrying sheets and blankets that he'd gathered from an airing cupboard. I was unpacking our clothes and piling them on top of the old wooden dresser, having wiped away a sheen of dust first. The flat clearly hadn't been cleaned in a long time and the air was itchy with it.

'It's fine,' I said.

'I know it's small. We use it for witnesses sometimes, but it's mostly women and children.' He seemed about to say something, but then shook his head. 'They usually want to be in the same room.'

'Domestic violence, I guess.'

My father didn't answer, but the strained atmosphere between us went up a notch, and I knew the hit had landed. What was between us remained unspoken but was growing louder, in the way that silence sometimes can.

'It's fine,' I said again. 'How long will we be here?'

'Shouldn't be more than a day or two. Maybe not even that. It's potentially a big case, though. We need to make sure we don't miss anything.'

'You think the man you've arrested killed Neil Spencer?'

'Possibly. Like I said, I think the remains we've found in your house are from a similar crime. There was always speculation that Frank Carter – the killer back then – had an accomplice of some kind. Norman Collins was never officially a suspect, but he was too interested in the case. I never thought he was directly involved, but . . .'

'But?'

'Maybe I got that wrong.'

'Yeah, I guess maybe you did.'

My father said nothing. The knowledge that I might have hurt him again brought a kind of thrill, but it was a small, disappointing one. He seemed so beaten down and uncomfortable. In his own way, perhaps he felt as powerless right now as I did.

'Okay.'

We moved back through to the sitting room, where Jake was kneeling down and drawing. There was a settee and a chair, a small table on wheels, and an old television balanced on a wooden chest of drawers with a mess of cables behind it. The whole place felt cold and bleak. I tried not to think about what was happening in our house – our real home – right now. Whatever problems it had thrown up, it felt like paradise compared to this.

But you'll deal with it. And this will be over soon.

And Pete Willis would be out of my life again.

'I'll leave you to it,' he said. 'Good to meet you, Jake.'

'Good to meet you too, Pete,' Jake said, not looking up from his picture. 'Thank you for this delightful flat.'

He hesitated. 'You're welcome.'

Out on the landing, I closed the door to the sitting room. There was a window here, but it was early evening now and the light coming in was dim. Willis seemed reluctant to leave, and so we stood in the gloom for a moment, his face full of shadow.

'You have everything you need?' he said finally.

'I think so.'

'Jake seems like a good kid.'

'Yes,' I said. 'He is.'

'He's creative. Just like you.'

I didn't reply. The silence between us was tingling now. As much as it was possible to tell in this half-light, Willis looked as though he wished he hadn't spoken. But then he explained himself.

'I saw the books you've written in the house.'

'You didn't know before?'

He shook his head.

'I'd have thought you might have been interested,' I said. 'Maybe looked me up, or something.'

'Did you look me up?'

'No, but that's different.'

As soon as I said it, I hated myself for it, because it acknowledged that power balance again – the idea that it was his job to look for me, to be concerned about me, to care about me, rather than the other way around. I didn't want him to imagine that was true. It wasn't. He was nothing to me.

'A long time ago,' he said, 'I decided it would be best for me to keep out of your life. Your mother and I decided between us.'

'That's one way of putting it.'

'I suppose so. It's my way of putting it. And I've honoured that. It's not always been easy. I've often wondered. But it's been for the best . . .'

He trailed off, suddenly looking weaker than ever.

Spare me the self-pity.

But I didn't say it. Whatever my father had done in the past, he'd obviously moved on since. He didn't look or smell like an alcoholic now. He was in good shape. And despite the weariness, there was an air of calm to him. I reminded myself again that this man and I were strangers to each other. We weren't father and son. We weren't enemies.

We were nothing.

He was looking off towards the window, towards the day slowly dying outside.

'Sally – your mother, I mean. What happened to her?'

Glass smashing.

My mother screaming.

I thought of everything that had followed. The way she did her best for me in spite of all the difficulties she faced as a single mother. The pain and ignominy of her death. Like Rebecca, taken far too young, long before either she or I deserved such a loss.

'She's dead,' I told him.

He was silent. For a moment, he even seemed broken. But then he gathered himself.

'When?'

'That's none of your business.'

The anger in my voice surprised me – but apparently not my father. He stood there, absorbing the force of the blow.

'No,' he said quietly. 'I suppose not.'

And then he started walking down the stairs to the front door. I watched him go. When he was halfway down I spoke again, just loud enough for him to hear.

'I remember that last night, you know. The night before you were gone. The last time you ever saw me. I remember how drunk you were. How red in the face you were. What you did. Throwing that glass at her. The way she screamed.'

He stopped on the stairs and stood completely still.

'I remember it all,' I said. 'So how dare you ask about her now?'

He didn't reply.

And then he continued silently down the stairs, leaving me with nothing but the sick and angry thud of my heartbeat.

Thirty-five

After leaving the safe house, Pete drove too fast along empty roads, heading straight home. The kitchen cabinet was calling to him, and he was going to surrender to it. Now that the decision was made, the urge was stronger than ever, and it felt like his whole life depended on getting there as quickly as possible.

Back home, he locked the door and drew the curtains. The house around him was still and silent, and it seemed as empty with him standing in it as it must have done before his arrival. Because after all, what did he add to it? He looked around at the spartan furnishings in the front room. It was the same throughout the house – every space just as ascetic and carefully organized. The truth was that he had lived in an empty house for years. The meagre detritus of a life barely lived, a real life avoided, was no less sad because it was tidy and clean.

Empty. Pointless.

Worthless.

The voice was gleeful in its victory. He stood there, breathing slowly, aware of his heart pounding. But he'd been here many times before, and this was the way it always worked. When the compulsion to drink was at its strongest, everything bolstered it. Any event or observation, good or bad, could be turned around and made to fit.

But it was all a lie.

You've been here before.

You can do this.

The urge fell silent for a moment, but then began to howl inside his head, conscious of the trick he was attempting to pull. He'd let it drive him home on auto-pilot, allowed it to believe that he was giving in, but now he was taking the wheel again.

The pain circled in his chest, swirling and unbearable.

You've been here before.

You can do this.

The table. The bottle and the photograph.

Tonight, he added a glass, and after a moment's hesitation, he opened the bottle and poured two fingers of vodka. Because why not? Either he would drink or he wouldn't. It wasn't how far down the road he went; it was whether he arrived at the end.

His phone buzzed. He picked it up to find a message from Amanda, filling him in on her interview with Norman Collins. They had Collins on the murder of Dominic Barnett, it seemed, but the situation with Neil Spencer was hazier, and Collins had decided to lawyer up.

'You think the man you've arrested killed Neil Spencer?' Tom had asked.

'Possibly,' he'd replied – and it was clear that the man was involved somehow. But if it wasn't Collins who had abducted and murdered Neil, it meant the actual killer was still out there. Any relief he'd felt after arresting Collins evaporated entirely at that thought, just as surely as it had twenty years ago when he'd seen Miranda and Alan Smith in the department's reception and realized the nightmare was far from over.

It shouldn't be his problem now. Tom was his son, albeit long estranged, and that conflict of interest meant he should talk to Amanda tomorrow and recuse himself from the investigation. He supposed it would bring relief of its own to be free from this pressure. And yet, having been dragged in this deep – having been forced to confront Carter again, and to look at Neil Spencer's body on the waste ground last night – he wanted to see this through, however damaging it might be.

He put the phone to one side, then stared at the glass, trying to analyse how he felt about seeing Tom again after so many years. The encounter should have shaken him to the core, he supposed, and yet he felt oddly calm. Over the years, he had grown numb to the fact of his fatherhood, as though it was something he had learned at school that no longer had any bearing on his life. Memories of Sally were on the right side of the pain threshold for him to bear, but his failure towards Tom had been absolute, and Pete had done his best never to think about that. It was better to have nothing to do with his son's life, and whenever he had found himself imagining what kind of man Tom might have become, he had quickly shoved those thoughts away. They were too hot to touch.

But now he knew.

He had no right to think of himself as a father, but it was impossible not to evaluate the man he had met that afternoon. A writer. That made sense, of course. Tom had always been creative as a little boy – always making up stories Pete couldn't follow, or playing out elaborate scenarios with his toys. Jake appeared to be a lot like Tom had been at that age: a sensitive and clever child. From the little Pete had learned, it was obvious Tom had suffered hardship and tragedy throughout his life, and yet he was capably raising Jake alone. There could be little doubt that his son had grown into a good man.

Not worthless. Not useless or a failure.

Which was good.

Pete ran his fingertip around the edge of the glass. It was good that Tom had succeeded in overcoming the miserable childhood he had offered him. Good that he had absented himself from Tom's life before he could poison it any more than he already had. Because it was clear that he had. Even after all this time, he was remembered. His impact had been terrible enough to leave a lasting impression.

I remember that last night.

Pete could still picture the look of hatred on his son's face when he'd said that. He picked up the glass. Put it down again. That wasn't quite right, though, was it? He deserved hatred – he was more than aware of that – but hatred had to be earned. Pete had been drinking almost constantly by the time Sally and Tom left him, and his days and nights had been a blur, but he remembered that particular evening with absolute clarity. Tom's description of what had happened was impossible.

Did it matter?

Perhaps not. If his son's memory was not literally true then, like Pete's own feelings of failure, it presumably still felt true enough, and that was the kind of truth that mattered most in the end.

He looked at the familiar photograph of him and Sally. It had been taken before Tom was conceived, but Pete thought it was possible to see the knowledge of impending fatherhood in the young man's expression if you wanted to. The squint against the sun. The half-smile that looked like it would soon disappear. It was as though the man in the photo already knew he was about to fail badly and lose everything.

Sally still looked so happy.

He had lost her a long time ago, but had maintained the fantasy that she was alive somewhere, leading a contented, loving life. Keeping up the miserable belief that his own loss had been her and Tom's gain. But now he knew the truth. There had been no gain. Sally was dead.

It felt like everything was.

Again, he picked up the glass, but this time, he kept hold of it, watching the silky liquid fold over on itself. It looked so innocent until it did that — so much like water until you moved it and saw the mist hiding there.

He'd been here before. He could survive this.

But why bother?

He looked around the room, weighing again the emptiness of his existence. There was nothing to him. He was a man made of air. A life with no heft. There was nothing good in his past that could be rescued, and nothing in his future that was worth trying to save.

Except that wasn't true, was it? Neil Spencer's killer might still be out there. If the boy's murder stemmed from some past failing of his, then it was his responsibility to put it right, whatever the personal repercussions might be. Whether he liked it or not, he was back in the nightmare now, and he thought that he needed to see it through to the end, even if it broke him. There was a conflict of interest, yes, but if he was careful then perhaps nobody would ever know. He doubted Tom would ever want their distant history aired.

That was one reason to stay sober.

And also —

Thank you for this delightful flat.

Pete smiled as he remembered Jake's words earlier. It had been such a strange thing to say, but it was funny. He was a funny kid. A nice kid. He was creative. He was a character. Probably a handful to deal with too, just like Tom had been at times.

Pete allowed himself to think about Jake for a few moments more. He could imagine sitting down and talking to the boy. Playing with him, the same way he might – and should – have done with Tom when he had been a child. It was foolish, of course. There was nothing there. In a couple of days, his involvement with the pair of them would be over, and he'd probably never see them again.

But even so, he decided that he wasn't going to drink.

Not tonight.

Easy to throw the glass, of course. Always easy to do that. Instead, he stood up, walked through to the kitchen, and poured it slowly away into the sink. He watched the liquid trailing away down the plughole, and alongside the urge in his chest he thought about Jake again and felt something he hadn't experienced in years. There was no reason to it. No sense. And yet there it was.

Hope.

PART FOUR

Thirty-six

The next morning, when I dropped Jake off at school, I was still quietly amazed by how well he'd adapted to our new circumstances. Last night in the safe house, he had dropped off to sleep without complaint, leaving me to sit alone in the front room afterwards with my laptop and my thoughts. When I'd finally gone to bed, I'd gazed down at him, and his face had looked so serene that I'd wondered if he was actually more at peace here than he was in our new home. I'd wondered what, if anything, he was dreaming about.

But then I often thought that.

For myself, even as tired as I was, the unfamiliar surroundings had made it harder to sleep than ever, so it was a relief when he was well behaved and easy to manage that morning. Perhaps he was treating this all as some kind of exciting adventure. Whatever the reason, I was grateful for it. I was so exhausted, and my nerves so on edge, that I wasn't sure I'd have been up to any real challenges.

We drove to the school, and then I walked him to the playground.

'Are you okay, mate?'

'I'm fine, Daddy.'

'All right, then. Here you go.' I handed him his water bottle and book bag. 'I love you.'

'I love you too.'

He walked off to the door, the bag swinging beside his leg. Mrs Shelley was waiting there. I hadn't had the conversation with Jake that I'd promised I would. I'd just have to hope that today was a little easier for him, or at least that he didn't punch anyone.

'You *still* look like shit.'

Karen fell into step beside me as I walked back out through the gates. She was still dressed up in her huge coat, despite the warmth of the morning.

'Yesterday, you were worried about offending me when you said that.'

'Yeah, but it didn't, did it?' She shrugged. 'I slept on it and figured it was probably okay.'

'Then you slept a lot better than I did.'

'That I can see.' She stuffed her hands into her pockets. 'What are you up to now? Fancy grabbing a coffee, or do you have to run off and be tired somewhere else?'

I hesitated. I had nothing to do. I'd told my father I needed my laptop for work, but the likelihood of me accomplishing anything in this state was pretty minimal. Today was likely to be a case of treading water and hoping some kind of land would eventually appear – killing time, basically – and looking at Karen now, I figured there were worse ways to do that.

'Sure,' I said. 'That would be nice.'

We walked down to the main road, where she led me past the small corner shop and village post office to a delicatessen called the Happy Pig. There were meadow scenes painted on the front windows, and the inside was rustic and crammed with wooden tables, like a farmhouse kitchen.

'Bit pretentious.' She pushed open the door and a bell tinkled. 'But the coffee's acceptable.'

'As long as it's got caffeine in.'

It certainly smelled good. We ordered at the counter, standing beside each other a little awkwardly while we waited and not speaking for the moment. Then we took our drinks over to a table and sat down.

Karen shrugged her coat off. She was wearing a white blouse and blue jeans underneath it, and I was surprised by how slim she looked without the armour on. Was it armour? I thought it might be. There was a scattering of wooden rings around her wrists, which rattled slightly as she reached up with both hands and gathered her hair back, tying it into a loose ponytail.

'So,' she said. 'What *is* going on with you?'

'It's a long story. How much do you want to know?'

'Oh, everything.'

I considered that. As a writer, one of the things I'd always believed was that you didn't talk about your stories until they were finished. If you did, there was less of an urge to write them down – almost as though the story just needed to be told in some capacity, and the pressure reduced the more you recounted the tale.

So with that in mind, I decided to tell Karen everything.

Almost everything, anyway.

She already knew about the junk in my garage and my visit from the man who'd turned out to be Norman Collins, but Jake's near abduction in the middle of the night made her raise her eyebrows. Then what I'd learned from Mrs Shearing, and the events that had unfolded yesterday. The discovery of the body. The safe house.

And last of all, my father.

The impression I'd gained so far of Karen was that she was fairly frivolous: prone to playful sarcasm and jokey asides. But by the time I'd finished explaining, she looked horrified and deadly serious.

'Shit,' she said quietly. 'They haven't released any details to the media yet – just that remains had been found at a property. I had no idea it was yours.'

'I think they're playing it close to their chests. From what

I can make out, they think it's the remains of a kid called Tony Smith. He was one of Frank Carter's victims.'

'His poor parents.' Karen shook her head. 'Twenty years. Although I guess they must have known after such a long time. Maybe it'll even be a relief for them to finally have some closure.'

I remembered my father's words.

'Everybody deserves to go home,' I said.

Karen looked off to one side. It seemed like she wanted to ask more, but wasn't sure if she should for some reason.

'This man they've arrested,' she said.

'Norman Collins.'

'Norman Collins, right. How did *he* know about it?'

'I don't know. Apparently, he always had an interest in the case.' I sipped my coffee. 'My father seems to think he might have been Carter's accomplice all along.'

'And that he killed Neil Spencer too?'

'I'm not sure.'

'I hope so . . . well,' she corrected herself, 'I mean, I know that's an awful thing to say, but at least that way they've got the bastard. Christ, if you hadn't woken up . . .'

'I know. I don't even want to think about it.'

'It's fucking terrifying.'

It was – but of course, not wanting to think about it didn't mean I could stop myself.

'I read up about him last night,' I said. 'Carter, I mean. A bit morbid, but it seemed like I needed to know. The Whisper Man. Some of the details were just horrific.'

Karen nodded. '"If you leave a door half open, soon you'll hear the whispers spoken." I asked Adam about that, after you mentioned it. It's a rhyme some of the kids say. He'd never even heard of Carter, of course, but I guess that must be where it originated. Passed down.'

'A warning against the bogeyman.'

'Yeah. Except this one was real.'

I thought about the rhyme. Adam had heard it without realizing what it meant, and maybe it extended beyond Featherbank. Things like that often spread among children, so perhaps one of the kids at Jake's old school had repeated it, and that was where he'd learned it.

It had to be something like that, of course. The little girl hadn't taught him it, because she wasn't real.

But that didn't explain the butterflies. Or the boy in the floor.

Karen seemed to read my mind.

'What about Jake? How's he handling all this?'

'All right, I think.' I shrugged, a little helplessly. 'I don't know. He and I . . . we sometimes find it hard to talk to each other. He's not the easiest of kids.'

'There's no such thing,' Karen said.

'And I'm not the easiest of men.'

'And again. But what about you, though? It must have been strange seeing your father after all this time. Have you really had no contact with him at all?'

'None. My mother left with me when it all got too much. I haven't seen him since.'

'Too much?'

'The drinking,' I said. 'The violence . . .'

But then I tailed off. It was easier to explain it like that than to go into detail, but the truth was, that final night aside, I had no actual memory of my father being physically violent towards my mother or me. The drinking, yes, although I didn't really understand that at the time; I just knew that he was angry all the time, that he disappeared for days, that there was too little money, that my parents argued furiously. And I remembered the resentment and bitterness that would radiate out from him – the sense of threat that pervaded the air, as though something bad might happen at any moment. I remembered being afraid. But actual violence might have been pushing it.

'I'm sorry to hear that,' Karen said.

I shrugged again, feeling awkward now.

'Thanks. But yes, it was strange seeing him. I remember him, of course, but he's not like he was. He doesn't look like a drinker now. His whole manner seems different. Quieter.'

'People change.'

'They do. And it's fine, really. We're both completely different people now. I'm not a kid any more. He's not really my father. It doesn't matter at all.'

'I'm not sure I believe you.'

'Well, it is what it is.'

'That I believe.' Karen had finished her coffee and now she began slipping on her coat. 'And on that note, I'm going to have to love you and leave you, I'm afraid.'

'You have to go and be tired somewhere?'

'No, I slept well, remember?'

'Right.' I swirled around the dregs of my own drink. She didn't seem inclined to tell me where she was going, and it occurred to me that I barely knew anything about her at all. 'We spent the whole time talking about me, you realize? That doesn't seem fair.'

'Because you're much more interesting than I am, especially right now. Perhaps it's something you can write about in one of your books.'

'Maybe.'

'Yeah, I'm sorry. I googled you.' She looked momentarily embarrassed. 'I'm good at finding things out. Don't tell anyone.'

'Your secret is safe.'

'Glad to hear it.' She paused, as though there was something else she wanted to say. But then she shook her head, clearly thinking better of it. 'See you later?'

'You will. Take care.'

I drained the last of my coffee as she left, wondering what she might have been about to say just then. And also thinking about the fact that she'd googled me. What did that mean?

And was it wrong that I quite liked it?

Thirty-seven

'Are you finished with that, love?'

The man shook his head, momentarily unsure where he was and what was being asked of him. Then he saw the waitress smiling at him, looked down at the table, and realized he'd finished his coffee.

'Yes.' He leaned back. 'Sorry, I was miles away there.'

She smiled again as she picked up his empty cup.

'Can I get you anything else?'

'Maybe in a minute.'

He had no intention of ordering anything, but even though the shop was only half full it made sense to be polite and observe social mores. He didn't want to be remembered as someone who overstayed their welcome. He didn't want to be remembered at all.

And he was good at that – although it was true that people made it easy for him. So many of them seemed to be lost in the noise of existence, all but sleepwalking through their lives, oblivious to the world around them. Hypnotized by their mobile phones. Ignoring the others they passed. People were self-centred and uncaring, and they paid little attention to things on their periphery. If you didn't stand out, you vanished as quickly from their minds as a dream.

He stared at Tom Kennedy, sitting two tables away.

Kennedy had his back to him, and now that the woman had left, the man could stare if he wanted. When she had been there, facing him, he had sipped his coffee and pretended to study his own phone, making himself an unremarkable part of the shop's scenery. But listening carefully the whole time, of course. Conversations mingled around you if you let them, becoming an impenetrable background hum, but if you focused you could pull one out and follow it easily. All it required was concentration, like delicately tuning a radio until the static disappeared and you were left with a clear signal.

How right he had been, he thought now.

We sometimes find it hard to talk to each other.

He's not the easiest of kids.

Well, the man was sure that Jake would flourish under *his* care. He would give the boy the home he deserved and provide the love and attention he needed. And then he himself would feel healed and whole as well.

And if not . . .

Time had a way of dulling sensations. He found it much easier now to think about what he had done to Neil Spencer. The shivers he'd experienced afterwards had long since faded, and he could handle the memories more dispassionately now – in fact, there was almost pleasure in doing so. Because that boy had deserved it, hadn't he? And if there had been moments of tranquillity and happiness in the two months beforehand, when everything had seemed good, there had also been a sense of calm and rightness in the aftermath of that final day that had been comforting in its own way too.

But no.

It wouldn't come to that.

Tom Kennedy stood up and made his way to the door. The man stared down at his phone, idly tapping the screen as Kennedy passed him.

The man sat for a few seconds more, thinking about the other things he'd heard. Who was Norman Collins? The name was completely unfamiliar to him. One of the others, he supposed, but he had no idea why this Collins had been arrested now. It suited him well enough, though. The police would be distracted. Kennedy might be less on edge. Which meant that he just needed to pick his moment, and everything would be well.

He stood up.

The greater the noise, the easier it was to slip silently in without being noticed.

Thirty-eight

I've been looking for you for so long.

Pete got out of the car and made his way into the hospital, then took the elevator down to the basement, where the city's pathology unit was based. One wall of the elevator was mirrored, though, and he looked fine. Calm, even. The pieces within might be broken, but from the outside he was like a carefully wrapped present that would only rattle if you shook it.

He couldn't remember ever feeling this apprehensive.

He'd been searching for Tony Smith for twenty years. On some level, he wondered if the boy's absence had even sustained him – if it had given him a sense of purpose and a reason to continue, albeit one that had always been kept occluded in the background of his thoughts. Regardless, however much he had tried not think about it, the case had never been closed for him.

So he had to be present when it was.

He hated the autopsy suites in here, and always had. The smell of antiseptic never quite masked the underlying stench, and the harsh light and polished metallic surfaces only served to emphasize the mottled bodies on display. Death was tangible here – laid out and made prosaic. These rooms were about weights and angles, and clipboards scribbled with spare details of chemistry and biology, all of it so cold and clinical. Every time he visited, he realized that the most important parts of a human life – the emotions, the character, the experiences – were conspicuous by their absence.

The pathologist, Chris Dale, walked Pete over to a gurney at the far side of the suite. As he followed the man, Pete felt light and faint, and had to fight the urge to turn around.

'Here's our boy.'

Dale spoke quietly. He was famed throughout the department for his brusque and dismissive manner when it came to dealing with the police, saving his respect for those he always referred to as his patients.

Our boy.

The way Dale said it made it clear that the remains were now under his protection. That the indignities they'd been subjected to were over, and that they would be looked after now.

Our boy, Pete thought.

The bones were laid out in the shape of a small child, but age had separated many of them, and not a scrap of flesh remained. Pete had seen a number of skeletons over the years. In some ways, they were easier to look at than more recently deceased victims, who looked like human beings but, in their eerie stillness, somehow *not*. A skeleton was so far removed from everyday experience that it could be viewed with less emotion. And yet the reality always hit home: the fact that people die, and after a short amount of time only objects remain, the bones little more than a scattering of possessions, abandoned where they fall.

'We've yet to do a full post-mortem,' Dale said. 'That's scheduled for later. What I can tell you in the meantime is that these are the remains of a male child who was around six years of age at the time of his death. I can't even guess at the cause of death for the moment, and we might never know, but he's been deceased for some time.'

'Twenty years?'

'Possibly.' Dale hesitated, knowing what Pete was asking,

then gestured at a second gurney beside them. 'We also have these additional items, which were recovered from the scene. There's the box itself, of course – the remains were brought here in it to help preserve them. The clothes were underneath the bones.'

Pete took a step closer. The clothes were old and matted with cobwebs, but Dale and his team had extracted them carefully, and they rested now in the same intact, neatly folded pile they had been stored in. He didn't need to move them to see what they were.

Blue jogging bottoms. Little black polo shirt.

He turned and looked again at the remains. The case had exerted such a hold on him all these years, and yet this was the first time he'd ever seen Tony Smith in real life. Until now, there had only ever been the photographs of a little boy frozen forever in time. With just the slightest of differences in circumstances, Pete might have passed a twenty-six-year-old Tony Smith on the street today without ever having heard the name. He stared down at the small, broken frame that had once supported and held a human being, along with all the inherent possibilities of what he might have become.

All their hopes and dreams, and look what I've gone and done.

Pete pushed Frank Carter's words out of his head, and stared down in silence for a few seconds, wanting to take in the enormity of the moment. Except he realized that it wasn't there, no more than Tony Smith himself was present in the empty shell of bones on the gurney. Pete had been held in orbit by this missing little boy for so long, his whole life circling the mystery of his whereabouts. That centre of gravity was gone now, and yet his trajectory felt unaltered.

'We found several of these in the box,' Dale said.

Pete turned to see the pathologist leaning forward, hands in his pockets, staring at the cardboard box that Tony Smith had been found in. Moving closer, Pete saw the man's attention was directed towards a butterfly stuck in the cobwebs there. It was obviously dead, but the coloured patterns on its wings remained clear and vivid.

'The Corpse Moth,' Pete said.

The pathologist looked at him with surprise.

'I never took you for a butterfly fan, Detective.'

'I saw a documentary once.' Pete shrugged. He'd always figured that he watched and read simply to kill time, and was slightly surprised himself to find that some of the knowledge had stuck. 'I have a lot of evenings to fill.'

'That I can believe.'

Pete dredged his memory for details. This breed of butterfly was native to the country, but relatively rare. The programme he'd watched had followed a team of eccentric men trailing through fields and hedgerows trying to catch sight of it. They'd found one at the end. The Corpse Moth was attracted to carrion. Pete himself had never seen one, but ever since watching the documentary, he'd found himself scanning the country lanes and hedgerows he searched on weekends, wondering if their presence might provide some indication that he was looking in the right place.

His phone buzzed in his pocket, and he took it out to find a message from Amanda. He read it quickly: an update on the case. After a night in the cells, it appeared that Norman Collins had re-evaluated his 'no comment' position and was now prepared to talk to them. She wanted Pete back there as soon as possible.

He put the phone away, but lingered for a moment, looking at the cardboard box in front of him. It was strapped with overlapping layers of brown parcel tape: a container that had clearly been sealed and reopened and sealed again many times over the years. The box would now be sent for forensic analysis in the hope of finding fingerprints. Pete's gaze moved over its surface now, imagining the invisible hands that might have touched it over the years. He pictured people pressing their fingertips against it, the cardboard a surrogate skin encasing the bones secreted within.

Prized among collectors.

For a moment, he wondered if such people had imagined a heartbeat. Or if they had gloried in the absence of one.

Thirty-nine

Seated across from Amanda and Pete in the interview room, Norman Collins' lawyer sighed heavily.

'My client is prepared to admit to the murder of Dominic Barnett,' he said. 'He categorically denies any involvement in the abduction and murder of Neil Spencer.'

Amanda stared at him, waiting.

'However, my client is prepared to make a full and frank statement regarding his knowledge of the remains found on Garholt Street yesterday. He has no desire for you to waste resources on him, potentially endangering another child, and he believes what he has to say may help you locate the individual actually responsible for the murder.'

'Which we very much appreciate.'

Amanda smiled politely, even though she knew bullshit when she heard it. Sitting mutely on the other side of the desk, Collins looked diminished and wounded. He was not a man built for imprisonment, and a night in custody had erased the smugness he'd displayed in here yesterday. The fact that he was finally going to talk brought her little pleasure, because it was clearly motivated by self-interest rather than any desire to save lives. There was no better nature in there; he'd simply had time to realize that talking to them – giving his side of the story – might do him some good in the long run. That it might look better for him if he cooperated and was seen to help.

But now wasn't the time to show disgust. Not if he really *could* help.

She leaned back. 'So – talk to us, Norman.'

'I don't know where to begin.'

'You knew that Tony Smith's remains were in that house, didn't you? Let's start there.'

Collins was silent for a few seconds, staring down at the table between them, composing himself. Amanda glanced at Pete, sitting beside her, and saw that he was doing the same. She was worried about him. He seemed more subdued than ever, and had hardly spoken to her after arriving at the department. It seemed like there had been something he was on the verge of telling her, but for some reason he had held it back. This was going to be hard for him, she knew. He'd come straight from viewing what were almost certainly the remains of Tony Smith, a boy he had sought out for so long, and now he was set to hear the truth about what had happened all that time ago. The years might have hardened him on the surface, but she didn't want to think of all his old wounds tearing open again.

'I understand what you think of my interests,' Collins said quietly.

Amanda turned her attention back to him.

'And I understand what many people think of them. But the fact remains that I am well respected in my field. And I've acquired a reputation over the years as a collector.'

A collector.

He made it sound benign – respectable almost – but she had seen details of his collection. What kind of individual was drawn to the material that he had spent so many years acquiring? She pictured Collins and the people like him as rats scurrying around in the dark underbelly of the internet. Doing their deals and making their plans. Chewing at the wires of society. When Collins looked up at her now, the disgust she felt must have been obvious on her face.

'It's really no different from the interests other people have,' he said defensively. 'I learned long ago that my hobby was considered niche by most, and abhorrent by a few. But there are others who share it. And I have proved trustworthy over the years, which has allowed me access to more important pieces than others.'

'You're a serious dealer?'

'A serious dealer in serious things.' He licked his lips. 'And like any such dealings, there are open forums, and there are private ones. My interest in the Whisper Man case was well known in the latter. And several years ago, I was made aware that a certain . . . experience might be open to me. Assuming I was willing to pay, of course.'

'What was this *experience*?'

He stared back at her for a moment, and then answered as though it was the most natural thing in the world.

'To spend time with Tony Smith, of course.'

A moment of silence.

'How?' she said.

'In the first instance, I was told to visit Victor Tyler in prison. Everything was arranged through Tyler. Frank Carter knew about it, but he had no interest in being directly involved. The procedure was that Tyler would vet the people who came to him. I was pleased to pass that particular test. Upon receipt of funds delivered to Tyler's wife, I was directed to an address.' Collins grimaced. 'I wasn't surprised to be sent to Julian Simpson.'

'Why?'

'He was an unsavoury sort. Poor personal hygiene.' Collins tapped his head. 'Not entirely all there. People used to make fun of him, but they were all frightened of him really. The house too. It's a strange-looking place, don't you think? I remember children used to dare each other to go into the garden. They'd take photographs of each other there. Even before then – back when I was a child – people thought of it as the local scary house.'

Amanda glanced at Pete again. His face was inscrutable, but she could imagine what he must be thinking. Julian Simpson's name had never come up in the case at the time. The police had known nothing of the man or his scary-looking house. And that was entirely understandable. There were people like Simpson in every community, their reputations among the young not necessarily based on anything tangible, and certainly not to the extent that adults would think anything of them.

But regardless, she knew Pete would blame himself for this.

'What happened next?' she asked Collins.

'I went to the house on Garholt Street,' he said. 'After paying more money to Simpson, I was made to wait in a downstairs room. After a time, he returned with a sealed cardboard box. He cut it open carefully. And there . . . there he was.'

'For the record, Norman?'

'Tony Smith.'

Amanda could hardly bring herself to ask the question.

'And what did you do with Tony's remains?'

'Do with them?' Collins sounded genuinely shocked. 'I didn't *do* anything with them. I'm not a monster – not like some of the others. And I wouldn't have wanted to damage an exhibit like that, even if it had been allowed. No, I simply stood there. Paying my respects. Imbibing the atmosphere. You may find this hard to understand, but it was one of the most powerful hours of my life.'

Jesus, Amanda thought.

He looked like a man remembering some lost love.

Of all the scenarios she had been imagining taking place, his answer was simultaneously the most banal and the most horrifying. The time spent with a murdered little boy's body had clearly bordered on a religious experience for him, and imagining him standing there, believing he had some special connection with the sad remains in a box at his feet, was as awful in its own way as anything she could have thought of.

Beside her, Pete leaned forward slowly.

'You said "not like some of the others".'

Whatever toll the account was taking on him, he just sounded weary right now – tired all the way down to his soul, Amanda thought.

'Who were the others, Norman? And what did they do?'

Collins swallowed.

'This was after Dominic Barnett took over – after Julian died. I think the two of them were friends, but Barnett didn't have the same level of respect. Things deteriorated under his care.'

'Is that why you killed him?' Amanda said.

'To protect the exhibit! And Barnett wouldn't grant me access any more – not after the last time. Tony needed to be kept safe.'

'Tell us about *the others*, Norman,' Pete said patiently.

'This was after Barnett took over.' Collins hesitated. 'I'd visited several times over the years, but for me it was always the same. I was paying my respects, and I wanted to be on my own with Tony. But once Barnett was in charge, there started to be others there too. And they were not as respect-ful as me.'

'What did they do?'

'I didn't see anything,' Collins said. 'I left – I was dis-gusted. And Barnett refused to refund me. He even sneered at me. But what could I do?'

'Why were you so disgusted?' Pete said.

'The last night I went, there were five or six other people there. All people fascinated by the case. A mixture of types – you'd be surprised, honestly – and I got the impression that some of them had travelled a great distance. All of us were strangers to each other. But it was clear that some of them were there for different reasons than I was.' Collins swallowed. 'Barnett had a mattress in the room. He'd put a red light bulb in. It was . . .'

'Sexual?' Amanda volunteered.

'Yes. I suppose so.' Collins shook his head and stared down at the table, as though this was beyond even his capacity to understand. 'Not with the body – with each other. But that was bad enough. I couldn't be part of something like that.'

'So you left?'

'Yes. When I'd visited in the past, it was like being in a church. It was quiet, beautiful. I felt the presence of *God*. But that time, with the light, those people . . .'

He trailed off again.

'Norman?'

Finally, he looked up.

'It was like standing in hell.'

'Do you believe him?' Amanda said.

They were back in the incident room. Pete was leaning on his desk, staring intently down at the CCTV photographs of the people who had visited Victor Tyler in prison over the years. Her own gaze moved across them. There were men and women here. The young and the old.

'A mixture of types,' Collins had told them. 'You'd be surprised, honestly.'

'I believe Collins didn't kill Neil Spencer.' Pete waved his hand over the photographs. 'But as to this . . .'

And then he fell silent, expressing the same disbelief that she was feeling herself. In the course of her career, she had witnessed enough horror that people's capacity for cruelty was no longer shocking. She had stood at crime scenes and accidents and watched the crowds gather or the passing vehicles slow down for a glimpse of the carnage. She understood the pull of death. But not this.

'Do you know why they called him the Whisper Man?' Pete said quietly.

'Because of Roger Hill.'

'That's right.' He nodded slowly. 'Roger was Carter's first victim. The family home was being renovated at the time, and Roger told his parents he'd heard someone whispering outside his window before he was abducted. Carter owned the scaffolding firm that was working on the place. That was what first brought him to our attention.'

'Grooming his victim.'

'Yes. Carter had the opportunity there, but the strange thing is, the parents of the other boys all claimed their children heard whispers too. There was no obvious connection to Carter, but they heard it all the same.'

'Maybe they did.'

'Maybe so. Or perhaps it's just that the name was in the newspaper by then, and it planted ideas in people's heads. Who knows? Whatever, it stuck. The Whisper Man. I've always hated that name.'

She waited.

'Because I wanted him to be forgotten, you see? I didn't want him to have a title. But right now, it seems to fit him perfectly. Because the whole time, he's been whispering. And people – these people – have been listening.' He spread the photographs out with his hand. 'And I think one of them more closely than the others.'

Amanda looked at the photographs again. He was right, she thought. From everything Collins had said, it was clear that many of the individuals in front of her now had walked a fair distance down a path towards outright evil. It wasn't a stretch to believe that one of them – drawn ever onwards by Frank Carter's whispers – had walked further down that path than the others. The best of these people were evil sycophants, but one of them was something worse.

A student.

Somewhere among these people, she thought, they would find Neil Spencer's killer.

Forty

After Jake had gone to bed that night, I sat in the front room of the safe house with a glass of white wine and my laptop.

Even though I was still attempting to process the events of the last few days, I was also aware that I did need to write. It seemed impossible in the present circumstances, but the money I had left wouldn't last forever. Even more urgently than that, it felt important to be working on something, not just to distract myself from what was happening, but because it had always been that way. That was who I was. That was what I needed to reclaim.

Rebecca.

I deleted the rest of what I'd written and stared at her name. My idea the other day had been to begin to write down my feelings and trust that some kind of narrative would eventually emerge from the fog. But it was difficult to pin down my feelings right now, never mind attempting to translate them into something as simple as words.

My mind drifted back to what Karen had said in the cafe this morning: 'Perhaps it's something you can write about in one of your books.' And the fact that she'd looked me up online. I knew how I felt about that now, because it brought a small flash of excitement. She was interested in me. Was I attracted to her? Yes. I just wasn't sure I was allowed to be. I looked at Rebecca's name on the screen. The excitement dissipated, replaced by guilt.

Rebecca.

I typed quickly.

I know exactly what you'd think about that, because you were always so much more practical than me. You'd want me to get on with my life. You'd want me to be happy. You'd be sad, of course, but you'd tell me that's the way life works. In fact, you'd more than likely tell me not to be so fucking stupid.

But the thing is, I'm not sure I'm *ready* to let you go yet.

Maybe it's *me* that feels I shouldn't be happy. That I don't deserve —

The doorbell rang.

I closed the laptop and headed downstairs, anxious that the doorbell didn't ring again and wake up Jake. At the door, I rubbed my eyes a little, grateful that I hadn't started crying. Even more so when I opened the door and saw my father standing there.

'DI Willis,' I said.

He nodded once. 'Can I come in?'

'Jake's asleep.'

'I figured. But it won't take long. And I'll be quiet, I promise. I just wanted to give you an update on where things are at.'

A part of me was reluctant to let him in, but that was childish — and anyway, he was just a policeman. When this was all over and done with, I'd never have to see him again. The fact he seemed so beaten down, almost deferential, helped as well. Right now, in fact, I felt I was the more powerful of the two of us. I opened the door wider.

'All right.'

He followed me upstairs and into the front room.

'We're finishing up at the house,' he said. 'You and Jake will be able to go back home tomorrow morning.'

'That's good. What about Norman Collins?'

'We've charged him with the murder of Dominic Barnett. He's confirmed that the remains in the house belong to the one victim of Carter's we never found. Tony Smith. Collins knew all along.'

'How?'

'That's a long story. The details don't matter for now.'

'Don't they? Well, what about Neil Spencer? And the attempt to abduct Jake?'

'We're working on that.'

'That's reassuring.' I picked up my wine and took a sip. 'Oh, I'm sorry – where are my manners? Would you like a glass?'

'I don't drink.'

'You used to.'

'Which is why I don't now. Some people can manage it, and others can't. It took me a while to realize that. I'm guessing you're a man who can.'

'Yes.'

He sighed. 'I also guess that with everything that's happened over the years, it must have been hard for you. But you seem like a man who can do a lot of things well. That's a good thing. I'm pleased about that.'

I wanted to fight back against that. Not just him having any right to pass judgement on me, but the words themselves. He was utterly mistaken – I couldn't do anything well, and I wasn't handling life at all. But of course, there was no way I was going to display any kind of weakness in front of my father, and so I said nothing.

'Anyway,' he said. 'Yes. I used to drink. There were lots of reasons for that – reasons, not excuses. I struggled with a lot of things back then.'

'Like being a good husband.'

'Yes.'

'Like fatherhood.'

'That too. The responsibility of it. I never knew how to be a father. I never really wanted to be. And you were a difficult baby – much better when you were older, though. You were always creative. You used to make up stories even back then.'

I couldn't remember that.

'Did I?'

'Yes. You were sensitive. Jake seems a lot like you.'

'Jake's too sensitive, I think.'

My father shook his head. 'There's no such thing.'

'There is, if it makes life difficult.' I thought about all the friends I never made, or who never made me. 'And you wouldn't know. You weren't there.'

'No, I wasn't. And like I said, it was for the best.'

'Well, that's something we can agree on.'

With that, it seemed like there was nothing left to say. He turned around, as though about to leave, but then he hesitated, and a moment later he turned back.

'But I was thinking about what you said last night,' he told me. 'About seeing me throw the glass at your mother before I left.'

'And?'

'You didn't,' he said. 'That didn't happen. You weren't in the house that night. You were having a sleepover with a friend from school.'

I was about to say something, but then stopped. It was my turn to hesitate. My first instinct was that my father was lying – that he had to be, because I remembered that night so clearly. And that I hadn't had any friends. But was that really true back then? And whatever my father had once been, it didn't strike me that he was a liar now. In fact, as much as I didn't want to allow it, he had the air of somebody who had become scrupulously honest with himself about his faults. Perhaps, over the years, he'd needed to be.

I turned the memory over in my head.

Glass smashing.

My father shouting.

My mother screaming.

I could see the image with absolute clarity in my head, but was it possible that I was wrong? The picture was more vivid than any other childhood memory I could think of. Was it too vivid? Could it have been more an emotion than an actual recollection? A summing-up of how I felt rather than a specific event that had actually occurred.

'But actually, that was more or less how it happened,' my father said quietly. 'To my eternal shame, that was what I did. I didn't throw the glass *at* her, because the stupid thing is, it was the *glass* I was angry with. But it was close enough.'

'I remember seeing it.'

'I don't know. Maybe Sally told you.'

'She never said anything bad about you.' I shook my head. 'You know that, right? Even after everything.'

He smiled sadly. It was clear that yes, he could believe that, and that it reminded him of how much he'd lost.

'Then I don't know,' he said. 'But I wanted to tell you something else too, for whatever it's worth now. Not much, but still. You said it was the last time I ever saw you. That's not true either.'

I gestured around. 'Obviously . . .'

'I mean back then. Your mother threw me out, and that was for the best. I respected that. I was almost relieved, to be honest – or at least, it felt like what I deserved. But there were times afterwards, before the two of you moved away, when if I was sober Sally would let me back in. She didn't want to disrupt you or cause any confusion, and I didn't either. So it was always after you'd gone to bed. I'd come into your room when you were asleep, and give you a cuddle. You never woke up. You never knew. But I did that.'

I stood there silently.

Because once again, I didn't believe that my father was lying, and his words had shaken me. I remembered Mister Night, my imaginary friend from childhood. The invisible man who would come into my bedroom at night and hug me while I was sleeping. Even worse, I remembered how *comforting* it had been. How it wasn't something I had been frightened of. And how, when Mister Night had disappeared from my life, I'd been bereft for a time, as though I'd lost an important part of myself.

'I'm not making excuses,' my father said. 'I just wanted you to know that things were complicated. That *I* was. I'm sorry.'

'Okay.'

And then there really was nothing else to say.

He started off down the stairs, and I was still too shaken to do anything but let him go.

Forty-one

The next morning, I made sure Jake was ready earlier than usual, so that we had time to call back home before I took him to school. My father was already outside, waiting for us in his car. He rolled down the window as we walked over to him.

'Hello,' my father said.

'Good morning, Pete,' Jake said gravely. 'How are you today?'

My father's face lit up slightly at that, amused by the overly formal tone my son could sometimes adopt. He matched it in return.

'Very well, thank you. How are you, Jake?'

'I'm fine. It was interesting staying here, but I'm looking forward to going home now.'

'I can imagine.'

'But not to going to school afterwards.'

'I can imagine that too. But school is very important.'

'Yes,' Jake said. 'Apparently so.'

My father started to laugh at that, but then glanced at me and stopped. Perhaps he thought interacting with Jake like this might annoy me. The strange thing was that, while it had done on that first afternoon in the police station, it didn't so much now. I liked it when people were impressed with my son; it made me feel proud of him. Stupid to think that way, of course – he was a person in his own right, not some accomplishment of mine – but the feeling was always there, and if anything, with my father, it was stronger than usual. I wasn't sure why. Did I want to rub his face in fatherhood, or was it some subconscious desire to impress him? I didn't like what either option said about me.

'We'll see you there.' I turned away. 'Come on, Jake.'

The journey wasn't a long one, but it took time in the morning traffic. Jake spent most of it in the back of the car, kicking the passenger seat aimlessly and whistling a tune to himself. Every now and then, I'd glance in the rear-view mirror and see him, head turned to one side, squinting through the window the way he often did, as though confused to see a world out there but only mildly interested in it.

'Daddy, why don't you like Pete?'

'You mean DI Willis.' I took the turning into our street. 'And it's not a case of not liking him. I don't know him. He's a policeman, not a friend.'

'He is friendly, though. I like him.'

'You don't know him either.'

'But if you don't know him and don't like him, why can't I not know him and like him instead?'

I was too tired for such contortions.

'It's not that I don't like him.'

Jake didn't reply, and I had no desire to argue the point any further. Children pick up on atmosphere very well, and my son was even more sensitive than most. It was probably obvious to him that I was lying.

And yet, was it really a lie? Our conversation last night had stayed with me and, perhaps because of that, it was easier to identify with my father now – to see him as a man, like me, who had found fatherhood difficult. Regardless, he was no more the man I remembered than I was still that child.

How long does it take, and how much does a person have to change, before the person you hated is gone, replaced by someone new? Pete was someone else now.

I didn't not like him. The truth was that I didn't know him at all.

When we reached our house, there was no sign of police activity any more – even the tape had been removed. And there wasn't the extensive media presence I'd been concerned might greet us: just a small group of people talking amongst themselves. They didn't seem that interested as I parked up in the driveway. Jake was, though.

'Are we going to be on *television*?' he said excitedly.

'Absolutely not.'

'Oh.'

Pete had been following our car the whole journey. He parked up sideways behind us now, then got out quickly. The reporters approached him, and I peered round to watch as he spoke to them.

'What's going on, Daddy?'

'Hang on.'

Jake was straining to see as well.

'Is that – ?' he said.

'Oh fuck.'

There was a moment of silence in the car after that. I stared at the small group that had gathered around my father, dimly aware that he was smiling politely at them, explaining things with a conciliatory shrug, and that a few of the reporters were nodding. But my attention was focused on one of them in particular.

'You said the F word, Daddy.'

Jake sounded awed.

'Yes, I did.' I turned away from the sight of Karen, standing among the reporters, a notepad in her hand. 'And yes. That's Adam's mother back there.'

*

'Are we going to be on television, Pete?' Jake said.

I closed the front door behind us and put the chain on.

'I've already told you that, Jake. No, we are not.'

'I'm just asking Pete as well.'

'No,' Pete said. 'You aren't. Just like your daddy told you. That's what I was talking to the people outside about. They're reporters, and so they're interested in what happened here, but I was reminding them that it's nothing to do with you two.'

'It sort of is,' Jake said.

'Well, sort of. But not really. If you'd known more, or were more closely involved, then it would be different.'

I shot Jake a look at that, hoping he'd understand from my expression that this was not the time to say anything else about the boy in the floor. He glanced at me and nodded, but wasn't about to let the matter drop quite so easily.

'Daddy *did* find him.'

'Yes,' Pete said. 'But that's not information that's been released to the people out there. As far as they're concerned, the two of you are not really part of the story. That's the best way to keep it for now, I think.'

'Okay.' Jake sounded disappointed. 'Can I look around and see what they've done?'

'Of course.'

He disappeared upstairs. Pete and I waited by the front door.

'I meant what I said,' he told me after a moment. 'You don't need to worry. The media won't want to prejudice any trial. I can't stop you talking to them, obviously, but all they know is the remains were found here, so I don't think they'll be that interested in you. And they'll be very careful around Jake.'

I nodded, feeling sick. That might be all the media officially knew, but I'd told Karen so much yesterday that it was hard to keep track of it all. She knew about the night-time visitor attempting to abduct Jake. The fact that it was me who had found the body. That Pete was my father – my abusive father. And I was quite sure I'd said things I couldn't even remember right now.

'I'm good at finding things out,' she'd said.

At the time, it had just been a conversation with a friend; I hadn't realized I was spilling everything to a fucking reporter.

And it hurt.

She should have told me. It had felt like she'd been genuinely interested in me, but now I wasn't so sure about that. On the one hand, there was no way she could have known I was connected to the case. But on the other, at no point in our conversation had she suggested that she really wasn't the person I should be telling everything to.

My father frowned. 'Are you okay?'

'Yes.'

But I would have to check the damage from that conversation later. In the meantime, there was no way I was going to tell my father about it.

'Are we safe here?' I said.

'Yes. Norman Collins isn't going to be released any time soon, and even if he was, there's nothing of interest to him here any more. Not for any of the others either.'

'Others?'

He hesitated

'People have always been interested in this house. Collins told me it was the neighbourhood scary house. Kids would dare each other to come near it. Take photographs and things.'

'The scary house. I'm tired of hearing about that.'

'That's just kids' stuff anyway,' Pete said. 'Tony Smith's remains are gone. That was all Collins was ever interested in. Not you or Jake.'

Not me or Jake. But I kept thinking back to seeing Jake at the bottom of the stairs that night, with the man talking to him through the letter box. I couldn't remember the exact words I'd heard, but I could recall enough to know he'd been trying to persuade Jake to open the door, and I wasn't convinced it had only been the keys to the garage he was interested in.

'What about Neil Spencer?' I said. 'Has Collins been charged with his murder?'

'No. But we have a number of suspects now. We're closing in. And believe me, I wouldn't let you both come back here if I didn't think it was safe.'

'You couldn't stop me.'

'No.' He looked away. 'I'd certainly argue the case, though, especially with Jake living here. Neil Spencer's abduction was opportunistic; he was out walking alone. This isn't a man who wants attention. You should obviously keep an eye on Jake, but there's no reason to think either of you are in any danger.'

Did he sound convinced? I wasn't sure, but it was difficult to read him today. He looked exhausted. When I'd first seen him, it had been obvious he was in good physical shape, but today he really looked his age.

'You look tired,' I said.

He nodded.

'I am tired. And I have to do something that I'm not looking forward to.'

'What?'

'It doesn't matter,' he said simply. 'What matters is that it has to be done.'

This whole case must have taken a toll on him, I realized, and that was apparent in his whole demeanour right now. *What matters is that it has to be done.* Before me now, I saw a man weighed down by so much, struggling to cope with the load. He looked like I often felt.

'My mother,' I said suddenly.

He looked back at me and waited, not asking the question.

'She died,' I said.

'You told me that.'

'You said you wanted to know what happened. She had a difficult life, but she was a good person. I couldn't have asked for a better parent. It was cancer. She didn't deserve what happened to her, but she didn't suffer either. It happened very quickly.'

That was a lie – my mother's death had been prolonged and painful – and I had no idea why I was telling it. There was no duty incumbent on me to make Pete feel better, or to ease any pain or guilt he felt. And yet a part of me was still pleased to see the weight on him lift a little.

'When?'

'Five years ago.'

'So she got to meet Jake?'

'Yes. He doesn't remember her. But yes.'

'Well, I'm glad about that, at least.'

There was a moment of silence. And then Jake came downstairs, and we both turned slightly away from each other at the same time, as though some tension between us had snapped.

'Everything's exactly the same, Daddy.' Jake sounded almost suspicious.

'We do a good job of searching through things carefully,' Pete said. 'And cleaning up after ourselves too.'

'Admirable.'

Jake turned and walked back into the front room.

Pete shook his head. 'He's a character, that one.'

'Yes. He is that.'

'I'll be in touch about any developments,' he said. 'But in the meantime, if you need anything – and I mean, anything at all – my details are there.'

'Thank you.'

I watched my father walk off down the driveway, head bowed slightly, and turned the card around in my hand. As he got into his car, I looked past him at the reporters gathered beyond it. Most of them had left now. I scanned the faces that remained, looking for Karen.

But she was gone.

Forty-two

This is the last time, Pete told himself. *Remember that.*

The thought was something to cling to while he sat in the bright white interview room at the prison, waiting for the monster to arrive. He had been here so many times over the years, and each occasion had left him shaken. But after today, there would be no reason for him ever to return. Tony Smith – always the focus of these visits in the past – had been found, and if Frank Carter refused to talk about the man they were looking for now, Pete had already made the decision that he would walk out of this room and not look back. And he'd never have to suffer the crawling aftermath of being in Carter's presence again.

This is the last time.

The thought helped, but only a little. The air in the silent room felt full of anticipation and threat, the locked door on the far side throbbing with menace. Because Carter must also know this was likely to be their last meeting, and Pete was sure he would be determined to make it count. Until now, the fear of these encounters had always been mental and emotional. He had never been physically afraid before. But right now, he was glad for the width of the desk dividing the room and the strength of the shackles the man would be wearing. He even wondered if, subconsciously, all those hours in the gym had been spent preparing himself in case a moment like that ever happened.

His heart leapt as he heard the door being unlocked.

Keep calm.

The familiar routine unfolded: the guards entering first; Carter taking his time. Pete steadied himself by concentrating on the envelope he'd brought, which was on the desk in front of him now. He stared at that and waited, ignoring the bulk of the man who finally approached, then sat down heavily across from him. Let the tables be turned for once – Carter could wait. Pete remained silent until the guards had retreated and he heard the door closing. Only then did he look up.

Carter was staring at the envelope too, a curious expression on his face.

'Have you written me a letter, Peter?'

Pete didn't reply.

'I've often thought I might write one to you.' Carter looked up and smiled. 'Would you like that?'

Pete suppressed the shudder he felt. There was little chance of Carter discovering his home address directly, but the idea of receiving even forwarded correspondence was intolerable.

Again, he said nothing.

Carter shook his head in disapproval.

'I told you last time, Peter. That's the problem with you, you know? I make this big effort to talk to you. I go to all these great lengths to tell you things and be helpful. And sometimes it feels like you're not listening to me at all.'

'It ends where it begins,' Pete said. 'I understand that now.'

'A bit too late for Neil Spencer, though.'

'What I'm interested in is how you knew that, Frank.'

'And like I said, that's the problem with you.' Carter leaned back. The weight of him made the chair creak. 'You don't listen. Honestly, what do I care about some fucking kid? That's not even what I was referring to.'

'No?'

'Not at all.' He leaned forward again, suddenly more engaged, and Pete resisted the urge to flinch. 'Hey, here's another one. Do you remember what you said about people in the outside world forgetting me?'

Pete thought back, then nodded. 'You told me it wasn't true.'

'That's right. Ha ha! And you understand that now, I guess? You get how wrong you were. Because all along, there was this whole bunch of people out there you didn't know about who have stayed really interested in me.'

Carter's eyes gleamed at that. Pete could only imagine the amount of pleasure he must have taken over the years, knowing he had fans like Norman Collins visiting the house where Tony Smith's remains had been left, treating the place as though it was some kind of shrine. Even more than that, he must have delighted in holding a secret over Pete for all this time – knowing that while Pete had been searching incessantly for the missing child, others had been finding Tony so very easily.

'Yes, Frank. I was wrong. I know that now. And I'm sure the whole experience was very flattering for you. The Whisper Man.' He pulled a face. 'Your legend living on.'

Carter grinned. 'In so many ways.'

'So let's talk about some of the others.'

Carter said nothing, but he glanced down at the envelope and his smile broadened. He wasn't going to be tricked into talking about Neil Spencer's killer. Pete knew that if he was going to learn anything, he would have to read between the lines, and that meant keeping the man talking. And while Carter might be deliberately vague on some subjects, Pete was sure he would be more than happy to talk about the visitors to the house over the years, at least now that the secret was out.

'All right,' Pete said. 'Why Victor Tyler?'

'Ah, Vic's a good man.'

'That's an interesting way of putting it. But what I actually meant is, why use an intermediary to arrange all this?'

'It wouldn't do much good to be accessible, would it, Peter?' Carter shook his head. 'If everyone could see God, how many people would bother going to church? It's better to keep some distance. Better for them too, of course. Safer. I imagine you've checked my visits over the years?'

'I'm the only person you see.'

'And what an honour, right?' He laughed.

'What about the money?'

'What about it?'

'Tyler was paid – or his wife was, at least. Simpson was too, and then Barnett after him. But not you.'

'What do I care about money?' Carter looked affronted. 'Everything I want in life is free now. Vic – like I said, he's a good man, a decent man. And Julian did right by me too. It's only fair they should get something for that. Never knew Barnett, and couldn't care less. But it's good those people paid to visit the place. They should fucking pay. I'm worth it, aren't I?'

'No.'

Carter laughed again. 'Maybe after you arrest them all, they'll even end up in here with me. That'll be a real kick for them, won't it? They'd enjoy that, I bet.'

Not as much as you, Pete thought.

He picked up the envelope and took out the photographs he had brought with him: a thin pile of CCTV stills taken of the visitors Victor Tyler had received over the years. An image of Norman Collins was on top, and he slid it carefully across the table to Carter.

'Do you recognize this man?'

Carter barely glanced at it.

'No.'

A second photograph. 'What about this man?'

'I don't know any of these fucking people, Peter.' Carter rolled his eyes. 'How many times do I have to tell you? You don't listen. You want to know who these people are, go ask Vic.'

'We will.'

In fact, he and Amanda had interviewed Tyler an hour earlier, and Tyler had enjoyed the situation substantially less than his friend Carter appeared to be doing. He was angry and refusing to cooperate. Pete supposed that was understandable, given that his wife was also implicated, but silence wasn't going to save either of them. Likewise, the visitors they'd identified – amongst whom Pete was sure they would find Neil Spencer's killer – were in the process of being hunted down and questioned.

All except one.

Pete slid another photograph across the table. It showed a younger man, perhaps in his twenties or early thirties. Average height and build. Black glasses. Shoulder-length brown hair. He had visited Tyler on a number of occasions, most recently in the week before Neil Spencer had been killed.

'What about this man?'

Carter didn't look at it. He stared at Pete and smiled.

'This is the one you're interested in, isn't it?'

Pete didn't reply.

'You're so predictable, Peter. So obvious. You soften me up with two, then hit me with the one that matters so you can watch my reaction. This is your guy, isn't it? Or at least, you think it is?'

'You're very clever, Frank. Do you recognize this man?'

Carter stared back for a moment longer. But even as he

did, his cuffed hands reached out and brought the photograph closer to him. The movement was uncanny, as though his hands were being operated by something separate from the rest of him. His head didn't move. His expression didn't change.

Then he looked down, studying the image.

'Ah,' he said softly.

Pete watched the man's huge chest rising and falling as he breathed slowly, taking in the details before him.

'Tell me about this man, Peter,' Carter said.

'I'm more interested in what you know.'

Pete waited him out. Eventually, Carter looked up, then tapped the photograph gently with one huge finger.

'This man is a bit smarter than the others, isn't he? He used a false name to visit, but he had the paperwork to back it up. You've looked into it, and you know it wasn't real.'

That was true. The man had provided identification at the time of his visits: his name was Liam Adams, he was twenty-nine years old, and he lived with his parents, thirty miles away from Featherbank. Officers had arrived at the property first thing that morning, only to be met with blank incomprehension – and then horror – on the faces of Liam's parents.

Because their son had died over a decade ago.

'Go on,' Pete told Carter.

'Do you know how easy it is to buy a new identity, Peter? Much simpler than you imagine. And like I said, he's clever, this one. If you want to send a message to someone these days, you have to be, don't you? This right here –' Carter lowered his voice – 'this is a man who takes care.'

'Tell me more about him, Frank.'

But instead of answering, Carter stared down at the photograph again for a few more seconds, studying it. It was as though he was looking at someone he'd heard a great deal about and was now curious to see finally. But then he sniffed loudly, suddenly uninterested in whatever he saw, and pushed the photo back across the table.

'I've told you everything I know.'

'I don't believe you.'

'And like I said, that's always been your problem.'

Carter smiled at him, but his eyes had gone blank now.

'You just don't listen, Peter.'

Pete didn't let his frustration out until he was back at the car, where Amanda was waiting for him. He clambered into the passenger seat and slammed the door, the photographs he was carrying spilling from his hand into the footwell.

'Shit.'

He leaned over and gathered them together, even though only one was important. After he'd rammed the others back into the envelope, he kept that picture out, resting it on top of his knees. A man with a dead teenager's name, with black glasses and brown hair that could easily be a disguise, or have been changed by now. The man could be almost any age. He could be almost anyone.

'I am guessing,' Amanda said, 'that Carter was not forthcoming?'

'He was his usual charming self.'

Pete ran a hand through his hair, angry with himself. The last time, yes, and he had survived it. But as always, he had come out of the conversation with nothing, even though Carter knew something.

'Fucker,' he said.

'Tell me,' Amanda said.

He took a moment to compose himself, and then ran through the conversation in detail. The idea that he didn't listen to Carter was rubbish; of course he listened to him. Every conversation with Carter seeped into him. The words were the opposite of sweat, soaking in and leaving him clammy on the inside.

When he was done, Amanda considered it.

'You think Carter knows who this man is?'

'I'm not sure.' Pete looked down at the photograph. 'Maybe. He certainly knows *something* about him. Or perhaps he doesn't, and he's just enjoying seeing me scrabble around, trying to make sense of his every fucking word.'

'You're swearing more than usual, Pete.'

'I'm angry.'

You just don't listen.

'Run through it again,' Amanda said patiently. 'Not this visit. The last one. That's what he said you hadn't been listening to, right?'

Pete hesitated, then thought back.

'It always ends where it starts,' he said. 'It started at the waste ground, so that's where Neil Spencer was always going to be returned to. Except Carter said that wasn't what he'd meant.'

'So what did he mean?'

'Who knows?' Pete wanted to throw up his hands. 'Then there was the dream about Tony Smith. But that wasn't real. He just made that up to taunt me.'

Amanda was silent for a few seconds.

'But if so,' she said, 'he made it up a certain way. And you said it yourself – that's why you visit him. You've always hoped he'd give something away without meaning to.'

Pete was ready to protest, but she was right. If the dream hadn't been real then Carter must have conjured it up himself, choosing to describe it in the way he had. And it was possible some truth had slipped out through the gaps there.

He ran through it in his mind now.

'He wasn't sure it was Tony.'

'In the dream?'

'Yes.' Pete nodded. 'The boy's T-shirt was pulled up over his face, so he couldn't see it properly. He said that was the way he liked it.'

'Just like Neil Spencer.'

'Yes.'

'None of which was ever made public.' Amanda shook her head in frustration. 'And Carter was a sadist. Why wouldn't he want to see the faces of his victims?'

Pete had no answer to that. Carter had always refused to discuss his motivations. But while there had never been any apparent sexual element to the murders, Amanda was right: he had hurt those children badly, and it was clear he was a sadist. As to why he covered their faces, there were countless possible explanations for that. If you asked five different profilers – and they had at the time – you got five different answers. Perhaps it was to make the victims physically easier to control. Or to muffle sound. To disorientate them. To scare them. To stop them seeing him. To stop him seeing them. One of the reasons profiling was such bullshit was that different offenders almost always had massively different reasons for the exact same behaviour, and –

Pete hesitated.

'All these bastards are the same,' he said quietly.

'What?'

'That's what Carter told me.' He frowned. 'Something like that, anyway. When he was talking about which of the children it was in the dream. "All those little bastards are the same. Any one of them will do."'

'Go on.'

But he fell silent again, trying to think through the

implications and feeling that some kind of understanding was suddenly within reach. It hadn't mattered to Carter who he had been hurting. More than that, he hadn't wanted to see the victims' faces at all.

But why?

To stop *him* seeing them.

Was that perhaps because he had wanted to imagine someone else in their place? Pete stared down at the photograph again – at the man who could be anyone – and recalled the strange look on Carter's face. Despite himself, he had been curious about the man in the photo. Once again, it had been as though he was seeing someone he had been interested in for a long time but was only now finally laying eyes on. It made Pete think of something else. How he had fought so hard not to think of Tom over the years, and yet had found it impossible not to evaluate him when they had met. How even though traces of the boy remained, the man was so different from the little boy he remembered.

Because children change so much.

I've told you everything I know.

And now, Pete remembered a different child. Another little boy – small and scared and malnourished – hiding behind his mother's legs as Pete unlocked the door to Frank Carter's extension.

A little boy who would now be in his late twenties.

Bring my family to me, Pete remembered. *That bitch and that little cunt.*

He looked up at Amanda, finally understanding.

'That's what I didn't listen to.'

Forty-three

Just before lunchtime, there was a knock at the door.

I looked up from my laptop. The first thing I'd done after dropping Jake at school that morning had been to google Karen. She'd been easy enough to find: Karen Shaw had bylines for hundreds of online articles at the local paper, including pieces that covered the abduction and murder of Neil Spencer. I'd read each of them with an increasingly sick feeling in my stomach: not just fear over what she might write next – all those private details I'd revealed to her yesterday in the coffee shop – but also a sense of betrayal. I'd allowed myself to imagine that she was genuinely interested in me, and now I felt stupid, as though I'd been conned in some way.

The knock came again: a quiet, tentative sound, as though whoever was outside was undecided if they wanted me to hear or not. And I thought I knew who I would find out there. I put the laptop to one side and went to the door.

Karen, standing on the front step.

I leaned against the wall and folded my arms.

'Are you bugged under that thing?'

I nodded at the big overcoat. She winced.

'Can I come in for a minute?'

'What for?'

'I just . . . want to explain. It won't take long.'

'There's no need.'

'I think there is.'

She looked contrite – ashamed, even – but I remembered my mother telling me that explanations and apologies were almost always for the person making them, and I felt an urge to tell Karen she could make herself feel better on her own time. But her apparent vulnerability right now was such a stark contrast to her manner during our previous encounters that I couldn't. It looked like she was doing this because it really did matter to her.

I leaned away from the wall.

'All right.'

We went through to the front room. A part of me was slightly embarrassed by the state of the place: my dirty plate from breakfast was on the settee by the laptop, and Jake's pens and drawings were still scattered all over the floor. But I wasn't going to apologize to Karen for the mess. It didn't matter what she thought, did it? Before this morning, it would have done – there was no point denying that now. Foolish, but true.

She stopped at the far end of the room, still wrapped up in her big coat, as though unsure whether she'd been invited in or not.

'Can I get you a drink?'

She shook her head. 'I just wanted to explain about this morning. I know how it must have looked.'

'I'm not really sure how it looked. Or what to think.'

'I'm sorry. I should have told you.'

'Yes.'

'And I almost did. You might not believe me, but I was actually kicking myself yesterday morning. In the coffee shop, I mean, the whole time you were telling me all that stuff.'

'You still let me, though.'

'Well, you kind of didn't give me chance.' She risked a slight smile at that: a flash of the Karen I was more used to. 'Honestly, it seemed like you had a lot to get off your chest, and on that level I was glad to be of use. It was a pain listening to it all as a journalist, though.'

'Was it really?'

'Yeah. Because I knew I wouldn't be able to use any of it.'

'I'm sure you could.'

'Well, yes, in the sense that it wasn't officially off the record, I suppose I could. But it wouldn't be fair on you or Jake. I wouldn't do that to you. It's more about personal ethics than professional ones.'

'Right.'

'Which is fucking typical, frankly.' She gave a bitter laugh. 'Biggest story in the history of the area since I moved here, and I've got an angle none of the majors have. And I can't use it.'

I didn't reply. It was true she hadn't used it – at least not yet. Her most recent article had been posted this morning, and it had only included the same basic details as all the other news outlets. What I'd told her went way above and beyond what was already out there, and it was also very obviously part of her beat. But however tempting it must have been, she hadn't revealed any of it so far. Did I believe her now when she said she wouldn't? I thought I did.

'Have you talked to any of the others?' she said.

'No.' I was about to repeat my father's line about not knowing anything, but that would have been a pointless lie in the circumstances. 'The rest of them left early on. There have been a few phone calls on the landline, but I've just ignored those.'

'Irritating.'

'I never answer the phone anyway.'

'No, I don't like phones much either.'

'It's more that nobody ever calls me.'

Not really a joke, but she smiled. And that was okay, I thought. The conversation had grown quieter the longer we'd been speaking, and some of the tension in the room had dissipated now. It was almost a surprise to me how much of a relief that was.

'Are they likely to keep trying?' I said.

'It depends on what happens. From experience, if they won't leave you alone, then it might be worth talking to one of them.' She held her hand up. 'Not necessarily me. In fact, as much as it kills me to say this, a part of me would probably prefer it wasn't.'

'Why?'

'Because we're friends, Tom, and that makes it harder to be objective. Like I said, I was kicking myself yesterday. You do realize that I didn't take you for a coffee because I sniffed a story, right? It was a total surprise, what you told me. How could I possibly have known? But the point is, if you get an account out there once, there'll be less interest. See what happens, though.'

I thought about it.

'But I could talk to you?'

'Yes, you could. And you know what? All that aside, it'd be nice to go for a coffee again at some point, wouldn't it?'

'Maybe I could get some dirt on you.'

She smiled. 'Yeah. Maybe you could.'

I thought about it.

'Sure you can't stay for a drink?'

'Sadly, yes – I wasn't just saving face before. I really do need to get back.' She was about to head out of the room, but then something occurred to her. 'What about tonight? I could probably get my mother to babysit Adam. We could grab a drink or something?'

Her mother to babysit.

Not a husband or partner.

I supposed I'd been assuming she was single, and I wasn't

sure now whether the confirmation was deliberate or accidental. Regardless, I very much wanted to say yes. Jesus, how astonishing would it be to go out for a drink with a woman? I couldn't remember the last time. But even more than that, I realized that I very much wanted to go for a drink with *her*. That I'd spent the morning feeling hurt and foolish for a fairly obvious reason.

But of course, it wasn't possible.

'I'd probably struggle with a babysitter,' I said.

'Right. I get you. Hang on a second.' She reached into her coat and produced a card. 'I realized you hadn't got my details. All my contact stuff is on there. If you want it, I mean.'

Yes, I wanted it.

'Thanks.' I took the card. 'I've not got one of my own.'

'Duh. Just text me so I've got your number.'

'Obviously. Duh indeed.'

She paused at the front door.

'How's Jake today?'

'Miraculously well,' I said. 'I really have no idea how.'

'I do. Like I said, you're too hard on yourself.'

And then she headed off down the path. I watched her go for a moment, then looked down at the card in my hand. Thinking. It was the second card I'd received today, and both were complicated in their different ways. But God, a drink out with Karen would be good. It felt like something people did, and that it should really be possible for me to do it as well.

Once I was back in the front room, I took out my phone and thought about the situation a whole lot more.

Hesitating. Unsure.

Just text me so I've got your number.

In the end, it wasn't the first message I sent.

Forty-four

Back at the department, the operations room was alive with activity. While most of the officers were continuing with their existing actions, a small number were now focused on the key task of tracking down Frank Carter's son, Francis, and that knowledge had galvanized everyone. The renewed energy in the room was tangible. After two months of moving in circles and following fruitless leads, it felt like a new path had opened up for them.

Not that it would necessarily go anywhere, Amanda reminded herself. It was always best not to get your hopes up.

But always so hard not to.

'No,' Pete said.

He added another sheet of paper to the pile on the desk between them.

'No,' she replied, adding one of her own.

After Frank Carter's trial and conviction, Francis and his mother had moved away, and because of the infamy of the case, they had been given new identities – an opportunity to begin fresh lives, without the shadow of the monster they had lived with hanging over them. Jane Carter had become Jane Parker; Francis had become David. After that, the pair of them had effectively disappeared. They were common, anonymous names, which was presumably one reason why they had been chosen. The task facing Amanda and Pete now was to find the correct David Parker out of the thousands living in the country.

Next sheet. This David Parker was forty-five years old. The one they were looking for would be twenty-seven.

'No,' she said.

And so it went.

They worked through the names mostly in silence. Pete was intent on the pages before him, and she presumed that his focus was a way of distracting himself. The conversation he'd had with Frank Carter must have shaken him as much as all the others, but there was an added tension now. Pete had met Carter's son when Francis was a child. He had effectively saved the boy. Knowing Pete as she was beginning to, it was easy to imagine what was going through his head right now. He would be asking hard questions of himself. What if Pete's actions back then had planted a seed that had grown into this fresh horror? What if, despite his best intentions, this was all somehow his fault?

'We can't be sure that Francis is involved,' she said.

'No.'

Pete added another sheet of paper to the pile.

Amanda sighed to herself, frustrated by the knowledge that nothing she could say right now was going to rescue Pete from his thoughts. But what she had said was true. As terrible an upbringing as Francis Carter might have suffered, she had seen plenty of people emerge from horrific, abusive childhoods and grow into decent adults. There were as many paths out of hell as there were people, and the vast majority of them ascended.

She was also familiar enough with the original investigation to know that Pete had done nothing wrong – that he had worked the case as well as anybody could, even going above and beyond in his dogged pursuit of Jane Carter. He had followed his gut instinct, focused on Frank Carter, and eventually brought the man down. While he hadn't been able to save Tony Smith in time, it was impossible to save everyone. There would always be mistakes you never saw in time.

And thinking about Neil Spencer, she knew she needed to cling to that herself. She didn't want to believe that the things you missed – the things you never even had the opportunity to hit – could weigh you down so much that they threatened to drown you.

She turned her attention back to the paperwork, working her way steadily through the list of David Parkers.

'No.'

The papers piling up.

'No.'

The words formed a predictable pattern. *No. No. No.* It was only when she'd done three in a row without a response that she noticed Pete had been silent for longer than he should have been. She looked up at him hopefully, but then realized he had stopped paying attention to the forms on the table. Instead, he had his mobile phone in his hands, and was staring at that.

'What?' she said.

'Nothing.'

And yet it clearly wasn't. In fact, she couldn't quite believe her eyes. Because Pete appeared to be smiling. Could that actually be the case? It was the smallest of expressions, but she realized she'd never seen even that much before. He'd always been so stern and serious – so dark, like a house in which the owner stubbornly refused to turn on any lights. Right now, though, a single room seemed to be illuminated. A text message, she guessed. Maybe it was a woman? Or a man, of course; after all, she knew next to nothing about his private life. Regardless, she liked seeing this unfamiliar expression on his face. It was a welcome break from the intensity she had become used to, and which made her worry about him.

She wanted this new light to stay.

'What?' She asked it more teasingly this time.

'Just someone asking if I'm free for something this evening.' He put the phone on the table, the smile disappearing. 'Which obviously I'm not.'

'Don't be ridiculous.'

Pete looked at her.

'I'm serious,' she told him. 'Technically speaking, this is my case, not yours. I'll stay as long as I have to, but listen, you are going home at the end of the day.'

'No.'

'Yes. And you can do whatever you want when you get there. I'll keep you up to date with any developments.'

'It should be me.'

'It absolutely should not. Even if we find the right David Parker, we have no idea how or even if he's involved. It's just a conversation. And I think it would be better for him and for you if someone else handles that. I know how much this case means to you, but you can't live in the past, Pete. Other things matter too.' She nodded at his phone. 'Sometimes you've got to leave it at the door at the end of the day. Do you know what I mean?'

He was silent for a moment, and she thought he was about to protest again. But then he nodded.

'You can't live in the past,' he repeated. 'You're right about that. More right than you know.'

'Oh, I know how right I am. Believe me.'

He smiled. 'All right then.'

Then he picked up his phone again, and began tapping a reply a little awkwardly, as though he didn't get many texts and wasn't used to sending ones in return. Or maybe he was just nervous about this one in particular. Regardless, she was pleased for him. There was that slight smile on his face again, and it was good to see. To know it was possible.

Alive, she realized, watching him. That was what it was.

After everything he'd been through, he seemed like a man who was finally looking forward to something.

Forty-five

I'd arranged with my father for him to arrive at seven o'clock that evening, and he was so prompt in his timing that I wondered whether he'd arrived early and been sitting outside until the designated time. Perhaps out of respect for me – the idea that if he was being allowed into my and Jake's life then it had to be precisely on my terms – but actually, I thought he was most likely the same with everyone. A man for whom discipline was important.

He was dressed neatly in suit trousers and shirt, as though he'd come straight from work, but he looked fresh and his hair was damp, so it was obvious he'd showered and changed first. He smelled clean too. As he followed me inside, I realized I'd checked that subconsciously. If he still drank, he would have started by now, and it wasn't too late for me to pull this whole event.

Jake was kneeling on the floor of the front room, hunched over a drawing.

'Pete's here,' I told him.

'Hi, Pete.'

'Could you at least pretend to look up?'

Jake sighed to himself, but put the cap on the pen he'd been using. His fingers were covered with ink.

'Hi, Pete,' he said again.

My father smiled.

'Good evening, Jake. Thank you for allowing me to look after you for a bit tonight.'

'You're welcome.'

'We both appreciate it,' I said. 'It should only be a couple of hours at most.'

'However long you need. I brought a book.'

I glanced at the thick paperback he was holding. I couldn't see enough of the cover to read the title, but there was a black and white photograph of Winston Churchill on the front. It was exactly the kind of worthy, weighty tome that I'd have struggled to force myself through, and it made me feel self-conscious. My father had transformed himself, physically and mentally, into this quietly impressive man. I couldn't help but feel slightly inadequate in comparison.

Stupid, though.

You're too hard on yourself.

My father put his book down on the settee.

'Can you show me around?'

'You've been here before.'

'In a different capacity,' he said. 'This is your home. I'd prefer to hear it from you.'

'Okay. We're just nipping upstairs, Jake.'

'Yes, I know.'

He was already drawing again. I led the way upstairs, pointing my father to the bathroom and then Jake's bedroom.

'He'd normally have a bath, but just skip that tonight,' I said. 'In half an hour or so, he comes up for bed. Pyjamas are there on the duvet. His book's down there. We normally read a chapter together before lights out, and we're about halfway through that one.'

My father looked down at it quizzically.

'*Power of Three?*'

'Yeah, Diana Wynne Jones. It's probably a bit old for him, but he likes it.'

'That's fine.'

'And like I said, I won't be out for long.'

'Are you doing anything nice?'

I hesitated.

'Just grabbing a drink with a friend.'

I didn't want to go into any more detail than that. For one thing, it made me feel curiously teenage to admit I was going on something that might be considered a date. Of course, my father and I had skipped that whole awkward period of my growing up, so perhaps it was natural to feel a little strange now. We'd never had the chance to develop the language to talk about it, or not to.

'I'm sure that will be nice,' he said.

'Yes.'

I thought it would be too, and that brought another teenage sensation: butterflies in my stomach. Not that it was a date, of course. It would be foolish to go into the evening thinking of it as one. That way disappointment lay. And both Karen and I had kids at our respective homes, so it wasn't like anything could really happen. How the hell did people manage that anyway? I really had no idea. I hadn't dated in so long that I might as well have been a teenager.

Butterflies.

Which reminded me that I hadn't locked the front door after letting my father in. It was ridiculous, but the excitement was immediately replaced by a small flush of fear.

'Come on,' I said. 'Let's head back down.'

Forty-six

The ceiling was creaking as Daddy and Pete moved around upstairs. They were talking, Jake could tell, but he couldn't make out the exact words. It was going to be about him though, obviously – instructions about how to put him to bed, and things like that. That was okay. He wanted go to bed as soon as possible.

Because he very much wanted this day to be over with.

That was the thing about going to sleep. It kind of *scrubbed* things.

Arguments, worries, whatever.

You could be scared or upset about something, and you might think sleep was impossible, but at some point it happened, and when you woke up in the morning the feeling was gone for a while, like a storm that had passed during the night. Or maybe it was like being put to sleep before a big operation. Which happened sometimes, Daddy had told him. The doctors put you to sleep, and you missed all the horrible stuff they had to do and just woke up better again afterwards.

Right now, what he wanted was the fear to go away.

Except *fear* wasn't quite the right word for it. When you were afraid, it was of something specific – like being told off – but what he was feeling was more like a bird that didn't have anywhere to land. Ever since this morning, there had just been the sensation that something bad was going to happen, but he wasn't sure what. But if Jake was certain of one thing right now, it was that he didn't want Daddy to go out tonight.

But the feeling wasn't real, so the sooner he went to sleep, the better. He would be scared – or whatever the name for this feeling was – but when he woke up in the morning, Daddy would be back home, and everything would be all right again.

'No, you're right to be scared.'

Jake jumped.

The little girl was sitting beside him, her legs straight out in front of her. He hadn't seen her since that first day at school, and yet the hash of scabs on her knee still looked red and raw, and her hair, as ever, was splayed out to one side. He could tell from her face that, once again, she wasn't in the mood for playing – that she knew something was wrong too. She looked more scared than he was.

'He shouldn't go out,' she said.

Jake looked back down at his drawing. Just like the feeling, he knew that the little girl wasn't real. Even if she seemed to be. Even if he so desperately wanted her to be.

'Nothing bad is going to happen,' he whispered.

'Yes, it is. You *know* it is.'

He shook his head. It was important to be sensible and grown-up about this, because Daddy was relying on him to be a good boy. So he continued to work on his picture, as though she wasn't really there. Which, of course, she wasn't.

Even so, he could sense her exasperation.

'You don't want him to meet her,' she said.

Jake kept drawing.

'You don't want your mummy replaced, do you?'

Jake stopped drawing.

No, of course he didn't want that. And that wasn't going to happen, was it? But he couldn't deny there had been something a little strange about Daddy's behaviour when he was talking about what was going to happen tonight. Again, the feeling wasn't precise enough to put a name to, but everything did seem a little off-balance and wrong, like there was something he wasn't being told. But nobody was going to replace Mummy. And Daddy didn't want that either.

But then he remembered the things Daddy had written.

They had talked about that, though, hadn't they? Just like things in books, it wasn't real. And besides, Daddy had been so sad recently, and this was something that might help with that. It was important. Jake needed to let Daddy be Daddy, so that he could be himself for Jake again too.

He had to be brave.

A moment later, the little girl rested her head on his shoulder, her hair stiff and unyielding against his neck.

'I'm so scared,' she said softly. 'Don't let him go, Jake.'

She was about to say something else, but then he heard heavy footsteps on the stairs, and the little girl was gone.

Forty-seven

When we got back downstairs, Jake was still sitting on the floor by his picture, pen in hand. But he'd stopped drawing now and was staring off into space. In fact, he looked as if he was about to cry. I walked over and crouched down beside him.

'You okay, mate?'

He nodded, but I didn't believe him.

'What's the matter?'

'Nothing.'

'Hmmm.' I frowned. 'Not sure I believe you on that one. Are you worried about tonight?'

He hesitated.

'Maybe a little.'

'Well, that's understandable. But you'll be fine. To be honest, I'd have thought you'd be looking forward to spending time with someone else for a change.'

He looked at me then, and while he still seemed so small and fragile, I didn't think I'd ever seen such an old expression on his face before now.

'Do you think I don't *want* to be with you?' he said.

'Oh, Jake. Come here.'

I adjusted my position so that he could sit on my knee for a cuddle. He perched on me, and then pressed his small body against mine.

'I don't think that at all. That wasn't what I meant.'

Except, it had been. Kind of, anyway. One of my biggest fears since Rebecca's death was that I couldn't connect with him. That we were strangers to each other. And a part of me did feel he might be better off without me and my fumbling attempts at fatherhood – that when he walked into school without a backward glance, it was how he felt all of the time.

It made me wonder if he thought the same about me. Maybe my going out this evening had made him feel I didn't want to be with him. That I'd booked him into the 567 Club because I wanted to be rid of him. While I did need my own time and space, nothing could have been further from the truth.

How sad that was, I thought. Both of us feeling the same. Both of us trying to meet in the middle but somehow always missing each other.

'And I want to be with you too,' I said. 'I won't be out for long, I promise.'

He tightened his grip on me slightly.

'Do you have to go?'

I took a deep breath.

The answer, I supposed, was no, I didn't have to, and I was reluctant to leave if it was going to upset him badly.

'I don't have to,' I said. 'But it will be fine, I promise. You'll go to bed soon, fall asleep, and when you wake up I'll be home again.'

He was silent, thinking over what I'd just told him. But the whole time, his anxiety seemed to be creeping into me as well. Apprehension. Dread, almost – the sudden fear that something bad was going to happen. It was silly, and there was no reason to think that. Even so, I could stay home, and I was about to tell him just that, but he nodded before I had the chance.

'Okay.'

'Right,' I said. 'Good. I love you, Jake.'

'I love you too, Daddy.'

He disentangled himself from me, and I stood up. My father had been waiting by the door the whole time and I walked over to him.

'Jake okay?'

'Yes. He'll be fine. But any problems at all, you've got my mobile number.'

'I have. But it'll be fine. Just strange for him, I guess.' He raised his voice a little. 'But we'll get along grand, Jake. You're going to be good for me, right?'

Jake, who was drawing again now, nodded in reply.

I watched him for a moment, crouched down and concentrating on his picture, and I felt an indescribable burst of love for him. But it was one that hardened into determination. We were going to get back on track, the two of us. Everything was going to be okay. I wanted to be with him, and he wanted to be with me, and somehow, between us, we would figure out a way to make that work.

'A couple of hours,' I told my father again. 'That's all it will be.'

Forty-eight

'We're nearly there,' DS Dyson said.

'I know,' Amanda told him.

She'd made Dyson drive, if only to keep him off his phone for an hour. They were fifty miles away from Featherbank now, heading along one edge of a large university campus. A corner took them into what was obviously the student heartland of the city, the houses all red brick and cramped together on thin streets. Each was at least three or four storeys high: buildings where five or six people could live together in groups, or landlords could rent out single rooms, creating collections of random strangers who stayed strangers. A square mile of disparate people. A place it was cheap and easy to disappear into.

And this was where David Parker, previously known as Francis Carter, had chosen to make his home.

The ID was a solid one – right age, and a close visual match for the build of Victor Tyler's prison visitor. They'd found him an hour before Pete had been due to leave, which had worried her at first, as she had been concerned he might overturn whatever arrangement he'd made earlier and insist on being involved. And she could tell that he had wanted to. But instead, he had watched quietly as Amanda made arrangements with the local force to visit the address, and when it had been time for him to leave, he had done so without complaint – just wished her luck and asked her to keep him informed of any developments. With the decision already made, she thought he might even have been relieved.

281

If only she could say the same – a part of her wished it was Pete with her right now. Because while everything they'd talked about back at the department remained true – they had no concrete evidence that Francis Carter was involved in the case at all, and this was going to be a routine visit in the first instance – she could feel it all the same. A tingle in her stomach, halfway between fear and excitement. It was telling her that she was close. That something was going to happen, and that she needed to be on guard and ready for it when it did.

Dyson turned down a steep hill. Each house here was lower than the one before it, so the roofs formed a black saw-blade pattern against the darkening sky. Francis Carter – or David Parker – was renting a one-bedroom flat in the basement of a large shared house.

Did that fit?

It worked for her in some ways, but not in others. If Parker was their man, he would certainly want his own place for privacy. But at the same time, could he really have kept a child here for two months without anyone seeing or hearing? Or had Neil been kept elsewhere?

The car slowed.

You're about to find out.

Dyson parked up under a street light that seemed to bleach the world of colour, and they both got out of the car. The house was four storeys high and seemed squeezed in by the properties beside it. No lights on at the front. There was a low brick wall with a rusted iron gate that Amanda opened quietly before stepping on to the path. To her left was a messy garden, too small and wretched for anyone to tend, and then steep steps led up to the front door. But just past the garden, a second set of steps led down below ground level into an area barely wide enough for a single person to stand. From the top, Amanda could see a front window. The door to Parker's flat was presumably directly underneath the main door above, obscured from view.

She led the way down, the garden rising up to her left, replaced by the brick wall overshadowing the steps. The air was much colder here; it felt like descending into a grave. The window was a dirty square of black, with cobwebs in the corners. Parker's front door was barely visible in the shadows.

She knocked hard and called out.

'Mr Parker? David Parker?'

No reply.

She gave it a few seconds more, then knocked again.

'David?' she said. 'Are you in there?'

Again, she was met by nothing but silence. Beside her, Dyson had his hands over his eyes, staring in through the window as best he could.

'Can't see a thing.' He leaned away from the grimy window pane. 'What do we do now?'

Amanda tried the door handle and was surprised when it turned with a creak. The door opened slightly. Immediately, the thick, heavy stink of mould wafted out from the flat.

'Not safe, leaving it unlocked like that, in this neighbourhood,' Dyson said.

Because he wasn't close enough to smell what she could. *Not safe at all*, she thought, but perhaps not in the way he was meaning. The room within was pitch black, and the tingling sensation in her stomach was stronger than ever. It was telling her that something dangerous was waiting in there.

'Stay alert,' she told Dyson.

Then she pulled out a torch and stepped carefully inside, one coat sleeve held protectively over her nose and mouth, the other playing the beam slowly over the room before her. The air was so dusty that it looked like sand was swirling in the light. She moved the beam around and caught flashes of detritus: tattered grey furniture; tangles of old clothes strewn across the wiry carpet; paperwork scattered on the surface of a rickety wooden table. The walls and ceiling were mottled with damp. There was a kitchen area along the wall to the right, and as she ran the light steadily along the filthy plates and bowls there, she saw things moving, casting large shadows as they scuttled away out of sight.

'Francis?' she called.

But it was obvious that nobody lived here any more. The place had been abandoned. Someone had walked out of here, closed the front door without bothering to lock it behind them, and never returned. She clicked the light switch beside her up and down. Nothing. The rent had been paid a year in advance, but apparently not the utilities.

Dyson stopped beside her.

'Jesus.'

'Wait here,' she said.

Then she stepped gingerly through the debris scattered around the room. There were two doors at the back. She opened one and found the bathroom, moving the torchlight back and forth and resisting the urge to gag. It stank far worse in here than it did in the front room. The sink at the far end was half full of dank water, with sodden towels lying knotted on the floor, their surfaces speckled with rot.

She closed the door and moved over to the second. This one had to lead to the bedroom. Bracing herself for what she might find, she turned the handle, pushed it open, and shone the torch inside.

'Anything?'

She ignored the question and stepped carefully over the threshold.

There was dust in the air here too, but it was clear that this room had not been neglected and uncared for like the rest of the property. The carpet was soft, and looked newer than the rest of the furnishings. While there was no furniture in here, she could see imprints in the carpet where items had rested: a large flattened rectangle formed under what might have been a chest of drawers; a single square that she could only guess at; four small squares spaced out far enough that they might have been the legs of a long table placed against one wall. The latter were deep too – the table must have had something heavy stored on top of it.

No obvious marks from a bed, though.

But then she noticed something, and quickly moved the torchlight back to the far wall. She could tell that it had been painted more recently than the rest of the flat, but it had also been amended. Around the base, someone had added careful drawings. Blades of grass seemed to grow out of the floor, with simple flowers dotted here and there and bees and butterflies hovering above.

She remembered the photographs she'd seen of the inside of Frank Carter's extension.

Oh God.

Slowly, she moved the beam upwards.

Close to the ceiling, an angry sun stared back at her with black eyes.

Forty-nine

Your daddy liked these books when he was younger.

Pete almost said that as he knelt down beside Jake's bed and picked up the book. The light in the bedroom was so soft, and Jake looked so small, lying there beneath the blankets, that he was momentarily transported back to a different time. He remembered reading to Tom when he had been a little boy. The Diana Wynne Jones books had been one of his son's favourites.

Power of Three. He couldn't recall the contents, but the cover was immediately familiar, and his fingertips tingled as he touched it. It was a very old edition. The covers were frayed at the edges, and the spine was so worn that the title was lost in the string of creases. Was this the actual copy he himself had read so many years ago? It was, he thought. Tom had kept it and was now reading it to his own son instead. Not just a story passed down through time, from father to son, but the exact same pages containing it.

Pete felt a sense of wonder at that.

Your daddy liked these books when he was younger.

But he caught himself before saying it. Not only was Jake unaware of Pete's relationship to him, but it was not Pete's place to reveal it, and it never would be. That was fine. If he wanted to claim he had changed over the years and was no longer the terrible father from Tom's worst memories, he could hardly lay claim to any of the better ones either.

If that man was gone, all of him had to be. With a new man in his place.

'Well, then.'

The light in the room made his voice quiet and gentle.

'Where are we up to?'

Afterwards, he sat downstairs in silence, the book he had brought untouched for the moment. The warmth he'd felt upstairs had been carried down with him, and he wanted to absorb it for a while.

For so long now, he'd buried himself in distractions: he'd used books and food and television – ritual in general – as a way of clicking fingers at one side of his own mind to distract it from glancing in more dangerous directions. But he didn't feel that now. The voices that plagued him were silent. The urge to drink was not alive tonight. He could still sense it there, in the same way that a stubbed-out candle smokes a little, but the fire and the brightness of it were gone.

It had been so lovely to read to Jake. The boy had been quiet and attentive, and then, after a page or two, he had wanted to take over. Although his delivery was faltering, it was obvious that his vocabulary was impressive. And it had been impossible not to feel the peace of the room. However much Pete had messed up Tom's own childhood, his son hadn't passed that on.

Pete checked on Jake fifteen minutes later and found the boy already fast asleep. He stood there for a moment, marvelling at how tranquil Jake appeared.

This is what you lose by drinking.

He'd told himself that so many times while looking at the photograph of Sally, his mind skirting the memories of the life he'd lost. Most of the time it had been enough, but sometimes it hadn't, and these past months had been the toughest of tests. Somehow he had resisted. Looking down at Jake now, he was monumentally glad about that, as though he had somehow dodged a bullet he hadn't known was coming. Although the future was uncertain, at least it was there.

Look what you gain by stopping.

That thought was so much better. It was the difference between regret and relief, between a cold hearth full of dead, grey ash and a fire that was still alight. He hadn't lost this. He might not have found it fully yet either. But he hadn't lost it.

Back downstairs, he did read for a little while, but he was distracted by thoughts of the investigation, and kept checking his phone for updates. There were none. It felt like Amanda should have been there by now, and Francis Carter should either be in custody or being questioned, and he hoped that was the case. Too busy to update him was too busy in the right direction.

Francis Carter.

He remembered the boy clearly. Although, of course, Francis Carter was an entirely different person now: a grown man, formed from that boy but distinct from him. Pete had only interacted with the child on a handful of occasions twenty years ago; the majority of the interviews had needed to be handled carefully by specially trained officers. Francis had been small and pale and haunted, staring down at the table with hooded eyes, giving one-word answers at most. The extent of the trauma he must have suffered living with his father had been obvious. He was a vulnerable child who had been through hell.

Carter's words came back to him now.

His top is all pulled up over his face so I can't see it properly, which is the way I like it.

The children had all been the same to him; any one would do. And he hadn't wanted to see their faces. But why? Could it possibly be, Pete wondered, because Carter had wanted to imagine the victims were his own son? A boy he couldn't touch without being caught, so the hatred he felt had to be acted out on other children instead?

Pete sat very still for a moment.

If that were the case, how might a child feel in response to that? That he was worthless and deserved to die too, perhaps. Guilt over the lives lost in his place. A heartfelt desire to make amends. An urge to help children like him, because by doing so he could somehow begin to heal himself.

This is a man who takes care.

Carter, talking about the man in the photograph he'd been shown.

Smiling at him.

You just don't listen, Peter.

Neil Spencer had been held captive for two months, but had been well looked after the whole time. Someone had taken care of him – until something went wrong, whereupon Neil had been killed and his body dumped at the exact spot of his abduction. Pete remembered what he'd thought when the boy's body was discovered on the waste ground that night. That it was like someone had returned a present they no longer wanted. He thought about it differently now.

Maybe it was more like a failed experiment.

Upstairs, Jake started screaming.

Fifty

I'd arranged to meet Karen in a pub a few streets away from my house, not far from the school. It was the village local, called simply the Featherbank, and I felt more than a little awkward as I arrived. It was a warm evening, and the beer garden adjoining the street was full of people. Through the large windows, the inside also seemed to be teeming as well. Just as when I'd walked into the playground on Jake's first day, it felt like I was entering a place where everybody knew each other, and where I didn't belong and never would.

I spotted Karen at the bar and made my way through the throng, packed in on all sides by hot bodies and laughter. Tonight, her big coat was nowhere in evidence. She was wearing jeans and a white top. I felt even more nervous as I stood beside her.

'Hey,' I said over the noise.

'Hey there.' She smiled at me, then leaned in and said, 'Excellent timing. What can I get you?'

I scanned the nearest pumps and picked something at random. She paid, handed me my pint, and then eased away from the bar and nodded for me to follow her through the crowd, deeper into the pub. As I did, I wondered if I'd entirely misjudged this evening, and she was taking me to meet a group of friends. But there was a door just past the bar, and she pushed through that into a different beer garden, this time secluded at the back of the pub and surrounded by trees. There were circular wooden tables spaced out on the grass, and a small play area, where a few children were making their way across low rope bridges while their parents sat drinking nearby. It was less busy out here, and Karen led me over to an empty table towards the far end.

'We could have brought the kids,' I said.

'If we were insane, yes.' She sat down. 'Assuming you're not being incredibly irresponsible, I'm guessing you managed to find a babysitter?'

I sat down beside her.

'Yes. My father.'

'Wow.' She blinked. 'After what you told me before, that must be strange.'

'It's weird, yeah. I wouldn't have asked him normally, but . . . well. I wanted to come out for a drink, and beggars can't be choosers.'

She raised her eyebrows.

I blushed. 'I mean about him, not you.'

'Ha! This is all off the record, by the way.' She put her hand on my arm, and left it there for a couple of seconds longer than she needed to. 'I'm glad you could come, anyway,' she said.

'Me too.'

'Cheers, by the way.'

We clinked glasses.

'So. You don't have any concerns about him?'

'My father?' I shook my head. 'Honestly, no. Not on that level. I don't know how I feel about it, to be honest. It's not a permanent thing. It's not any kind of thing, really.'

'Yes. That's a sensible way of looking at it. People worry too much about the nature of things. Sometimes it's better just to go with them. What about Jake?'

'Oh, he probably likes him more than he does me.'

'I'm sure that's not true.'

I remembered how Jake had been just before I left and fought down the guilt it brought.

'Maybe,' I said.

'Like I've told you, you're too hard on yourself.'

'Maybe,' I said again.

I sipped my drink. A part of me remained on edge, but I realized now that it wasn't anything to do with spending time with Karen. In fact, it was surprising how relaxed I felt now that I was here, and how natural it was to be sitting this close to her, a little closer than friends normally would. No, the nerves were because I was still worried about Jake. It was hard to stop thinking about him. Hard to shake the gut feeling that as much as I wanted to be here, there was somewhere else it was far more important for me to be instead.

I took another sip of my drink and told myself not to be stupid.

'You said your mum's looking after Adam?'

'Yeah.'

Karen rolled her eyes and then started to explain her whole situation. She'd moved back to Featherbank last year, choosing the village mainly because her mother lived here. While there had never been any love lost between the two of them, the woman was good with Adam, and Karen had figured the support would help while she established herself on her own two feet again.

'Adam's father isn't on the scene?'

'Do you think I'd be out with you if he was?'

Karen smiled. I shrugged slightly helplessly, and she let me off.

'No, he isn't. And maybe that's rough on Adam, but sometimes kids are better off that way, even if they don't always realize it at the time. Brian — that's my ex — let's just say that he was like your father in some ways. A lot of ways.'

She took a sip of her own drink, and while the silence wasn't uncomfortable, it still felt like a natural point to leave that particular subject. Some conversations need to wait, if they even have to be had at all. In the meantime, I watched the children clambering over the play equipment in the far corner of the garden. The evening was settling in now. The air was growing darker, with midges flickering in the trees around us.

But it was still warm. Still nice.

Except . . .

I looked off in a different direction now. My internal compass had already worked out where my house was from here, and I wasn't even that far away from Jake: probably only a few hundred metres as the crow flies. But it seemed too far. And looking back at the children again, I thought it wasn't just that it was becoming gloomy but that the light seemed wrong, somehow. That everything was off-kilter and odd.

'Oh,' Karen said, reaching into her bag. 'I just remembered. I've got something. This is a bit embarrassing, but will you sign it for me?'

My most recent book. The sight of it reminded me how far behind I was on any kind of follow-up, and that made me panic slightly. But it was clearly meant as a nice gesture, and also kind of a silly one, so I forced myself to smile.

'Sure.'

She handed me a pen. I opened the book on the title page and started writing.

To Karen.

I paused. I could never think what to write.

I'm really glad to have met you. I hope you don't think this is shit.

When you signed books for people, some waited to read what you'd put. Karen was not one of those people. She laughed as she saw what I'd written.

'I'm sure I won't. Anyway, what makes you think I'm going to read it? This is going straight on eBay, mate.'

'Which is fine, although I wouldn't plan your retirement yet.'

'Don't worry.'

The air around us was darker still. I looked over at the play area again, and saw a little girl in a blue and white dress standing there, staring back at me. Our eyes met for a moment, and everything else in the beer garden faded into the background. And then she grinned and ran towards one of the rope bridges, another little girl running after her, laughing.

I shook my head.

'Are you okay?' Karen said.

'Yes.'

'Hmmm. I'm not sure I believe you. Is it Jake?'

'I suppose so.'

'You're worried about him?'

'I don't know. Maybe. It's probably nothing, just that this is the first time I've been out on an evening without him. And I am having a good time, honestly. But it feels . . .'

'Really fucking strange?'

'A little bit, yeah.'

'I get you.' She smiled sympathetically. 'It was the same for me when I first started leaving Adam with my mum. It's like there's something tethering you to home and it's stretching too thin. There's this need inside you to get back.'

I nodded, even though it felt much more than that. The sensation inside me was that something was terribly wrong. But I was probably just being overdramatic about exactly what she was describing.

'And it's fine,' Karen said. 'Honestly. Early days. Let's just finish these and you can get back home, and maybe we can do this again sometime. Assuming you want to?'

'I definitely want to.'

'Good.'

She was looking at me, both of us holding eye contact, and the space between us felt weighted with possibility. I realized that this was a moment when I could lean in for a kiss, and that if I did, she would lean forward too. That we would both close our eyes as our lips met, and that the kiss would be as gentle as breath. I also knew that if I didn't, one of us would have to turn away. But the moment would have been there, and we would both know it, and at some point it would happen again.

Might as well be now then.

And I was about to do just that when my phone started ringing.

Fifty-one

It had been in the afternoon, and he and Daddy were coming back from school. It was usually Mummy who picked him up on that day, because it was supposed to be one of Daddy's days to work, but that wasn't what happened.

Daddy wrote stories for a living, and people paid him to read them, which Jake personally thought was exceptionally cool. And Daddy sometimes agreed that, yes, it was. For one thing, he didn't have to wear a suit and go into an office every day and be told what to do like lots of other parents did. But it was also hard, because it didn't seem like a job to other people.

Jake didn't know all the ins and outs of it, but he was dimly aware that this had caused problems between his parents at one point, in that Daddy was doing most of the pick-ups and drop-offs, and that meant he wasn't writing quite so many stories. The solution was that Mummy started picking him up more often. This had been meant to be one of her days. But then Daddy turned up and explained that Mummy wasn't feeling well, and so he'd had to come instead.

That was the way he said it. *Had to* come instead.

'Is she okay?' Jake said.

'She's fine,' Daddy said. 'She was just a bit light-headed when she got back from work, and so she's having a lie-down.'

Jake believed him, because of course Mummy was fine. But Daddy seemed more tense than normal, and Jake wondered if his most recent story had been going even less well than usual, and that having to come out to collect Jake was . . . well. What was the opposite of icing on a cake?

Jake often felt like he was a problem for Daddy. That things would be a bit easier if he wasn't around.

And in the car, Daddy asked the usual questions about his day, and how things had been, and what he'd done. As always, Jake did his best not to answer them. There was nothing exciting to say, and he didn't think Daddy was really all that interested anyway.

They parked up outside the house.

'Can I go in and see Mummy?'

He half expected Daddy to say no, although he wasn't sure why – maybe because it was something that Jake really wanted to do, and so Daddy would say no just to spoil his fun. But that wasn't very fair, because Daddy just smiled and ruffled his hair.

'Of course, mate. Just be gentle with her, okay?'

'I will.'

The door was unlocked, and he ran into the house without taking his shoes off. That was something Mummy would normally tell him off for, because she liked to keep the place clean and tidy, but they weren't dirty or anything, and he wanted to see her and try to make her feel better. He ran through the kitchen and into the front room.

And then he stopped.

Because there was something wrong. The curtains at the far end of the room were open, and the afternoon sun was coming in at an angle, lighting up half the room. It looked peaceful, and everything was very still and silent. But that was the problem. Even when someone was hiding from you, you could usually tell that they were there somewhere, because people took up space and that altered the pressure somehow. The house right now didn't feel like that at all.

It felt empty.

Daddy was still outside, probably doing something with the car. Jake walked slowly across the front room, but it was more like the room was walking backwards past him. The silence was so huge that it felt like he might bruise it if he wasn't careful.

To the side of the window, the door was open. It led to the small area at the bottom of the stairs. As Jake stepped closer, he could see more and more of it.

The marbled glass of the back door.

The only sound now was his own heartbeat.

The white wallpaper.

Approaching so slowly that he was barely moving.

The knotted, wooden handrail.

He looked down at the floor.

Mummy —

'*Daddy!*'

Jake screamed the word before he was even properly awake. Then he tucked himself down entirely beneath the covers and shouted it again, his small heart beating hard. He hadn't had the nightmare since the old house, and the shock of it had got a whole lot bigger while it had been gone.

He waited.

He wasn't sure what time it was, or how long he'd been asleep, but surely it had been long enough that Daddy must be home by now? A moment later, he heard steady footsteps coming up the stairs.

Jake risked poking his head out. The hall light was still on, and a shadow stretched into the room as someone came in.

'Hey,' the man said softly. 'What's the matter?'

Pete, Jake remembered. He liked Pete well enough, but the fact remained that Pete was not Daddy, and Daddy was who he wanted and needed to be walking over to him right now.

Pete was very old, but he sat down cross-legged beside the bed in a quick, decisive movement.

'What's wrong?'

'I had a bad dream. Where's Daddy?'

'He's not back yet. Bad dreams are horrible, aren't they? What was this one about?'

Jake shook his head. He'd never even told Daddy what the nightmare was about, and he wasn't sure he ever would.

'That's okay.' Pete nodded to himself. 'I have bad dreams too, you know? Quite often, in fact. But I actually think it's all right to have them.'

'How can it be all right?'

'Because sometimes really bad things happen to us, and we don't like to think about them, so they get buried really deep in our heads.'

'Like earworms?'

'I suppose so, yes. But they have to come out eventually. And bad dreams can be our brain's way of dealing with that. Breaking it all down into smaller and smaller pieces, until eventually there's nothing left any more.'

Jake considered that. The nightmare had been even more frightening than ever, so it felt more like his mind was building something up rather than breaking it down. But then, it always ended at the same point, before he could properly remember seeing Mummy lying on the floor. Maybe Pete was right. Perhaps his own mind was so scared that it had to build itself up for that sight before it could begin to break it down.

'I know it doesn't make it any easier,' Pete said. 'But you know what? A nightmare can never, ever hurt you. There's nothing to be scared of.'

'I know that,' Jake said. 'But I still want my daddy.'

'He'll be back soon, I'm sure.'

'I need him now.' With the return of the nightmare, along with the little girl's warning earlier, Jake was more sure than ever that something was wrong. 'Can you ring him and get him to come home?'

Pete was silent for a moment.

'Please?' Jake said. 'He won't mind.'

'I know he won't,' Pete agreed, taking out his mobile phone.

Jake watched anxiously as Pete swiped through, pressed the screen, and then held it up to his ear.

Downstairs, the front door opened.

'Ah, there's your dad now.' Pete cancelled the call. 'I guess that's okay then. Will you be all right up here for a minute while I go down and get him?'

No, Jake thought, *I won't*. He didn't want to spend another second up here in the darkness by himself. But at least Daddy was home now, and he felt a flood of relief at that.

'Okay.'

Pete stood up and walked out of the room, and Jake heard the creak of his footfall on the stairs, and then him calling out Daddy's name.

Jake stared at the wedge of illuminated hallway beyond the bedroom door, listening carefully. For a few seconds, there was nothing but silence. But then he heard something he couldn't identify. Movement of some kind, as though furniture was being shifted about. And people talking, only with sounds instead of words, like when you were trying really hard to do something and the effort made you make a noise.

Another loud sound. Something heavy falling over.

And then silence again.

Jake thought about calling out for Daddy, but for some reason his heart was thudding hard in his chest again, as hard as it had been when he'd first woken up from the nightmare, and the silence was ringing so much that it felt like he was back inside it, back in their old front room.

He stared at the empty hallway, waiting.

A few seconds later, there was a new sound. Footfall on the stairs again. Someone was coming up, but they were moving slowly and carefully, as though they were scared of the silence too.

And then someone whispered his name.

Fifty-two

'I'm sure everything's fine.'

Hurrying along behind me, Karen tried to make it sound breezy. And no doubt she was right – I was almost certainly overreacting, walking so quickly that she was struggling to keep up. She had come with me without us discussing it. But if she hadn't, I might even have been running right now. Because while she was right, and there was most likely nothing to worry about, I still felt it in my heart. The certainty that something was terribly wrong.

I took out my mobile and tried phoning my father again. He had called me back at the pub, but it had cut off before I'd had a chance to answer. Which meant that something must have happened. But when I'd tried to call him back, he hadn't picked up.

The phone rang and rang now.

He still wasn't picking up.

'Fuck.'

I cancelled the call as we reached the bottom of my street. Maybe he'd dialled by accident, or changed his mind about needing to talk to me. But I remembered how deferential he'd been earlier on, and how quietly pleased he'd seemed to be asked to look after Jake and be allowed into our lives, in however small a way. He wouldn't have called me if he could possibly have helped it. Not unless it had been important.

The field to the right was thick with the evening gloom. There seemed to be nobody out there right now, but it was already too dark to see to the far side. I started to walk even more quickly, aware that I was probably coming across as an absolute lunatic to Karen. But I was beginning to panic now, however irrational it was, and that mattered more.

Jake . . .

I reached the driveway.

The front door was open, a block of light slanted out across the path.

If you leave a door half open . . .

And then I really did start running.

'Tom –'

I reached the door, but then stopped at the threshold. There were smears of bloody footprints all over the wood at the bottom of the stairs.

'Jake?' I shouted inside.

The house was silent. I stepped carefully inside, my heart pounding fast and hard in my ears.

Karen had reached me now.

'What – ? Oh God.'

I looked to my right, into the front room, and the sight that awaited me there made no sense whatsoever. My father was lying on his side with his back to me, curled up on the floor by the window, almost as though he'd gone to sleep there. But he was surrounded by blood. I shook my head. There was blood all over the side of his body. Further up, it was pooling around his head. He was completely still. And for a moment, unable to process what I was seeing, so was I.

Beside me, Karen took a sharp, shocked intake of breath. I turned slightly and saw that she'd gone pale. Her eyes were wide and she was holding her hand over her mouth.

Jake, I thought.

'Tom –'

But I didn't hear anything after that, because the thought of my son had brought me back to life, galvanizing me into action. I moved past her, around her, then headed straight up the stairs as quickly as I could. Praying. Thinking: *Please!*

'Jake!'

There was blood on the upstairs landing too, pressed into the carpet by the shoes of whoever had committed the atrocity downstairs. Someone had attacked my father, and then they'd come up here, up here to . . .

My son's room.

I stepped in. The bed sheet had been folded neatly back. Jake was not there. Nobody was there. I stood there for a few seconds, frozen in place, dread itching at my skin.

Downstairs, Karen was on her phone, talking frantically. Ambulance. Police. Urgent. A jumble of words that made no sense to me right then. It felt like my mind was going to shut down – as though my skull had suddenly opened up and exposed my brain to a vast, incomprehensible kaleidoscope of horror.

I walked across to the bed.

Jake was gone. But that wasn't possible, because Jake couldn't be gone.

This wasn't happening.

The Packet of Special Things was lying on the floor by the bed. It was when I picked that up, knowing that he would never have gone anywhere willingly without it, that the reality of it hit me full force.

The Packet was here and Jake wasn't.

This wasn't a nightmare. It was actually happening.

My son was gone.

That was when I tried to scream.

PART FIVE

Fifty-three

The first forty-eight hours after a child disappears are the most crucial.

When Neil Spencer disappeared, the first two hours of that period had been wasted, because nobody had realized he was gone. With Jake Kennedy, the investigation began within minutes of his father and his friend arriving home. At that point, Amanda had been with Dyson in a police department fifty miles away. They had driven back as quickly as possible.

Outside Tom Kennedy's house now, she checked her watch. Just after ten o'clock at night. All the machinery that rolled out when a child went missing was already in motion. The odd-looking house beside her was brightly lit and busy with activity, shadows moving across the curtains, while up and down the street, officers were standing at porches, interviewing neighbours. Torchlight moved over the field across the road. Statements were being taken; CCTV was being gathered; people were out searching.

In different circumstances, Pete himself would have been out with the search teams. But not tonight, of course. Trying to keep calm, she took out her phone and called the hospital for an update, then listened as dispassionately as she could to the news. Pete remained unconscious and in a critical condition. Christ. She remembered how formidable he had been for a man his age, but it appeared to have counted for little this evening. Perhaps he hadn't been concentrating for some reason and had been taken unawares; he had received few defensive wounds, but had been stabbed several times in the side, neck and head. The attack had been unnecessarily frenzied – clearly attempted murder, and the hours ahead would reveal whether that attempt had been successful. She was told that it was touch and go as to whether he would survive the night. She could only hope that his fitness would serve him now where it had failed him before.

You can do it, Pete, she thought.

He would pull through. He had to.

She put the phone down and then quickly checked the online case file for updates. No developments as yet. Officers had already taken statements from Tom Kennedy and the woman he had been out with, Karen Shaw. Amanda recognized the name; Shaw was a local crime reporter. According to their accounts, they'd simply met up for a drink as friends. Their children were in the same year at school, so maybe that was all it was, but Amanda hoped for everyone's sake that Shaw was more trustworthy than most of her profession. Especially now.

Because she still didn't know why Pete had been at the house.

She remembered how alive he'd seemed that afternoon, reading the message he'd received and then making his arrangements. At the time, she'd suspected a date of some kind. In reality, it must have been this – and whatever this turned out to be, the fact remained that Pete was involved in the case and shouldn't have been here off duty. It was a breach of professionalism.

And what bothered her more was the knowledge that she'd effectively pushed him into it. She'd wanted him to be happy. If she hadn't pressed him, he would still be alive.

He is still alive.

She had to cling to that. More than anything else, she

needed to be professional and focused right now. She couldn't afford to let her emotions out. Guilt. Fear. Anger. Once let loose, any one of them would charge off, dragging the others along like dogs chained in a pack. And that was no good at all.

Pete was still alive.

Jake Kennedy was still alive.

She was not going to lose either of them. But there was only one that she could do anything about right now.

And so, finally, she shut down the case file and got out of the car.

Inside the house, Amanda stepped gingerly over the dance of dried blood at the bottom of the stairs, then walked cautiously into the front room, preparing herself for the sight she knew awaited her.

Several CSIs were at work in here, measuring, analysing and taking photographs, but she tuned them out, focusing instead on the overturned coffee table and, inevitably, the blood smeared on the furniture and pooled on the floor. There was enough of it that she could smell it in the air. Her career had brought her face-to-face with worse than this, but knowing it had been Pete attacked in here meant what she was seeing now was impossible to accept.

She watched the CSIs for a moment. The forensic work was so sombre, so thorough that it felt like the room was already being treated as a murder scene. As though everybody in here knew a truth that she had yet to catch up with.

She went through to the spare room. The walls were lined with bookcases, with several boxes on the floor still to be unpacked. Tom Kennedy was pacing back and forth between them, following an elaborate path, the same way an animal might wear away the ground in an enclosure. Karen Shaw was sitting in a chair by a computer table, holding one elbow, her other hand at her mouth, staring at the floor.

Tom noticed Amanda and came to a stop. She recognized the expression on his face. People dealt with situations like this in different ways — some almost preternaturally calm, others distracting themselves with motion and activity — but in every case, the behaviour was about displacement. Right now, Tom Kennedy was panicking and struggling to contain it. If he couldn't move in the direction of his son then he needed to be moving somewhere. After he stopped walking, his body began to tremble.

'Tom,' she told him. 'I know this is difficult. I know this is terrifying for you. But I need you to listen to me and I need you to believe me. We are going to find Jake. I promise you.'

He stared back at her. It was obvious that he didn't believe her, and perhaps it wasn't a promise she could keep. But she meant it all the same. The determination was burning inside her. She wouldn't stop, wouldn't rest, until she'd found Jake and caught the man who had taken him. Who had taken Neil Spencer before him. Who had hurt Pete so badly.

I am not losing another child on my watch.

'We believe we know who's taken him, and we're going to find him. Like I said, I give you my word. Every available officer is focused on hunting this man down and finding your son. We are going to bring him home safe.'

'Who is he?'

'I can't tell you that right now.'

'My son is alone with him.'

She could tell from his face that right now he was picturing every terrible possibility — that a reel of the worst imaginable horrors was unfolding in his head.

'I know it's hard, Tom,' she said. 'But I also want you to remember that, assuming this is the same man who took Neil Spencer, Neil was well cared for at first.'

'And then murdered.'

She had no answer to that. Instead, she thought about the abandoned flat she had visited a few hours earlier, and the way that Francis Carter had recreated the decorations in his father's extension. He must have seen the horrors in there as a child, and it seemed that he had never truly escaped that room – that a part of him had remained trapped there, unable to move on. Yes, he had looked after Neil Spencer for a time. But then some darker impulse had emerged, and there was no reason to think he would contain it any better with Jake than he had with Neil. The opposite, in fact – once the dam was broken, killers like this had a tendency to accelerate.

But she was not prepared to entertain that idea right now.

Tom, of course, had no such luxury.

'Why Jake?'

'We don't know for certain.' The desperation in his question was also familiar to her. Faced with tragedy and horror, it was natural to search for explanations: reasons why the tragedy could not have been prevented, to help ease the pain; or ways in which the horror could have been avoided, serving only to stoke the guilt. 'We believe the suspect may have had an interest in this house, the same way that Norman Collins did. It's likely he discovered your son was living here, and probably decided upon him as a target as a result of that.'

'Fixated on him, you mean.'

'Yes.'

A few beats of silence.

'How is he?' Tom said.

Amanda thought he must still be talking about Jake, but

then she realized he was staring past her towards the front room, and understood he was asking after Pete.

'He's in intensive care,' she said. 'That's the last I've heard. His condition is critical, but . . . well, Pete's a fighter. If anyone can make it through, it's him.'

Tom nodded to himself, as though that resonated with him on some level. Which didn't make sense, because he had barely known Pete at all. Once again, she remembered how pleased Pete had been that afternoon. How suddenly alive he had seemed.

'Why was he here?' she said. 'He shouldn't have been.'

'He was babysitting Jake.'

'Why Pete, though?'

Tom fell silent. She watched him. It was clear that he was considering what to tell her, choosing his words carefully. And suddenly, she realized she had seen this expression before too. The tilt of Tom Kennedy's head. The angle of his jawline. The serious expression. Standing in front of her now, his hollow face illuminated by the light above, Tom Kennedy looked almost exactly like Pete.

Christ, she thought.

But then he shook his head and moved slightly, and the resemblance disappeared.

'He left me his card. He said, if we needed anything, to get in touch. And he and Jake . . . well, Jake liked him. They liked each other.'

The explanation stumbled to an end, and Amanda continued to stare at him. Although she could no longer see the similarity outright, she hadn't imagined it. She could press it home, but she decided that it wasn't important – not right now. If she was correct, the repercussions of that could be dealt with later.

Right now, in fact, she needed to be back at the department, making good on the promise she'd given, as best she could.

'Okay,' she said. 'What's going to happen next is that I'm going to leave here, and I'm going to find your son and bring him home.'

'What do I do?'

Amanda glanced back towards the front room. It went without saying that Tom couldn't stay here overnight.

'You don't have family in the area, do you?'

'No.'

'You can come to mine,' Karen said. 'It's not a problem.' She hadn't spoken until now.

Amanda looked at her. 'Are you sure about that?'

'Yes.'

Amanda could tell from Karen's expression that she understood the severity of the situation. Tom was silent for a moment, considering the offer. Despite Amanda's reservations about the journalist, she hoped to God he said yes. She could do without the headache of booking him into the safe house again right now. And it was obvious that he wanted to say yes – that he was a man on the verge of collapse – and so Amanda decided to give him a push.

'Okay then.' She held out her card. 'Those are my details. Direct line. I'll get family liaison out to you first thing in the morning anyway. But for now, if you need anything, you call me. I've got your number too. Any developments at all, and that includes about Pete, and you'll hear from me the same minute.'

She hesitated, then lowered her voice slightly.

'The same fucking minute, Tom. I promise you.'

Fifty-four

The day was dead and the night was cool.

The man stood in his driveway, warming his hands on a mug of coffee. The front door of his house was open behind him, the inside dark and silent. The world was so quiet that he imagined he could hear the steam rising from the cup.

He had made his home on an out-of-the-way street in an undesirable area, a few miles from Featherbank itself. It was partly for financial reasons, but mainly for privacy. One of the neighbouring houses was vacant, while the occupants of the other kept to themselves, even when they weren't drinking. The hedges on either side of his small driveway were overgrown, shielding his comings and goings from view, and there was never anything in the way of traffic. This wasn't a street you came to, nor was it anywhere you would pass through on your way to somewhere else. It was, put simply, a place you avoided.

Francis liked to think that his presence here had contributed to that. That if you did find yourself driving past for some reason, you would understand on some primal level that it was not a location in which to linger.

Much like Jake Kennedy's former home, of course.

The scary house.

The man remembered that monstrosity from his own childhood. It appeared to have been common knowledge amongst the other children that the place was dangerous, although none of them had known why. Some said it was haunted; others claimed that a former murderer lived there.

All without reason, of course – it was solely down to the way it looked. If they hadn't approached Francis with the same mentality, he would have been able to tell them the real reason the house was frightening. But there had been nobody for him to tell.

It felt like a long time ago. He wondered if the police had found the remnants of his old life yet. If so, it didn't matter; he'd left little behind but dust. He remembered how easy it had been – how simple it was, on one level, to become other people if you wanted. It had cost less than a thousand pounds to acquire a new identity from a man sixty miles south of here. Ever since, he had been building a shell around himself to enable him to begin his transformation, the same way that a caterpillar emerges from its own cocoon, vibrant and powerful and unrecognizable.

And yet traces of the frightened, hateful boy he had once been remained. Francis had not been his name in years, but it was still how he thought of himself. He could remember his father making him watch the things he did to those boys. From the look on his father's face, Francis had understood only too well that the man had hated him, and that he would have done the same to Francis if he could. The boys he killed had only ever been stand-ins for the child he despised most of all. Francis had always been well aware of how worthless and disgusting he was.

He couldn't save the boys he'd seen murdered all those years ago, just as he couldn't help or comfort the child he had once been. But he could make amends. Because there were so many children like him in the world, and it wasn't too late to rescue and protect them.

He and Jake would be good for each other.

Francis sipped his coffee, then stared up at the night sky and its meaningless patterns of constellations. His thoughts drifted to the violence back at the house. His skin was still singing with the thrill of that, and he knew it was a sensation his mind should avoid. Because even though he had known in advance the evening would involve a physical confrontation, it had been surprising how natural it had been when it came to it. He had killed once, and it had been easy to kill again. It was as though what he'd been forced to do to Neil had turned a key inside him, unlocking desires he'd only been dimly aware of beforehand.

It had felt good, hadn't it?

Coffee slopped over his hand, and he looked down to see that his hand was trembling slightly.

He forced himself to calm down.

But a part of him didn't want to. It was much easier now to remember what he'd done to Neil Spencer, and he couldn't deny that there had been enjoyment in the act of killing. He had simply been afraid to acknowledge it until now. Thinking back, he could imagine that his father had been there with him.

Watching.

Nodding along in approval.

Now you understand, don't you, Francis?

Yes. Now he understood why his father had hated him so much. For being such a worthless creature. But he wasn't any more, and he wondered what it might be like to look into his father's eyes now. Whether they could forgive each other for what they had once been in the light of what they had since become.

I'm like you, you see?

You don't have to hate me any more.

Francis shook his head. Jesus Christ, what was he thinking? What had happened with Neil had been a mistake. He needed to concentrate now, because he had Jake to care for.

To keep safe. To love.

Because that was what all children wanted and needed, wasn't it? To be loved and cherished by their parents. His heart ached at the thought.

They wanted that more than anything.

He sipped the last of his coffee and grimaced. It had gone cold, so he poured the dregs into the weeds at the side of the doorstep then went back inside, leaving the silent world out there for the silent one within.

Time to say goodnight to the boy.

No more mistakes.

And yet, as he headed upstairs to Jake, he kept thinking about killing Neil Spencer and how it had made him feel.

I'm like you, you see?

And he wondered if perhaps it hadn't been so terrible a mistake, after all.

Fifty-five

When you woke up from a nightmare, things were supposed to be okay.

Not like this.

When Jake had first opened his eyes, he had been confused. It was too bright in his room. The light was on, and that wasn't right. And then he'd realized this wasn't his bedroom at all, but some other child's, and that wasn't right either. But his head was so groggy that he couldn't make sense of it, beyond feeling a tightening knot of wrongness in his heart. The world had swum around him when he'd sat up. And then a memory had come back to him, and the knot had tightened more quickly, squeezing panic out into his whole body.

He was supposed to be at home. And he had been. But then there had been the man coming up the stairs, and then into his room, and then something on his face. And then . . .

Nothing.

Until he woke up here.

That had been perhaps ten minutes ago. At first, he had thought that this must be another nightmare – a new one – because it certainly felt like one. But he knew, even before he pinched himself in desperation, that it was too real for that. The fear was too strong. If he had been asleep, it would have woken him up by now. He remembered hearing about the man who had taken Neil Spencer and hurt him, and then he wondered if maybe this was a nightmare after all, just not the kind you got to wake up from. The world was full of bad men. Full of bad dreams that didn't always happen when you were asleep.

He glanced to one side now.

The little girl was here with him!

'You're –'

'Shhh. Keep your voice down.' She looked around the small room and swallowed hard. 'You mustn't let him know that I'm here.'

Which, of course, she wasn't – he knew that deep down. But he was so grateful to see her that he wasn't going to think about that. She was right, though. It wouldn't be okay for the man to hear him talking to anyone. It would be . . .

'Really bad?' he whispered.

She nodded seriously.

'Where am I?' he said.

'I don't know where you are, Jake. You're where you are, and so that's where I am too.'

'Because you won't leave me?'

'I'll never leave you. *Ever.*' She looked around again. 'And I'll do my best to help you, but I can't protect you. This is a very serious situation. You know that, don't you? It's a long, long way from being right.'

Jake nodded. Everything was wrong, and he wasn't safe, and it was suddenly too much.

'I want my daddy.'

Maybe that was a pathetic thing to say, but once it was out, he couldn't stop himself. So he whispered it again and again, and then he started to cry, thinking that if you wanted something hard enough then it might come true. It wouldn't, though. It felt like Daddy was the distance of the whole world away from him right now.

'Please try not to make any noise.' She rested her hand on his shoulder. 'You have to be brave.'

'I want my daddy.'

'He'll find you. You know he will.'

'I want my daddy.'

'Come on, Jake. Please.' Her hand tightened on him, half-way between reassuring and scared. 'I need you to calm down.'

He tried to stop crying.

'That's better.'

She moved her hand and was silent for a moment, listening.

'I think it's okay for now. So what we need to do is find out as much as possible about where we are. Because that might tell us how we can get out. Okay?'

He nodded. He was still scared, but what she was saying made sense.

He stood up and looked around the room.

The wall on one side of the room only went up to chest height before it began sloping inwards, the way that roofs did, so that meant he must be in an attic. He'd never been in an attic before. He'd always pictured them as dark, dusty places with bare floorboards and cardboard boxes and spiders, but this one was neatly carpeted, and the walls had been painted bright white, with grass drawn on at the bottom, and bees and butterflies fluttering above. It might have been nice, if it hadn't been harshly lit by a bare bulb in the ceiling, giving everything an unreal quality, as though bits of the drawings might start coming to life at any moment. There was an open chest full of soft toys against the sloping wall. A small wardrobe against another. He looked behind him. The bed was decked out in *Transformers* sheets that looked old and worn.

So he was in some other child's room. Except it didn't feel right or natural in here, as though it had never really been meant to be lived in by a real boy.

There was a door in the opposite wall. He walked across and pushed it open nervously. A small toilet and sink. There was a towel in a circular hoop and soap on the basin. He closed the door again. Turning around, there was a narrow corridor leading off from one corner of the room, but it only went a little way before there was another wall. He stepped into the space and found himself at the top of a dark staircase. At the bottom, there was a closed door.

A wooden handrail in the wall . . .

Jake stepped back quickly before he could see the bottom of the stairs properly. He ran back into the room and over to the bed.

No, no, no.

The stairs were almost exactly the same as the ones in the old house.

And that meant he must not see what was –

His heart was beating far too quickly now. It felt like he couldn't breathe.

'Sit down, Jake.'

He couldn't even do that.

'It's okay,' the little girl said gently. 'Just breathe.'

He closed his eyes and really concentrated. It was hard at first, but then the air started to get in, and his heart rate began to slow.

'Sit down.'

He did as she told him, and then she put her hand on his shoulder again, saying nothing for the moment beyond soft, reassuring hushing noises. When his breathing was under control again, she moved her hand, but still didn't speak. He could tell she wanted him to go down and check the door, but there was absolutely no way he could do that. Not ever. The stairs were out of bounds. It wouldn't matter, even if –

'It's probably locked anyway,' she said.

Jake nodded, feeling relieved – because she was right, and that meant he didn't need to go down there. What if the man made him, though? That was too much to think about. Too scary. He wouldn't be able to, and he didn't think this man would carry him.

'Do you remember what your daddy wrote to you that time?' the little girl asked.

'Yes.'

'Say it then.'

'Even when we argue we still love each other very much.'

'That's true,' she said. 'But this man, he isn't like that.'

'What do you mean?'

'I think what you have to do here is be very, very good. I don't think you can afford to have any arguments here.'

She was right, he thought. If he was bad here, it wouldn't be like with Daddy, where things were okay again afterwards. He thought if the Whisper Man got angry with him then things might end up very far from okay indeed.

The girl stood up suddenly.

'Get into bed. Do it quickly.'

She looked so frightened that he knew there wasn't enough time to ask why. He pulled the covers back and clambered in. As he lay down on the strange little bed, he heard a key turn in the lock downstairs.

The man was coming.

'Close your eyes,' she said urgently. 'Pretend to be asleep.'

Jake clenched his eyes shut. It was usually easy to pretend to be asleep – he did it at home all the time, because he knew Daddy would keep checking on him while he was awake, and he didn't want to be difficult. It was harder here, but as he heard the stairs creaking, he forced himself to breathe slowly and steadily, the way sleeping people did, and he relaxed his eyes a little, because sleeping people didn't squeeze them shut, and then –

And then the man was in the room.

Jake could hear the sound of gentle breathing, and then felt the man as a terrible presence close by. The skin on his face began to itch and he could tell the man was right next to the bed, looking down at him. Staring at him. Jake kept his eyes closed. If he was asleep then he couldn't be being bad, could he? There was no risk of an argument. He'd gone to bed like a good boy, without being told.

There were a few seconds of silence.

'Look at you,' the man whispered.

His voice sounded full of wonder, as though for some reason he hadn't expected to find a little boy up here. Jake forced himself not to flinch as a strand of hair was moved out of his face.

'So perfect.'

The voice was familiar, wasn't it? Jake thought so, but he wasn't sure. And he wasn't about to open his eyes to find out. The man stood up, then moved away quietly.

'I'm going to look after you, Jake.'

There was a click, and the darkness beyond his closed eyes deepened.

'You're safe now. I promise.'

Jake kept breathing slowly and steadily as the man went back down the stairs, and then as the door closed again and the key turned in the lock. Even then, he didn't dare open his eyes. He was thinking about what the little girl had said about Daddy. That he would find him.

Even when we argue we still love each other very much.

He believed that. It was one of the reasons why it didn't really matter when they argued. Daddy loved him and wanted him to be safe, and however angry they both might get, they would always end up back in the same place afterwards, as though none of it had ever happened.

But there was also a small part of him that knew he made Daddy's life very difficult indeed. That he was often a distraction rather than a help. He thought about how Daddy had gone out without him tonight. And he wondered if, wherever Daddy was right now, he might even be feeling glad he didn't have Jake to bother him any more.

No.

Daddy was going to find him.

Finally, Jake opened his eyes. The room was pitch black now, apart from the little girl, who was standing by the bed, perfectly illuminated. She was as bright as a candle flame, but the light didn't leave her edges and radiate around the tiny attic room.

'What are we doing, Jake?' she whispered.

'I don't know.'

'What are we being?'

Now, he understood.

'*Brave*,' he whispered back. 'We're being brave.'

Fifty-six

I lurched awake, immediately disorientated and confused by my surroundings. The room around me was dark and unfamiliar and full of strange shadows. Where was I? I had no idea, only that it wasn't right for me to be here. That wherever this was, I was supposed to be somewhere else, and that I desperately needed to be –

Karen's front room.

I remembered now. Jake was missing.

I sat very still on the settee for a moment, my heart beating hard.

My son had been taken.

The idea seemed unreal, but I knew it was true, and the tendrils of panic it brought were like a shot of adrenaline, knocking the leftover dregs of sleep away. How had I fallen asleep at all in this state? I was exhausted, but the terror humming inside me right now was already almost too much to bear. Perhaps I had been so tired and broken that my body had simply shut down for a while.

I checked my phone. It was nearly six o'clock in the morning, so I hadn't been asleep for long. Karen had gone to bed in the early hours. She'd been adamant about staying up with me to wait for news, but had also been so wiped out by the evening's events that I'd finally convinced her that one of us should grab some rest. Before she went upstairs, she'd told me to wake her up if there were any developments. There had been no messages or missed calls since. The situation hadn't changed.

Except that Jake had now been with whoever had taken him for a few more hours.

I stood up, flicked on the light switch and began pacing back and forth across the front room. If I didn't move, I felt sure my feelings would overwhelm me. The aching need to be with Jake kept smacking up against the knowledge that I couldn't reach him, and my heart was twisting and contorting inside me from the tension of that.

I kept picturing his face, the image so vivid that when I closed my eyes I imagined I could stretch out my hand and touch the soft skin of his cheek. He must be so scared right now, I knew. He would be lost and bewildered and terrified. He would be wondering where I was and why I hadn't found him.

If he was anything at all any more.

I shook my head. I couldn't think like that. DI Beck had told me last night that they were going to find him, and I had to allow myself to believe her. Because if not – if he was dead – then there was nothing beyond that. It would be the end of the world: a hammer blow to the head of life, scrambling all coherent thought. After that, there would only ever be static.

He is alive.

I imagined he was calling out to me, and that somehow I could hear it in my heart. But it didn't feel like imagination, more like his actual voice, crying out on a wavelength I was almost but not quite tuned into. He was alive. There was no way I could know that. But there had been so many inexplicable events recently that was it really so impossible?

It didn't matter if it was.

He was alive. I could still feel him, so he had to be.

And so I formed the words in my head, clearly and precisely, and then flung them out into the universe as hard as possible, hoping the message might reach him. That he might receive it in his own heart and feel the truth of it.

I love you, Jake.

And I am going to find you.

The house came to life shortly afterwards.

Karen had told me to help myself to anything in the kitchen. I was leaning on the counter in there, drinking black coffee and watching the dawn light creasing at the horizon, when the floorboards began creaking overhead. I set the kettle boiling again. A few minutes later, Karen came down, already dressed, but still looking exhausted.

'Anything?' she said.

I shook my head.

'You've not phoned them?'

'Not yet.' I was reluctant to. For one thing, without me bothering them, they could concentrate on finding Jake. For another, it also meant I didn't have to hear anything I might not want to. 'I will, but if there was anything they'd have called already.'

The kettle clicked off. Karen spooned instant coffee into a mug.

'What have you told Adam?' I said.

'Nothing. He knows you're here and that you slept on the settee, but I haven't said anything else.'

'I'll stay out of the way.'

'You don't have to.'

Even so, I kept to the kitchen after Adam came downstairs. Karen made him his breakfast and he ate it watching television in the front room. Outside the kitchen window, the day was already brightening. A new morning. I listened half-heartedly to whatever programme was playing in the other room, amazed by how life was carrying on. How it always does. You only notice how astonishing that is when a part of you gets left behind.

Karen gave me a key before she left with Adam.

'What time is the liaison officer getting here?' she said.

'I don't know.'

She put a hand on my arm. 'Call them, Tom.'

'I will.'

She looked at me for a moment, her face sad and serious, then she leaned in and kissed me on the cheek.

'I'll take the car. I'll be back soon.'

'Okay.'

When the front door closed, I fell back down on the settee. My phone was there, and yes, I could call the police, but I was sure that DI Beck would have phoned if there had been any news, and I didn't want to be told what I already knew.

That Jake was still out there.

That he was still in danger.

And so instead, I reached out for the item I'd brought with me from the house. My son's Packet of Special Things.

Even if I couldn't be with him physically, I could think of one way I could at least feel closer to him. I was conscious of the weight and importance of what I was holding. Jake had never told me I couldn't look inside it, but he hadn't needed to. His collection was for him, not for me. He was old enough to be entitled to his own secrets. And so, however tempted I had sometimes been, I had never violated that trust.

Forgive me, Jake.

I opened the clasp.

I just need to feel you close to me.

Fifty-seven

When Francis woke up, the house was silent.

For a while, he lay very still in bed, staring at the ceiling and listening. No sound at all. No movement that he could detect either. But he could sense the boy's presence directly above him, and the house felt fuller as a result. There was a feeling of potential to it.

There is a child up there.

The peace and quiet were encouraging, because of course that was how things should be. It meant that Jake understood the situation and was happy with it. Perhaps he was even excited to be in his new home.

Francis thought back to how easily the boy had settled in last night — already asleep and comfortable when he had gone up to check on him. With Neil Spencer, there had been so much crying and shouting at first that, even with the neighbours he did and didn't have, Francis had been glad for the soundproofing he'd installed behind the walls of the attic. With Neil, he'd been too patient, writing that period off as a tantrum, whereas now he understood that Neil had been bad from the start, and there had been no chance of it ending any other way.

Perhaps Jake really was different.

He isn't, Francis.

His father's voice.

They're all the same.

All hateful little bastards that disappoint you in the end.

Maybe that was true, but he shook the thought away for now. He had to give Jake a chance. Nowhere near as many chances as he'd given Neil Spencer, obviously, but an opportunity to enjoy and appreciate a happy home where he was looked after and truly cared for.

Francis went for a shower, which always made him feel vulnerable. With the door closed and the water loud in his ears, it was impossible to hear the rest of the house, and when he closed his eyes he could imagine something creeping into the bathroom and standing just outside the shower curtain. He sluiced the foam from his face quickly, and opened his eyes to see the water trailing away down the plughole. He'd had to unblock that after dealing with Neil. He could unblock it again if it came to it.

You know what you want to do.

His heart was beating a little too fast.

Downstairs, he prepared coffee and breakfast for himself, made the phone call he needed to make, then set about getting food for Jake. He wiped crumbs off the counter with his forearm, then put two crumpets into the toaster. Both were leftovers, with speckles of mould around the rims, but that was good enough. Francis had no idea what Jake liked to drink, but there was an open orange Fruit Shoot on the side, the one Neil hadn't had a chance to finish, and that would do as well.

Start as you mean to go on.

He carried the plate and plastic bottle upstairs, and then paused on the landing, pressing his ear against the door to the attic.

Silence.

But then he wasn't so sure. He thought he could hear something. Was Jake whispering to someone? If he was, it was so quiet that it was impossible for Francis to make out the words. Impossible even to be sure that it was happening.

Francis listened carefully.

Silence.

Then the whispering sound again.

It raised the hairs on his neck. There was nobody else up there – nobody that Jake could be talking to – and yet Francis suddenly had an irrational fear that there might be. That in bringing this child into his house, he had somehow brought someone or something else with him. Something dangerous.

Maybe he's talking to Neil.

But that was stupid; Francis didn't believe in ghosts. As a child, he would sometimes go near the door to his father's extension and imagine one of the little boys standing on the other side, bright and pale, waiting patiently. There had even been times when he'd thought he could hear breathing through the wood. But none of it had been real. The only ghosts that existed were in your head. They spoke through you, not to you.

He unlocked the door and opened it, then climbed the stairs slowly, not wanting to scare the child. But the whispering sound had stopped, and that annoyed him. He didn't like the idea that Jake was keeping secrets from him.

In the attic, the boy was sitting on the bed with his hands on his knees, and Francis was at least pleased to see that he had already dressed himself from the selection of clothes he'd provided in the drawers. Although he was less pleased to note that the chest of toys didn't appear to have been touched. Weren't they good enough, or something? Francis had kept those for a long time, and they meant a lot to him; the boy should have been grateful for the opportunity to play with them. He looked around for the pyjamas Jake had been wearing, and saw they were folded neatly in a pile on the bed. That was good. He would need them when it came to returning the boy later.

'Good morning, Jake,' he said brightly. 'I see you've got dressed already.'

'Good morning. I couldn't find my school clothes.'

'I thought you could have a day off.'

Jake nodded. 'That's nice. Is my daddy going to be picking me up?'

'Well, *that* is a complicated question.' Francis walked over to the bed. The boy seemed almost eerily calm. 'And one I don't think you need to worry about for the moment. All you need to know is that you're safe now.'

'Okay.'

'And that I'm going to look after you.'

'Thank you.'

'Who were you talking to?'

The boy looked confused. 'Nobody.'

'Yes, you were. Who was it?'

'Nobody.'

Francis felt a sudden urge to strike the boy in the face as hard as he could.

'We don't lie in this house, Jake.'

'I'm not lying.' Jake looked off to one side, and for a moment Francis had the odd sense that he was hearing a voice that wasn't really there. 'Maybe I was talking to myself. I'm sorry if I was. Sometimes that happens when I'm thinking about stuff. I get distracted.'

Francis was silent, considering the answer. It made a degree of sense. He sometimes got lost in a dream world too. Which meant that Jake was like him, and that was good on one level, because it gave him something to fix.

'We'll work on that together,' he said. 'Here, I brought you some breakfast.'

Jake took the plate and bottle and said thank you without being prompted, which was another good thing. Presumably he'd learned some manners from somewhere. But he also looked down at what he was now holding and didn't begin eating. The mould was still visible, Francis noticed. Clearly, it wasn't good enough for him.

It had been good enough for Francis as a boy.

'Are you not hungry, Jake?'

'Not right now.'

'You have to eat if you're going to grow up big and strong.' Francis smiled patiently. 'What would you like to do afterwards?'

Jake was silent for a moment.

'I don't know. Maybe I'd like to do some drawing.'

'We can do that! I'll help you with it.'

Jake smiled.

'Thank you.'

But he said Francis's name afterwards, and Francis went very still. The boy recognized him, of course, but a good home was no place for informality. A child needed discipline. There had to be a clearly delineated hierarchy.

'Sir,' Francis said. 'That's what you'll call me here. Do you understand?'

Jake nodded.

'Because in this house, we show respect for our elders. Do you understand?'

Jake nodded again.

'And we appreciate the things they do for us.' Francis gestured at the plate. 'I've gone to a lot of trouble. Eat your breakfast, please.'

For a moment, the eerie calm on Jake's face faded away and the boy looked like he was going to start crying. He stared off to one side again.

Francis's fist clenched at his side.

Just disobey me once, he thought.

Just once.

But then Jake looked back at him, the calm restored now, and picked up one of the crumpets. In the light up here, the mould was obvious around the edge.

'Yes,' he said. 'Sir.'

Fifty-eight

It felt like a transgression as I opened the Packet and looked inside at the contents.

It was an assortment of paper, material and trinkets, much of which overlapped with my own past and memories. The first thing I saw was a coloured wristband, pulled taut at the plastic clasp where Rebecca had stretched it over her hand rather than cut it off. It was from a music festival we'd been to in the early days of our relationship, long before Jake had even been thought of, never mind born. Rebecca and I had camped with friends – who had slowly drifted away over the subsequent years – and spent the weekend drinking and dancing, not caring about the rain or the cold. We had been young and carefree, and looking at it now, the wristband seemed like a talisman from a better time.

Excellent choice, Jake.

I recognized a small brown packet, and my vision blurred slightly as I opened it and tipped the contents into my palm. A tooth, so impossibly small that it felt like air on my skin. It was the first one Jake had lost, not long after Rebecca died. That night, I'd slipped money under his pillow, along with a note from the tooth fairy explaining that she wanted him to keep the tooth because it was special. I hadn't seen it again until now.

I replaced it carefully in its envelope, and then unfolded a piece of paper that turned out to be the picture I'd drawn for him: a crude attempt at the two of us standing side by side, with that message underneath.

Even when we argue we still love each other very much.

The tears came at that. There had been so many arguments over the years. Both of us so similar, and yet failing to understand each other. Both of us reaching out to the other and always somehow missing. But God, it was true. I loved him through every single second of it. I loved him so much. I hoped that, wherever he was right now, he knew that.

I worked my way through the other items. They felt sacred to the touch, but also sometimes oblique in their mystery. There were several more bits of paper, and while some of it made sense – one of the few party invitations he'd ever received – much of it was incomprehensible to me. There were faded tickets and receipts, scribbled notes Rebecca had made, all so apparently meaningless that I couldn't fathom why Jake had dignified them as being special. Maybe it was even the smallness and apparent insignificance of them that he liked. These were adult things that he lacked the experience to decode. But his mother had cared enough to keep them, and so perhaps, if he studied them for long enough, he might understand her better.

Then a much older sheet of paper – torn from a small ring-bound notebook, so that one end was frayed. I unfolded it and immediately recognized Rebecca's handwriting. A poem she'd written – presumably as a teenager, based on how faded the ink was. I started to read it.

> If you leave a door half open, soon you'll hear the
>   whispers spoken.
> If you play outside alone, soon you won't be going home.
> If your window's left unlatched, you'll hear him
>   tapping at the glass.
> If you're lonely, sad and blue, the Whisper Man will
>   come for you.

I read it again, the front room receding around me, then examined the writing once more to make sure. It was Rebecca's – I was certain of it. A less mature version than the one I was familiar with, but I knew my wife's handwriting.

This was where Jake had learned the rhyme.

From his mother.

Rebecca had known it when she was younger, and she had written it down. I did the maths in my head and realized that Rebecca would have been thirteen years old at the time of Frank Carter's crimes. Perhaps the murders he committed were the kind of thing that would have caught the attention of a girl that age.

But that didn't explain where she had heard the rhyme.

I put the note to one side.

There were a number of photographs in the Packet, all of them so old that they must have been taken with an old-fashioned camera. I remembered doing the same as a child on holidays, and my mother and I had also done what Rebecca and her parents apparently had with these, writing a date and description on the back.

2 August 1983 – two days old.

I turned the photograph over, and saw a woman sitting on a settee, cradling a baby against her. Rebecca's mother. I had known her briefly: an enthusiastic woman, with a sense of adventure she'd passed on to her daughter. Here, she looked desperately tired but excited. The baby was asleep, swaddled in a yellow woollen blanket. From the date, I knew it had to be Rebecca, even if it was impossible to believe she had ever been so small.

21 April 1987 – playing Poohsticks.

This one showed Rebecca's father standing on a slatted wooden bridge with lush green foliage in the background, holding her up so she could dangle a stick over the water rushing past below. She was facing the camera, grinning. Not yet four years old, but I could already see the woman she would become. Even back then, she had the smile that I could still picture so clearly in my head.

3 September 1988 – first day at school.

Here was Rebecca as a little girl, dressed in a blue jumper and pleated grey skirt, standing proudly in front of . . .

Rose Terrace school.

I stared at the photograph for several seconds.

The school was familiar by now, and the photograph was certainly of Rebecca – but those two things did not go together. And yet there was no mistaking either of them. Those were the same railings, the same steps. The word GIRLS was carved into the black stone above the door. And that was my wife, as a child, standing outside.

First day at school.

Rebecca had lived here in Featherbank.

I was stunned by the discovery. How had I not known that? We had visited Rebecca's parents on the south coast several times before they died, and while I was dimly aware that they'd moved when she was younger, that had certainly been *home* for her: where she had thought of herself as being from. But then, maybe that was simply where, as a teenager, her life had flowered – where the friends she made and the stories she gathered had been the ones she carried into adulthood. Because the evidence was right in front of me. Rebecca had lived here as a child – or at least close enough to attend the school.

Close enough to have heard the Whisper Man rhyme.

I thought about how focused Jake had been on our new house when he'd seen it on my iPad – how all the others in the search results had become invisible to him after viewing the photographs of it online. It couldn't be a coincidence. I quickly flicked through the other photographs that he had kept. Most were snaps that had been taken on holiday, but a few of the locations were more familiar: Rebecca eating an ice cream on New Road Side. High up on a swing in the local park. Riding a tricycle on the pavement by the main road.

And then —

And then our house.

The sight of it was as incongruous as the school photograph had been. Rebecca in a place where she simply shouldn't and couldn't be. Here, she was standing on the pavement outside our new home, one foot placed backwards on the driveway. The building behind, with its odd angles and misplaced windows, looked frightening, looming over the little girl who was just far enough over the threshold of the property to get the kudos for daring.

The local scary house. The kids would dare each other to go near it. Take photographs and things.

That was why the house had leapt out at Jake when he had seen it. Because he'd seen it before, with his mother standing in front of it.

And then I looked properly at Rebecca in the photograph. She appeared to be about seven or eight years old, and was wearing a blue-and-white checked dress that was high enough to see a graze on her knee. And it must have been a breezy day when it was taken, because her hair was swept out to one side.

She was the same girl Jake had drawn in the window with him in his picture.

I fought back tears again as I finally understood.

As ridiculous as it was, I'd almost begun to believe there was more to my son's invisible friend than his imagination alone. And I supposed that there was. Except he wasn't seeing ghosts or spirits. His imaginary friend was simply the mother he missed so much, conjured up as a little girl his own age. Someone who would play with him the way she always used to. Someone who could help him through the terrible new world he'd found himself in.

I turned the photograph over.

1 June 1991, it said. *Being brave.*

I remembered how, when we'd first moved in, he had been running from room to room, as though looking for someone, and my heart broke for him. I'd let him down so badly. It would have been hard for him regardless, but I could and should have done more to help him through it. Been more attentive, more present, less wrapped up in my own suffering. But I hadn't. And so he'd been forced to find solace with a memory instead.

I put the photograph down.

I'm so sorry, Jake.

And then, for what it was worth, I searched through the rest of the material he'd kept. Each piece hurt to look at. Because I was certain now that I had lost my son forever, and that this was as close as I would ever be to him again, for whatever was left of my life.

But then I unfolded the last piece of paper he'd kept. And when I saw what was there, I went still again. It took a moment to understand what I was seeing and what it meant.

And then I grabbed my mobile phone, already on my way to the front door.

Fifty-nine

'Slow down,' Amanda said. 'What have you found?'

She had been working non-stop through the night, and now – approaching nine o'clock in the morning – she could feel every minute of it. Her body was beyond weary. Her bones were aching and her thoughts were skittish and distracted. The last thing she really needed was Tom Kennedy gabbling down the phone at her, especially when he sounded as disjointed and out of it as she felt.

'I told you,' he said. 'A picture.'

'A picture of a butterfly.'

'Yes.'

'Can you please slow down and explain to me what that means?'

'It was in Jake's Packet of Special Things.'

'His what?'

'He collects things – keeps them. Things that have some kind of meaning for him. This picture was in there. It's one of the butterflies that were in the garage.'

'Okay.'

Amanda looked around the heaving operations room. It seemed as chaotic right now as the contents of her head. *Focus.* There was a picture of a butterfly. It clearly meant something to Tom Kennedy, but she still had no idea why.

'Jake drew this picture?'

'No! That's the point. It's too elaborate. It looks like something that a grown-up has done. He *was* drawing them, though, the evening after his first day at school. I think someone gave it to him to copy. Because how could he have seen them otherwise? They were in the garage, right?'

'The garage.'

'So he had to have seen them somewhere else. And this must be where. Someone drew it for him. Someone who'd seen them.'

'Someone who'd been in your garage?'

'Or the house. That's what you said, isn't it? That there were more people like Norman Collins who knew the body was there. That the man you think took Jake is one of these people.'

Amanda was silent for a moment, considering that. Yes, that was what they were thinking. And while Kennedy's discovery probably meant nothing, the night hadn't brought much else to go on either.

'Who drew the picture?' she said.

'I don't know. It looks recent, so I think maybe it was someone at the school. Jake brought it home after his first day, and that's why he was copying it.'

The school.

In the days following Neil Spencer's disappearance, they'd talked to everyone who'd had any degree of regular contact with the boy, and that had included the teaching staff. But there had been nothing suspicious about any of them. And of course, Jake had only been at the school for a few days. This picture, assuming it had any relevance at all, could have come from anywhere.

'But you're not sure?'

'No,' Tom said. 'But there's something else too. That evening, Jake was talking to someone who wasn't there. He does that, right? He has imaginary friends. Only this time he said it was "the boy in the floor". So how can he have known about that, along with the butterflies, unless someone talked to him about it?'

'I don't know.'

She resisted the urge to point out that it could simply be a coincidence, and that even if it wasn't, there was still no reason to focus on the school. Instead, she turned to what seemed to her a far more fucking pertinent issue right now.

'You didn't think to mention this before?'

The phone went silent. Maybe it was a low blow to have delivered: the man's son was missing, after all, and some things only made sense in hindsight. Pictures and imaginary friends. Monsters whispering outside windows. Adults didn't always listen hard enough to children. But if Tom Kennedy had told them about this earlier, and if she had listened to him, then things might be different right now. She wouldn't be sitting here exhausted, with Pete in hospital and Jake Kennedy missing. It was impossible to keep the accusation out of her voice.

'Tom? Why didn't you say anything?'

'I didn't know what it meant,' he said.

'Well, maybe it doesn't mean anything, but . . . oh, for fuck's sake, hang on a second.'

An alert had come through on her screen. Amanda opened the message. Liz Bamber, the family liaison officer, had arrived at Karen Shaw's home but nobody was answering the door. Amanda frowned and pushed the phone against her ear. Now that Tom had stopped talking, she could hear traffic in the background.

'Where are you?' she asked him.

'I'm on my way to the school.'

Christ. She leaned forward urgently.

'Don't do that, please.'

'But —'

'But nothing. It won't help.'

She closed her eyes and rubbed her forehead. What the

hell was he thinking? Except, of course, his son was missing and so he wasn't thinking properly at all.

'Listen to me,' she said. 'Listen right now. I need you to go back to Karen Shaw's house. There's an officer, Sergeant Liz Bamber, waiting for you there. I'm going to ask her to bring you to the department. We can discuss this picture then. Okay?'

He didn't reply. She could imagine him thinking it over. Torn between his determination to help Jake and the authority in her voice.

'Tom? Let's not make this any worse.'

'Okay.'

He hung up.

Damn it. She wasn't sure whether she believed him or not, but she supposed there was nothing she could do about it for now. In the meantime, she pinged a message back to Liz, relaying her instructions, and then leaned back in her chair and tried to rub some life into her face.

Another report was delivered to her desk. She opened her eyes again to find more useless witness statements. None of the neighbours had seen or heard anything. Somehow, Francis Carter – or David Parker, or whatever he was calling himself – had walked into a house, committed the attempted murder of an experienced officer, abducted a child, and disappeared without attracting any attention whatsoever. The luck of the Devil. Literally.

But not just luck, of course. Twenty years ago, he might have been a fragile, vulnerable little boy, but it was clear that the years since had seen him grow into a disturbed and dangerous man. One who was good at moving unnoticed and undetected.

She sighed.

The school, then, for what it was worth.

Let's take another look.

Sixty

Go back to Karen Shaw's house.

For a moment, it had felt like I might. DI Beck was police, after all, and my instinct was to do what the police told me. And her words had stung me. On top of every other way I'd failed, there was too much that I hadn't told the police, and the fact I'd been trying to protect Jake at the time didn't change the fact that I could have prevented this.

Which meant he was missing because of me.

I couldn't blame DI Beck for not taking me seriously in the light of that, but she hadn't seen what Jake had drawn. Someone had made that picture for him to copy, and they had done so recently.

So why had Jake kept it?

What was so special about it?

I remembered what had happened after that first day. The argument we'd had. The words he'd read on my computer screen. The distance between us. I could only think of one explanation for why that picture had ended up in his Packet of Special Things, and it was that Jake had decided to keep it because someone had shown him the kindness and support that I hadn't.

And it was that thought that made my decision for me.

I made it to the school just in time. The doors were still open, and there were a few parents and children milling around in the playground. I'd been considering going to the office – and would have done, if necessary – but the office had a security door that separated it from the rest of the school. Here, I could get straight into Jake's classroom if I needed to.

I ran through the gates, my heart pounding, straight past Karen, who was just leaving.

'Tom —'

'A minute.'

Mrs Shelley was standing by the open door, the last of the children trailing in past her. She looked alarmed at the sight of me. I imagined I looked as frantic as I felt.

'Mr Kennedy —'

'Who drew this?' I unfolded the sheet of paper and showed her the picture of the butterfly. 'Who drew it?'

'I don't —'

'Jake is *missing*,' I said. 'Do you understand? Someone has taken my son. Jake came home with this picture after his first day of school. I need to know who drew it.'

She shook her head. I was babbling too much information for her to process, and I fought down the urge to grab her and shake her and try to make her understand how important this was. And then I realized Karen was standing beside me, gently resting her hand on my arm.

'Tom. Try to calm down.'

'I am calm.' My gaze didn't leave Mrs Shelley as I tapped the picture of the butterfly. 'Who drew this for Jake? Was it another child? A teacher? Was it you?'

'I don't know!' She was flustered; I was scaring her. 'I'm not sure. It might have been George.'

My grip tightened on the paper.

'George?'

'He's one of our teaching assistants. But —'

'Is he here now?'

'He should be.'

She glanced back, and that was all the time it took for me to move past her into the corridor beyond.

'Mr Kennedy!'

'Tom –'

I ignored them both, glancing sideways into the cloak-room, where the children from Jake's class were hanging up their things – where Jake should have been – and then started running, rounding the corner ahead and entering the main hall, which was filled with children traipsing towards the classrooms on all sides. I dodged between them, then stopped in the middle, the hall spinning around me as I looked here and there, not knowing which room might be Jake's, and where George might be. I was in trouble here, I knew that deep down, but it didn't matter. Because if I didn't find Jake my life was over anyway, and if George was here then he couldn't be hurting –

Adam.

I recognized Karen's son putting his water bottle into a trolley at the far end of the hall, then walking through a door. I ran across, noticing one of the receptionists and an older man, the caretaker, heading down a far corridor towards the hall. Mrs Shelley must have called ahead. An intruder in the school would warrant that, I guessed.

'Mr Kennedy!' the receptionist shouted.

But I reached the classroom before they did, moving quickly inside, still just about self-aware enough not to barge the children in front of me out of the way. The room was a cacophony of colour, the walls painted yellow and adorned with what seemed like hundreds of laminated sheets: multi-plication tables; pictures of fruit and numbers; small, cartoonish figures performing tasks with their occupations written beside them. I looked across the sea of tiny tables and chairs, searching for an adult. An older woman was standing at the far end of the room, staring at me in confusion, clutching a register on a clipboard, but she was the only grown-up I could see.

And then I felt a hand on my arm.

I turned to find the old caretaker standing beside me, a firm expression on his face.

'You can't be in here.'

'All right.'

I fought the urge to shake his hand off me. There was no point – whoever George was, he wasn't here. But the frustration at that realization made me shake the man's hand off anyway.

'All right.'

Outside the classroom, the caretaker pointedly closed the door. Mrs Shelley was walking towards me, her phone in her hand. I wondered if she'd already used it to call the police. If so, maybe they'd start taking me seriously now.

'Mr Kennedy –'

'I know. I shouldn't be in here.'

'You're trespassing.'

'Put me on amber then.'

She started to say something, but then stopped herself. More than anything else, she looked concerned.

'You said Jake is missing?'

'Yes,' I said. 'Someone took him last night.'

'I'm sorry. I can't imagine what . . . obviously I understand that you're upset.'

I wasn't sure she could. The panic was like a live wire inside me now.

'I need to find George,' I said.

'He's not here.'

The receptionist. She was standing with her arms folded, and she looked considerably less forgiving than Mrs Shelley.

'Where is he?' I said.

'Well, I imagine he's at home. He called in sick a little while ago.'

The alarm went up a notch, because that couldn't be a coincidence. And it meant he was with Jake *right now*.

'Where does he live?'

'I'm not at liberty to reveal staff details.'

I thought about marching straight past her and getting into the main office. The caretaker was standing there, blocking the way, but the man was in his sixties and I could win that fight if I tried. There would be police and charges to answer then, but it would be worth it if I had enough time in the office to search the cabinets and find the information I wanted. But not much use to me if I couldn't. And not much use to Jake if I ended up in custody.

'You'll give it to the police?' I said.

'Of course.'

I turned and walked across the hall, back the way I'd come. They followed me, making sure I left. Once outside, the door was closed and locked behind me. The playground was almost entirely empty now, but Karen was waiting for me by the gate, an anxious look on her face.

'Thank fuck,' she said. 'You know you could have got arrested for that?'

'I need to find him.'

'This George? Who is he?'

'Classroom assistant. He drew something for Jake to copy – a butterfly. One of the ones they found with the boy's body in the garage.'

Karen looked sceptical. And hearing myself say it out loud again, I didn't blame her. But just as with Beck, it was impossible to make other people understand. The person who had taken Jake had known about the remains, so they would know about the butterflies and the boy in the floor. My son wasn't psychic. He was vulnerable and lonely, and he had to have learned about those things from someone. Someone with access to him.

Someone with access to him right now.

'The police?' Karen said.

'They don't believe me either.'

She sighed.

'I know,' I said. 'But I'm right, Karen. And I need to find Jake. I can't bear the thought of him being hurt. Of him not being with me. Of it all being my fault. I *need* to find him.'

She was silent for a moment, considering that. And then she sighed again.

'George Saunders,' she said. 'He's the only George listed on the school website. I got his address while you were inside.'

'Christ.'

'I told you,' she said. 'I'm good at finding things out.'

Sixty-one

'I don't think you should be drawing that.'

The little girl sounded nervous. She was pacing back and forth across the small attic bedroom. Every now and then, she'd stop and look down at his work. Before now, she hadn't said anything, but that was when he'd been drawing the house and its elaborate garden, the way he was supposed to, copying the intricate scene George had drawn for him. Before he'd given up and started drawing a battle scene instead.

Round and round, the circles went.

Force fields. Or portals. He couldn't decide which, and maybe it didn't matter. Something for protection or something for escape: either would do. Anything that would make him safe or take him away from here, from George, from the awful presence he could feel throbbing just out of sight at the bottom of the stairs. He wasn't sure George had even locked the door when he left earlier, and he thought the little girl wanted him to sneak down and try it. No way. Even with a clear path to the front door, there was no –

'Please stop, Jake.'

And he did. His hand was trembling so much he could hardly hold the pen. He was pressing it down so hard that the portal was beginning to cut through the paper.

'I've done it as well as I can,' he said. 'I can't do it.'

George had given him four sheets to work on, and he'd used three already trying to replicate the picture of the house and its garden. But it was too complicated. A part of him suspected George had done that deliberately – that it was a test, the same way that the disgusting breakfast had been. With the tests at school, you could tell that the teachers wanted you to pass, but he didn't think that George wanted that at all. When Mrs Shelley had put him on amber that first day, Jake thought that she probably hadn't wanted to. But with George, it felt like he was looking for any excuse to put him straight on to red.

So he'd tried. He'd done his best. And there was one sheet left, so he was drawing a battle. It was good to be creative, wasn't it?

Daddy always liked his pictures.

But he didn't want to think about Daddy right now. He started drawing again. Round and round. And maybe the little girl was right, but he couldn't stop himself now. It was all that was holding back the panic, even though his hand seemed to be totally out of control. So maybe this was panic, after all –

The door opened at the bottom of the stairs.

Round and round.

The sound of his footfall coming up.

And then there was so much ink on the sheet that the paper tore. The figure popped out.

You're safe now, Jake thought.

And then George entered the room.

He was smiling, but it was all wrong. Jake thought it was like George had put on a parent costume, except it was uncomfortable and didn't fit, and what he really wanted to do was take it off as quickly as possible. Jake didn't want to see what might be underneath. He stood up, his heart trembling as hard as his body was.

'Now then!' George walked across. 'Let's see how you've done.'

He stopped a short distance away. He could see the picture.

The smile disappeared.

'What the fuck is that?'

Jake blinked at the swear word. As he did, he realized there were tears in his eyes. He had started crying without even noticing, and the urge to let himself go – to break down and sob – was tremendous. It was only the look on George's face that stopped him. George wouldn't want real emotion. If Jake broke down, George would simply wait until he was finished and then give him something to really cry about.

'That's not what I told you to draw.'

'Show him the others,' the little girl said quickly.

Jake rubbed his eyes and then pointed down at the drawings he'd been told to do.

I want my daddy.

The words were bubbling up inside him, threatening to come out.

'I did my best,' he said. 'I couldn't do it.'

George looked down, examining the pictures blankly. The room was silent for a few seconds, the air humming with threat.

'These aren't good enough.'

Despite himself, the comment stung Jake. He knew he was no good at drawing, but Daddy always said he liked them anyway, because –

'I tried my best.'

'No, Jake. Evidently you *didn't*. Because you gave up, didn't you? You had another sheet to practise on, and you decided to do . . . this instead.' George waved his hand contemptuously at the battle scene. 'Things in this house cost money. We do not waste them.'

'Say sorry,' the little girl told him.

'I'm sorry, sir.'

'Sorry isn't good enough, Jake. Not good enough at all.'

George was staring down at him very gravely. It looked like he was struggling to control himself, because his hands were trembling. And Jake knew that the drawing was just an excuse. Deep down, George wanted to be angry with him. His hands were trembling because he was trying to decide if this was enough of an infringement to do so.

He made up his mind.

'And so you're going to have to be punished.'

And then George became totally still. The costume came away. Jake could see all the goodness and kindness falling away from him, as though they had only ever been pretend, things that could be discarded as easily as pulling off a T-shirt. There was a monster standing in front of him.

He was alone here with it.

And it was going to hurt him.

Jake retreated until the back of his calves were against the small bed.

'I want my daddy.'

'What?'

'Daddy! I want my daddy!'

George started to move closer, but then Jake jumped at the sound of an alarm somewhere in the house below, and George stopped where he was. Very slowly, he turned his head and stared back towards the staircase. The rest of his body remained angled towards Jake.

Not an alarm, Jake realized.

Someone was ringing the doorbell.

Sixty-two

On the first floor, seething with rage, Francis ducked quickly into his bedroom and pulled on a white robe. He was supposed to be sick, after all. He also forced himself to calm down enough to hide the rage he felt. It was good to keep it close to the surface, though. Accessible. He might need it.

The fucking doorbell.

Still ringing. He headed downstairs. It wouldn't be the police, he decided. If anything ever brought them to his door, their arrival would be considerably less polite even than this. He looked out through the spyglass in the front door, the bell ringing loudly and incessantly in his ear. The glass gave a fish-eye view of the steps and garden, and he saw Tom Kennedy leaning on the bell, a look of wild determination on his face. Francis recoiled slightly. How the fuck had Kennedy found him? What could have brought him here but not the police?

And why would he even want his son back?

Francis stepped back from the door. There was no need to answer it – surely Kennedy would go away soon. It was madness to think the man might stay there much longer.

And yet the doorbell continued ringing.

Francis thought again about the look on the man's face, and he wondered if perhaps Kennedy really was insane. If that was what losing a child, even one as blatantly uncared for as Jake, might do to a man.

Or if perhaps he'd misjudged things.

He rested his forehead against the door, bare inches from

the man outside now, feeling Kennedy's presence as a tingle in the front of his skull. Was it possible that Jake was loved, after all? That his father cared about him so much that his abduction had driven him to such extremes? The idea sent an explosion of loss and hopelessness through Francis. It wouldn't be fair if that was true. None of this was fair. Little boys didn't matter that much to anyone. He had known it all along, deep down, but he was certain of it now. They were worthless. They deserved nothing but –

The bell kept ringing.

'All *right*,' he called out loudly.

Kennedy must have heard him, but he didn't relent. Francis walked quickly into the kitchen, selected a small, sharp knife from the draining rack and slid it into the pocket of the robe. Finally, the bell stopped. Francis put the feeling of loss away inside him and brought the anger back up again, keeping it just out of sight.

Get rid of him.

Deal with the boy.

Then he put on his best face and went back to the door.

Sixty-three

'All *right*.'

I was so surprised when I heard the voice from behind the door that I forgot to take my finger off the bell.

I'd given up expecting anyone to answer. By that point, it was more that I had nowhere else to be and nothing else to do. I wasn't even sure how long I'd been standing there. I had just become intent on ringing that bell, as though by holding it down I could somehow save Jake.

I stepped back, then turned around and looked at Karen. She was waiting in the car, watching me anxiously, her phone pressed to her ear. She'd insisted on phoning the police, so I'd left her with DI Beck's details. She stared back at me now, shaking her head.

I turned back to the door, with no idea what was going to happen next. I'd been running on adrenaline since looking through Jake's Packet of Special Things, and now that I was here, I had no idea what the hell I was going to say to George Saunders, or what I was even going to do.

A key in the lock.

The memory of seeing my father last night came back to me. The injuries that had been inflicted on him. He had been a fit, capable man, and yet whoever had attacked him had overwhelmed him easily. He had been unarmed, and perhaps taken by surprise, but even so. What use was I going to be?

I hadn't thought this through well enough.

The door opened.

I expected it to be on a chain, with Saunders only half visible, perhaps peering guiltily out. But he opened it fully and confidently, and I was immediately taken aback by the sight of him. He was average-looking in every way, and while I guessed he was in his twenties, he looked much younger. There was a soft, childlike sense to him. I didn't think I'd ever seen anyone appear so harmless.

'George Saunders?' I said.

He nodded sleepily, then pulled the white robe he was wearing more tightly around him. His black hair was messy and unkempt, and the expression on his face suggested that he had only just woken up, and was both bewildered and slightly irritated about it.

'You work at Rose Terrace school, right?'

He squinted at me.

'Yeah. Right.'

'My son goes there. I think you might teach him.'

'Oh. Well, no, I don't teach. I'm just an assistant.'

'Year Three. Jake Kennedy.'

'Right. Yeah, I think he's in my class. But what I meant is, it's his teacher you'd need to talk to.' He frowned, but more out of sleepy confusion than suspicion, as though the thought had only just occurred to him. 'And at the school, too. How did you even get my address?'

I looked at him. His face was pale, and he was shivering slightly despite the heat of the morning. He really did *look* ill. And yes, slightly perturbed by my presence, but not unduly concerned about it being me in particular. Just uneasy about a parent turning up on his doorstep.

'It's not really about his schoolwork,' I said.

'What is it about then?'

'Jake is missing.'

Saunders shook his head, not understanding.

'Someone *took him*,' I said. 'Just like Neil Spencer.'

'Oh Jesus.' He looked genuinely aghast at that. 'I'm so sorry. When did this . . . ?'

'Last night.'

'Oh Jesus,' he said again, then closed his eyes and rubbed his forehead. 'That is awful. *Awful*. I haven't really had much to do with Jake, but he seems like such a nice kid.'

He is, I thought.

But I also noted Saunders' use of the present tense, and began doubting my earlier suspicions. The evidence that had led me here was paper-thin, and in the flesh Saunders looked like someone who wouldn't hurt a fly. Couldn't, even. And he seemed genuinely surprised by the news that Jake had been abducted – the man was clearly upset.

I held up the picture of the butterfly.

'Did you draw this for him?'

Saunders peered at it.

'No. I've never seen that before.'

'You didn't draw this?'

'No.'

He took a step back. I was holding the sheet of paper up, my hand trembling, and he was responding exactly the way anyone would when faced with a man like me on their doorstep.

'What about the boy in the floor?' I said.

'What?'

'The *boy in the floor*.'

He stared at me, obviously horrified now. It was the kind of horror that came from gradually understanding he was being accused of something. And if he was faking it, then he was a phenomenal actor.

This is a mistake, I thought.

But even so.

'Jake!' I shouted past him.

'What are you – ?'

I leaned up against the door frame, almost chest to chest with Saunders now, and shouted again.

'Jake!'

No answer.

After a few seconds of silence, Saunders swallowed. The noise it made was so hard that I could hear it.

'Mr . . . Kennedy?'

'Yes.'

'I can understand you're upset. I *really* can. But you're scaring me. I don't know what's going on, but I really think you should go now.'

I looked at him. The fear in his eyes was obvious, and I thought it was real. His whole body was frozen in a flinch. He was the kind of timid man you could force down into a huddle just by raising your voice, and it seemed I was halfway there.

Saunders was telling the truth.

Jake wasn't here, and I –

And I –

I shook my head, taking a step back myself.

Lost now. Completely lost. It had been a mistake coming here. I needed to do as I'd been told and get back to Karen's house before I could do any more damage. Before I could fuck things up any more than I already had.

'I'm sorry,' I said.

'Mr Kennedy –'

'I'm sorry. I'm going now.'

Sixty-four

Wait here.

What choice did he have? None.

Jake sat on the bed, gripping the edges with his hands. When George had left, he'd locked the door at the bottom of the stairs. The bell had still been ringing then. The sound had continued for another minute or so, before finally stopping, and so Jake assumed that George must have answered it, and was probably still talking to whoever was at the door. Otherwise, surely he would be back up here? Doing what he'd been planning to do before whoever it was called round.

Maybe not if I'm good, he thought.

Maybe if he waited here then George would like him again.

'You know that's not true, Jake.'

He turned his head. The little girl was sitting on the bed beside him, and she had her serious face on again. But it was different now. She looked scared, but also full of quiet determination.

'He's a bad man,' she said, 'and he wants to hurt you. And he's going to hurt you if you let him.'

Jake wanted to cry.

'How am I supposed to stop him?'

She smiled softly, as though they both knew the answer to that question. *No, no, no.* Jake looked over at the corner of the room, where the short corridor led to the stairs. There was no way he could go down there. He couldn't face what might be waiting at the bottom.

'I can't do that!'

'But what if it's Daddy at the door?'

Which was exactly what Jake had hardly been daring to think. That maybe Daddy did want to find him after all, and that somehow he had, and that he was downstairs now.

It was too much to hope for.

'Daddy would come up and get me.'

'Only if he knows you're here. He might not be sure.' She thought about it. 'Maybe you need to meet him halfway.'

Jake shook his head. It was too much to ask.

'I can't go down there.'

The little girl was silent for a moment. Then, 'Tell me about the nightmare,' she said quietly.

Jake shut his eyes.

'It's about finding Mummy, isn't it?'

'Yes.'

'And you've never told anybody about it before, not even Daddy. Because you're so scared of it. But you can tell me now.'

'I can't.'

'Yes, you can,' she whispered. 'I'll help you. You walk into the front room, and the house feels empty. Daddy's not there, is he? He's still outside. So you walk across the front room.'

'Don't,' Jake said.

'It's sunny.'

He scrunched his eyes shut, but it didn't help. He could remember the angle of sunlight through their old back window.

'You walk so slowly, because you can feel that something is wrong. Something is missing. Somehow, you already know that.'

And now he could see the back door, the wall, the handrail.

All revealed in stages.

And then –

'And then you see her,' the little girl said. 'Don't you?'

This wasn't a nightmare, so there was no way to wake up and stop the image from appearing. Yes, he saw Mummy. She was lying at the bottom of the stairs, her head tilted to one side and her cheek resting against the carpet. Her face was pale, even slightly blue, and her eyes were closed. It had been a heart attack, Daddy told him afterwards, which didn't make sense because that was something that happened to older people. But Daddy said that sometimes it happened to younger people too, maybe if their hearts were too . . .

And then he'd trailed off and started crying. They both had.

But that was afterwards. In that moment, he'd just stood there, understanding what he was seeing in a way his mind couldn't make sense of, because the feelings were all too big.

'I saw her,' he said.

'And?'

'And it was Mummy.'

Just Mummy. Not a monster. The monstrous thing was how it had made him feel and what it meant. In that moment, it had seemed like a part of him was lying there instead, and that he would never have the words to describe the world of emotions that exploded inside him, as huge as the way the Big Bang had made the universe.

But it had just been Mummy. He didn't need to be scared of her.

'We need to go downstairs now.' The little girl put her hand on his shoulder. 'There's nothing to be frightened of.'

Jake opened his eyes and looked at her. She was still there, and somehow more real than ever, and he didn't think he had ever seen anyone who loved him so much.

'Will you go with me?' he said.

She smiled.

'Of course I will. *Always*, my gorgeous boy.'

Then she stood up, and reached out and took his hands, pulling him to his feet.

'What are we being?' she said.

Sixty-five

'I'm sorry. I'm going now.'

I wasn't even sure who I was apologizing to. Saunders, I supposed, for arriving on his doorstep, and accusing him, frightening him, without any real evidence. But the apology also went deeper than that. It was to Jake. To Rebecca. To myself, even. Somehow, I'd let all of us down.

I looked back at Karen. She was still holding the phone to her ear, but she shook her head at me again.

'Look,' Saunders said carefully. 'It's okay. Like I said, I know you're upset. And I can't imagine what you must be going through right now. But . . .'

He trailed off.

'I know,' I said.

'I'm happy to talk to the police. And I hope you find him. Your son. I hope this is all some kind of mistake.'

'Thank you.'

I nodded, and I was about to head back to the car when I heard a noise coming from somewhere in the house behind me. I stopped. Then turned back to Saunders. It was a distant hammering sound, and someone was shouting, but so indistinct that it was barely audible.

Saunders had heard it too. The expression on his face had changed while my back had been turned, and he no longer looked quite so ill or soft or harmless. It was as though the humanity had only ever been a disguise, and now it had fallen away and I was facing something entirely alien.

He closed the door quickly.

'Jake!'

I got up the step just in time to wedge my leg in. The door slammed agonizingly on the side of my knee, but I ignored the pain and pushed against it, bracing one hand inside the door jamb, and then my back against the wood, heaving as hard as I could. Saunders was grunting on the other side, pressing back against me. But I was bigger than him, and the sudden burst of adrenaline was adding to my weight.

Jake was somewhere inside this house, and if I didn't reach him then Saunders was going to kill him. I knew Saunders couldn't escape from this. He wouldn't try. But if he managed to keep me out, he could still hurt my son.

'Jake!'

Suddenly the resistance was gone.

Saunders must have stepped away. The door shot open, and I barrelled into the front room, half barging into him, half falling. He hit me half-heartedly in the side as I collided with him, and then he tumbled backwards and we landed hard, me on top of him, his head tilted to one side against the floorboards, my right forearm across his jaw. My left hand was pinning his right arm to the floor at the elbow. His body heaved upwards, trying to fight me off, but I was larger than him and I was suddenly sure that I could hold him.

But then he lurched up against me again and I felt his hand at my side, where he'd hit me so ineffectively, and I registered the pain there. Not overwhelming in itself, but sickening and awful. Deep, internal, wrong. I glanced down and saw the ball of his fist still pressed against me, and then the blood that was beginning to soak into the white robe he was wearing.

The knife he was holding was embedded somewhere inside me, and when he rose up against me, screaming in rage, my whole world shrieked with him.

Jake!

I wasn't sure if I shouted it or simply thought it.

Saunders was baring his teeth inches from my face, spitting and trying to bite me. I pressed down on him, my vision beginning to fragment into tiny stars at the edges. And then, when he lurched up again, the blade moved with him, and those stars exploded. If I let him up now, he would kill me and then kill Jake, so I pressed down harder on him, and the knife moved again, and that explosion of stars blurred into white light that gradually filled my vision. But I couldn't let him up. I would hold him down as he killed me.

Jake.

The hammering and shouting was still coming from somewhere above me. I could make out the words now. My son was up there, and he was calling for me.

Jake.

The stars disappeared as the light overwhelmed me.

I'm sorry.

Sixty-six

Adrenaline had a way of waking you up.

Francis Carter, Amanda thought.

Or David Parker, or whatever he was calling himself.

Back at the department, she'd worked her way through the school's employees, looking for a male in his late twenties. There were four men working there, including the caretaker, and only one of them was an approximate age match. George Saunders was twenty-four years old, while Francis Carter would be twenty-seven by now. But when it came to buying a fake identity, the age only needed to be approximate.

Saunders had been spoken to after Neil Spencer went missing, and the interview hadn't sounded any alarm bells. She had read the transcript. Saunders had been erudite and convincing. He had no alibi for the exact period of the abduction, but that wasn't so surprising. No record. No warning signs at all. Nothing to pursue.

Except that a new search now revealed that the real George Saunders had died three years earlier.

Reality felt heightened as Amanda drove into the street. She parked at the top, outside a property that appeared to be derelict, a little way back from the target house, and then a van pulled in behind her, with two more vehicles approaching from the opposite direction and coming to a stop a short distance down the hill. All of them kept away from the eyeline of the house, so that if Saunders were to look out of his window right now, he would see nothing. That was important. The last thing they needed was for him to barricade himself in and for them to end up dealing with a hostage situation.

Not that it would come to that, she thought. If he was cornered, Saunders would simply kill Jake Kennedy.

Her phone had been buzzing the whole way. She took it out now. Four missed calls. The first three were all from an unknown number. The fourth was from the hospital. Which meant there was news about Pete.

Something fell away inside her. She remembered how determined she had been last night – that she would not lose Pete, that she would find Jake Kennedy. How stupid to think like that. But she put those feelings away for now, gathering herself together, because there was only one of those things she could do something about right now.

I'm not losing another child on my watch.

She got out of the car.

The street was silent. It felt almost wholly deserted here, an area of the city that was slowly dying in its sleep. She heard the side of the van behind her rumbling open, and then the scuff of shoes on tarmac. Down the hill, officers were congregating on the pavement. The plan had been that she would go in first, ostensibly alone, and try to get Francis to open the door and allow her inside the property. At that point, there would be a flurry of activity, and he would be taken down in seconds.

But then Amanda saw Karen Shaw's car parked up ahead. And as she walked down the street, she realized the door to George Saunders' house was open, and she began running.

'*Everybody, move!*'

Through the front garden, up the path, and then through the open door into what turned out to be a living room. There was a mess of bodies on the floor, blood everywhere, but it wasn't immediately obvious who was hurt and who wasn't.

'Help me, please.'

That was Karen Shaw. Amanda moved over. Shaw was kneeling on one of Francis Carter's arms, trying to hold it still. Between them, Tom Kennedy was pressing down on Francis Carter. Carter himself was pinned in place, eyes shut tight, desperately attempting to move, even though the weight of the two of them together was enough to keep him in place.

From somewhere above them, Amanda could hear a hammering noise and shouting.

'Daddy! Daddy!'

Officers swarmed in past her, a dozen bodies overtaking the scene.

'Don't move him,' Karen shouted. 'He's been stabbed.'

Amanda could see the spread of blood soaking into Carter's bathrobe. Tom Kennedy was completely still. She couldn't tell if he was alive or not.

If she had lost him today as well . . .

'Daddy! Daddy!'

That, at least, she could still do something about.

She ran to the stairs.

PART SIX

Sixty-seven

Pete remembered hearing that your life flashed before your eyes when you died.

It was true, he realized now, but of course it also happened the whole time you were alive. How *fast* things went, he thought. As a boy, he had marvelled at the lifespans of butterflies and mayflies, some of them alive for only days or even hours, and it had seemed unimaginable. But he understood now that it was true for everything – that it was only a matter of perspective. The years accumulated faster and faster, like friends linking arms in an ever-expanding circle, reeling faster and faster as midnight approached. And then, suddenly, it was done.

Unfurling backwards.

Flashing before your eyes, as it did for him now.

He looked down at a child, sleeping peacefully in a room barely lit by the soft light from the hall. The little boy was lying on his side, his hair swept back behind his ear, with one hand clutching the other in front of his face. Everything was calm. A child, warm and loved, was sleeping safely and without fear. An old book, its pages splayed open, lay on the floor by the bed.

Your daddy liked these books when he was younger.

And then here was a quiet country lane. It was summertime and the whole world was in bloom. He looked around, blinking. The hedgerows on either side of the warm tarmac were lustrous and thick with life, while the trees reached together overhead, their leaves forming a canopy that coloured the world in shades of lime and lemon. Butterflies flickered across the fields. How beautiful it was here. He had been too focused to notice that before — too busy looking without looking. He saw it so clearly now that he wondered how he could have been so distracted as to miss it then.

Here — a flash — was a scene so abhorrent that his mind refused to countenance it. He heard the nasal buzz of the flies that were darting mindlessly through the wine-stained air, and he saw an angry sun staring down at the children on the floor that were not children any more, and then somehow, mercifully, time reversed more quickly. He stepped backwards. A door swung shut. A padlock clicked.

Nobody should have to see hell even once.

There was no need to look inside it ever again.

Here was a beach. The sand underneath his legs was as soft and fine as silk, hot from the bright white sun that seemed to fill the sky above. In front of him, the sea was a froth of silver feathers. A woman was sitting so close to him that he could feel the tiny hairs on her bare upper arm tingling against his own skin. With her other hand she was holding out a camera, pointing it at them both. He did his best to smile, squinting against the light. He was so happy right then — he hadn't realized it at the time, but he was. He loved her so much, but for some reason he had never known how to articulate that. He did now; it was so simple. When the photograph was taken, he turned his head to look at the woman, and he gave himself permission to feel the words as well as speaking them.

'*I love you.*'

She smiled at him.

Here was a house. It was squat and ugly and throbbing with hatred, much like the man he knew resided within, and while he didn't want to go inside, he had no choice. He was small – a child again now – and this was his home. The front door rattled and the carpet breathed out dust beneath his feet. The air was thick and grey with resentment. In the front room, a bitter old man sat in an armchair by an open fire, his paunch pushing out so far against the dirty jumper that it rested on his thighs. There was a sneer on the man's face. There was always that, whenever there was anything at all.

What a disappointment he was. It was clear to him how useless he was, how nothing he did was ever good enough.

But it wasn't true.

You don't know me, he thought.

You never did.

As a child, his father had been a language he was unable to speak, but he was fluent now. The man wanted him to be someone else, and that had been confusing. But he could read the whole book of his father now and he knew that none of it had ever been about *him*. His own book was separate, and always had been. He had only ever needed to be himself, and it had just taken time – too much time – to understand that.

Here was a child's bedroom, windowless and small, only twice the width of the single bed.

He lay down, breathing in deeply the suddenly familiar smell of the sheets and pillow. The comfort blanket from his cot was tucked between the mattress and the wood. Instinctively, he reached out for it, curling a corner of the soft cloth in his hand, bringing it to his face, closing his eyes and breathing in.

This was the end, he realized. The tangle of his life had been unpicked and set out like a tapestry before him, and he saw and understood it clearly now, all of it so obvious in hindsight.

He wished he could have it again.

Here was a door opening. An angle of light from the shabby hallway fell over Pete, and then a different man walked tentatively into the room, moving slowly and carefully, limping slightly, as though he had been hurt and his body was tender in some way. The man approached the bed and, with difficulty, knelt down beside it.

After watching Pete sleeping for a time, unsure what he was going to do, the man finally came to a decision. He leaned across and embraced him as best he could.

And even though Pete was all but lost in deeper dreams by then, he sensed the embrace, or at least imagined he did, and for a moment he felt understood and forgiven. As though a cycle had been completed, or something found.

As though a missing piece of him had finally been returned.

Sixty-eight

The letter was waiting for Amanda when she got home, but she didn't open it straight away.

It was obvious from the HMP Whitrow stamping who it was going to be from, and she was unwilling to face that right now. Frank Carter had haunted Pete for twenty years – taunting him, playing with him – and she was damned if she was going to read him gloating about that on the day Pete died. Not that Carter could have known when he sent this, of course – but then, the man seemed to know everything, somehow.

Fuck him, though. She had better, more important things to do.

She left the letter on the dining-room table, poured herself a large measure of wine, and then raised the glass.

'Here's to you, Pete,' she said quietly. 'Safe journey.'

And then, despite herself, she started crying – which was ridiculous. She'd never been prone to tears. Had always taken pride in being calm and dispassionate. But the investigation had changed her. And there was nobody here to see it right now, she supposed, so she decided it was fine to let herself go. It felt good. She wasn't even crying for Pete, she realized after a while, so much as allowing all the emotion of the past few months to come pouring out.

Pete, yes. But also Neil Spencer. Tom and Jake Kennedy.

All of it.

It was as though she had been holding her breath for

weeks, and the sobbing now was a deep exhalation she had desperately needed.

She drank the wine and poured another glass.

Having spoken to Tom, and knowing what she did now, she imagined getting drunk probably wasn't what Pete would have wanted. But he would also have understood. In fact, she could imagine the understanding look he would be giving her if he could see her right now – it would be just like some of the others he'd given her. A look that said: *I've been there, and I get it, but it's not something we can talk about, can we?*

He'd understand, all right. The Whisper Man case had taken up the last twenty years of his life. After everything that had happened, she imagined it might end up doing the same to her if she wasn't careful. Perhaps that was all right, though – maybe that was the way it was even meant to be. Some investigations stayed with you, sinking their claws in and hanging on, so that you would always have to drag them behind you no matter how hard you tried to dislodge them. Before this, she had always imagined she would be impervious to that – she would be a climber like Lyons, not weighed down the way Pete had been – but she knew herself a little better now. This was something she was going to be carrying for a long time. That was the kind of copper it had turned out she was. Not the sensible kind at all.

So be it.

She downed the wine and poured a third.

There were positives to cling to, of course, and despite everything, it was important to do that. Jake Kennedy had been found in time. Francis Carter was in prison. And she would always be the woman who had caught him. She had worked herself to the bone, doing everything she could, and she had not been found wanting. When the hour came, she had filled every fucking second of it.

Eventually, she steeled herself and opened the letter. She was drunk enough by then not to care any more what Frank Carter might have to say. What did he matter? Let the fucker write what he wanted. His words would bounce off her, and he would still be rotting where he was afterwards, and she would still be here. It wasn't like with Pete. Carter had nothing to hold over her. No way of hurting her.

A single sheet of paper, almost entirely empty.

Then the words Carter had written:

If Peter can still hear, tell him thank you.

Sixty-nine

Francis sat in his cell, waiting.

He had spent these two weeks in prison in a state of anticipation, but something in the world had clicked today, and he had known that it was finally time. Past lights out, he was sitting patiently on his bunk in the darkness, still fully dressed, his hands resting on his thighs. He listened to the metallic echoes and the catcalls of the other convicts gradually dying away around him. He stared almost blindly at the rough brickwork of the opposite wall.

Waiting.

He was a grown man, and he was not afraid.

They had done their best to make him so, of course. When he'd first been brought to the prison, the guards had been professional but also either unable or unwilling to hide their hatred for him. Francis had killed a little boy, after all, and – perhaps even worse in their eyes – a police officer. The body search had been overly robust. Because he was on remand, he was supposed to be separated from the convicted prisoners, but there had been frequent bangs and clatters against his door, and threats hissed and whispered from the walkway outside. Beyond the occasional call to knock it off, the guards had sounded bored and done little to stop it. Francis thought they enjoyed it.

Let them.

He waited. It was warm in the cell, but his skin was singing, his body was trembling slightly. But not with fear.

Because he was a grown man. And he was not afraid.

The first time he'd seen his father was a week ago, in the prison canteen. Even at mealtimes, Francis was kept away from the other inmates, and so he had been seated at a table by himself, with a guard watching over him as he ate the slop that had been provided. Francis thought they gave him the most disgusting portions they could, but if that were the case then the joke was on them. He had eaten much worse. And he had survived far harsher treatment than this. Spooning up a mouthful of cold mashed potato, he had told himself for the hundredth time that this was all just a test. Whatever they threw at him, he would endure. He would earn what –

And then he had turned his head and seen his father.

Frank Carter walked through the door to the canteen as if he owned the whole prison, ducking slightly, his presence immediately immense in the hall. A mountain of a man. The guards, most of them shorter than him by a head, kept a respectful distance. A group of other inmates flanked him, all of them wearing orange prison uniforms, but his father stood out among them, clearly the leader of the group. He did not appear to have aged. To Francis, his father seemed almost preternaturally large and powerful, as though, if he wanted, he could walk through the walls of the prison and emerge unscathed, covered with dust.

As though he could do anything.

'Hurry up, Carter.' The guard prodded him in the back.

Francis ate the mash, thinking that the man could soon be made to regret doing that. Because his father was king in here, and that made Francis royalty. As he ate, he stole surreptitious glances over at the table where his father was holding court. The prisoners there were laughing, but it was too far away for Francis to tune out the other noises and hear what they were saying. His father wasn't laughing, though. And while Francis thought some of the others occasionally looked his way, his father never did. No, Frank Carter just ate quickly, occasionally dabbing at his beard with a napkin but otherwise staring straight ahead of him as he chewed, as though he had serious business on his mind.

'I said *hurry up.*'

In the intervening days, Francis had seen Carter on a handful of other occasions, and each time it was the same. He was impressed anew by the size of the man – always towering over the figures around him, like a father surrounded by children. And each time, he had seemed entirely unaware of Francis. Unlike the coterie of fawning men around him, he never even looked in Francis's direction. But Francis *felt* him constantly. Lying alone in his cell at night, his father was a solid presence, throbbing somewhere just out of reach beyond the thick door and the steel walkways.

The anticipation had built steadily until, today, he had known the moment was coming.

I am a grown man, Francis thought now.

And I am not afraid.

The prison had fallen as silent as it ever did. There were still distant noises, but his own cell was so quiet that he could hear himself breathing.

He waited.

And waited.

Until, finally, he heard the footfall approaching on the walkway outside, the sound simultaneously both cautious and excited. Francis stood up, his heart beating with hope, listening more carefully now. It was more than one person. There was soft laughter followed by hushing sounds. The rattling of keys. Which made sense – his father would have access to anything he wanted in here.

But there was also something almost taunting about the noise.

Outside the cell, someone whispered his name.

Fraaaaancis.

A key turned in the lock.

And then the door opened.

Frank Carter stepped into the cell, the solid bulk of the man filling the doorway. There was just enough light for Francis to be able to see his father's face, to see the expression there, and —

And —

He was a child again.

And he was terrified.

Because Francis remembered the expression on his father's face only too well. It was the look he had always worn when he would come to Francis's bedroom at night and order him to get up, to get downstairs, because there was something he needed to see. Back then, the hatred he saw had been constrained by necessity and directed at others in his place. But here and now, finally, there was no longer any need for constraint.

Help me, Francis thought.

But there was nobody to help him here. No more than there had been anyone all those years ago. There was nobody to call out to who would come.

There never had been.

The Whisper Man walked slowly towards him. With his hands trembling, Francis reached down and took hold of the bottom of his T-shirt.

And then he pulled it up to cover his face.

Seventy

'Are you all right, Daddy?'

'What?'

I shook my head. I was sitting by Jake's bed, holding *Power of Three* open at the last page, staring into space. We had just finished the book, and then I had got distracted. Lost in thought.

'I'm fine,' I said.

From Jake's expression, it was clear that he didn't believe me – and he was right, of course. I was a long way from being fine. But I didn't want to tell him about seeing my father for the last time at the hospital that day. In time, perhaps I would, but there was still so much he didn't know, and I wasn't sure I had the words yet to explain any of it, or to make him understand.

Nothing ever changed on that level.

'Just this book.' I closed it and ran my hand thoughtfully over the cover. 'I haven't read it since I was a kid, and I guess it brought back memories. Made me feel a bit like I was your age again.'

'I don't believe you were ever my age.'

I laughed. 'Hard to believe, isn't it? Cuddle?'

Jake pulled the sheet away, then clambered out. I put the book down as he perched on my knee.

'*Carefully.*'

'Sorry, Daddy.'

'It's okay. Just reminding you.'

It had been nearly two weeks since my injuries at the hands

of George Saunders, a man I now knew had once been called Francis Carter. I still wasn't sure how close I'd come to dying that day. I couldn't even remember most of it. A lot of what happened that morning was a blur, as though the panic I had been experiencing had blanked it all out and stopped me from retaining it. The first day in hospital was much the same; my life only swam back into focus slowly. I was left now with bandages across one side of my body, an inability to put my weight down properly on that foot, and a handful of impressions that were little more than memories of a dream: Jake shouting for me; the desperation I had felt; the *need* to reach him.

The fact that I had been ready to die for him.

He hugged me now, very gently. Even so, I had to do my best not to wince. I was grateful that he didn't need me to carry him up and down the stairs in this house. After what had happened, I'd been worried he might be more scared than ever, and that the behaviour might return, but the truth was that he'd dealt with the horrors of that day far better than I'd imagined. Perhaps better than I had.

I hugged him back as best I could. It was all I could ever do. And then, after he'd clambered back into bed, I stood in the doorway, watching him for a moment. He looked so peaceful, warm and safe, with the Packet of Special Things resting on the floor beside him. I hadn't told him that I had looked inside it that morning, or what I had found there, or the truth about the little girl. That was something else that – for the moment at least – I didn't have the words for.

'Goodnight, mate. I love you.'

He yawned.

'Love you too, Daddy.'

The stairs were hard for me right now, so after I turned off the light, I went into my own room for a while, waiting for him to go to sleep. I sat on the bed and opened my laptop, turning my attention to the most recent file and reading what was there.

Rebecca.

I know exactly what you'd think about that, because you were always so much more practical than me. You'd want me to get on with my life. You'd want me to be happy . . .

And so on. It took me a moment to understand what I'd written, because I hadn't touched the document since that final night in the safe house, which seemed like a lifetime ago now. It was about Karen – how I felt guilty for having feelings for her. That also seemed very distant. She had come to see me in the hospital. She'd taken Jake to school for me and helped to look after him as I gradually recuperated. There was a growing closeness between us. What happened had brought us together, but it had also knocked us off a more predictable track, and that kiss hadn't happened yet. But I could still feel it there . . . waiting.

You'd want me to be happy.

Yes.

I deleted everything apart from Rebecca's name.

My intention before had been to write about my life with Rebecca, the grief I felt over her death, and the way the loss of her had affected me. I still wanted to do that, because it felt like she would be an important part of whatever I did write. She didn't end when her life did because, even without the existence of ghosts, that's simply not the way things work. But I realized now that there was so much more, and that I wanted to write about all of it. The truth about everything that had happened.

Mister Night.

The boy in the floor.

The butterflies.

The little girl with the strange dress.

And the Whisper Man, of course.

It was a daunting prospect, because it was all such a jumble, and there was so much I didn't know and perhaps never would. But then again, I wasn't sure that in itself was a problem. The truth of something can be in the feeling of it as much as the fact.

I stared at the screen.

Rebecca.

Only one word, and even that was wrong. Jake and I had moved to this house for a fresh start, and as much as Rebecca was an integral part of the story, I realized it shouldn't be about her. That was the whole point. My focus needed to be elsewhere now.

I deleted her name. I hesitated, then typed:

Jake.

There is so much I want to tell you, but we've always found it hard to talk to each other, haven't we?

So I'll have to write to you instead.

That was when I heard Jake whispering.

I sat completely still, listening to the silence that followed the noise, and which now seemed to fill the house more ominously than before. Seconds ticked by – long enough for me to believe I had imagined the sound.

But then it came again.

In his room on the other side of the hall, Jake was talking very quietly to someone.

I put the laptop to one side and stood up carefully, then made my way out into the hall as silently as I could. My heart was sinking a little. Over the last two weeks, there had been no sign at all of the little girl or the boy in the floor, and although I was happy to let Jake be himself, I had been relieved about that. I didn't relish the possibility of them returning now.

I stood in the hallway, listening.

'Okay,' Jake whispered. 'Good night.'

And then nothing.

I waited a little longer, but it was clear that the conversation was over. After a few more seconds, I walked across the hall and stepped up into his room. There was enough light from behind me to see that Jake was lying very still in his bed, entirely alone in the room.

I moved over.

'Jake?' I whispered.

'Yes, Daddy?'

He sounded barely there.

'Who were you talking to just now?'

But there was no reply, beyond the gentle rise and fall of the covers over him, and the steady sound of his breathing. Perhaps he had just been half asleep, I thought, and talking to himself.

I tucked the covers over him a little better, and was about to head back to the door when he spoke again.

'Your daddy read that book to you when you were young,' he said.

For a moment, I said nothing. I just stared down at Jake, lying there with his back to me. The silence was ringing now. The room suddenly felt colder than it had before, and a shiver ran through me.

Yes, I thought. *He probably did.*

It hadn't been a question, though, and there was no way Jake could have known. I didn't even remember it happening myself. But of course, I'd told Jake the book was a childhood favourite of mine, so I supposed it was a natural assumption for him to make. It didn't necessarily mean anything.

'He did.' I looked around the empty room. 'Why did you say that?'

But my son was already dreaming.

Acknowledgements

I owe a huge debt of gratitude to a number of people – firstly my fabulous agent, Sandra Sawicka, along with Leah Middleton and everyone else at Marjacq. Joel Richardson is my editor at Michael Joseph, and his patience and advice along the way have been invaluable. I would also like to thank Emma Henderson, Sarah Scarlett, Catherine Wood, Lucy Beresford-Knox, Elizabeth Brandon and Alex Elam for their hard work and support, Shan Morley Jones for catching my mistakes, and Lee Motley for creating such beautiful cover art. I have been bowled over by each and every one of you, and I cannot thank you enough.

In addition, the crime fiction community is famous for its warmth and generosity, and I'm constantly grateful to enjoy the support and friendship of so many amazing writers, readers and bloggers. You're all ace. I need to raise an extra large glass – a beaker, even – to the Blankets. You know who you are.

Finally, thanks to Lynn and Zack for absolutely everything – not least putting up with me. This book is dedicated to both of you, with so much love.

He just wanted a decent book to read ...

Not too much to ask, is it? It was in 1935 when Allen Lane, Managing Director of Bodley Head Publishers, stood on a platform at Exeter railway station looking for something good to read on his journey back to London. His choice was limited to popular magazines and poor-quality paperbacks – the same choice faced every day by the vast majority of readers, few of whom could afford hardbacks. Lane's disappointment and subsequent anger at the range of books generally available led him to found a company – and change the world.

'We believed in the existence in this country of a vast reading public for intelligent books at a low price, and staked everything on it'
Sir Allen Lane, 1902–1970, founder of Penguin Books

The quality paperback had arrived – and not just in bookshops. Lane was adamant that his Penguins should appear in chain stores and tobacconists, and should cost no more than a packet of cigarettes.

Reading habits (and cigarette prices) have changed since 1935, but Penguin still believes in publishing the best books for everybody to enjoy. We still believe that good design costs no more than bad design, and we still believe that quality books published passionately and responsibly make the world a better place.

So wherever you see the little bird – whether it's on a piece of prize-winning literary fiction or a celebrity autobiography, political tour de force or historical masterpiece, a serial-killer thriller, reference book, world classic or a piece of pure escapism – you can bet that it represents the very best that the genre has to offer.

Whatever you like to read – trust Penguin.

Mark Haddon

THE CURIOUS INCIDENT OF THE DOG IN THE NIGHT-TIME

VINTAGE BOOKS

London

Published by Vintage 2004

This edition printed for World Book Night 2011

Copyright © Mark Haddon 2003

Cover illustration © Marc Boutavant; cover design © Suzanne Dean;
hand lettering © Tim Marrs

First published in Great Britain in 2003 by
Jonathan Cape

Vintage
Random House, 20 Vauxhall Bridge Road,
London SW1V 2SA

www.vintage-books.co.uk

Addresses for companies within The Random House Group Limited
can be found at: www.randomhouse.co.uk/offices.htm

The Random House Group Limited Reg. No. 954009

A CIP catalogue record for this book
is available from the British Library

ISBN 9780099560852

The Random House Group Limited supports The Forest
Stewardship Council (FSC), the leading international forest
certification organisation. All our titles that are printed on
Greenpeace approved FSC certified paper carry the FSC logo.
Our paper procurement policy can be found at
www.rbooks.co.uk/environment

FSC

Mixed Sources

Product group from well-managed
forests and other controlled sources

Cert no. SGS - COC - 2061
www.fsc.org
© 1996 Forest Stewardship Council

Printed and bound in Great Britain by
Clays Ltd, St Ives Plc

This book
is dedicated to
Sos

With thanks to
Kathryn Heyman, Clare Alexander,
Kate Shaw and Dave Cohen

ACKNOWLEDGEMENTS

Underground logo, fabric designs and line diagram reproduced with kind permission of Transport for London. Kuoni advert reproduced with kind permission of Kuoni Advertising. A level Maths question reproduced with kind permission of OCR. Every effort has been made to trace other copyright holders, and the publishers will be happy to correct mistakes or omissions in future editions.

2

It was 7 minutes after midnight. The dog was lying on the grass in the middle of the lawn in front of Mrs Shears' house. Its eyes were closed. It looked as if it was running on its side, the way dogs run when they think they are chasing a cat in a dream. But the dog was not running or asleep. The dog was dead. There was a garden fork sticking out of the dog. The points of the fork must have gone all the way through the dog and into the ground because the fork had not fallen over. I decided that the dog was probably killed with the fork because I could not see any other wounds in the dog and I do not think you would stick a garden fork into a dog after it had died for some other reason, like cancer for example, or a road accident. But I could not be certain about this.

I went through Mrs Shears' gate, closing it behind me. I walked onto her lawn and knelt beside the dog. I put my hand on the muzzle of the dog. It was still warm.

The dog was called Wellington. It belonged to Mrs Shears who was our friend. She lived on the opposite side of the road, two houses to the left.

Wellington was a poodle. Not one of the small poodles that have hairstyles, but a big poodle. It had curly black fur, but when you got close you could see that the skin underneath the fur was a very pale yellow, like chicken.

I stroked Wellington and wondered who had killed him, and why.

3

My name is Christopher John Francis Boone. I know all the countries of the world and their capital cities and every prime number up to 7,507.

Eight years ago, when I first met Siobhan, she showed me this picture

and I knew that it meant 'sad', which is what I felt when I found the dead dog.

Then she showed me this picture

and I knew that it meant 'happy', like when I'm reading about the Apollo space missions, or when I am still awake at three or four in the morning and I can walk up and down the street and pretend that I am the only person in the whole world.

Then she drew some other pictures

but I was unable to say what these meant.

I got Siobhan to draw lots of these faces and then write down next to them exactly what they meant. I kept the piece of paper in my pocket and took it out when I didn't understand what someone was saying. But it was very difficult to decide which of the diagrams was most like the face they were making because people's faces move very quickly.

When I told Siobhan that I was doing this, she got out a pencil and another piece of paper and said it probably made people feel very

and then she laughed. So I tore the original piece of paper up and threw it away. And Siobhan apologised. And now if I don't know what someone is saying I ask them what they mean or I walk away.

5

I pulled the fork out of the dog and lifted him into my arms and hugged him. He was leaking blood from the fork-holes.

I like dogs. You always know what a dog is thinking. It has four moods. Happy, sad, cross and concentrating. Also, dogs are faithful and they do not tell lies because they cannot talk.

I had been hugging the dog for 4 minutes when I heard screaming. I looked up and saw Mrs Shears running towards me from the patio. She was wearing pyjamas and a housecoat. Her toenails were painted bright pink and she had no shoes on.

She was shouting, 'What in fuck's name have you done to my dog?'

I do not like people shouting at me. It makes me scared that they are going to hit me or touch me and I do not know what is going to happen.

'Let go of the dog,' she shouted. 'Let go of the fucking dog for Christ's sake.'

I put the dog down on the lawn and moved back 2 metres.

She bent down. I thought she was going to pick the dog up herself, but she didn't. Perhaps she noticed how much blood there was and didn't want to get dirty. Instead, she started screaming again.

I put my hands over my ears and closed my eyes and rolled forward till I was hunched up with my forehead pressed onto the grass. The grass was wet and cold. It was nice.

7

This is a murder mystery novel.

Siobhan said that I should write something I would want to read myself. Mostly I read books about science and maths. I do not like proper novels. In proper novels people say things like, 'I am veined with iron, with silver and with streaks of common mud. I cannot contract into the firm fist which those clench who do not depend on stimulus.'[1] What does this mean? I do not know. Nor does Father. Nor do Siobhan or Mr Jeavons. I have asked them.

Siobhan has long blonde hair and wears glasses which are made of green plastic. And Mr Jeavons smells of soap and wears brown shoes that have approximately 60 tiny circular holes in each of them.

But I do like murder mystery novels. So I am writing a murder mystery novel.

In a murder mystery novel someone has to work out who the murderer is and then catch them. It is a puzzle. If it is a good puzzle you can sometimes work out the answer before the end of the book.

Siobhan said that the book should begin with something to grab people's attention. That is why I started with the dog. I also started with the dog because it happened to me and I find it hard to imagine things which did not happen to me.

Siobhan read the first page and said that it was different. She

---

[1] I found this book in the library in town when Mother took me into town once.

put this word into inverted commas by making the wiggly quotation sign with her first and second fingers. She said that it was usually people who were killed in murder mystery novels. I said that two dogs were killed in **The Hound of the Baskervilles**, the hound itself and James Mortimer's spaniel, but Siobhan said they weren't the victims of the murder, Sir Charles Baskerville was. She said that this was because readers cared more about people than dogs, so if a person was killed in the book readers would want to carry on reading.

I said that I wanted to write about something real and I knew people who had died but I did not know any people who had been killed, except Edward's father from school, Mr Paulson, and that was a gliding accident, not murder, and I didn't really know him. I also said that I cared about dogs because they were faithful and honest, and some dogs were cleverer and more interesting than some people. Steve, for example, who comes to school on Thursdays, needs help to eat his food and could not even fetch a stick. Siobhan asked me not to say this to Steve's mother.

11

Then the police arrived. I like the police. They have uniforms and numbers and you know what they are meant to be doing. There was a policewoman and a policeman. The policewoman had a little hole in her tights on her left ankle and a red scratch in the middle of the hole. The policeman had a big orange leaf stuck to the bottom of his shoe which was poking out from one side.

The policewoman put her arms round Mrs Shears and led her back towards the house.

I lifted my head off the grass.

The policeman squatted down beside me and said, 'Would you like to tell me what's going on here, young man?'

I sat up and said, 'The dog is dead.'

'I'd got that far,' he said.

I said, 'I think someone killed the dog.'

'How old are you?' he asked.

I replied, 'I am 15 years and 3 months and 2 days.'

'And what, precisely, were you doing in the garden?' he asked.

'I was holding the dog,' I replied.

'And why were you holding the dog?' he asked.

This was a difficult question. It was something I wanted to do. I like dogs. It made me sad to see that the dog was dead.

I like policemen, too, and I wanted to answer the question properly, but the policeman did not give me enough time to work out the correct answer.

'Why were you holding the dog?' he asked again.

'I like dogs,' I said.

'Did you kill the dog?' he asked.

I said, 'I did not kill the dog.'

'Is this your fork?' he asked.

I said, 'No.'

'You seem very upset about this,' he said.

He was asking too many questions and he was asking them too quickly. They were stacking up in my head like loaves in the factory where Uncle Terry works. The factory is a bakery and he operates the slicing machines. And sometimes the slicer is not working fast enough but the bread keeps coming and there is a blockage. I sometimes think of my mind as a machine, but not always as a bread-slicing machine. It makes it easier to explain to other people what is going on inside it.

The policeman said, 'I am going to ask you once again . . .'

I rolled back onto the lawn and pressed my forehead to the ground again and made the noise that Father calls groaning. I make this noise when there is too much information coming into my head from the outside world. It is like when you are upset and you hold the radio against your ear and you tune it halfway between two stations so that all you get is white noise and then you turn the volume right up so that this is all you can hear and then you know you are safe because you cannot hear anything else.

The policeman took hold of my arm and lifted me onto my feet.

I didn't like him touching me like this.
And this is when I hit him.

13

This will not be a funny book. I cannot tell jokes because I do not understand them. Here is a joke, as an example. It is one of Father's.

His face was drawn but the curtains were real.

I know why this is meant to be funny. I asked. It is because *drawn* has three meanings, and they are **1)** drawn with a pencil, **2)** exhausted, and **3)** pulled across a window, and meaning **1** refers to both the face and the curtains, meaning **2** refers only to the face, and meaning **3** refers only to the curtains.

If I try to say the joke to myself, making the word mean the three different things at the same time, it is like hearing three different pieces of music at the same time which is uncomfortable and confusing and not nice like white noise. It is like three people trying to talk to you at the same time about different things.

And that is why there are no jokes in this book.

17

The policeman looked at me for a while without speaking. Then he said, 'I am arresting you for assaulting a police officer.'

This made me feel a lot calmer because it is what policemen say on television and in films.

Then he said, 'I strongly advise you to get into the back of the police car because if you try any of that monkey-business again, you little shit, I will seriously lose my rag. Is that understood?'

I walked over to the police car which was parked just outside the gate. He opened the back door and I got inside. He climbed into the driver's seat and made a call on his radio to the police-woman who was still inside the house. He said, 'The little bugger just had a pop at me, Kate. Can you hang on with Mrs S while I drop him off at the station? I'll get Tony to swing by and pick you up.'

And she said, 'Sure. I'll catch you later.'

The policeman said, 'Okey-doke,' and we drove off.

The police car smelt of hot plastic and aftershave and take-away chips.

I watched the sky as we drove towards the town centre. It was a clear night and you could see the Milky Way.

Some people think the Milky Way is a long line of stars, but it isn't. Our galaxy is a huge disc of stars millions of light years across and the solar system is somewhere near the outside edge of the disc.

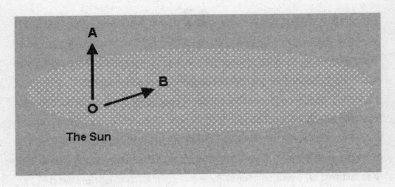

The Sun

When you look in direction A, at 90° to the disc, you don't see many stars. But when you look in direction B, you see lots more stars because you are looking into the main body of the galaxy, and because the galaxy is a disc you see a stripe of stars.

And then I thought about how, for a long time, scientists were puzzled by the fact that the sky is dark at night, even though there are billions of stars in the universe and there must be stars in every direction you look, so that the sky should be full of starlight because there is very little in the way to stop the light reaching earth.

Then they worked out that the universe was expanding, that the stars were all rushing away from one another after the Big Bang, and the further the stars were away from us the faster they were moving, some of them nearly as fast as the speed of light, which was why their light never reached us.

I like this fact. It is something you can work out in your own mind just by looking at the sky above your head at night and thinking without having to ask anyone.

And when the universe has finished exploding all the stars will slow down, like a ball that has been thrown into the air, and they will come to a halt and they will all begin to fall towards the centre of the universe again. And then there will be nothing to stop us seeing all the stars in the world because they will all be moving towards us, gradually faster and faster, and we will know that the world is going to end soon because when we look up into the sky at night there will be no darkness, just the blazing light of billions and billions of stars, all falling.

Except that no one will see this because there will be no people left on the earth to see it. They will probably have become extinct by then. And even if there are people still in existence they will not see it because the light will be so bright and hot that everyone will be burnt to death, even if they live in tunnels.

19

Chapters in books are usually given the cardinal numbers **1**, **2**, **3**, **4**, **5**, **6** and so on. But I have decided to give my chapters prime numbers **2**, **3**, **5**, **7**, **11**, **13** and so on because I like prime numbers.

This is how you work out what prime numbers are.

First, you write down all the positive whole numbers in the world.

1	2	3	4	5	6	7	8	9	10
11	12	13	14	15	16	17	18	19	20
21	22	23	24	25	26	27	28	29	30
31	32	33	34	35	36	37	38	39	40
41	42	43	44	45	46	47	48	49	etc.

Then you take away all the numbers that are multiples of 2. Then you take away all the numbers that are multiples of 3. Then you take away all the numbers that are multiples of 4 and 5 and 6 and 7 and so on. The numbers that are left are the prime numbers.

	2	3		5		7			
11		13				17		19	
		23						29	
31						37			
41		43				47			etc.

The rule for working out prime numbers is really simple, but no one has ever worked out a simple formula for telling you whether a very big number is a prime number or what the next one will be. If a number is really, really big, it can take a computer years to work out whether it is a prime number.

Prime numbers are useful for writing codes and in America they are classed as Military Material and if you find one over 100 digits long you have to tell the CIA and they buy it off you for $10,000. But it would not be a very good way of making a living.

Prime numbers are what is left when you have taken all the patterns away. I think prime numbers are like life. They are very logical but you could never work out the rules, even if you spent all your time thinking about them.

23

When I got to the police station they made me take the laces out of my shoes and empty my pockets at the front desk in case I had anything in them that I could use to kill myself or escape or attack a policeman with.

The sergeant behind the desk had very hairy hands and he had bitten his nails so much that they had bled.

This is what I had in my pockets

1. A Swiss Army Knife with 13 attachments including a wire-stripper and a saw and a toothpick and tweezers.

2. A piece of string.

3. A piece of a wooden puzzle which looked like this

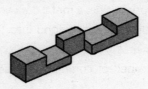

4. 3 pellets of rat food for Toby, my rat.

5. £1.47 (this was made up of a £1 coin, a 20p coin, two 10p coins, a 5p coin and a 2p coin).

6. A red paperclip.

7. A key for the front door.

I was also wearing my watch and they wanted me to leave this at the desk as well but I said that I needed to keep my watch on because I needed to know exactly what time it was. And when they tried to take it off me I screamed, so they let me keep it on.

They asked me if I had any family. I said I did. They asked me who my family was. I said it was Father, but Mother was dead. And I said it was also Uncle Terry but he was in Sunderland and he was Father's brother, and it was my grandparents, too, but three of them were dead and Grandma Burton was in a home because she had senile dementia and thought that I was someone on television.

Then they asked me for Father's phone number.

I told them that he had two numbers, one for at home and one which was a mobile phone and I said both of them.

It was nice in the police cell. It was almost a perfect cube, 2 metres long by 2 metres wide by 2 metres high. It contained approximately 8 cubic metres of air. It had a small window with bars and, on the opposite side, a metal door with a long, thin hatch near the floor for sliding trays of food into the cell and a sliding hatch higher up so that policemen could look in and check that prisoners hadn't escaped or committed suicide. There was also a padded bench.

I wondered how I would escape if I was in a story. It would be difficult because the only things I had were my clothes and my shoes which had no laces in them.

I decided that my best plan would be to wait for a really sunny day and then use my glasses to focus the sunlight on a piece of my clothing and start a fire. I would then make my escape when they saw the smoke and took me out of the cell. And if they didn't notice I would be able to wee on the clothes and put them out.

I wondered whether Mrs Shears had told the police that I had killed Wellington and whether, when the police found out that she had lied, she would go to prison. Because telling lies about people is called *Slander*.

29

I find people confusing.

This is for two main reasons.

The first main reason is that people do a lot of talking without using any words. Siobhan says that if you raise one eyebrow it can mean lots of different things. It can mean 'I want to do sex with you' and it can also mean 'I think that what you just said was very stupid.'

Siobhan also says that if you close your mouth and breathe out loudly through your nose it can mean that you are relaxed, or that you are bored, or that you are angry and it all depends on how much air comes out of your nose and how fast and what shape your mouth is when you do it and how you are sitting and what you said just before and hundreds of other things which are too complicated to work out in a few seconds.

The second main reason is that people often talk using metaphors. These are examples of metaphors

I laughed my socks off.
He was the apple of her eye.
They had a skeleton in the cupboard.
We had a real pig of a day.
The dog was stone dead.

The word metaphor means carrying something from one place to another, and it comes from the Greek words μετα (which means *from one place to another*) and φερειν (which means *to carry*) and it is when you describe something by using a word for something that it isn't. This means that the word metaphor is a metaphor.

I think it should be called a lie because a pig is not like a day and people do not have skeletons in their cupboards. And when I try and make a picture of the phrase in my head it just confuses me because imagining an apple in someone's eye doesn't have anything to do with liking someone a lot and it makes you forget what the person was talking about.

My name is a metaphor. It means *carrying Christ* and it comes from the Greek words χριστος (which means *Jesus Christ*) and φερειν and it was the name given to St Christopher because he carried Jesus Christ across a river.

This makes you wonder what he was called before he carried Christ across the river. But he wasn't called anything because this is an apocryphal story which means that it is a lie, too.

Mother used to say that it meant Christopher was a nice name because it was a story about being kind and helpful, but I do not want my name to mean a story about being kind and helpful. I want my name to mean me.

31

It was 1:12 a.m. when Father arrived at the police station. I did not see him until 1:28 a.m. but I knew he was there because I could hear him.

He was shouting, 'I want to see my son,' and 'Why the hell is he locked up?' and, 'Of course I'm bloody angry.'

Then I heard a policeman telling him to calm down. Then I heard nothing for a long while.

At 1:28 a.m. a policeman opened the door of the cell and told me that there was someone to see me.

I stepped outside. Father was standing in the corridor. He held up his right hand and spread his fingers out in a fan. I held up my left hand and spread my fingers out in a fan and we made our fingers and thumbs touch each other. We do this because sometimes Father wants to give me a hug, but I do not like hugging people, so we do this instead, and it means that he loves me.

Then the policeman told us to follow him down the corridor to another room. In the room was a table and three chairs. He told us to sit down on the far side of the table and he sat down on the other side. There was a tape recorder on the table and I asked whether I was going to be interviewed and he was going to record the interview.

He said, 'I don't think there will be any need for that.'

He was an inspector. I could tell because he wasn't wearing a uniform. He also had a very hairy nose. It looked as if there were two very small mice hiding in his nostrils.[2]

He said, 'I have spoken to your father and he says that you didn't mean to hit the policeman.'

I didn't say anything because this wasn't a question.

He said, 'Did you mean to hit the policeman?'

I said, 'Yes.'

He squeezed his face and said, 'But you didn't mean to hurt the policeman?'

I thought about this and said, 'No. I didn't mean to hurt the policeman. I just wanted him to stop touching me.'

Then he said, 'You know that it is wrong to hit a policeman, don't you?'

I said, 'I do.'

He was quiet for a few seconds, then he asked, 'Did you kill the dog, Christopher?'

I said, 'I didn't kill the dog.'

He said, 'Do you know that it is wrong to lie to a policeman and that you can get into a very great deal of trouble if you do?'

I said, 'Yes.'

He said, 'So, do you know who killed the dog?'

I said, 'No.'

He said, 'Are you telling the truth?'

[2] This is not a *metaphor*, it is a *simile*, which means that it really did look like there were two very small mice hiding in his nostrils and if you make a picture in your head of a man with two very small mice hiding in his nostrils you will know what the police inspector looked like. And a simile is not a lie, unless it is a bad simile.

I said, 'Yes. I always tell the truth.'

And he said, 'Right. I am going to give you a caution.'

I asked, 'Is that going to be on a piece of paper like a certificate I can keep?'

He replied, 'No, a caution means that we are going to keep a record of what you did, that you hit a policeman but that it was an accident and that you didn't mean to hurt the policeman.'

I said, 'But it wasn't an accident.'

And Father said, 'Christopher, please.'

The policeman closed his mouth and breathed out loudly through his nose and said, 'If you get into any more trouble we will take out this record and see that you have been given a caution and we will take things much more seriously. Do you understand what I'm saying?'

I said that I understood.

Then he said that we could go and he stood up and opened the door and we walked out into the corridor and back to the front desk where I picked up my Swiss Army Knife and my piece of string and the piece of the wooden puzzle and the 3 pellets of rat food for Toby and my £1.47 and the paperclip and my front door key which were all in a little plastic bag and we went out to Father's car which was parked outside and we drove home.

37

I do not tell lies. Mother used to say that this was because I was a good person. But it is not because I am a good person. It is because I can't tell lies.

Mother was a small person who smelt nice. And she sometimes wore a fleece with a zip down the front which was pink and it had a tiny label which said **Berghaus** on the left bosom.

A lie is when you say something happened which didn't happen. But there is only ever one thing which happened at a particular time and a particular place. And there are an infinite number of things which didn't happen at that time and that place. And if I think about something which didn't happen I start thinking about all the other things which didn't happen.

For example, this morning for breakfast I had Ready Brek and some hot raspberry milkshake. But if I say that I actually had Shreddies and a mug of tea[3] I start thinking about Coco-Pops and lemonade and porridge and Dr Pepper and how I wasn't eating my breakfast in Egypt and there wasn't a rhinoceros in the room and Father wasn't wearing a diving suit and so on and even writing this makes me feel shaky and scared, like I do when I'm standing on the top of a very tall building and there are thousands of houses and cars and people below me and my head is so full of all these things that I'm afraid that I'm going to forget to stand up straight and hang onto the rail and I'm going to fall over and be killed.

[3] But I wouldn't have Shreddies and tea because they are both brown.

This is another reason why I don't like proper novels, because they are lies about things which didn't happen and they make me feel shaky and scared.

And this is why everything I have written here is true.

41

There were clouds in the sky on the way home, so I couldn't see the Milky Way.

I said, 'I'm sorry,' because Father had had to come to the police station, which was a bad thing.

He said, 'It's OK.'

I said, 'I didn't kill the dog.'

And he said, 'I know.'

Then he said, 'Christopher, you have to stay out of trouble, OK?'

I said, 'I didn't know I was going to get into trouble. I like Wellington and I went to say hello to him, but I didn't know that someone had killed him.'

Father said, 'Just try and keep your nose out of other people's business.'

I thought for a little and I said, 'I am going to find out who killed Wellington.'

And Father said, 'Were you listening to what I was saying, Christopher?'

I said, 'Yes, I was listening to what you were saying, but when someone gets murdered you have to find out who did it so that they can be punished.'

And he said, 'It's a bloody dog, Christopher, a bloody dog.'

I replied, 'I think dogs are important, too.'

He said, 'Leave it.'

And I said, 'I wonder if the police will find out who killed him and punish the person.'

Then Father banged the steering wheel with his fist and the car weaved a little bit across the dotted line in the middle of the road and he shouted, 'I said leave it, for God's sake.'

I could tell that he was angry because he was shouting, and I didn't want to make him angry so I didn't say anything else until we got home.

When we came in through the front door I went into the kitchen and got a carrot for Toby and I went upstairs and I shut the door of my room and I let Toby out and gave him the carrot. Then I turned my computer on and played 76 games of Minesweeper and did the Expert Version in 102 seconds, which was only 3 seconds off my best time which was 99 seconds.

At 2:07 a.m. I decided that I wanted a drink of orange squash before I brushed my teeth and got into bed so I went downstairs to the kitchen. Father was sitting on the sofa watching snooker on the television and drinking whisky. There were tears coming out of his eyes.

I asked, 'Are you sad about Wellington?'

He looked at me for a long time and sucked air in through his nose. Then he said, 'Yes, Christopher, you could say that. You could very well say that.'

I decided to leave him alone because when I am sad I want to be left alone. So I didn't say anything else. I just went into the kitchen and made my orange squash and took it back upstairs to my room.

43

Mother died 2 years ago.

I came home from school one day and no one answered the door, so I went and found the secret key that we keep under a flowerpot behind the kitchen door. I let myself into the house and carried on making the Airfix Sherman Tank model I was building.

An hour and a half later Father came home from work. He runs a business and he does heating maintenance and boiler repair with a man called Rhodri who is his employee. He knocked on the door of my room and opened it and asked whether I had seen Mother.

I said that I hadn't seen her and he went downstairs and started making some phone calls. I did not hear what he said.

Then he came up to my room and said he had to go out for a while and he wasn't sure how long he would be. He said that if I needed anything I should call him on his mobile phone.

He was away for 2½ hours. When he came back I went downstairs. He was sitting in the kitchen staring out of the back window down the garden to the pond and the corrugated iron fence and the top of the tower of the church on Manstead Street which looks like a castle because it is Norman.

Father said, 'I'm afraid you won't be seeing your mother for a while.'

He didn't look at me when he said this. He kept on looking through the window.

Usually people look at you when they're talking to you. I know that they're working out what I'm thinking, but I can't tell what they're thinking. It is like being in a room with a one-way mirror in a spy film. But this was nice, having Father speak to me but not look at me.

I said, 'Why not?'

He waited for a very long time, then he said, 'Your mother has had to go into hospital.'

'Can we visit her?' I asked, because I like hospitals. I like the uniforms and the machines.

Father said, 'No.'

I said, 'Why can't we?'

And he said, 'She needs rest. She needs to be on her own.'

I asked, 'Is it a psychiatric hospital?'

And Father said, 'No. It's an ordinary hospital. She has a problem . . . a problem with her heart.'

I said, 'We will need to take food to her,' because I knew that food in hospital was not very good. David from school, he went into hospital to have an operation on his leg to make his calf muscle longer so that he could walk better. And he hated the food, so his mother used to take meals in every day.

Father waited for a long time again and said, 'I'll take some in to her during the day when you're at school and I'll give it to the doctors and they can give it to your mum, OK?'

I said, 'But you can't cook.'

Father put his hands over his face and said, 'Christopher. Look. I'll buy some ready-made stuff from Marks and Spencer's and take those in. She likes those.'

I said I would make her a Get Well card, because that is what you do for people when they are in hospital.

Father said he would take it in the next day.

47

In the bus on the way to school next morning we passed 4 red cars in a row which meant that it was a **Good Day**, so I decided not to be sad about Wellington.

Mr Jeavons, the psychologist at the school, once asked me why 4 red cars in a row made it a **Good Day**, and 3 red cars in a row made it a **Quite Good Day**, and 5 red cars in a row made it a **Super Good Day**, and why 4 yellow cars in a row made it a **Black Day**, which is a day when I don't speak to anyone and sit on my own reading books and don't eat my lunch and *Take No Risks*. He said that I was clearly a very logical person, so he was surprised that I should think like this because it wasn't very logical.

I said that I liked things to be in a nice order. And one way of things being in a nice order was to be logical. Especially if those things were numbers or an argument. But there were other ways of putting things in a nice order. And that was why I had **Good Days** and **Black Days**. And I said that some people who worked in an office came out of their house in the morning and saw that the sun was shining and it made them feel happy, or they saw that it was raining and it made them feel sad, but the only difference was the weather and if they worked in an office the weather didn't have anything to do with whether they had a good day or a bad day.

I said that when Father got up in the morning he always put his trousers on before he put his socks on and it wasn't logical but he always did it that way, because he liked things in a nice order, too. Also whenever he went upstairs he went up two at a time always starting with his right foot.

Mr Jeavons said that I was a very clever boy.

I said that I wasn't clever. I was just noticing how things were, and that wasn't clever. That was just being observant. Being clever was when you looked at how things were and used the evidence to work out something new. Like the universe expanding, or who committed a murder. Or if you see someone's name and you give each letter a value from 1 to 26 (**a = 1**, **b = 2** *etc*.) and you add the numbers up in your head and you find that it makes a prime number, like **Jesus Christ** (151), or **Scooby Doo** (113), or **Sherlock Holmes** (163), or **Doctor Watson** (167).

Mr Jeavons asked me whether this made me feel safe, having things always in a nice order and I said it did.

Then he asked if I didn't like things changing. And I said I wouldn't mind things changing if I became an astronaut, for example, which is one of the biggest changes you can imagine, apart from becoming a girl or dying.

He asked whether I wanted to become an astronaut and I said I did.

He said that it was very difficult to become an astronaut. I said that I knew. You had to become an officer in the air force and you had to take lots of orders and be prepared to kill other human beings, and I couldn't take orders. Also I didn't have 20/20 vision which you needed to be a pilot. But I said that you could still want something that is very unlikely to happen.

Terry, who is the older brother of Francis, who is at the school, said I would only ever get a job collecting supermarket trollies or cleaning out donkey shit at an animal sanctuary and they didn't let spazzers drive rockets that cost billions of pounds. When I told this to Father he said that Terry was jealous of my being cleverer than him. Which was a stupid thing to think because we weren't in a competition. But Terry is stupid, so *quod erat demonstrandum* which is Latin for *Which is the thing that was going to be proved*, which means *Thus it is proved*.

I'm not a spazzer, which means spastic, not like Francis, who is a spazzer, and even though I probably won't become an astronaut I am going to go to university and study Mathematics, or Physics, or Physics and Mathematics (which is a Joint Honour School), because I like mathematics and physics and I'm very good at them. But Terry won't go to university. Father says Terry is most likely to end up in prison.

Terry has a tattoo on his arm of a heart-shape with a knife through the middle of it.

But this is what is called a digression, and now I am going to go back to the fact that it was a Good Day.

Because it was a Good Day I decided that I would try and find out who killed Wellington because a Good Day is a day for projects and planning things.

When I said this to Siobhan she said, 'Well, we're meant to be writing stories today, so why don't you write about finding Wellington and going to the police station.'

And that is when I started writing this.

And Siobhan said that she would help with the spelling and the grammar and the footnotes.

53

Mother died two weeks later.

I had not been into hospital to see her but Father had taken in lots of food from Marks and Spencer's. He said that she had been looking OK and seemed to be getting better. She had sent me lots of love and had my Get Well card on the table beside her bed. Father said that she liked it very much.

The card had pictures of cars on the front. It looked like this.

I did it with Mrs Peters at school who does art, and it was a lino cut, which is when you draw a picture on a piece of lino and Mrs Peters cuts round the picture with a Stanley knife and then you put ink on the lino and press it onto the paper, which is why all the cars looked the same because I did one car and pressed it onto the paper 9 times. And it was Mrs Peters' idea to do lots of cars, which I liked. And I coloured all the cars in with red paint to make it a **Super Super Good Day** for Mother.

Father said that she died of a heart attack and it wasn't expected.

I said, 'What kind of heart attack?' because I was surprised.

Mother was only 38 years old and heart attacks usually happen to older people, and Mother was very active and rode a bicycle and ate food which was healthy and high in fibre and low in saturated fat like chicken and vegetables and muesli.

Father said that he didn't know what kind of heart attack she had and now wasn't the moment to be asking questions like that.

I said that it was probably an aneurysm.

A heart attack is when some of the muscles in the heart stop getting blood and die. There are two main types of heart attack. The first is an embolism. That is when a blood clot blocks one of the blood vessels taking blood to the muscles in the heart. And you can stop this happening by taking aspirin and eating fish. Which is why Eskimos don't get this sort of heart attack because they eat fish and fish stops their blood clotting, but if they cut themselves badly they can bleed to death.

But an aneurysm is when a blood vessel breaks and the blood doesn't get to the heart muscles because it is leaking. And some people get aneurysms just because there is a weak bit in their blood vessels, like Mrs Hardisty who lived at number 72 in our street who had a weak bit in the blood vessels in her neck and died just because she turned her head round to reverse her car into a parking space.

On the other hand it could have been an embolism, because

your blood clots much more easily when you are lying down for a long time, like when you are in hospital.

Father said, 'I'm sorry, Christopher, I'm really sorry.'

But it wasn't his fault.

Then Mrs Shears came over and cooked supper for us. And she was wearing sandals and jeans and a T-shirt which had the words **WINDSURF** and **CORFU** and a picture of a windsurfer on it.

And father was sitting down and she stood next to him and held his head against her bosoms and said, 'Come on, Ed. We're going to get you through this.'

And then she made us spaghetti and tomato sauce.

And after dinner she played Scrabble with me and I beat her 247 points to 134.

59

I decided that I was going to find out who killed Wellington even though Father had told me to stay out of other people's business.

This is because I do not always do what I am told.

And this is because when people tell you what to do it is usually confusing and does not make sense.

For example, people often say 'Be quiet,' but they don't tell you how long to be quiet for. Or you see a sign which says **KEEP OFF THE GRASS** but it should say **KEEP OFF THE GRASS AROUND THIS SIGN** or **KEEP OFF ALL THE GRASS IN THIS PARK** because there is lots of grass you are allowed to walk on.

Also people break rules all the time. For example, Father often drives at over 30 mph in a 30 mph zone and sometimes he drives when he has been drinking and often he doesn't wear his seatbelt when he is driving his van. And in the Bible it says *Thou shalt not kill* but there were the Crusades and two World Wars and the Gulf War and there were Christians killing people in all of them.

Also I don't know what Father means when he says 'Stay out of other people's business' because I do not know what he means by 'other people's business' because I do lots of things with other people, at school and in the shop and on the bus, and his job is going into other people's houses and fixing their boilers and their heating. And all of these things are other people's business.

Siobhan understands. When she tells me not to do something she tells me exactly what it is that I am not allowed to do. And I like this.

For example, she once said, 'You must never punch Sarah or hit her in any way, Christopher. Even if she hits you first. If she does hit you again, move away from her and stand still and count from 1 to 50, then come and tell me what she has done, or tell one of the other members of staff what she has done.'

Or, for example, she once said, 'If you want to go on the swings and there are already people on the swings, you must never push them off. You must ask them if you can have a go. And then you must wait until they have finished.'

But when other people tell you what you can't do they don't do it like this. So I decide for myself what I am going to do and what I am not going to do.

That evening I went round to Mrs Shears' house and knocked on the door and waited for her to answer it.

When she opened the door she was holding a mug of tea and she was wearing sheepskin slippers and she had been watching a quiz programme on the television because there was a television on and I could hear someone saying, 'The capital city of Venezuela is . . . a) Maracas, b) Caracas, c) Bogota or d) Georgetown.' And I knew that it was Caracas.

She said, 'Christopher, I really don't think I want to see you right now.'

I said, 'I didn't kill Wellington.'

And she replied, 'What are you doing here?'

I said, 'I wanted to come and tell you that I didn't kill Wellington. And also I want to find out who killed him.'

Some of her tea spilled onto the carpet.

I said, 'Do you know who killed Wellington?'

She didn't answer my question. She just said, 'Goodbye, Christopher,' and closed the door.

Then I decided to do some detective work.

I could see that she was watching me and waiting for me to leave because I could see her standing in her hall on the other side of the frosted glass in her front door. So I walked down the path and out of the garden. Then I turned round and saw that she wasn't standing in her hall any longer. I made sure that there was no one watching and climbed over the wall and walked down the side of the house into her back garden to the shed where she kept all her gardening tools.

The shed was locked with a padlock and I couldn't go inside so I walked round to the window in the side. Then I had some good luck. When I looked through the window I could see a fork that looked exactly the same as the fork that had been sticking out of Wellington. It was lying on the bench by the window and it had been cleaned because there was no blood on the spikes. I could see some other tools as well, a spade and a rake and one of those long clippers people use for cutting branches which are too high to reach. And they all had the same green plastic handles like the fork. This meant that the fork belonged to Mrs Shears. Either that or it was a *Red Herring*, which is a clue which makes you come to a wrong conclusion or something which looks like a clue but isn't.

I wondered if Mrs Shears had killed Wellington herself. But if she had killed Wellington herself why did she come out of the house shouting, 'What in fuck's name have you done to my dog?'

I thought that Mrs Shears probably didn't kill Wellington. But whoever had killed him had probably killed him with Mrs Shears' fork. And the shed was locked. This meant that it was someone who had the key to Mrs Shears' shed, or that she had left it unlocked, or that she had left her fork lying around in the garden.

I heard a noise and turned round and saw Mrs Shears standing on the lawn looking at me.

I said, 'I came to see if the fork was in the shed.'

And she said, 'If you don't go now I will call the police again.'

So I went home.

When I got home I said hello to Father and went upstairs and fed Toby, my rat, and felt happy, because I was being a detective and finding things out.

61

Mrs Forbes at school said that when Mother died she had gone to heaven. That was because Mrs Forbes is very old and she believes in heaven. And she wears tracksuit trousers because she says that they are more comfortable than normal trousers. And one of her legs is very slightly shorter than the other one because of an accident on a motorbike.

But when Mother died she didn't go to heaven because heaven doesn't exist.

Mrs Peters' husband is a vicar called the Reverend Peters, and he comes to our school sometimes to talk to us, and I asked him where heaven was and he said, 'It's not in our universe. It's another kind of place altogether.'

The Reverend Peters makes a funny ticking noise with his tongue sometimes when he is thinking. And he smokes cigarettes and you can smell them on his breath and I don't like this.

I said that there wasn't anything outside the universe and there wasn't another kind of place altogether. Except that there might be if you went through a black hole, but a black hole is what is called a *Singularity*, which means it is impossible to find out what is on the other side because the gravity of a black hole is so big that even electromagnetic waves like light can't get out of it, and electromagnetic waves are how we get information about things which are far away. And if heaven was on the other side of a black hole dead people would have to be fired into space on rockets to get there, and they aren't, or people would notice.

I think people believe in heaven because they don't like the idea of dying, because they want to carry on living and they don't like the idea that other people will move into their house and put their things into the rubbish.

The Reverend Peters said, 'Well, when I say that heaven is outside the universe it's really just a manner of speaking. I suppose what it really means is that they are with God.'

And I replied, 'But where is God?'

And the Reverend Peters said that we should talk about this on another day when he had more time.

What actually happens when you die is that your brain stops working and your body rots, like Rabbit did when he died and we buried him in the earth at the bottom of the garden. And all his molecules were broken down into other molecules and they went into the earth and were eaten by worms and went into the plants and if we go and dig in the same place in 10 years there will be nothing except his skeleton left. And in 1,000 years even his skeleton will be gone. But that is all right because he is a part of the flowers and the apple tree and the hawthorn bush now.

When people die they are sometimes put into coffins which means that they don't mix with the earth for a very long time until the wood of the coffin rots.

But Mother was cremated. This means that she was put into a coffin and burnt and ground up and turned into ash and smoke. I do not know what happens to the ash and I couldn't ask at the crematorium because I didn't go to the funeral. But the smoke goes out of the chimney and into the air and sometimes I look up into the sky and I think that there are molecules of Mother up there, or in clouds over Africa or the Antarctic, or coming down as rain in the rainforests in Brazil, or in snow somewhere.

67

The next day was Saturday and there is not much to do on a Saturday unless Father takes me out somewhere on an outing to the boating lake or to the garden centre, but on this Saturday England were playing Romania at football which meant that we weren't going to go on an outing because Father wanted to watch the match on the television. So I decided to do some more detection on my own.

I decided that I would go and ask some of the other people who lived in our street if they had seen anyone killing Wellington or whether they had seen anything strange happening in the street on Thursday night.

Talking to strangers is not something I usually do. I do not like talking to strangers. This is not because of **Stranger Danger** which they tell us about at school, which is where a strange man offers you sweets or a ride in his car because he wants to do sex with you. I am not worried about that. If a strange man touched me I would hit him, and I can hit people very hard. For example, when I punched Sarah because she had pulled my hair I knocked her unconscious and she had concussion and they had to take her to the Accident and Emergency Department at the hospital. And also I always have my Swiss Army Knife in my pocket and it has a saw blade which could cut a man's fingers off.

I do not like strangers because I do not like people I have never met before. They are hard to understand. It is like being in France, which is where we went on holiday sometimes when Mother was alive, to camp. And I hated it because if you went into a shop or a restaurant or on a beach you couldn't understand what anyone was saying which was frightening.

It takes me a long time to get used to people I do not know. For example, when there is a new member of staff at school I do not talk to them for weeks and weeks. I just watch them until I know that they are safe. Then I ask them questions about themselves, like whether they have pets and what is their favourite colour and what do they know about the Apollo space missions and I get them to draw a plan of their house and I ask them what kind of car they drive, so I get to know them. Then I don't mind if I am in the same room as them and don't have to watch them all the time.

So talking to the other people in our street was brave. But if you are going to do detective work you have to be brave, so I had no choice.

First of all I made a plan of our part of the street which is called Randolph Street, like this

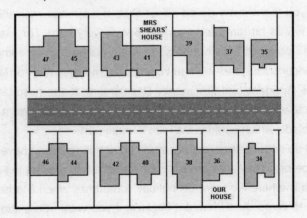

Then I made sure I had my Swiss Army Knife in my pocket and I went out and I knocked on the door of number 40 which is opposite Mrs Shears' house which means that they were most likely to have seen something. The people who live at number 40 are called Thompson.

Mr Thompson answered the door. He was wearing a T-shirt which said

Beer.
Helping ugly people
have sex for
2,000 years.

Mr Thompson said, 'Can I help you?'

I said, 'Do you know who killed Wellington?'

I did not look at his face. I do not like looking at people's faces, especially if they are strangers. He did not say anything for a few seconds.

Then he said, 'Who are you?'

I said, 'I'm Christopher Boone from number 36 and I know you. You're Mr Thompson.'

He said, 'I'm Mr Thompson's brother.'

I said, 'Do you know who killed Wellington?'

He said, 'Who the fuck is Wellington?'

I said, 'Mrs Shears' dog. Mrs Shears is from number 41.'

He said, 'Someone killed her dog?'

I said, 'With a fork.'

He said, 'Jesus Christ.'

I said, 'A garden fork,' in case he thought I meant a fork you eat your food with. Then I said, 'Do you know who killed him?'

He said, 'I haven't a bloody clue.'

I said, 'Did you see anything suspicious on Thursday evening?'

He said, 'Look, son, do you really think you should be going around asking questions like this?'

And I said, 'Yes, because I want to find out who killed Wellington, and I am writing a book about it.'

And he said, 'Well, I was in Colchester on Thursday, so you're asking the wrong bloke.'

I said, 'Thank you,' and I walked away.

There was no answer at house number 42.

I had seen the people who lived at number 44, but I did not know what their names were. They were black people and they were a man and a lady with two children, a boy and a girl. The lady answered the door. She was wearing boots which looked like army boots and there were 5 bracelets made out of a silver-coloured metal on her wrist and they made a jangling noise. She said, 'It's Christopher, isn't it?'

I said that it was, and I asked her if she knew who killed Wellington. She knew who Wellington was so I didn't have to explain, and she had heard about him being killed.

I asked if she had seen anything suspicious on Thursday evening which might be a clue.

She said, 'Like what?'

And I said, 'Like strangers. Or like the sound of people arguing.'

But she said she hadn't.

And then I decided to do what is called *Trying a Different Tack*, and I asked her whether she knew of anyone who might want to make Mrs Shears sad.

And she said, 'Perhaps you should be talking to your father about this.'

And I explained that I couldn't ask my father because the investigation was a secret because he had told me to stay out of other people's business.

She said, 'Well, maybe he has a point, Christopher.'

And I said, 'So, you don't know anything which might be a clue.'

And she said, 'No,' and then she said, 'You be careful, young man.'

I said that I would be careful and then I said thank you to her for helping me with my questions and I went to number 43 which is the house next to Mrs Shears' house.

The people who live at number 43 are Mr Wise and Mr Wise's mother who is in a wheelchair which is why he lives with her so he can take her to the shops and drive her around.

It was Mr Wise who answered the door. He smelt of body odour and old biscuits and off popcorn which is what you smell of if you haven't washed for a very long time, like Jason at school smells because his family is poor.

I asked Mr Wise if he knew who had killed Wellington on Thursday night.

He said, 'Bloody hell, policemen really are getting younger, aren't they?'

Then he laughed. I do not like people laughing at me, so I turned and walked away.

I did not knock at the door of number 38 which is the house next to our house because the people there take drugs and Father says that I should never talk to them, so I don't. And they play loud music at night and they make me scared sometimes when I see them in the street. And it is not really their house.

Then I noticed that the old lady who lives at number 39, which is on the other side of Mrs Shears' house, was in her front garden, cutting her hedge with an electric hedge-trimmer. Her name is Mrs Alexander. She has a dog. It is a Dachshund, so she was probably a good person because she liked dogs. But the dog wasn't in the garden with her. It was inside the house.

Mrs Alexander was wearing jeans and training shoes which old people don't normally wear. And there was mud on the jeans. And the trainers were New Balance trainers. And the laces were red.

I went up to Mrs Alexander and said, 'Do you know anything about Wellington being killed?'

Then she turned the electric hedge-trimmer off and said, 'I'm afraid you're going to have to say that again. I'm a little deaf.'

So I said, 'Do you know anything about Wellington being killed?'

And she said, 'I heard about it yesterday. Dreadful. Dreadful.'

I said, 'Do you know who killed him?'

And she said, 'No, I don't.'

I replied, 'Somebody must know because the person who

killed Wellington knows that they killed Wellington. Unless they were a mad person and didn't know what they were doing. Or unless they had amnesia.'

And she said, 'Well, I suppose you're probably right.'

I said, 'Thank you for helping me with my investigation.'

And she said, 'You're Christopher, aren't you?'

I said, 'Yes. I live at number 36.'

And she said, 'We haven't talked before, have we?'

I said, 'No. I don't like talking to strangers. But I'm doing detective work.'

And she said, 'I see you every day, going to school.'

I didn't reply to this.

And she said, 'It's very nice of you to come and say hello.'

I didn't reply to this either because Mrs Alexander was doing what is called chatting where people say things to each other which aren't questions and answers and aren't connected.

Then she said, 'Even if it's only because you're doing detective work.'

And I said, 'Thank you,' again.

And I was about to turn and walk away when she said, 'I have a grandson your age.'

I tried to do chatting by saying, 'My age is 15 years and 3 months and 3 days.'

And she said, 'Well, almost your age.'

Then we said nothing for a little while until she said, 'You don't have a dog, do you?'

And I said, 'No.'

She said, 'You'd probably like a dog, wouldn't you?'

And I said, 'I have a rat.'

And she said, 'A rat?'

And I said, 'He's called Toby.'

And she said, 'Oh.'

And I said, 'Most people don't like rats because they think they carry diseases like bubonic plague. But that's only because they lived in sewers and stowed away on ships coming from foreign countries where there were strange diseases. But rats are very clean. Toby is always washing himself. And you don't have to take him out for walks. I just let him run around my room so that he gets some exercise. And sometimes he sits on my shoulder or hides in my sleeve like it's a burrow. But rats don't live in burrows in nature.'

Mrs Alexander said, 'Do you want to come in for tea?'

And I said, 'I don't go into other people's houses.'

And she said, 'Well, maybe I could bring some out here. Do you like lemon squash?'

I replied, 'I only like orange squash.'

And she said, 'Luckily I have some of that as well. And what about Battenberg?'

And I said, 'I don't know because I don't know what Battenberg is.'

She said, 'It's a kind of cake. It has four pink and yellow squares in the middle and it has marzipan icing round the edge.'

And I said, 'Is it a long cake with a square cross-section which is divided into equally sized, alternately coloured squares?'

And she said, 'Yes, I think you could probably describe it like that.'

I said, 'I think I'd like the pink squares but not the yellow squares because I don't like yellow. And I don't know what marzipan is so I don't know whether I'd like that.'

And she said, 'I'm afraid marzipan is yellow, too. Perhaps I should bring out some biscuits instead. Do you like biscuits?'

And I said, 'Yes. Some sorts of biscuits.'

And she said, 'I'll get a selection.'

Then she turned and went into the house. She moved very slowly because she was an old lady and she was inside the house for more than 6 minutes and I began to get nervous because I didn't know what she was doing in the house. I didn't know her well enough to know whether she was telling the truth about getting orange squash and Battenberg cake. And I thought she might be ringing the police and then I'd get into much more serious trouble because of the caution.

So I walked away.

And as I was crossing the street I had a stroke of inspiration about who might have killed Wellington. I was imagining a **Chain of Reasoning** inside my head which was like this

1. Why would you kill a dog?

    a) Because you hated the dog.

    b) Because you were mad.

    c) Because you wanted to make Mrs Shears upset.

2. I didn't know anyone who hated Wellington, so if it was **a)** it was probably a stranger.

3. I didn't know any mad people, so if it was **b)** it was also probably a stranger.

4. Most murders are committed by someone who is known to the victim. In fact, you are most likely to be murdered by a member of your own family on Christmas Day. This is a fact. Wellington was therefore most likely to have been killed by someone known to him.

5. If it was **c)** I only knew one person who didn't like Mrs Shears, and that was Mr Shears who knew Wellington very well indeed.

This meant that Mr Shears was my **Prime Suspect**.

Mr Shears used to be married to Mrs Shears and they lived together until two years ago. Then Mr Shears left and didn't come back. This was why Mrs Shears came over and did lots of cooking for us after Mother died, because she didn't have to cook for Mr Shears any more and she didn't have to stay at home and be his wife. And also Father said that she needed company and didn't want to be on her own.

And sometimes Mrs Shears stayed overnight at our house and I liked it when she did because she made things tidy and she arranged the jars and pans and tins in order of their height on the shelves in the kitchen and she always made their labels face outwards and she put the knives and forks and spoons in the correct compartments in the cutlery drawer. But she smoked cigarettes and she said lots of things I didn't understand, e.g. 'I'm going to hit the hay,' and, 'It's brass monkeys out there,' and, 'Let's rustle up some tucker.' And I didn't like it when she said things like that because I didn't know what she meant.

And I don't know why Mr Shears left Mrs Shears because nobody told me. But when you get married it is because you want to live together and have children, and if you get married in a church you have to promise that you will stay together until death do us part. And if you don't want to live together you have to get divorced and this is because one of you has done sex with some-body else or because you are having arguments and you hate each other and you don't want to live in the same house any more and have children. And Mr Shears didn't want to live in the same house as Mrs Shears any more so he probably hated her and he might have come back and killed her dog to make her sad.

I decided to try and find out more about Mr Shears.

71

All the other children at my school are stupid. Except I'm not meant to call them stupid, even though this is what they are. I'm meant to say that they have learning difficulties or that they have special needs. But this is stupid because everyone has learning difficulties because learning to speak French or understanding Relativity is difficult, and also everyone has special needs, like Father who has to carry a little packet of artificial sweetening tablets around with him to put in his coffee to stop him getting fat, or Mrs Peters who wears a beige-coloured hearing aid, or Siobhan who has glasses so thick that they give you a headache if you borrow them, and none of these people are Special Needs, even if they have special needs.

But Siobhan said we have to use those words because people used to call children like the children at school *spaz* and *crip* and *mong* which were nasty words. But that is stupid too because sometimes the children from the school down the road see us in the street when we're getting off the bus and they shout, 'Special Needs! Special Needs!' But I don't take any notice because I don't listen to what other people say and only sticks and stones can break my bones and I have my Swiss Army Knife if they hit me and if I kill them it will be self-defence and I won't go to prison.

I am going to prove that I'm not stupid. Next month I'm going to take my A level in Maths and I'm going to get an A grade. No one has ever taken an A level at our school before and the headmistress, Mrs Gascoyne, didn't want me to take it at first. She said they didn't have the facilities to let us sit A levels. But Father had an argument with Mrs Gascoyne and he got really cross. Mrs Gascoyne said they didn't want to treat me differently from everyone else in the school because then everyone would want to be treated differently and it would set a precedent. And I could always do my A levels later, at 18.

I was sitting in Mrs Gascoyne's office with Father when she said these things. And Father said, 'Christopher is getting a crap enough deal already, don't you think, without you shitting on him from a great height as well. Jesus, this is the one thing he is really good at.'

Then Mrs Gascoyne said that she and Father should talk about this at some later point on their own. But Father asked her whether she wanted to say things she was embarrassed to say in front of me, and she said no, so he said, 'Say them now, then.'

And she said that if I sat an A level I would have to have a member of staff looking after me on my own in a separate room. And Father said he would pay someone £50 to do it after school and he wasn't going to take no for an answer. And she said she'd go away and think about it. And the next week she rang Father at home and told him that I could take the A level and the Reverend Peters would be what is called the invigilator.

And after I've taken A level Maths I am going to take A level Further Maths and Physics and then I can go to university. There is not a university in our town, which is Swindon, because it is a small place. So we will have to move to another town where there is a university because I don't want to live on my own or in a house with other students. But that will be all right because Father wants to move to a different town as well. He sometimes says things like, 'We've got to get out of this town, kiddo.' And sometimes he says, 'Swindon is the arsehole of the world.'

Then, when I've got a degree in Maths, or Physics, or Maths and Physics, I will be able to get a job and earn lots of money and I will be able to pay someone who can look after me and cook my meals and wash my clothes, or I will get a lady to marry me and be my wife and she can look after me so I can have company and not be on my own.

73

I used to think that Mother and Father might get divorced. That was because they had lots of arguments and sometimes they hated each other. This was because of the stress of looking after someone who has Behavioural Problems like I have. I used to have lots of Behavioural Problems, but I don't have so many now because I'm more grown up and I can take decisions for myself and do things on my own like going out of the house and buying things at the shop at the end of the road.

These are some of my Behavioural Problems

A. Not talking to people for a long time.[4]

B. Not eating or drinking anything for a long time.[5]

C. Not liking being touched.

D. Screaming when I am angry or confused.

E. Not liking being in really small places with other people.

F. Smashing things when I am angry or confused.

G. Groaning.

H. Not liking yellow things or brown things and refusing to touch yellow things or brown things.

I. Refusing to use my toothbrush if anyone else has touched it.

J. Not eating food if different sorts of food are touching each other.

[4] Once I didn't talk to anyone for 5 weeks.
[5] When I was 6 Mother used to get me to drink strawberry-flavoured slimming meals out of a measuring jug and we would have competitions to see how fast I could drink a quarter of a litre.

K. Not noticing that people are angry with me.

L. Not smiling.

M. Saying things that other people think are rude.[6]

N. Doing stupid things.[7]

O. Hitting other people.

P. Hating France.

Q. Driving Mother's car.[8]

R. Getting cross when someone has moved the furniture.[9]

Sometimes these things would make Mother and Father really angry and they would shout at me or they would shout at each other. Sometimes Father would say, 'Christopher, if you do not behave I swear I shall knock the living daylights out of you,' or

[6] People say that you always have to tell the truth. But they do not mean this because you are not allowed to tell old people that they are old and you are not allowed to tell people if they smell funny or if a grown-up has made a fart. And you are not allowed to say, 'I don't like you,' unless that person has been horrible to you.

[7] Stupid things are things like emptying a jar of peanut butter onto the table in the kitchen and making it level with a knife so it covers all the table right to the edges, or burning things on the gas stove to see what happened to them, like my shoes or silver foil or sugar.

[8] I only did this once by borrowing the keys when she went into town on the bus, and I hadn't driven a car before and I was 8 years old and 5 months so I drove it into the wall, and the car isn't there any more because Mother is dead.

[9] It is permitted to move the chairs and the table in the kitchen because that is different but it makes me feel dizzy and sick if someone has moved the sofa and the chairs around in the living room or the dining room. Mother used to do this when she did the hoovering, so I made a special plan of where all the furniture was meant to be and did measurements and I put everything back in its proper place afterwards and then I felt better. But since Mother died Father hasn't done any hoovering so that is OK. And Mrs Shears did the hoovering once but I did groaning and she shouted at Father and she never did it again.

Mother would say, 'Jesus, Christopher, I am seriously considering putting you in a home,' or Mother would say, 'You are going to drive me into an early grave.'

79

When I got home Father was sitting at the table in the kitchen and he had made my supper. He was wearing a lumberjack shirt. The supper was baked beans and broccoli and two slices of ham and they were laid out on the plate so that they were not touching.

He said, 'Where have you been?'

And I said, 'I have been out.' This is called a white lie. A white lie is not a lie at all. It is where you tell the truth but you do not tell all of the truth. This means that everything you say is a white lie because when someone says, for example, 'What do you want to do today?' you say, 'I want to do painting with Mrs Peters,' but you don't say 'I want to have my lunch and I want to go to the toilet and I want to go home after school and I want to play with Toby and I want to have my supper and I want to play on my computer and I want to go to bed.' And I said a white lie because I knew that Father didn't want me to be a detective.

Father said, 'I have just had a phone call from Mrs Shears.'

I started eating my baked beans and broccoli and two slices of ham.

Then Father asked, 'What the hell were you doing poking round her garden?'

I said, 'I was doing detective work trying to find out who killed Wellington.'

Father replied, 'How many times do I have to tell you, Christopher?'

The baked beans and the broccoli and the ham were **cold** but I didn't mind this. I eat very slowly so my food is nearly always cold.

Father said, 'I told you to keep your nose out of other people's business.'

I said, 'I think Mr Shears probably killed Wellington.'

Father didn't say anything.

I said, 'He is my Prime Suspect. Because I think someone might have killed Wellington to make Mrs Shears sad. And a murder is usually committed by someone known . . .'

Father banged the table with his fist really hard so that the plates and his knife and fork jumped around and my ham jumped sideways so that it touched the broccoli so I couldn't eat the ham or the broccoli any more.

Then he shouted, 'I will not have that man's name mentioned in my house.'

I asked, 'Why not?'

And he said, 'That man is evil.'

And I said, 'Does that mean he might have killed Wellington?'

Father put his head in his hands and said, 'Jesus wept.'

I could see that Father was angry with me, so I said, 'I know you told me not to get involved in other people's business but Mrs Shears is a friend of ours.'

And Father said, 'Well, she's not a friend any more.'

And I asked, 'Why not?'

And Father said, 'OK, Christopher. I am going to say this for the last and final time. I will not tell you again. Look at me when I'm talking to you, for God's sake. Look at me. You are not to go asking Mrs Shears about who killed that bloody dog. You are not to go asking anyone about who killed that bloody dog. You are not to go trespassing in other people's gardens. You are to stop this ridiculous bloody detective game right now.'

I didn't say anything.

Father said, 'I am going to make you promise, Christopher. And you know what it means when I make you promise.'

I did know what it meant when you say you promise something. You have to say that you will never do something again and then you must never do it because that would make the promise a lie. I said, 'I know.'

Father said, 'Promise me you will stop doing these things. Promise that you will give up this ridiculous game right now, OK?'

I said, 'I promise.'

83

I think I would make a very good astronaut.

To be a good astronaut you have to be intelligent and I'm intelligent. You also have to understand how machines work and I'm good at understanding how machines work. You also have to be someone who would like being on their own in a tiny spacecraft thousands and thousands of miles away from the surface of the earth and not panic or get claustrophobia or homesick or insane. And I like really little spaces, so long as there is no one else in them with me. Sometimes when I want to be on my own I get into the airing cupboard in the bathroom and slide in beside the boiler and pull the door closed behind me and sit there and think for hours and it makes me feel very calm.

So I would have to be an astronaut on my own, or have my own part of the spacecraft which no one else could come into.

And also there are no yellow things or brown things in a spacecraft so that would be OK, too.

And I would have to talk to other people from Mission Control, but we would do that through a radio link-up and a TV monitor so they wouldn't be like real people who are strangers, but it would be like playing a computer game.

Also I wouldn't be homesick at all because I'd be surrounded by lots of the things I like, which are machines and computers and outer space. And I would be able to look out of a little window in the spacecraft and know that there was no one else near me for thousands and thousands of miles which is what I sometimes pretend at night in the summer when I go and lie on the lawn and look up at the sky and I put my hands round the sides of my face so that I can't see the fence and the chimney and the washing line and I can pretend I'm in space.

And all I could see would be stars. And stars are the places where the molecules that life is made of were constructed billions of years ago. For example, all the iron in your blood which stops you being anaemic was made in a star.

And I would like it if I could take Toby with me into space, and that might be allowed because they sometimes do take animals into space for experiments, so if I could think of a good experiment you could do with a rat that didn't hurt the rat, I could make them let me take Toby.

But if they didn't let me I would still go because it would be a Dream Come True.

89

The next day at school I told Siobhan that Father had told me I couldn't do any more detecting which meant that the book was finished. I showed her the pages I had written so far, with the diagram of the universe and the map of the street and the prime numbers. And she said that it didn't matter. She said the book was really good as it was and that I should be very proud of having written a book at all, even if it was quite short and there were some very good books which were very short like **Heart of Darkness** which was by Conrad.

But I said that it wasn't a proper book because it didn't have a proper ending because I never found out who killed Wellington so the murderer was still At Large.

And she said that was like life, and not all murders were solved and not all murderers were caught. Like Jack the Ripper.

I said I didn't like the idea that the murderer was still At Large. I said I didn't like to think that the person who killed Wellington could be living somewhere nearby and I might meet him when I went out for a walk at night. And this was possible because a murder was usually committed by a person who was known to the victim.

Then I said, 'Father said I was never to mention Mr Shears' name in our house again and that he was an evil man and maybe that meant he was the person who killed Wellington.'

And she said, 'Perhaps your father just doesn't like Mr Shears very much.'

And I asked, 'Why?'

And she said, 'I don't know, Christopher. I don't know because I don't know anything about Mr Shears.'

I said, 'Mr Shears used to be married to Mrs Shears and he left her, like in a divorce. But I don't know if they were actually divorced.'

And Siobhan said, 'Well, Mrs Shears is a friend of yours, isn't she? A friend of you and your father. So perhaps your father doesn't like Mr Shears because he left Mrs Shears. Because he did something bad to someone who is a friend.'

And I said, 'But Father says Mrs Shears isn't a friend of ours any more.'

And Siobhan said, 'I'm sorry Christopher. I wish I could answer all these questions, but I simply don't know.'

Then the bell went for the end of school.

The next day I saw 4 yellow cars in a row on the way to school which made it a **Black Day** so I didn't eat anything at lunch and I sat in the corner of the room all day and read my A level Maths course book. And the next day, too, I saw 4 yellow cars in a row on the way to school which made it another **Black Day** too, so I didn't speak to anyone and for the whole afternoon I sat in the corner of the Library groaning with my head pressed into the join between the two walls and this made me feel calm and safe. But on the third day I kept my eyes closed all the way to school until we got off the bus because after I have had 2 **Black Days** in a row I'm allowed to do that.

97

But it wasn't the end of the book because five days later I saw 5 red cars in a row which made it a **Super Good Day** and I knew that something special was going to happen. Nothing special happened at school so I knew something special was going to happen after school. And when I got home I went down to the shop at the end of our road to buy some liquorice laces and a Milky Bar with my pocket money.

And when I had bought my liquorice laces and a Milky Bar I turned round and saw Mrs Alexander, the old lady from number 39, who was in the shop as well. She wasn't wearing jeans now. She was wearing a dress like a normal old lady. And she smelt of cooking.

She said, 'What happened to you the other day?'

I asked, 'Which day?'

And she said, 'I came out again and you'd gone. I had to eat all the biscuits myself.'

I said, 'I went away.'

And she said, 'I gathered that.'

I said, 'I thought you might ring the police.'

And she said, 'Why on earth would I do that?'

And I said, 'Because I was poking my nose into other people's business and Father said I shouldn't investigate who killed Wellington. And a policeman gave me a caution and if I get into trouble again it will be a lot worse because of the caution.'

Then the Indian lady behind the counter said to Mrs

Alexander, 'Can I help you?' and Mrs Alexander said she'd like a pint of milk and a packet of Jaffa Cakes and I went out of the shop.

When I was outside the shop I saw that Mrs Alexander's Dachshund was sitting on the pavement. It was wearing a little coat made out of Tartan material which is Scottish and check. She had tied its lead to the drainpipe next to the door. I like dogs, so I bent down and I said hello to her dog and it licked my hand. Its tongue was rough and wet and it liked the smell on my trousers and started sniffing them.

Then Mrs Alexander came outside and said, 'His name is Ivor.'

I didn't say anything.

And Mrs Alexander said, 'You're very shy, aren't you, Christopher?'

And I said, 'I'm not allowed to talk to you.'

And she said, 'Don't worry. I'm not going to tell the police and I'm not going to tell your father because there's nothing wrong with having a chat. Having a chat is just being friendly, isn't it?'

I said, 'I can't do chatting.'

Then she said, 'Do you like computers?'

And I said, 'Yes. I like computers. I have a computer at home in my bedroom.'

And she said, 'I know. I can see you sitting at your computer in your bedroom sometimes when I look across the street.'

Then she untied Ivor's lead from the drainpipe.

I wasn't going to say anything because I didn't want to get into trouble.

Then I thought that this was a **Super Good Day** and something special hadn't happened yet so it was possible that talking to Mrs Alexander was the special thing that was going to happen. And I thought that she might tell me something about Wellington or about Mr Shears without me asking her, so that wouldn't be breaking my promise.

So I said, 'And I like maths and looking after Toby. And also I like outer space and I like being on my own.'

And she said, 'I bet you're very good at maths, aren't you?'

And I said, 'I am. I'm going to do my A level Maths next month. And I'm going to get an A grade.'

And Mrs Alexander said, 'Really? A level Maths?'

I replied, 'Yes. I don't tell lies.'

And she said, 'I apologise. I didn't mean to suggest that you were lying. I just wondered if I heard you correctly. I'm a little deaf sometimes.'

And I said, 'I remember. You told me.' And then I said, 'I'm the first person to do an A level from my school because it's a special school.'

And she said, 'Well, I am very impressed. And I hope you do get an A.'

And I said, 'I will.'

Then she said, 'And the other thing I know about you is that your favourite colour is not yellow.'

And I said, 'No. And it's not brown either. My favourite colour is red. And metal colour.'

Then Ivor did a poo and Mrs Alexander picked it up with her hand inside a little plastic bag and then she turned the plastic bag

71

inside out and tied a knot in the top so that the poo was all sealed up and she didn't touch the poo with her hands.

And then I did some reasoning. I reasoned that father had only made me do a promise about five things which were

1. Not to mention Mr Shears' name in our house.
2. Not to go asking Mrs Shears about who killed that bloody dog.
3. Not to go asking anyone about who killed that bloody dog.
4. Not to go trespassing in other people's gardens.
5. To stop this ridiculous bloody detective game.

And asking about Mr Shears wasn't any of these things. And if you are a detective you have to *Take Risks* and this was a **Super Good Day** which meant it was a good day for *Taking Risks*, so I said, 'Do you know Mr Shears?' which was like chatting.

And Mrs Alexander said, 'Not really, no. I mean, I knew him well enough to say hello and talk to a little in the street, but I didn't know much about him. I think he worked in a bank. The National Westminster. In town.'

And I said, 'Father says that he is an evil man. Do you know why he said that? Is Mr Shears an evil man?'

And Mrs Alexander said, 'Why are you asking me about Mr Shears, Christopher?'

I didn't say anything because I didn't want to be investigating Wellington's murder and that was the reason I was asking about Mr Shears.

But Mrs Alexander said, 'Is this about Wellington?'

And I nodded because that didn't count as being a detective.

Mrs Alexander didn't say anything. She walked to the little red box on a pole next to the gate to the park and she put Ivor's poo into the box, which was a brown thing inside a red thing which made my head feel funny so I didn't look. Then she walked back to me.

She sucked in a big breath and said, 'Perhaps it would be best not to talk about these things, Christopher.'

And I asked, 'Why not?'

And she said, 'Because.' Then she stopped and decided to start saying a different sentence. 'Because maybe your father is right and you shouldn't go around asking questions about this.'

And I asked, 'Why?'

And she said, 'Because obviously he is going to find it quite upsetting.'

And I said, 'Why is he going to find it upsetting?'

Then she sucked in another big breath and said, 'Because . . . because I think you know why your father doesn't like Mr Shears very much.'

Then I asked, 'Did Mr Shears kill Mother?'

And Mrs Alexander said, 'Kill her?'

And I said, 'Yes. Did he kill Mother?'

And Mrs Alexander said, 'No. No. Of course he didn't kill your mother.'

And I said, 'But did he give her stress so that she died of a heart attack?'

And Mrs Alexander said, 'I honestly don't know what you're talking about, Christopher.'

And I said, 'Or did he hurt her so that she had to go into hospital?'

And Mrs Alexander said, 'Did she have to go into hospital?'

And I said, 'Yes. And it wasn't very serious at first, but she had a heart attack when she was in hospital.'

And Mrs Alexander said, 'Oh my goodness.'

I said, 'And she died.'

And Mrs Alexander said, 'Oh my goodness,' again, and then she said, 'Oh Christopher, I am so, so sorry. I never realised.'

Then I asked her, 'Why did you say, "I think you know why your father doesn't like Mr Shears very much"?'

Mrs Alexander put her hand over her mouth and said, 'Oh dear, dear, dear.' But she didn't answer my question.

So I asked her the same question again, because in a murder mystery novel when someone doesn't want to answer a question it is because they are trying to keep a secret or trying to stop someone getting into trouble, which means that the answers to those questions are the most important answers of all, and that is why the detective has to put that person under pressure.

But Mrs Alexander still didn't answer. Instead she asked me a question. She said, 'So you don't know?'

And I said, 'Don't know what?'

She replied, 'Christopher, look, I probably shouldn't be telling you this.' Then she said, 'Perhaps we should take a little walk in the park together. This is not the place to be talking about this kind of thing.'

I was nervous. I did not know Mrs Alexander. I knew that she was an old lady and that she liked dogs. But she was a stranger. And I never go into the park on my own because it is dangerous and people inject drugs behind the public toilets in the corner. I wanted to go home and go up to my room and feed Toby and practise some maths.

But I was excited, too. Because I thought she might tell me a secret. And the secret might be about who killed Wellington. Or about Mr Shears. And if she did that I might have more evidence against him, or be able to *Exclude Him From My Investigations*.

So because it was a **Super Good Day** I decided to walk into the park with Mrs Alexander even though it scared me.

When we were inside the park Mrs Alexander stopped walking and said, 'I am going to say something to you and you must promise not to tell your father that I told you this.'

I asked, 'Why?'

And she said, 'I shouldn't have said what I said. And if I don't explain, you'll carry on wondering what I meant. And you might ask your father. And I don't want you to do that because I don't want you to upset him. So I'm going to explain why I said what I said. But before I do that you have to promise not to tell anyone I said this to you.'

I asked, 'Why?'

And she said, 'Christopher, please, just trust me.'

And I said, 'I promise.' Because if Mrs Alexander told me who killed Wellington, or she told me that Mr Shears had really killed Mother, I could still go to the police and tell them because you are allowed to break a promise if someone has committed a crime and you know about it.

And Mrs Alexander said, 'Your mother, before she died, was very good friends with Mr Shears.'

And I said, 'I know.'

And she said, 'No, Christopher. I'm not sure that you do. I mean that they were very good friends. Very, very good friends.'

I thought about this for a while and said, 'Do you mean that they were doing sex?'

And Mrs Alexander said, 'Yes, Christopher. That is what I mean.'

Then she didn't say anything for about 30 seconds.

Then she said, 'I'm sorry, Christopher. I really didn't mean to say anything that was going to upset you. But I wanted to explain. Why I said what I said. You see, I thought you knew. That's why your father thinks that Mr Shears is an evil man. And that will be why he doesn't want you going around talking to people about Mr Shears. Because that will bring back bad memories.'

And I said, 'Was that why Mr Shears left Mrs Shears, because he was doing sex with someone else when he was married to Mrs Shears?'

And Mrs Alexander said, 'Yes, I expect so.'

Then she said, 'I'm sorry, Christopher. I really am.'

And I said, 'I think I should go now.'

And she said, 'Are you OK, Christopher?'

And I said, 'I'm scared of being in the park with you because you're a stranger.'

And she said, 'I'm not a stranger, Christopher, I'm a friend.'

And I said, 'I'm going to go home now.'

And she said, 'If you want to talk about this you can come and see me any time you want. You only have to knock on my door.'

And I said, 'OK.'

And she said, 'Christopher?'

And I said, 'What?'

And she said, 'You won't tell your father about this conversation, will you?'

And I said, 'No. I promised.'

And she said, 'You go on home. And remember what I said. Any time.'

Then I went home.

101

Mr Jeavons said that I liked maths because it was safe. He said I liked maths because it meant solving problems, and these problems were difficult and interesting, but there was always a straightforward answer at the end. And what he meant was that maths wasn't like life because in life there are no straightforward answers at the end. I know he meant this because this is what he said.

This is because Mr Jeavons doesn't understand numbers.

Here is a famous story called **The Monty Hall Problem** which I have included in this book because it illustrates what I mean.

There used to a be a column called *Ask Marilyn* in a magazine called *Parade* in America. And this column was written by Marilyn vos Savant and in the magazine it said that she had the highest IQ in the world in the *Guinness Book of World Records Hall of Fame*. And in the column she answered maths questions sent in by readers. And in September 1990 this question was sent in by Craig F. Whitaker of Columbia, Maryland (but it is not what is called a direct quote because I have made it simpler and easier to understand).

You are on a game show on television. On this game show the idea is to win a car as a prize. The game show host shows you three doors. He says that there is a car behind one of the doors and there are goats behind the other two doors. He asks you to pick a door. You pick a door but the door is not opened. Then the game show host opens one of the doors you didn't pick to show a goat (because he knows what is behind the doors). Then he says that you have one final chance to change your mind before the doors are opened and you get a car or a goat. So he asks you if you want to change your mind and pick the other unopened door instead. What should you do?

Marilyn vos Savant said that you should always change and pick the final door because the chances are 2 in 3 that there will be a car behind that door.

But if you use your intuition you think that chance is 50:50 because you think there is an equal chance that the car is behind any door.

Lots of people wrote to the magazine to say that Marilyn vos Savant was wrong, even when she explained very carefully why she was right. 92% of the letters she got about the problem said that she was wrong and lots of these were from mathematicians and scientists. Here are some of the things that they said

I'm very concerned with the general public's lack of mathematical skills. Please help by confessing your error.
Robert Sachs, Ph.D., George Mason University

There is enough mathematical illiteracy in this country,

*and we don't need the world's highest IQ propagating
more. Shame!*
Scott Smith, Ph.D., University of Florida

*I am in shock that after being corrected by at least
three mathematicians, you still do not see your mistake.*
Kent Ford, Dickinson State University

*I am sure you will receive many letters from high school
and college students. Perhaps you should keep a few
addresses for help with future columns.*
W. Robert Smith, Ph.D., Georgia State University

*You are utterly incorrect . . . How many irate
mathematicians are needed to get you to change
your mind?*
E. Ray Bobo, Ph.D., Georgetown University

*If all those Ph.D.s were wrong, the country would be in
very serious trouble.*
Everett Harman, Ph.D., U.S. Army Research Institute

But Marilyn vos Savant was right. And here are 2 ways you can
show this.

Firstly you can do it by maths like this

Let the doors be called X, Y and Z.

Let C_X be the event that the car is behind door X and so on.

Let H_X be the event that the host opens door X and so on.

Supposing that you choose door X, the possibility that you win a car if you then switch your choice is given by the following formula:

$$P(H_Z \wedge C_Y) + P(H_Y \wedge C_Z)$$
$$= P(C_Y).P(H_Z \mid C_Y) + P(C_Z).P(H_Y \mid C_Z)$$
$$= (1/3.1) + (1/3.1) = 2/3$$

The second way you can work it out is by making a picture of all the possible outcomes like this

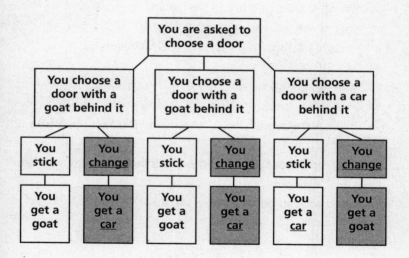

So, if you change, 2 times out of 3 you get a car. And if you stick, you only get a car 1 time out of 3.

And this shows that intuition can sometimes get things wrong. And intuition is what people use in life to make decisions. But logic can help you work out the right answer.

It also shows that Mr Jeavons was wrong and numbers are sometimes very complicated and not very straightforward at all. And that is why I like **The Monty Hall Problem**.

103

When I got home, Rhodri was there. Rhodri is the man who works for Father, helping him do heating maintenance and boiler repair. And he sometimes comes round to the house in the evening to drink beer with Father and watch the television and have a conversation.

Rhodri was wearing a pair of white dungarees which had dirty marks all over them and he had a gold ring on the middle finger of his left hand and he smelt of something I do not know the name of which Father often smells of when he comes home from work.

I put my liquorice laces and my Milky Bar in my special food box on the shelf which Father is not allowed to touch because it is mine.

Then Father said, 'And what have you been up to, young man?'

And I said, 'I went to the shop to get some liquorice laces and a Milky Bar.'

And he said, 'You were a long time.'

And I said, 'I talked to Mrs Alexander's dog outside the shop. And I stroked him and he sniffed my trousers.' Which was another white lie.

Then Rhodri said to me, 'God, you do get the third degree, don't you?'

But I didn't know what *the third degree* was.

And he said, 'So, how are you doing, Captain?'

And I said, 'I'm doing very well, thank you,' which is what you're meant to say.

And he said, 'What's 251 times 864?'

And I thought about this and I said, '216,864.' Because it was a really easy sum because you just multiply **864 x 1,000** which is **864,000**. Then you divide it by by **4** which is **216,000** and that's **250 x 864**. Then you just add another **864** on to it to get **251 x 864**. And that's **216,864**.

And I said, 'Is that right?'

And Rhodri said, 'I haven't got a bloody clue,' and he laughed.

I don't like it when Rhodri laughs at me. Rhodri laughs at me a lot. Father says it is being friendly.

Then Father said, 'I'll stick one of those Gobi Aloo Sag things in the oven for you, OK?'

This is because I like Indian food because it has a strong taste. But Gobi Aloo Sag is yellow so I put red food colouring into it before I eat it. And I keep a little plastic bottle of this in my special food box.

And I said, 'OK.'

And Rhodri said, 'So, it looks like Parky stitched them up, then?' But this was to Father, not to me.

And Father said, 'Well, those circuit boards looked like they'd come out of the bloody ark.'

And Rhodri said, 'You going to tell them?'

And Father said, 'What's the point? They're hardly going to take him to court, are they?'

And Rhodri said, 'That'll be the day.'

And Father said, 'Best to let sleeping dogs lie, I reckon.'

Then I went into the garden.

Siobhan said that when you are writing a book you have to include some descriptions of things. I said that I could take photographs and put them in the book. But she said the idea of a book was to describe things using words so that people could read them and make a picture in their own head.

And she said it was best to describe things that were interesting or different.

She also said that I should describe people in the story by mentioning one or two details about them, so that people could make a picture of them in their head. Which is why I wrote about Mr Jeavons' shoes with all the holes in them and the policeman who looked as if he had two mice in his nose and the thing Rhodri smelled of but I didn't know the name for.

So I decided to do a description of the garden. But the garden wasn't very interesting or different. It was just a garden, with grass and a shed and a clothes line. But the sky was interesting and different because usually skies look boring because they are all blue or all grey or all covered in one pattern of clouds and they don't look like they are hundreds of miles above your head. They look like someone might have painted them on a big roof. But this sky had lots of different types of clouds in it at different heights so you could see how big it was and this made it look enormous.

Furthest away in the sky were lots of little white clouds which looked liked fish scales or sand dunes which had a very regular pattern.

Then, next furthest away and to the west were some big

clouds which were coloured slightly orange because it was nearly evening and the sun was going down.

Then, closest to the ground was a huge cloud which was coloured grey because it was a rain cloud. And it was a big pointy shape and it looked like this

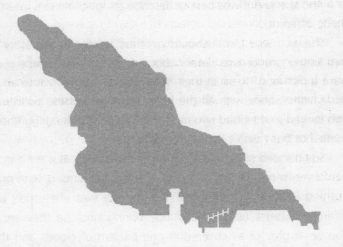

And when I looked at it for a long time I could see it moving very slowly and it was like an alien spaceship hundreds of kilometres long, like in *Dune* or *Blake's 7* or *Close Encounters of the Third Kind*, except that it wasn't made of solid material, it was made of droplets of condensed water vapour, which is what clouds are made of.

And it could have been an alien spaceship.

People think that alien spaceships would be solid and made of metal and have lights all over them and move slowly through the sky because that is how we would build a spaceship if we were able to build one that big. But aliens, if they exist, would probably be very different from us. They might look like big slugs, or be flat like reflections. Or they might be bigger than planets. Or they might not have bodies at all. They might just be information, like in a computer. And their spaceships might look like clouds, or be made up of unconnected objects like dust or leaves.

Then I listened to the sounds in the garden and I could hear a bird singing and I could hear traffic noise which was like the surf on a beach and I could hear someone playing music somewhere and children shouting. And in between these noises, if I listened very carefully and stood completely still, I could hear a tiny whining noise inside my ears and the air going in and out of my nose.

Then I sniffed the air to see if I could see what the air in the garden smelled like. But I couldn't smell anything. It smelled of nothing. And this was interesting, too.

Then I went inside and fed Toby.

107

The Hound of the Baskervilles is my favourite book.

In ***The Hound of the Baskervilles***, Sherlock Holmes and Doctor Watson get a visit from James Mortimer who is a doctor from the moors in Devon. James Mortimer's friend, Sir Charles Baskerville, has died of a heart attack and James Mortimer thinks that he might have been scared to death. James Mortimer also has an ancient scroll which describes the curse of the Baskervilles.

On this scroll it says that Sir Charles Baskerville had an ancestor called Sir Hugo Baskerville who was a wild, profane and godless man. And he tried to do sex with a daughter of a yeoman, but she escaped and he chased her across the moor. And his friends, who were dare-devil roisterers, chased after him.

And when they found him, the daughter of the yeoman had died of exhaustion and fatigue. And they saw a great, black beast, shaped like a hound, yet larger than any hound that ever mortal eye has rested on, and this hound was tearing the throat out of Sir Hugo Baskerville. And one of the friends died of fear that very night and the other two were broken men for the rest of their days.

James Mortimer thinks that the Hound of the Baskervilles might have scared Sir Charles to death and he is worried that his son and heir, Sir Henry Baskerville, will be in danger when he goes to the Hall in Devon.

So Sherlock Holmes sends Doctor Watson to Devon with Sir Henry Baskerville and James Mortimer. And Doctor Watson tries to work out who might have killed Sir Charles Baskerville. And Sherlock Holmes says he will stay in London, but he travels to Devon secretly and does investigations of his own.

And Sherlock Holmes finds out that Sir Charles was killed by a neighbour called Stapleton who is a butterfly collector and a distant relation of the Baskervilles. And Stapleton is poor, so he tries to kill Sir Henry Baskerville so that he will inherit the Hall.

In order to do this he has brought a huge dog from London and covered it in phosphorus to make it glow in the dark and it was this dog which scared Sir Charles Baskerville to death. And Sherlock Holmes and Watson and Lestrade from Scotland Yard catch him. And Sherlock Holmes and Watson shoot the dog, which is one of the dogs which gets killed in the story, which is not nice because it is not the dog's fault. And Stapleton escapes into the Grimpen Mire which is part of the moor, and he dies because he is sucked into a bog.

There are some bits of the story I don't like. One bit is the ancient scroll because it is written in old language which is difficult to understand, like this

> Learn then from this story not to fear the fruits of the past, but rather to be circumspect in the future, that those foul passions whereby our family has suffered so grievously may not again be loosed to our undoing.

And sometimes Sir Arthur Conan Doyle (who is the author) describes people like this

There was something subtly wrong with the face, some coarseness of expression, some hardness, perhaps of eye, some looseness of lip which marred its perfect beauty.

And I don't know what *some hardness, perhaps of eye* means, and I'm not interested in faces.

But sometimes it is fun not knowing what the words mean because you can look them up in a dictionary, like *goyal* (which is a deep dip) or *tors* (which are hills or rocky heights).

I like **The Hound of the Baskervilles** because it is a detective story which means that there are clues and Red Herrings.

These are some of the clues

1. Two of Sir Henry Baskerville's boots go missing when he is staying at a hotel in London – This means that someone wants to give them to the Hound of the Baskervilles to smell, like a bloodhound, so that it can chase him. This means that The Hound of the Baskervilles is not a supernatural being but a real dog.

2. Stapleton is the only person who knows how to get through the Grimpen Mire and he tells Watson to stay out of it for his own safety – This means that he is hiding something in the middle of the Grimpen Mire and doesn't want anyone else to find it.

3. Mrs Stapleton tells Doctor Watson to 'Go straight back to London instantly' – This is because she thinks Doctor Watson is Sir Henry Baskerville and she knows that her husband wants to kill him.

And these are some of the Red Herrings

1. Sherlock Holmes and Watson are followed when they are in London by a man in a coach with a black beard – This makes you think that the man is Barrymore who is the caretaker at Baskerville Hall because he is the only other person who has a black beard. But the man is really Stapleton who is wearing a false beard.

2. Selden, the Notting Hill murderer – This is a man who has escaped from a prison nearby and is being hunted down on the moors, which makes you think that he has something to do with the story, because he is a criminal, but he isn't anything to do with the story at all.

3. The Man on the Tor – This is a silhouette of a man that Doctor Watson sees on the moor at night and doesn't recognise, which makes you think it is the murderer. But it is Sherlock Holmes who has come to Devon secretly.

I also like **The Hound of the Baskervilles** because I like Sherlock Holmes and I think that if I were a proper detective he is the kind of detective I would be. He is very intelligent and he solves the mystery and he says

> *The world is full of obvious things which nobody by any chance ever observes.*

But he notices them, like I do. Also it says in the book

> *Sherlock Holmes had, in a very remarkable degree, the power of detaching his mind at will.*

And this is like me, too, because if I get really interested in something, like practising maths, or reading a book about the Apollo missions, or Great White sharks, I don't notice anything else and Father can be calling me to come and eat my supper and I won't hear him. And this is why I am very good at playing chess, because I detach my mind at will and concentrate on the board and after a while the person I am playing will stop concentrating and start scratching their nose, or staring out of the window and then they will make a mistake and I will win.

Also Doctor Watson says about Sherlock Holmes

> *. . . his mind . . . was busy in endeavouring to frame some scheme into which all these strange and apparently disconnected episodes could be fitted.*

And that is what I am trying to do by writing this book.

Also Sherlock Holmes doesn't believe in the supernatural, which is God and fairy tales and Hounds of Hell and curses, which are stupid things.

And I am going to finish this chapter with two interesting facts about Sherlock Holmes.

1. In the original Sherlock Holmes stories Sherlock Holmes is never described as wearing a deerstalker hat, which is what he is always wearing in pictures and cartoons. The deerstalker hat was invented by a man called Sidney Paget who did the illustrations for the original books.

2. In the original Sherlock Holmes stories Sherlock Holmes never says, 'Elementary, my dear Watson.' He only ever says this in films and on the television.

109

That night I wrote some more of my book and the next morning I took it into school so that Siobhan could read it and tell me if I had made mistakes with the spelling and the grammar.

Siobhan read the book during morning break when she has a cup of coffee and sits at the edge of the playground with the other teachers. And after morning break she came and sat down next to me and said she had read the bit about my conversation with Mrs Alexander and she said, 'Have you told your father about this?'

And I replied, 'No,'

And she said, 'Are you going to tell your father about this?'

And I replied, 'No.'

And she said, 'Good. I think that's a good idea, Christopher.' And then she said, 'Did it make you sad to find this out?'

And I asked, 'Find what out?'

And she said, 'Did it make you upset to find out that your mother and Mr Shears had an affair?'

And I said, 'No.'

And she said, 'Are you telling the truth, Christopher?'

And then I said, 'I always tell the truth.'

And she said, 'I know you do, Christopher. But sometimes we get sad about things and we don't like to tell other people that we are sad about them. We like to keep it a secret. Or sometimes we are sad but we don't really know we are sad. So we say we aren't sad. But really we are.'

And I said, 'I'm not sad.'

And she said, 'If you do start to feel sad about this. I want you to know that you can come and talk to me about it. Because I think talking to me will help you feel less sad. And if you don't feel sad but you just want to talk to me about it, that would be OK, too. Do you understand?'

And I said, 'I understand.'

And she said, 'Good.'

And I replied, 'But I don't feel sad about it. Because Mother is dead. And because Mr Shears isn't around any more. So I would be feeling sad about something that isn't real and doesn't exist. And that would be stupid.'

And then I practised maths for the rest of the morning and at lunch I didn't have the quiche because it was yellow, but I did have the carrots and the peas and lots of tomato ketchup. And for afters I had some blackberry and apple crumble, but not the crumble bit because that was yellow too, and I got Mrs Davis to take the crumble bit off before she put it onto my plate because it doesn't matter if different sorts of food are touching before they are actually on your plate.

Then, after lunch, I spent the afternoon doing art with Mrs Peters and I painted some pictures of aliens which looked like this

113

My memory is like a film. That is why I am really good at remembering things, like the conversations I have written down in this book, and what people were wearing, and what they smelled like, because my memory has a smelltrack which is like a soundtrack.

And when people ask me to remember something I can simply press **Rewind** and **Fast Forward** and **Pause** like on a video recorder, but more like a DVD because I don't have to Rewind through everything in between to get to a memory of something a long time ago. And there are no buttons, either, because it is happening in my head.

If someone says to me, 'Christopher, tell me what your mother was like,' I can Rewind to lots of different scenes and say what she was like in those scenes.

For example I could Rewind to 4th July 1992 when I was 9 years old, which was a Saturday, and we were on holiday in Cornwall and in the afternoon we were on the beach in a place called Polperro. And Mother was wearing a pair of shorts made out of denim and a light blue bikini top and she was smoking cigarettes called Consulate which were mint flavour. And she wasn't swimming. Mother was sunbathing on a towel which had red and purple stripes and she was reading a book by Georgette Heyer called *The Masqueraders*. And then she finished sunbathing and went into the water to swim and she said, 'Bloody Nora, it's cold.' And she said I should come and swim, too, but I don't like swimming because I don't like taking my clothes off. And she said I should just roll up my trousers and walk into the water a little way, so I did. And I stood in the water. And Mother said, 'Look. It's lovely.' And she jumped backwards and disappeared under the water and I thought a shark had eaten her and I screamed and she stood up out of the water again and came over to where I was standing and held up her right hand and spread her fingers out in a fan and said, 'Come on, Christopher, touch my hand. Come on now. Stop screaming. Touch my hand. Listen to me, Christopher. You can do it.' And after a while I stopped screaming and I held up my left hand and spread my fingers out in a fan and we made our fingers and thumbs touch each other. And Mother said, 'It's OK, Christopher. It's OK. There aren't any sharks in Cornwall,' and then I felt better.

Except I can't remember anything before I was about 4 because I wasn't looking at things in the right way before then, so they didn't get recorded properly.

And this is how I recognise someone if I don't know who they are. I see what they are wearing, or if they have a walking stick, or funny hair, or a certain type of glasses, or they have a particular way of moving their arms and I do a **Search** through my memories to see if I have met them before.

And this is also how I know how to act in difficult situations when I don't know what to do.

For example, if people say things which don't make sense, like, 'See you later, alligator,' or 'You'll catch your death in that,' I do a **Search** and see if I have ever heard someone say this before.

And if someone is lying on the floor at school I do a **Search** through my memory to find a picture of someone having an epileptic fit and then I compare the picture with what is happening in front of me so I can decide whether they are just lying down and playing a game, or having a sleep, or whether they are having an epileptic fit. And if they are having an epileptic fit I move any furniture out of the way to stop them banging their head and I take my jumper off and I put it underneath their head and I go and find a teacher.

Other people have pictures in their heads, too. But they are different because the pictures in my head are all pictures of things which really happened. But other people have pictures in their heads of things which aren't real and didn't happen.

For example, sometimes Mother used to say, 'If I hadn't married your father I think I'd be living in a little farmhouse in the South of France with someone called Jean. And he'd be, ooh, a local handyman. You know, doing painting and decorating for people, gardening, building fences. And we'd have a veranda with figs growing over it and there would be a field of sunflowers at the bottom of the garden and a little town on the hill in the distance and we'd sit outside in the evening and drink red wine and smoke Gauloises cigarettes and watch the sun go down.'

And Siobhan once said that when she felt depressed or sad she would close her eyes and she would imagine that she was staying in a house on Cape Cod with her friend Elly, and they would take a trip on a boat from Provincetown and go out into the bay to watch the humpback whales and that made her feel calm and peaceful and happy.

And sometimes, when someone has died, like Mother died, people say, 'What would you want to say to your mother if she was here now?' or 'What would your mother think about that?', which is stupid because Mother is dead and you can't say anything to people who are dead and dead people can't think.

And Grandmother has pictures in her head, too, but her pictures are all confused, like someone has muddled the film up and she can't tell what happened in what order, so she thinks that dead people are still alive and she doesn't know whether something happened in real life or whether it happened on television.

127

When I got home from school Father was still out at work, so I unlocked the front door and went inside and took my coat off. I went into the kitchen and put my things on the table. And one of the things was this book which I had taken into school to show to Siobhan. I made myself a raspberry milkshake and heated it up in the microwave and then went through to the living room to watch one of my *Blue Planet* videos about life in the deepest parts of the ocean.

The video was about the sea creatures who live around sulphur chimneys, which are underwater volcanoes where gases are ejected from the earth's crust into the water. Scientists never expected there to be any living organisms there because it was so hot and so poisonous, but there are whole ecosystems there.

I like this bit because it shows you that there is always something new that science can discover, and all the facts that you take for granted can be completely wrong. And also I like the fact that they are filming in a place which is harder to get to than the top of Mount Everest but is only a few miles away from sea-level. And it is one of the quietest and darkest and most secret places on the surface of the earth. And I like imagining that I am there sometimes, in a spherical metal submersible with windows that are 30 cm thick to stop them imploding under the pressure. And I imagine that I am the only person inside it, and that it is not connected to a ship at all, but it can operate under its own power and I can control the motors and move anywhere I want to on the sea bed and I can never be found.

Father came home at 5:48 p.m. I heard him come through the front door. Then he came into the living room. He was wearing a lime green and sky blue check shirt and there was a double knot on one of his shoes but not on the other. He was carrying an old advert for Fussell's Milk Powder which was made of metal and painted with blue and white enamel and covered with little circles of rust which were like bullet-holes, but he didn't explain why he was carrying this.

He said, 'Howdy, Pardner,' which is a joke he does.

And I said, 'Hello.'

I carried on watching the video and Father went into the kitchen.

I had forgotten that I had left my book lying on the kitchen table because I was too interested in the **Blue Planet** video. This is what is called *Relaxing Your Guard*, and it is what you must never do if you are a detective.

It was 5:54 p.m. when Father came back into the living room. He said, 'What is this?', but he said it very quietly and I didn't realise that he was angry because he wasn't shouting.

He was holding the book in his right hand.

I said, 'It's a book I'm writing.'

And he said, 'Is this true? Did you talk to Mrs Alexander?' He said this very quietly as well, so I still didn't realise that he was angry.

And I said, 'Yes.'

Then he said, 'Holy fucking Jesus, Christopher. How stupid are you?'

This is what Siobhan says is called a rhetorical question. It has a question mark at the end, but you are not meant to answer it because the person who is asking it already knows the answer. It is difficult to spot a rhetorical question.

Then Father said, 'What the fuck did I tell you, Christopher?' This was much louder.

And I replied, 'Not to mention Mr Shears' name in our house. And not to go asking Mrs Shears, or anyone, about who killed that bloody dog. And not to go trespassing in other people's gardens. And to stop this ridiculous bloody detective game. Except I haven't done any of those things. I just asked Mrs Alexander about Mr Shears because . . .'

But Father interrupted me and said, 'Don't give me that bollocks, you little shit. You knew exactly what you were bloody doing. I've read the book, remember.' And when he said this he held up the book and shook it. 'What else did I say, Christopher?'

I thought that this might be another rhetorical question, but I wasn't sure. I found it hard to work out what to say because I was starting to get scared and confused.

Then Father repeated the question, 'What else did I say, Christopher?'

I said, 'I don't know.'

And he said, 'Come on. You're the fucking memory man.'

But I couldn't think.

And Father said, 'Not to go around sticking your fucking nose into other people's business. And what do you do? You go around sticking your nose into other people's business. You go around raking up the past and sharing it with every Tom, Dick and Harry you bump into. What am I going to do with you, Christopher? What the fuck am I going to do with you?'

I said, 'I was just doing chatting with Mrs Alexander. I wasn't doing investigating.'

And he said, 'I ask you to do one thing for me, Christopher. One thing.'

And I said, 'I didn't want to talk to Mrs Alexander. It was Mrs Alexander who . . .'

But Father interrupted me and grabbed hold of my arm really hard.

Father had never grabbed hold of me like that before. Mother had hit me sometimes because she was a very hot-tempered person, which means that she got angry more quickly than other people and she shouted more often. But Father is a more level-headed person, which means he doesn't get angry as quickly and he doesn't shout as often. So I was very surprised when he grabbed me.

I don't like it when people grab me. And I don't like being surprised either. So I hit him, like I hit the policeman when he took hold of my arms and lifted me onto my feet. But Father didn't let go, and he was shouting. And I hit him again. And then I didn't know what I was doing any more.

I had no memories for a short while. I know it was a short while because I checked my watch afterwards. It was like someone had switched me off and then switched me on again. And when they switched me on again I was sitting on the carpet with my back against the wall and there was blood on my right hand and the side of my head was hurting. And Father was standing on the carpet a metre in front of me looking down at me and he was still holding my book in his right hand, but it was bent in half and all the corners were messed up, and there was a scratch on his neck and a big rip in the sleeve of his green and blue check shirt and he was breathing really deeply.

After about a minute he turned and he walked through to the kitchen. Then he unlocked the back door into the garden and went outside. I heard him lift the lid of the dustbin and drop something into it and put the lid of the dustbin back on. Then he came into the kitchen again, but he wasn't carrying the book any more. Then he locked the back door and put the key into the little china jug that is shaped like a fat nun and he stood in the middle of the kitchen and closed his eyes.

Then he opened his eyes and he said, 'I need a fucking drink.'

And he got himself a can of beer.

131

These are some of the reasons why I hate yellow and brown.

YELLOW

1. Custard

2. Bananas (bananas also turn brown)

3. Double Yellow Lines

4. Yellow Fever (which is a disease from tropical America and West Africa which causes a high fever, acute nephritis, jaundice and haemorrhages, and it is caused by a virus transmitted by the bite of a mosquito called *Aëdes aegypti*, which used to be called *Stegomyia fasciata*; and nephritis is inflammation of the kidneys)

5. Yellow Flowers (because I get hay fever from flower pollen, which is one of 3 sorts of hay fever, and the others are from grass pollen and fungus pollen, and it makes me feel ill)

6. Sweetcorn (because it comes out in your poo and you don't digest it so you are not really meant to eat it, like grass or leaves)

BROWN

1. Dirt

2. Gravy

3. Poo

4. Wood (because people used to make machines and vehicles out of wood, but they don't any more because wood breaks and goes rotten and has worms in sometimes, and now people make machines and vehicles out of metal and plastic which are much better and more modern)

5. Melissa Brown (who is a girl at school, who is not actually brown like Anil or Mohammed, it's just her name, but she tore my big astronaut painting into two pieces and I threw it away even after Mrs Peters sellotaped it together again because it looked broken)

Mrs Forbes said that hating yellow and brown is just being silly. And Siobhan said that she shouldn't say things like that and everyone has favourite colours. And Siobhan was right. But Mrs Forbes was a bit right, too. Because it is sort of being silly. But in life you have to take lots of decisions and if you don't take decisions you would never do anything because you would spend all your time choosing between things you could do. So it is good to have a reason why you hate some things and you like others. It is like being in a restaurant like when Father takes me out to a Berni Inn sometimes and you look at the menu and you have to choose what you are going to have. But you don't know if you are going to like something because you haven't tasted it yet, so you have favourite foods and you choose these, and you have foods you don't like and you don't choose these, and then it is simple.

137

The next day Father said he was sorry that he had hit me and he didn't mean to. He made me wash the cut on my cheek with Dettol to make sure that it wasn't infected, then he got me to put a plaster on it so it didn't bleed.

Then, because it was a Saturday he said he was going to take me on an expedition to show me that he was properly sorry, and we were going to Twycross Zoo. So he made me some sandwiches with white bread and tomatoes and lettuce and ham and strawberry jam for me to eat because I don't like eating food from places I don't know. And he said it would be OK because there wouldn't be too many people at the zoo because it was forecast to rain, and I was glad about that because I don't like crowds of people and I like it when it is raining. So I went and got my waterproof which is orange.

Then we drove to Twycross Zoo.

I had never been to Twycross Zoo before so I didn't have a picture of it in my mind before we got there, so we bought a guidebook from the information centre and then we walked round the whole zoo and I decided which were my favourite animals.

My favourite animals were

1. RANDYMAN, which is the name of the oldest **Red-Faced Black Spider Monkey** (*Ateles paniscus paniscus*) ever kept in captivity. Randyman is 44 years old which is the same age as Father. He used to be a pet on a ship and have a metal band round his stomach, like in a story about pirates.

2. The **PATAGONIAN SEALIONS** which are called Miracle and Star.

3. MALIKU, which is an **Orang-Utan**. I liked it especially because it was lying in a kind of hammock made out of a pair of stripy green pyjama bottoms and on the blue plastic notice next to the cage it said it made the hammock itself.

Then we went to the café and Father had plaice and chips and apple pie and ice cream and a pot of Earl Grey tea and I had my sandwiches and I read the guidebook to the zoo.

And Father said, 'I love you very much, Christopher. Don't ever forget that. And I know I lose my rag occasionally. I know I get angry. I know I shout. And I know I shouldn't. But I only do it because I worry about you, because I don't want to see you getting into trouble, because I don't want you to get hurt. Do you understand?'

I didn't know whether I understood. So I said, 'I don't know.'

And Father said, 'Christopher, do you understand that I love you?'

And I said, 'Yes,' because loving someone is helping them when they get into trouble, and looking after them, and telling them the truth, and Father looks after me when I get into trouble, like coming to the police station, and he looks after me by cooking meals for me, and he always tells me the truth, which means that he loves me.

And then he held up his right hand and spread his fingers out in a fan, and I held up my left hand and spread my fingers out in a fan and we made our fingers and thumbs touch each other.

Then I got out a piece of paper from my bag and I did a map of the zoo from memory as a test. The map was like this

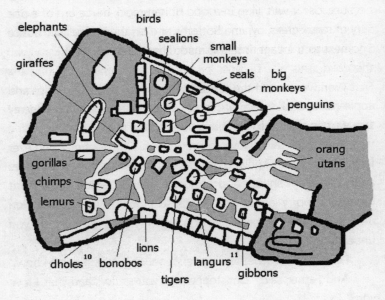

Then we went and looked at the giraffes. And the smell of their poo was like the smell inside the gerbil cage at school when we had gerbils, and when they ran their legs were so long it looked like they were running in slow motion.

Then Father said we had to get home before the roads got busy.

[10] The Dhole is *The Indian Wild Dog* and it looks like a fox.
[11] The Langur is *The Entellus Monkey*.

139

I like Sherlock Holmes, but I do not like Sir Arthur Conan Doyle who was the author of the Sherlock Holmes stories. That is because he wasn't like Sherlock Holmes and he believed in the supernatural. And when he got old he joined the Spiritualist Society which meant that he believed you could communicate with the dead. This was because his son died of influenza during the First World War and he still wanted to talk to him.

And in 1917 something famous happened called **The Case of the Cottingley Fairies**. 2 cousins called Frances Griffiths, who was 9 years old, and Elsie Wright, who was 16 years old, said they used to play with fairies by a stream called Cottingley Beck and they used Frances's father's camera to take 5 photographs of the fairies like this

But they weren't real fairies. They were drawings on pieces of paper that they cut out and stood up with pins, because Elsie was a really good artist.

Harold Snelling, who was an expert in fake photography, said

> These dancing figures are not made of paper nor any fabric; they are not painted on a photographic background – but what gets me most is that all these figures have moved during the exposure.

But he was being stupid because paper would move during an exposure, and the exposure was very long because in the photograph you can see a little waterfall in the background and it is blurred.

Then Sir Arthur Conan Doyle heard about the pictures and he said he believed they were real in an article in a magazine called **The Strand**. But he was being stupid, too, because if you look at the pictures you can see that the fairies look just like fairies in old books and they have wings and dresses and tights and shoes, which is like aliens landing on the earth and being like Daleks from **Doctor Who** or Imperial Stormtroopers from the Death Star in **Star Wars** or little green men like in cartoons of aliens.

And in 1981 a man called Joe Cooper interviewed Elsie Wright and Frances Griffiths for an article in a magazine called **The Unexplained** and Elsie Wright said all 5 photographs had been faked and Frances Griffiths said 4 had been faked but one was real.

And they said Elsie had drawn the fairies from a book called **Princess Mary's Gift Book** by Arthur Shepperson.

And this shows that sometimes people want to be stupid and they do not want to know the truth.

And it shows that something called Occam's razor is true. And Occam's razor is not a razor that men shave with but a law, and it says

Entia non sunt multiplicanda praeter necessitatem.

Which is Latin and it means

No more things should be presumed to exist than are absolutely necessary.

Which means that a murder victim is usually killed by someone known to them and fairies are made out of paper and you can't talk to someone who is dead.

149

When I went to school on Monday, Siobhan asked me why I had a bruise on the side of my face. I said that Father was angry and he had grabbed me so I had hit him and then we had a fight. Siobhan asked whether Father had hit me and I said I didn't know because I got very cross and it made my memory go strange. And then she asked if Father had hit me because he was angry. And I said he didn't hit me, he grabbed me, but he was angry. And Siobhan asked if he grabbed me hard, and I said that he had grabbed me hard. And Siobhan asked if I was frightened about going home, and I said I wasn't. And then she asked me if I wanted to talk about it any more, and I said that I didn't. And then she said, 'OK,' and we didn't talk about it any more, because grabbing is OK if it is on your arm or your shoulder when you are angry, but you can't grab someone's hair or their face. But hitting is not allowed, except if you are already in a fight with someone then it is not so bad.

And when I got home from school Father was still at work so I went into the kitchen and took the key out of the little china jug shaped like a nun and opened the back door and went outside and looked inside the dustbin to find my book.

I wanted to get my book back because I liked writing it. I liked having a project to do and I liked it especially if it was a difficult project like a book. Also I still didn't know who had killed Wellington and my book was where I had kept all the clues that I had discovered and I did not want them to be thrown away.

But my book wasn't in the dustbin.

I put the lid back on the dustbin and walked down the garden to have a look in the bin where Father keeps the garden waste, such as lawn-clippings and apples that have fallen off the trees, but my book wasn't in there either.

I wondered if Father had put it into his van and driven to the tip and put it into one of the big bins there, but I did not want that to be true because then I would never see it again.

One other possibility was that Father had hidden my book somewhere in the house. So I decided to do some detecting and see if I could find it. Except I had to keep listening really hard all the time so I would hear his van when he pulled up outside the house so he wouldn't catch me being a detective.

I started by looking in the kitchen. My book was approximately **25 cm x 35 cm x 1 cm** so it couldn't be hidden in a very small place, which meant that I didn't have to look in any really small places. I looked on top of the cupboards and down the back of drawers and under the oven and I used my special Maglite torch and a piece of mirror from the utility room to help me see into the dark spaces at the back of the cupboards where the mice used to get in from the garden and have their babies.

Then I detected in the utility room.

Then I detected in the dining room.

Then I detected in the living room where I found the missing wheel from my Airfix Messerschmitt Bf 109 G-6 model under the sofa.

Then I thought I heard Father coming through the front door and I jumped and I tried to stand up fast and I banged my knee on the corner of the coffee table and it hurt a lot, but it was only one of the drug people next door dropping something on the floor.

Then I went upstairs, but I didn't do any detecting in my own room because I reasoned that Father wouldn't hide something from me in my own room unless he was being very clever and doing what is called a *Double Bluff* like in a real murder mystery novel, so I decided to look in my own room only if I couldn't find the book anywhere else.

I detected in the bathroom, but the only place to look was in the airing cupboard and there was nothing in there.

Which meant that the only room left to detect in was Father's bedroom. I didn't know whether I should look in there because he had told me before not to mess with anything in his room. But if he was going to hide something from me the best place to hide it would be in his room.

So I told myself I would not mess with things in his room. I would move them and then I would move them back. And he would never know I had done it so he wouldn't be angry.

I started by looking under the bed. There were 7 shoes and a comb with lots of hair in it and a piece of copper pipe and a chocolate biscuit and a porn magazine called **Fiesta** and a dead bee and a Homer Simpson pattern tie and a wooden spoon, but not my book.

Then I looked in the drawers on either side of the dressing table, but these only contained aspirin and nail-clippers and batteries and dental floss and a tampon and tissues and a spare false tooth in case Father lost the false tooth he had to fill the gap where he knocked a tooth out when he fell off the ladder putting a bird-box up in the garden, but my book wasn't in there either.

Then I looked in his clothes cupboard. This was full of his clothes on hangers. There was also a little shelf at the top that I could see on to if I stood on the bed, but I had to take my shoes off in case I left a dirty footprint that would be a clue if Father decided to do some detecting. But the only things on the shelf were more porn magazines and a broken sandwich toaster and 12 wire coat hangers and an old hairdryer that used to belong to Mother.

In the bottom of the cupboard was a large plastic toolbox which was full of tools for doing Do It Yourself, like a drill and a paintbrush and some screws and a hammer, but I could see these without opening the box because it was made of transparent grey plastic.

Then I saw that there was another box underneath the toolbox so I lifted the toolbox out of the cupboard. The other box was an old cardboard box that is called a shirt box because people used to buy shirts in them. And when I opened the shirt box I saw my book was inside it.

Then I didn't know what to do.

I was happy because Father hadn't thrown my book away. But if I took the book he would know I had been messing with things in his room and he would be very angry and I had promised not to mess with things in his room.

Then I heard his van pulling up outside the house and I knew that I had to think fast and be clever. So I decided that I would leave the book where it was because I reasoned that Father wasn't going to throw it away if he had put it into the shirt box and I could carry on writing in another book that I would keep really secret and then, maybe later, he might change his mind and let me have the first book back again and I could copy the new book into it. And if he never gave it back to me I would be able to remember most of what I had written so I would put it all into the second secret book and if there were bits I wanted to check to make sure I had remembered them correctly I could come into his room when he was out and check.

Then I heard Father shutting the door of the van.

And that was when I saw the envelope.

It was an envelope addressed to me and it was lying under my book in the shirt box with some other envelopes. I picked it up. It had never been opened. It said

Christopher Boone
36 Randolph Street
Swindon
Wiltshire

Then I noticed that there were lots of other envelopes and they were all addressed to me. And this was interesting and confusing.

And then I noticed how the words Christopher and Swindon were written. They were written like this

Christopher

Swinden

I only know 3 people who do little circles instead of dots over the letter *i*. And one of them is Siobhan, and one of them was Mr Loxely who used to teach at the school, and one of them was Mother.

And then I heard Father opening the front door so I took one envelope from under the book and I put the lid back on the shirt box and I put the toolbox back on top of it and I closed the cupboard door really carefully.

Then Father called out, 'Christopher?'

I said nothing because he might be able to hear where I was calling from. I stood up and walked around the bed to the door, holding the envelope, trying to make as little noise as possible.

Father was standing at the bottom of the stairs and I thought he might see me, but he was flicking through the post which had come that morning so his head was pointing downwards. Then he walked away from the foot of the stairs towards the kitchen and I closed the door of his room very quietly and went into my own room.

I wanted to look at the envelope, but I didn't want to make

Father angry, so I hid the envelope underneath my mattress. Then I walked downstairs and said hello to Father.

And he said, 'So, what have you been up to today, young man?'

And I said, 'Today we did **Life Skills** with Mrs Gray. Which was **Using Money** and **Public Transport**. And I had tomato soup for lunch, and 3 apples. And I practised some maths in the afternoon and we went for a walk in the park with Mrs Peters and collected leaves for making collages.'

And Father said, 'Excellent, excellent. What do you fancy for chow tonight?'

Chow is food.

I said I wanted baked beans and broccoli.

And Father said, 'I think that can be very easily arranged.'

Then I sat on the sofa and I read some more of the book I was reading called **Chaos** by James Gleick.

Then I went into the kitchen and had my baked beans and broccoli while Father had sausages and eggs and fried bread and a mug of tea.

Then Father said, 'I'm going to put those shelves up in the living room, if that's all right with you. I'll make a bit of a racket, I'm afraid, so if you want to watch television we're going to have to shift it upstairs.'

And I said, 'I'll go and be on my own in my room.'

And he said, 'Good man.'

And I said, 'Thank you for supper,' because that is being polite.

And he said, 'No problem, kiddo.'

And I went up to my room.

And when I was in my room I shut the door and I took out the envelope from underneath my mattress. I held the letter up to the light to see if I could detect what was inside the envelope but the paper of the envelope was too thick. I wondered whether I should open the envelope because it was something I had taken from Father's room. But then I reasoned that it was addressed to me so it belonged to me so it was OK to open it.

So I opened the envelope.

Inside there was a letter.

And this was what was written in the letter

451c Chapter Road
Willesden
London NW2 5NG
0208 887 8907

Dear Christopher,

I'm sorry it's been such a very long time since I wrote my last letter to you. I've been very busy. I've got a new job working as a secretery for a factory that makes things out of steel. You'd like it a lot. The factory is full of huge machines that make the steel and cut it and bend it into watever shapes they need. This week they're making a roof for a cafe in a shopping centre in Birmingham. It's shaped like a huge flower and they're going to stretch canvas over it to make it look like an enormus tent.

Also we've moved into the new flat at last as you can see from the address. It's not as nice as the old one and I don't like Willesden very much, but it's easier for Roger to get to work and he's bought it (he only rented the other one), so we can get our own furnature and paint the walls the colour we want to.

And that's why it's such a long time since I wrote my last letter to you because it's been hard work packing up all our things and then unpacking them and then getting used to this new job.

I'm very tired now and I must go to sleep and I want to put this into the letterbox tomorrow morning, so I'll sign off now and write you another letter soon.

You haven't written to me yet, so I know that you are probably still angry with me. I'm sorry Christopher. But I still love you. I hope you don't stay angry with me forever. And I'd love it if you were able to write me a letter (but remember to send it to the new address!).

I think about you all the time.

Lots of Love,

Your Mum.

X X X X X X

Then I was really confused because Mother had never worked as a secretary for a firm that made things out of steel. Mother had worked as a secretary for a big garage in the centre of town. And Mother had never lived in London. Mother had always lived with us. And Mother had never written a letter to me before.

There was no date on the letter so I couldn't work out when Mother had written the letter and I wondered whether someone else had written the letter and pretended to be Mother.

And then I looked at the front of the envelope and I saw that there was a postmark and there was a date on the postmark and it was quite difficult to read, but it said

Which meant that the letter was posted on 16th October 1997, which was 18 months after Mother had died.

And then the door of my bedroom opened and Father said, 'What are you doing?'

I said, 'I'm reading a letter.'

And he said, 'I've finished the drilling. That David Attenborough nature programme's on telly if you're interested.'

I said, 'OK.'

Then he went downstairs again.

I looked at the letter and thought really hard. It was a mystery and I couldn't work it out. Perhaps the letter was in the wrong envelope and it had been written before Mother had died. But why was she writing from London? The longest she had been away was a week when she went to visit her cousin Ruth, who had cancer, but Ruth lived in Manchester.

And then I thought that perhaps it wasn't a letter from Mother. Perhaps it was a letter to another person called Christopher, from that Christopher's mother.

I was excited. When I started writing my book there was only one mystery I had to solve. Now there were two.

I decided that I would not think about it any more that night because I didn't have enough information and could easily *Leap to the Wrong Conclusions* like Mr Athelney Jones of Scotland Yard, which is a dangerous thing to do because you should make sure you have all the available clues before you start deducing things. That way you are much less likely to make a mistake.

I decided that I would wait until Father was out of the house. Then I would go into the cupboard in his bedroom and look at the other letters and see who they were from and what they said.

I folded the letter and hid it under my mattress in case Father found and got cross. Then I went downstairs and watched the television.

151

Lots of things are mysteries. But that doesn't mean there isn't an answer to them. It's just that scientists haven't found the answer yet.

For example, some people believe in the ghosts of people who have come back from the dead. And Uncle Terry said that he saw a ghost in a shoe shop in a shopping centre in Northampton because he was going down into the basement when he saw someone dressed in grey walk across the bottom of the stairs. But when he got to the bottom of the stairs the basement was empty and there were no doors.

When he told the lady on the till upstairs they said it was called Tuck and he was a ghost of a Franciscan Friar who used to live in the monastery which was on the same site hundreds of years ago, which was why the shopping centre was called **Greyfriars Shopping Centre**, and they were used to him and not frightened at all.

Eventually scientists will discover something that explains ghosts, just like they discovered electricity which explained lightning, and it might be something about people's brains, or something about the earth's magnetic field, or it might be some new force altogether. And then ghosts won't be mysteries. They will be like electricity and rainbows and non-stick frying pans.

But sometimes a mystery isn't a mystery. And this is an example of a mystery which isn't a mystery.

We have a pond at the school, with frogs in, which are there so we can learn how to treat animals with kindness and respect, because some of the children at school are horrible to animals and think it's funny to crush worms or throw stones at cats.

And some years there are lots of frogs in the pond, and some years there are very few. And if you drew a graph of how many frogs there were in the pond it would look like this (but this graph is what's called *hypothetical* which means that the numbers aren't the real numbers, it is just an *illustration*)

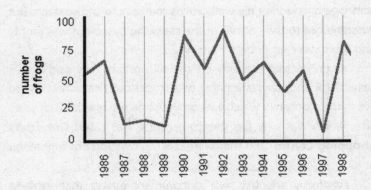

And if you looked at the graph you might think that there was a really cold winter in 1987 and 1988 and 1989 and 1997, or that there was a heron which came and ate lots of the frogs (sometimes there is a heron who comes and tries to eat the frogs, but there is chicken wire over the pond to stop it).

But sometimes it is nothing to do with cold winters or cats or herons. Sometimes it is just maths.

Here is a formula for a population of animals

$$N_{new} = \lambda \, (N_{old}) \, (1 - N_{old})$$

And in this formula **N** stands for the population density. When **N = 1** the population is the biggest it can get. And when **N = 0** the population is extinct. N_{new} is the population in one year, and N_{old} is the population in the year before. And λ is what is called a constant.

When λ is less than 1, the population gets smaller and smaller and goes extinct. And when λ is between 1 and 3, the population gets bigger and then it stays stable like this (and these graphs are hypothetical, too)

And when λ is between 3 and 3.57 the population goes in cycles like this

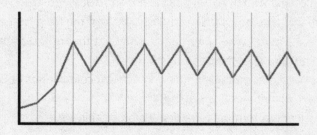

But when λ is greater than 3.57 the population becomes chaotic like in the first graph.

This was discovered by Robert May and George Oster and Jim Yorke. And it means that sometimes things are so complicated that it is impossible to predict what they are going to do next, but they are only obeying really simple rules.

And it means that, sometimes, a whole population of frogs, or worms, or people, can die for no reason whatsoever, just because that is the way the numbers work.

157

It was six days before I could go back into Father's room to look in the shirt box in the cupboard.

On the first day, which was a Wednesday, Joseph Fleming took his trousers off and went to the toilet all over the floor of the changing room and started to eat it, but Mr Davis stopped him.

Joseph eats everything. He once ate one of the little blocks of blue disinfectant which hang inside the toilets. And he once ate a £50 note from his mother's wallet. And he eats string and rubber bands and tissues and writing paper and paints and plastic forks. Also he bangs his chin and screams a lot.

Tyrone said that there was a horse and a pig in the poo, so I said he was being stupid, but Siobhan said he wasn't. They were small, plastic animals from the library that the staff use to make people tell stories. And Joseph had eaten them.

So I said I wasn't going to go into the toilets because there was poo on the floor, and it made me feel uncomfortable to think about it, even though Mr Ennison had come in and cleaned it up. And I wet my trousers and I had to put on some spare ones from the spare clothes locker in Mrs Gascoyne's room. So Siobhan said I could use the staff room toilets for two days, but only two days, and then I would have to use the children's toilets again. And we made this a deal.

On the second, third and fourth days, which were Thursday, Friday and Saturday, nothing interesting happened.

On the fifth day, which was a Sunday, it rained very hard. I like it when it rains hard. It sounds like white noise everywhere, which is like silence but not empty.

I went upstairs and sat in my room and watched the water falling in the street. It was falling so hard that it looked like white sparks (and this is a simile, too, not a metaphor). And there was no one around because everyone was staying indoors. And it made me think how all the water in the world was connected, and this water had evaporated from the oceans somewhere in the middle of the Gulf of Mexico or Baffin Bay, and now it was falling in front of the house and it would drain away into the gutters and flow to a sewage station where it would be cleaned and then it would go into a river and go back into the ocean again.

And in the evening on Monday Father got a phone call from a lady whose cellar had flooded and he had to go out and fix it in an emergency.

If there is only one emergency Rhodri goes and fixes it because his wife and his children went to live in Somerset which means he doesn't have anything to do in the evenings apart from playing snooker and drinking and watching the television, and he needs to do overtime to earn money to send to his wife to help her look after the children. And Father has me to look after. But this evening there were two emergencies, so Father told me to behave and to ring him on his mobile phone if there was a problem, and then he went out in the van.

So I went into his bedroom and opened up the cupboard and lifted the toolbox off the top of the shirt box and opened the shirt box.

I counted the letters. There were 43 of them. They were all addressed to me in the same handwriting.

I took one out and opened it.

Inside was this letter

3rd May   *451c Chapter Road*
                                             London NW2 5NG
                                             0208 887 8907

Dear Christopher,

We have a new fridge and cooker at last! Roger and I drove to the tip at the weekend to throw the old ones away. It's where people throw everything away. There are huge bins for three differant colours of bottles and cardboard and engine oil and garden waste and household waist and larger items (that's where we put the old fridge and cooker).

Then we went to a secondhand shop and bought a new cooker and a new fridge. Now the house feels a little bit more like home.

I was looking through some old photos last night, which made me sad. Then I found a photo of you playing with the train set we bought for you a couple of Christmas's ago. And that made me happy because it was one of the really good times we had together.

Do you remember how you played with it all day and

you refused to go to bed at night because you were still playing with it. And do you remember how we told you about train timetabels and you made a train timetabel and you had a clock and you made the trains run on time. And there was a little woodden station, too, and we showed you how people who wanted to go on the train went to the station and bought a ticket and then got on the train? And then we got out a map and we showed you the little lines which were the trains lines connecting all the stations. And you played with it for weeks and weeks and weeks and we bought you more trains and you knew where they were all going.

I liked remembering that a lot.

I have to go now. It's half past three in the afternoon. I know you always like to know exactly what time it is. And I have to go to the Co-op and buy some ham to make Roger's tea with. I'll put this letter in the post box on the way to the shop.

Love,

Your Mum

x x x x x x

Then I opened another envelope. This was the letter that was inside

Flat 1, 312 Lausanne Rd
London N8 5BV
0208 756 4321

Dear Christopher,

I said that I wanted to explain to you why I went away when I had the time to do it properly. Now I have lots of time. So I'm sitting on the sofa here with this letter and the radio on and I'm going to try and explain.

I was not a very good mother, Christopher. Maybe if things had been differant, maybe if you'd been differant, I might have been better at it. But that's just the way things turned out.

I'm not like your father. Your father is a much more pacient person. He just gets on with things and if things upset him he doesn't let it show. But that's not the way I am and there's nothing I can do to change that.

Do you remember once when we were shopping in town together? And we went into Bentalls and it was really crowded and we had to get a Christmas present for Grandma? And you were frightened because of all the people in the shop. It was the middle of Christmas shopping when everyone was in town. And I was talking to Mr Land who works on the kichen floor and went to school with me. And you crouched down on the floor and put your hands over your ears and you were in the way of everyone. So I got cross, because I don't like shopping at Christmas, either, and I told you to behave and I tried to pick you up and move you. But you shouted and you knocked those mixers off the shelf and there was a big crash. And everyone turned round to see what was going on. And Mr Land was realy nice about it but there were boxes and bits of broken bowl on the floor and everyone was staring and I saw that you had wet yourself and I was so cross and I wanted to take you out of the shop but you wouldn't let me touch you and you just lay on the floor and screamed and banged your hands and feet on the floor and the maniger came and asked what the problem was and I was at the end of my tether and I had to pay for two broken mixers and we just had to wait until you stoped screaming. And then I had to walk you all the way home which took hours because I knew you wouldn't go on the bus again.

And I remember that night I just cried and cried and cried and your father was really nice about it at first and he made you supper and he put you to bed and he said these things happen and it would be OK. But I said I couldn't take it anymore and eventually he got really cross and he told me I was being stupid and said I should pull myself together and I hit him, which was wrong, but I was so upset.

We had a lot of argumants like that. Because I often thought I couldn't take any more. And your father is really

134

pacient but I'm not, I get cross, even though I don't mean too. And by the end we stopped talking to each other very much because we knew it would always end up in an argumant and it would go nowere. And I felt realy lonley.

And that was when I started spending lots of time with Roger. I mean obviously we had always spent lots of time with Roger and Eileen. But I started seeing Roger on his own because I could talk to him. He was the only person I could really talk to. And when I was with him I didn't feel lonley anymore.

And I know you might not understand any of this, but I wanted to try to explain, so that you knew. And even if you don't understand now, you can keep this letter and read it later and maybe you might understand then.

And Roger told me that he and Eileen weren't in love with one another anymore, and that they hadn't been in love with one another for a long time. Which meant that he was feeling lonely too. So we had a lot in common. And then we realised that we were in love with one another. And he suggested that I should leave your father and that we should move into a house together. But I said that I couldn't leave you, and he was sad about that but he understood that you were realy important to me.

And then you and me had that argumant. Do you remember? It was about your supper one evening. I'd cooked you something and you wouldn't eat it. And you hadn't eaten for days and days and you were looking so *thin. And you started to shout and I got cross and I threw the food across the room. Which I know I shouldn't have done. And you grabbed the chopping board and you threw it and it hit my foot and broke my toes. Then, of course, we had to go to the hospital and I had that plaster put on my foot. And afterwards, at home, your father and I had a huge argumant. He blamed me for getting cross with you. And he said I should just give you what you wanted, even if it was just a plate of lettuce or a strawberry milkshake. And I said I was just trying to get you to eat something healthy. And he said you couldn't help it. And I said well I couldn't help it either and I just lost my rag. And he said that if he could keep his temper then I should bloody well keep my temper. And it went on and on like this.*

And I couldn't walk properly for a month, do you remember, and your father had to look after you. And I remember looking at the two of you and seeing you together and thinking how you were really differant with him. Much calmer. And you didn't shout at one another. And it made me so sad because it was like you didn't really need me at all. And somehow that was even worse than you and me arguing all the time because it was like I was invisible.

And I think that was when I realised you and your father were probably better off if I wasn't living in the house. Then he would only have one person to look after instead of two.

Then Roger said that he had asked the bank for a transfer. That means he asked them if he could have a job in London, and he was leaving. He asked me if I wanted to come with him. I thought about it for a long time, Christopher. Honestly, I did. And it broke my heart, but eventualy I decided it would be better for all of us if I went. So I said yes.

I meant to say goodbye. I was going to come back and pick up some clothes when you were back from school. And that was when I was going to explain what I was doing and say that I would come back and see you as often as I could and you could come down to London sometimes to stay with us. But when I rang your father he said I couldn't come back. He was really angry. He said I couldn't talk to you. I didn't know what to do. He said that I was being selfish and that I was never to set foot inside the house again. So I haven't. But I have written you these letters instead.

I wonder if you can understand any of this. I know it will be very difficult for you. But I hope you can understand a little.

Christopher, I never meant to hurt you. I thought that what I was doing was the best for all of us. I hope it is. And I want you to know that this is not your fault.

I used to have dreams that everything would get better. Do you remember, you used to say that you wanted to be an astranaut? Well, I used to have dreams where you

were an astranaut and you were on the television and I
thought that's my son. I wonder what it is that you want
to be now. Has it changed? Are you still doing maths? I
hope you are.

Please, Christopher, write to me sometime, or ring me
on the telephone. The numbers at the top of the letter.

Love and Kisses,

Your Mother
x x x x x x

Then I opened a third envelope. This was the letter that was
inside

18th September   *Flat 1*
                                        312 Lausanne Road
                                              London N8
                                           0208 756 4321

Dear Christopher,

Well, I said I'd write you every week, and I have. In fact,
this is the second letter this week, so I'm doing even better
than I said.

I have got a job! I'm working in Camden, at Perkin and
Rashid, which is a Chartered Survayors. That means they go

around looking at houses and work out how much they should cost and what work needs to be done on them and how much that work will cost. And also they work out how much new houses and offices and factories will cost to build.

It's a nice office. The other secretary is Angie. Her desk is covered in little teddy bears and furry toys and pictures of her children (so I've put a picture of you in a frame on my desk). She's really nice and we always go out for lunch together.

I don't know how long I'll stay here, though. I have to do a lot of adding up of numbers for when we send bills out to clients and I'm not very good at doing this (you'd be better at it than I am!).

The company is run by two men called Mr Perkin and Mr Rashid. Mr Rashid is from Pakistan and very stern and always wants us to work faster. And Mr Perkin is weird (Angie calls him Pervy Perkin). When he comes and stands next to me to ask a question he always puts his hand on my sholder and squots down so his face is really near mine and I can smell his toothpaste which gives me the creeps. And the pay is not very good, either. So I shall be looking for something better as soon as I get the chance.

I went up to Alexandra Palace the other day. It's a big park just round the corner from our flat, and the park is a huge hill with a big conference centre on the top and it made me think of you because if you came here we could *go there and fly kites or watch the planes coming into Heathrow airport and I know you'd like that.*

I have to go now, Christopher. I'm writing this in my lunch hour (Angie is off sick with the flu, so we can't have lunch together). Please write to me some time and tell me about how you are and what your doing at school.

I hope you got the present I sent you. Have you solved it yet? Roger and I saw it in a shop in Camden market and I know you've always liked puzles. Roger tried to get the two pieces apart before we wrapped it up and he couldn't do it. He said that if you managed to do it you were a genius.

Loads and loads of love,

Your Mother

x x x x

And this was the fourth letter

23rd August   *Flat 1*
312 Lausanne Road
London N8

Dear Christopher,

I'm sorry I didn't write last week. I had to go to the dentist and have two of my molars out. You might not remember

when we had to take you to the dentist. You wouldn't let
anyone put their hand inside your mouth so we had to put
you to sleep so that the dentist could take one of your
teeth out. Well, they didn't put me to sleep, they just gave
me what is called a local anathsetic which means that you
can't feel anything in your mouth, which is just as well
because they had to saw through the bone to get the
tooth out. And it didn't hurt at all. In fact I was laughing
because the dentist had to tug and pull and strain so much
and it seemed really funny to me. But when I got home the
pain started to come back and I had to lie on the sofa for
two days and take lots of painkillers . . .

Then I stopped reading the letter because I felt sick.

Mother had not had a heart attack. Mother had not died. Mother had been alive all the time. And Father had lied about this.

I tried really hard to think if there was any other explanation but I couldn't think of one. And then I couldn't think of anything at all because my brain wasn't working properly.

I felt giddy. It was like the room was swinging from side to side, as if it was at the top of a really tall building and the building was swinging backwards and forwards in a strong wind (this is a simile, too). But I knew that the room couldn't be swinging backwards and forwards, so it must have been something which was happening inside my head.

I rolled onto the bed and curled up in a ball.

My stomach hurt.

I don't know what happened then because there is a gap in my memory, like a bit of the tape had been erased. But I know that a lot of time must have passed because later on, when I opened my eyes again, I could see that it was dark outside the window. And I had been sick because there was sick all over the bed and on my hands and arms and face.

But before this I heard Father coming into the house and calling out my name, which is another reason why I know a lot of time had passed.

And it was strange because he was calling, 'Christopher . . .? Christopher . . .?' and I could see my name written out as he was saying it. Often I can see what someone is saying written out like it is being printed on a computer screen, especially if they are in another room. But this was not on a computer screen. I could see it written really large, like it was on a big advert on the side of a bus. And it was in my mother's hand-writing, like this

Christopher Christopher

And then I heard Father come up the stairs and walk into the room.

He said, 'Christopher, what the hell are you doing?'

And I could tell that he was in the room, but his voice sounded tiny and far away, like people's voices sometimes do when I am groaning and I don't want them to be near me.

And he said, 'What the fuck are you...? That's my cupboard, Christopher. Those are . . . Oh shit . . . Shit, shit, shit, shit, shit.'

Then he said nothing for a while.

Then he put his hand on my shoulder and moved me onto my side and he said, 'Oh, Christ.' But it didn't hurt when he touched me, like it normally does. I could see him touching me, like I was watching a film of what was happening in the room, but I could hardly feel his hand at all. It was just like the wind blowing against me.

And then he was silent again for a while.

Then he said, 'I'm sorry, Christopher. I'm so, so sorry.'

And then I noticed that I had been sick because I could feel something wet all over me, and I could smell it, like when someone is sick at school.

Then he said, 'You read the letters.'

Then I could hear that he was crying because his breath sounded all bubbly and wet, like it does when someone has a cold and they have lots of snot in their nose.

Then he said, 'I did it for your good, Christopher. Honestly I did. I never meant to lie. I just thought . . . I just thought it was better if you didn't know . . . that . . . that . . . I didn't mean to . . . I was going to show them to you when you were older.'

Then he was silent again.

Then he said, 'It was an accident.'

Then he was silent again.

Then he said, 'I didn't know what to say . . . I was in such a mess . . . She left a note and . . . Then she rang and . . . I said she was in hospital because . . . because I didn't know how to explain. It was so complicated. So difficult. And I . . . I said she was in hospital. And I know it wasn't true. But once I'd said that . . . I couldn't . . . I couldn't change it. Do you understand . . . Christopher . . .? Christopher . . .? It just . . . It got out of control and I wish . . .'

Then he was silent for a really long time.

Then he touched me on the shoulder again and said, 'Christopher, we have to get you cleaned up, OK?'

He shook my shoulder a little bit but I didn't move.

And he said, 'Christopher, I'm going to go to the bathroom and I'm going to run you a hot bath. Then I'm going to come back and take you to the bathroom, OK? Then I can put the sheets into the washing machine.'

Then I heard him get up and go to the bathroom and turn the taps on. I listened to the water running into the bath. He didn't come back for a while. Then he came back and touched my shoulder again and said, 'Let's do this really gently, Christopher. Let's sit you up and get your clothes off and get you into the bath, OK? I'm going to have to touch you, but it's going to be all right.'

Then he lifted me up and made me sit on the side of the bed. He took my jumper and my shirt off and put them on the bed. Then he made me stand up and walk through to the bathroom. And I didn't scream. And I didn't fight. And I didn't hit him.

163

When I was little and I first went to school, my main teacher was called Julie, because Siobhan hadn't started working at the school then. She only started working at the school when I was twelve.

And one day Julie sat down at a desk next to me and put a tube of Smarties on the desk, and she said, 'Christopher, what do you think is in here?'

And I said, 'Smarties.'

Then she took the top off the Smarties tube and turned it upside down and a little red pencil came out and she laughed and I said, 'It's not Smarties, it's a pencil.'

Then she put the little red pencil back inside the Smarties tube and put the top back on.

Then she said, 'If your Mummy came in now, and we asked her what was inside the Smarties tube, what do you think she would say?', because I used to call Mother *Mummy* then, not *Mother*.

And I said, 'A pencil.'

That was because when I was little I didn't understand about other people having minds. And Julie said to Mother and Father that I would always find this very difficult. But I don't find this difficult now. Because I decided that it was a kind of puzzle, and if something is a puzzle there is always a way of solving it.

It's like computers. People think computers are different from people because they don't have minds, even though, in the Turing test, computers can have conversations with people about the weather and wine and what Italy is like, and they can even tell jokes.

But the mind is just a complicated machine.

And when we look at things we think we're just looking out of our eyes like we're looking out of little windows and there's a person inside our head, but we're not. We're looking at a screen inside our heads, like a computer screen.

And you can tell this because of an experiment which I saw on TV in a series called *How the Mind Works*. And in this experiment you put your head in a clamp and you look at a page of writing on a screen. And it looks like a normal page of writing and nothing is changing. But after a while, as your eye moves round the page, you realise that something is very strange because when you try to read a bit of the page you've read before it's different.

And this is because when your eye flicks from one point to another you don't see anything at all and you're blind. And the flicks are called *saccades*. Because if you saw everything when your eye flicked from one point to another you'd feel giddy. And in the experiment there is a sensor which tells when your eye is flicking from one place to another and when it's doing this it changes some of the words on the page in a place where you're not looking.

But you don't notice that you're blind during saccades because your brain fills in the screen in your head to make it seem like you're looking out of two little windows in your head. And you don't notice that words have changed on another part of the page because your mind fills in a picture of things you're not looking at at that moment.

And people are different from animals because they can have pictures on the screens in their heads of things which they are not looking at. They can have pictures of someone in another room. Or they can have a picture of what is going to happen tomorrow. Or they can have pictures of themselves as an astronaut. Or they can have pictures of really big numbers. Or they can have pictures of chains of reasoning when they're trying to work something out.

And that is why a dog can go to the vet and have a really big operation and have metal pins sticking out of its leg but if it sees a cat it forgets that it has pins sticking out of its leg and chases after the cat. But when a person has an operation it has a picture in its head of the hurt carrying on for months and months. And it has a picture of all the stitches in its leg and the broken bone and the pins and even if it sees a bus it has to catch it doesn't run because it has a picture in its head of the bones crunching together and the stitches breaking and even more pain.

And that is why people think that computers don't have minds, and why people think that their brains are special, and different from computers. Because people can see the screen inside their head and they think there is someone in their head sitting there looking at the screen, like Captain Jean-Luc Picard in **Star Trek: The Next Generation**, sitting in his captain's seat looking at a big screen. And they think that this person is their special human mind which is called a *homunculus*, which means *a little man*. And they think that computers don't have this homunculus.

But this homunculus is just another picture on the screen in their heads. And when the homunculus is on the screen in their heads (because the person is thinking about the homunculus) there is another bit of the brain watching the screen. And when the person thinks about this part of the brain (the bit that is watching the homunculus on the screen) they put this bit of the brain on the screen and there is another bit of the brain watching the screen. But the brain doesn't see this happen because it is like the eye flicking from one place to another and people are blind inside their heads when they do the changing from thinking about one thing to thinking about another.

And this is why people's brains are like computers. And it's not because they are special but because they have to keep turning off for fractions of a second while the screen changes. And because there is something they can't see people think it has to be special, because people always think there is something special about what they can't see, like the dark side of the moon, or the other side of a black hole, or in the dark when they wake up at night and they're scared.

Also people think they're not computers because they have feelings and computers don't have feelings. But feelings are just having a picture on the screen in your head of what is going to happen tomorrow or next year, or what might have happened instead of what did happen, and if it is a happy picture they smile and if it is a sad picture they cry.

167

After Father had given me a bath and cleaned the sick off me and dried me off with a towel, he took me to my bedroom and put some clean clothes on me.

Then he said, 'Have you had anything to eat yet this evening?'
But I didn't say anything.

Then he said, 'Can I get you anything to eat, Christopher?'
But I still didn't say anything.

So he said, 'OK. Look. I'm going to go and put your clothes and the bedsheets into the washing machine and then I'll come back, OK?

I sat on the bed and looked at my knees.

So Father went out of the room and picked up my clothes from the bathroom floor and put them on the landing. Then he went and got the sheets from his bed and brought them out onto the landing together with my shirt and my jumper. Then he picked them all up and took them downstairs. Then I heard him start the washing machine and I heard the boiler starting up and the water in the water pipes going into the washing machine.

That was all I could hear for a long time.

I doubled 2s in my head because it made me feel calmer. I got to **33,554,432** which is 2^{25}, which was not very much because I've got to 2^{45} before, but my brain wasn't working very well.

Then Father came back into the room again and said, 'How are you feeling? Can I get you anything?'

I didn't say anything. I carried on looking at my knees.

And Father didn't say anything either. He just sat down on the bed next to me and put his elbows on his knees and looked down at the carpet between his legs where there was a little red piece of Lego with eight nobbles on.

Then I heard Toby waking up, because he is nocturnal, and I heard him rustling in his cage.

And Father was silent for a really long time.

Then he said, 'Look, maybe I shouldn't say this, but . . . I want you to know that you can trust me. And . . . OK, maybe I don't tell the truth all the time. God knows, I try, Christopher, God knows I do, but . . . Life is difficult, you know. It's bloody hard telling the truth all the time. Sometimes it's impossible. And I want you to know that I'm trying, I really am. And perhaps this is not a very good time to say this, and I know you're not going to like it, but . . . You have to know that I am going to tell you the truth from now on. About everything. Because . . . if you don't tell the truth now, then later on . . . later on it hurts even more. So . . .'

Father rubbed his face with his hands and pulled his chin down with his fingers and stared at the wall. I could see him out of the corner of my eye.

And he said, 'I killed Wellington, Christopher.'

I wondered if this was a joke, because I don't understand jokes, and when people tell jokes they don't mean what they say.

But then Father said, 'Please. Christopher. Just . . . let me explain.' Then he sucked in some air and he said, 'When your mum left . . . Eileen . . . Mrs Shears . . . she was very good to us. Very good to me. She helped me through a very difficult time. And I'm not sure I would have made it without her. Well, you know how she was round here most days. Helping out with the cooking and the cleaning. Popping over to see if we were OK, if we needed anything . . . I thought . . . Well . . . Shit, Christopher, I'm trying to keep this simple . . . I thought she might carry on coming over. I thought . . . and maybe I was being stupid . . . I thought she might . . . eventually . . . want to move in here. Or that we might move into her house. We . . . we got on really, really well. I thought we were friends. And I guess I thought wrong. I guess . . . in the end . . . it comes down to . . . Shit . . . We argued, Christopher, and . . . She said some things I'm not going to say to you because they're not nice, but they hurt, but . . . I think she cared more for that bloody dog than for me, for us. And maybe that's not so stupid, looking back. Maybe we are a bloody handful. And maybe it is easier living on your own looking after some stupid mutt, than sharing your life with other actual human beings. I mean, shit, buddy, we're not exactly low-maintenance, are we . . .? Anyway, we had this row. Well, quite a few rows to be honest. But after this particularly nasty little blow-out, she chucked me out of the house. And you know what that bloody dog was like after the operation. Bloody schizophrenic. Nice as pie one moment, roll over, tickle its stomach. Sink its teeth into your leg the next. Anyway, we're yelling at each other and it's in the garden relieving itself. So when she slams the door behind me the bugger's waiting for me. And . . . I know, I know. Maybe if I'd just given it a kick it would probably have backed off. But, shit, Christopher, when that red mist comes down . . . Christ, you know how it is. I mean, we're not that different, me and you. And all I could think was that she cared more about this bloody dog than she did about you or me. And it was like everything I'd been bottling up for two years just . . .'

Then Father was silent for a bit.

Then he said, 'I'm sorry, Christopher. I promise you, I never meant for it to turn out like this.'

And then I knew that it wasn't a joke and I was really frightened.

Father said. 'We all make mistakes, Christopher. You, me, your mum, everyone. And sometimes they're really big mistakes. We're only human.'

Then he held up his right hand and spread his fingers out in a fan.

But I screamed and pushed him backwards so that he fell off the bed and onto the floor.

He sat up and said, 'OK. Look. Christopher. I'm sorry. Let's leave it for tonight, OK? I'm going to go downstairs and you get some sleep and we'll talk in the morning.' Then he said, 'It's going to be all right. Honestly. Trust me.'

Then he stood up and took a deep breath and went out of the room.

I sat on the bed for a long time looking at the floor. Then I heard Toby scratching in his cage. I looked up and saw him staring through the bars at me.

I had to get out of the house. Father had murdered Wellington. That meant he could murder me, because I couldn't trust him, even though he had said, 'Trust me,' because he had told a lie about a big thing.

But I couldn't get out of the house straight away because he would see me, so I would have to wait until he was asleep.

The time was 11:16 p.m.

I tried doubling 2s again, but I couldn't get past 2^{15} which was **32,768**. So I groaned to make the time pass quicker and not think.

Then it was 1:20 a.m., but I hadn't heard Father come upstairs to bed. I wondered if he was asleep downstairs or whether he was waiting to come in and kill me. So I got out my Swiss Army Knife and opened the saw blade so that I could defend myself. Then I went out of my bedroom really quietly and listened. I couldn't hear anything, so I started going downstairs really quietly and really slowly. And when I got downstairs I could see Father's foot through the door of the living room. I waited for 4 minutes to see if it moved, but it didn't move. So I carried on walking till I got to the hallway. Then I looked round the door of the living room.

Father was lying on the sofa with his eyes closed.

I looked at him for a long time.

Then he snored and I jumped and I could hear the blood in my ears and my heart going really fast and a pain like someone had blown up a really big balloon inside my chest.

I wondered if I was going to have a heart attack.

Father's eyes were still closed. I wondered if he was pretending to be asleep. So I gripped the penknife really hard and I knocked on the doorframe.

Father moved his head from one side to the other and his foot twitched and he said, 'Gnnnn,' but his eyes stayed closed. And then he snored again.

He was asleep.

That meant I could get out of the house if I was really quiet so I didn't wake him up.

I took both my coats and my scarf from the hooks next to the front door and I put them all on because it would be cold outside at night. Then I went upstairs again really quietly, but it was difficult because my legs were shaking. I went into my room and I picked up Toby's cage. He was making scratching noises, so I took off one of the coats and put it over the cage to make the noise quieter. Then I carried him downstairs again.

Father was still asleep.

I went into the kitchen and I picked up my special food box. I unlocked the back door and stepped outside. Then I held the handle of the door down as I shut it again so that the click wasn't too loud. Then I walked down to the bottom of the garden.

At the bottom of the garden is a shed. It has the lawnmower and the hedge-cutter in, and lots of gardening equipment that mother used to use, like pots and bags of compost and bamboo canes and string and spades. It would be a bit warmer in the shed but I knew that Father might look for me in the shed, so I went round the back of the shed and I squeezed into the gap between the wall of the shed and the fence, behind the big, black, plastic tub for collecting rainwater. Then I sat down and I felt a bit safer.

I decided to leave my other coat over Toby's cage because I didn't want him to get cold and die.

I opened up my special food box. Inside was the Milky Bar and two liquorice laces and three clementines and a pink wafer biscuit and my red food colouring. I didn't feel hungry but I knew that I should eat something because if you don't eat something you can get cold, so I ate two clementines and the Milky Bar.

Then I wondered what I would do next.

173

Between the roof of the shed and the big plant that hangs over the fence from the house next door I could see the constellation **Orion**.

People say that **Orion** is called Orion because Orion was a hunter and the constellation looks like a hunter with a club and a bow and arrow, like this

But this is really silly because it is just stars, and you could join up the dots in any way you wanted, and you could make it look like a lady with an umbrella who is waving, or the coffee maker which Mrs Shears has, which is from Italy, with a handle and steam coming out, or like a dinosaur

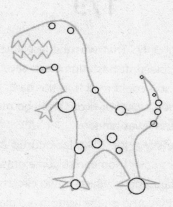

And there aren't any lines in space, so you could join bits of **Orion** to bits of **Lepus** or **Taurus** or **Gemini** and say that they were a constellation called **The Bunch of Grapes** or **Jesus** or **The Bicycle** (except that they didn't have bicycles in Roman and Greek times which was when they called **Orion** Orion).

And anyway, **Orion** is not a hunter or a coffee maker or a dinosaur. It is just Betelgeuse and Bellatrix and Alnilam and Rigel and 17 other stars I don't know the names of. And they are nuclear explosions billions of miles away.

And that is the truth.

179

I stayed awake until 3:47. That was the last time I looked at my watch before I fell asleep. It has a luminous face and lights up if you press a button so I could read it in the dark. I was cold and I was frightened Father might come out and find me. But I felt safer in the garden because I was hidden.

I looked at the sky a lot. I like looking up at the sky in the garden at night. In summer I sometimes come outside at night with my torch and my planisphere, which is two circles of plastic with a pin through the middle. And on the bottom is a map of the sky and on top is an aperture which is an opening shaped in a parabola and you turn it round to see a map of the sky that you can see on that day of the year from the latitude 51.5° North which is the latitude that Swindon is on, because the largest bit of the sky is always on the other side of the earth.

And when you look at the sky you know you are looking at stars which are hundreds and thousands of light years away from you. And some of the stars don't even exist any more because their light has taken so long to get to us that they are already dead, or they have exploded and collapsed into red dwarfs. And that makes you seem very small, and if you have difficult things in your life it is nice to think that they are what is called *negligible* which means that they are so small you don't have to take them into account when you are calculating something.

I didn't sleep very well because of the cold and because the ground was very bumpy and pointy underneath me and because

Toby was scratching in his cage a lot. But when I woke up properly it was dawn and the sky was all orange and blue and purple and I could hear birds singing which is called *The Dawn Chorus*. And I stayed where I was for another 2 hours and 32 minutes, and then I heard Father come into the garden and call out, 'Christopher . . .? Christopher . . .?'

So I turned round and I found an old plastic sack covered in mud that used to have fertiliser in it and I squeezed myself and Toby's cage and my special food box into the corner between the wall of the shed and the fence and the rainwater tub and I covered myself with the fertiliser sack. And then I heard Father coming down the garden and I took my Swiss Army Knife out of my pocket and got out the saw blade and held it in case he found us. And I heard him open the door of the shed and look inside. And then I heard him say, 'Shit.' And then I heard his footsteps in the bushes round the side of the shed and my heart was beating really fast and I could feel the feeling like a balloon inside my chest again and I think he might have looked round the back of the shed, but I couldn't see because I was hiding, but he didn't see me because I heard him walking back up the garden again.

Then I stayed still and I looked at my watch and I stayed still for 27 minutes. And then I heard Father start the engine of his van. I knew it was his van because I heard it very often and it was nearby and I knew it wasn't any of the neighbours' cars because the people who take drugs have a Volkswagen camper van and Mr Thompson who lives at number 40 has a Vauxhall Cavalier and the people who live at number 34 have a Peugeot and they all sound different.

And when I heard him drive away from the house I knew it would be safe to come out.

And then I had to decide what to do because I couldn't live in the house with Father any more because it was dangerous.

So I made a decision.

I decided that I would go and knock on Mrs Shears' door and I would go and live with her, because I knew her and she wasn't a stranger and I had stayed in her house before, when there was a power cut on our side of the street. And this time she wouldn't tell me to go away because I would be able to tell her who had killed Wellington and that way she would know that I was a friend. And also she would understand why I couldn't live with Father any more.

I took the liquorice laces and the pink wafer biscuit and the last clementine out of my special food box and put them in my pocket and hid the special food box under the fertiliser bag. Then I picked up Toby's cage and my extra coat and I climbed out from behind the shed. I walked up the garden and down the side of the house. I undid the bolt in the garden door and walked out in front of the house.

There was no one in the street so I crossed and walked up the drive to Mrs Shears' house and knocked on the door and waited and worked out what I was going to say when she opened the door.

But she didn't come to the door. So I knocked again.

Then I turned round and saw some people walking down the street and I was frightened again because it was two of the people who take drugs in the house next door. So I grabbed Toby's cage and went round the side of Mrs Shears' house and sat down behind the dustbin so they couldn't see me.

And then I had to work out what to do.

And I did this by thinking of all the things I could do and deciding whether they were the right decision or not.

I decided that I couldn't go home again.

And I decided that I couldn't go and live with Siobhan because she couldn't look after me when school was closed because she was a teacher and not a friend or a member of my family.

And I decided that I couldn't go and live with Uncle Terry because he lived in Sunderland and I didn't know how to get to Sunderland and I didn't like Uncle Terry because he smoked cigarettes and stroked my hair.

And I decided I couldn't go and live with Mrs Alexander because she wasn't a friend or a member of my family even if she had a dog, because I couldn't stay overnight in her house or use her toilet because she had used it and she was a stranger.

And then I thought that I could go and live with Mother because she was my family and I knew where she lived because I could remember the address from the letters which was 451c Chapter Road, London NW2 5NG. Except that she lived in London and I'd never been to London before. I'd only been to Dover to go to France, and to Sunderland to visit Uncle Terry and to Manchester to visit Aunt Ruth who had cancer, except she didn't have cancer when I was there. And I had never been anywhere apart from the shop at the end of the road on my own. And the thought of going somewhere on my own was frightening.

But then I thought about going home again, or staying where I was, or hiding in the garden every night and Father finding me and that made me feel even more frightened. And when I thought about that I felt like I was going to be sick again like I did the night before.

And then I realised that there was nothing I could do which felt safe. And I made a picture of it in my head like this

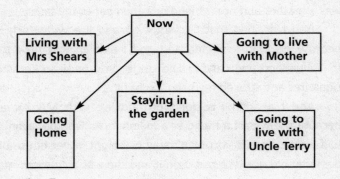

And then I imagined crossing out all the possibilities which were impossible, which is like in a maths exam, when you look at all the questions and you decide which ones you are going to do and which ones you are not going to do and you cross out all the ones which you are not going to do because then your decision is final and you can't change your mind. And it was like this

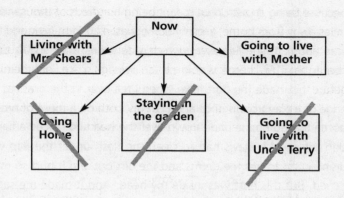

Which meant that I had to go London to live with Mother. And I could do it by going on a train because I knew all about trains from the train set, how you looked at the timetable and went to the station and bought a ticket and looked at the departure board to see if your train was on time and then you went to the right platform and got on board. And I would go from Swindon station where Sherlock Holmes and Doctor Watson stop for lunch when they are on their way to Ross from Paddington in **The Boscombe Valley Mystery**.

And then I looked at the wall on the opposite side of the little passage down the side of Mrs Shears' house where I was sitting and there was the circular lid of a very old metal pan leaning against the wall. And it was covered in rust. And it looked like the surface of a planet because the rust was shaped like countries and continents and islands.

And then I thought how I could never be an astronaut

because being an astronaut meant being hundreds of thousands of miles away from home, and my home was in London now and that was about 100 miles away which was more than 1,000 times nearer than my home would be if I was in space, and thinking about this made me hurt. Like when I fell over in the grass at the edge of a playground once and I cut my knee on a piece of broken bottle that someone had thrown over the wall and I sliced a flap of skin off and Mr Davis had to clean the flesh under the flap with disinfectant to get the germs and the dirt out and it hurt so much I cried. But this hurt was inside my head. And it made me sad to think that I could never become an astronaut.

And then I thought that I had to be like Sherlock Holmes and I had to *detach my mind at will to a remarkable degree* so that I did not notice how much it was hurting inside my head.

And then I thought I would need money if I was going to go to London. And I would need food to eat because it was a long journey and I wouldn't know where to get food from. And then I thought I would need someone to look after Toby when I went to London because I couldn't take him with me.

And then I *Formulated a Plan*. And that made me feel better because there was something in my head that had an order and a pattern and I just had to follow the instructions one after the other.

I stood up and I made sure there was no one in the street. Then I went to Mrs Alexander's house which is next door to Mrs Shears' house, and I knocked on the door.

Then Mrs Alexander opened the door, and she said, 'Christopher, what on earth has happened to you?'

And I said, 'Can you look after Toby for me?'

And she said, 'Who's Toby?'

And I said, 'Toby's my pet rat.'

Then Mrs Alexander said, 'Oh . . . Oh yes. I remember now. You told me.'

Then I held Toby's cage up and said, 'This is him.'

Mrs Alexander took a step backwards into her hallway.

And I said, 'He eats special pellets and you can buy them from a pet shop. But he can also eat biscuits and carrots and bread and chicken bones. But you mustn't give him chocolate because it's got caffeine and theobromine in, which are methylxanthines, and it's poisonous for rats in large quantities. And he needs new water in his bottle every day, too. And he won't mind being in someone else's house because he's an animal. And he likes to come out of his cage, but it doesn't matter if you don't take him out.'

Then Mrs Alexander said, 'Why do you need someone to look after Toby, Christopher?'

And I said, 'I'm going to London.'

And she said, 'How long are you going for?'

And I said, 'Until I go to university.'

And she said, 'Can't you take Toby with you?'

And I said, 'London's a long way away and I don't want to take him on the train because I might lose him.'

And Mrs Alexander said, 'Right.' And then she said, 'Are you and your father moving house?'

And I said, 'No.'

And she said, 'So, why are you going to London?'

And I said, 'I'm going to live with Mother.'

And she said, 'I thought you told me your mother was dead.'

And I said, 'I thought she was dead, but she was still alive. And Father lied to me. And also he said he killed Wellington.'

And Mrs Alexander said, 'Oh my goodness.'

And I said, 'I'm going to live with my mother because Father killed Wellington and he lied and I'm frightened of being in the house with him.'

And Mrs Alexander said, 'Is your mother here?'

And I said, 'No. Mother is in London.'

And she said, 'So you're going to London on your own?'

And I said, 'Yes.'

And she said, 'Look, Christopher, why don't you come inside and sit down and we can talk about this and work out what is the best thing to do.'

And I said, 'No. I can't come inside. Will you look after Toby for me?'

And she said, 'I really don't think that would be a good idea, Christopher.'

And I didn't say anything.

And she said, 'Where's your father at the moment, Christopher?'

And I said, 'I don't know.'

And she said, 'Well, perhaps we should try and give him a ring and see if we can get in touch with him. I'm sure he's worried about you. And I'm sure that there's been some dreadful misunderstanding.'

So I turned round and I ran across the road back to our house. And I didn't look before I crossed the road and a yellow Mini had to stop and the tyres squealed on the road. And I ran down the side of the house and back through the garden gate and I bolted it behind me.

I tried to open the kitchen door but it was locked. So I picked up a brick that was lying on the ground and I smashed it through the window and the glass shattered everywhere. Then I put my arm through the broken glass and I opened the door from the inside.

I went into the house and I put Toby down on the kitchen table. Then I ran upstairs and I grabbed my school bag and I put some food for Toby in it and some of my maths books and some clean pants and a vest and a clean shirt. Then I came downstairs and I opened the fridge and I put a carton of orange juice into my bag, and a bottle of milk that hadn't been opened. And I took two more clementines and two tins of baked beans and a packet of custard creams from the cupboard and I put them in my bag as well, because I could open them with the can opener on my Swiss Army Knife.

Then I looked on the surface next to the sink and I saw Father's mobile phone and his wallet and his address book and I felt *my skin . . . cold under my clothes* like Doctor Watson in **The Sign of the Four** when he sees the tiny footsteps of Tonga, the Andaman Islander, on the roof of Bartholomew Sholto's house in Norwood, because I thought Father had come back and he was in the house, and the pain in my head got much worse. But then I rewound the pictures in my memory and I saw that his van wasn't

167

parked outside the house, so he must have left his mobile phone and his wallet and his address book when he left the house. And I picked up his wallet and I took his bank card out because that was how I could get money because the card has a PIN number which is the secret code which you put into the machine at the bank to get money out and Father hadn't written it down in a safe place, which is what you're meant to do, but he had told me because he said I'd never forget it. And it was 3558. And I put the card into my pocket.

Then I took Toby out of his cage and put him into the pocket of one of my coats because the cage was very heavy to carry all the way to London. And then I went out of the kitchen door into the garden again.

I went out through the garden gate and made sure there wasn't anyone watching, and then I started walking towards the school because that was a direction I knew, and when I got to school I could ask Siobhan where the train station was.

Normally I would have got more and more frightened if I was walking to school, because I had never done it before. But I was frightened in two different ways. And one way was being frightened of being far away from a place I was used to, and the other was being frightened of being near where Father lived, and they were in *inverse proportion to one another*, so that the total fear remained a constant as I got further away from home and further away from Father like this

$$\textbf{Fear}_{total} \approx \textbf{Fear}_{new\ place} \ \textbf{x} \ \textbf{Fear}_{near\ Father} \approx \textbf{constant}$$

It takes 19 minutes for the bus to get to school from our house, but it took me 47 minutes to walk the same distance so I was very tired when I got there and I hoped that I could stay at school for a little while and have some biscuits and some orange juice before I went to the train station. But I couldn't, because when I got to the school I saw that Father's van was parked outside in the car park. And I knew it was his van because it said **Ed Boone Heating Maintenance & Boiler Repair** on the side with a crossed spanners sign like this

And when I saw the van I was sick again. But I knew I was going to be sick this time so I didn't sick all over myself and I was just sick onto the wall and the pavement, and there wasn't very much sick because I hadn't eaten much. And when I had been sick I wanted to curl up on the ground and do groaning. But I knew that if I curled up on the ground and did groaning then Father would come out of the school and he would see me and he would catch me and take me home. So I took lots of deep breaths like Siobhan says I have to do if someone hits me at school, and I counted fifty breaths and I concentrated very hard on the numbers and did their cubes as I said them. And that made the hurt less painful.

And then I cleaned the sick away from my mouth and I made a decision that I would have to find out how to get to the train station and I would do this by asking someone, and it would be a lady because when they talked to us about Stranger Danger at school they say that if a man comes up to you and talks to you and you feel frightened you should call out and find a lady to run to because ladies are safer.

So I got out my Swiss Army Knife and I flicked out the saw blade and I held it tightly in the pocket that Toby wasn't in so that I could stab someone if they grabbed hold of me and then I saw a lady on the other side of the street with a baby in a pushchair and a little boy with a toy elephant, so I decided to ask her. And this time I looked left and right and left again so that I wouldn't be run over by a car, and I crossed the road.

And I said to the lady, 'Where can I buy a map?'

And she said, 'Pardon?'

And I said, 'Where can I buy a map?' And I could feel the hand that was holding the knife shaking even though I wasn't shaking it.

And she said, 'Patrick, put that down, it's dirty. A map of where?'

And I said, 'A map of here.'

And she said, 'I don't know.' And then she said, 'Where do you want to get to?'

And I said, 'I'm going to the train station.'

And she laughed and she said, 'You don't need a map to get to the train station.'

And I said, 'I do, because I don't know where the train station is.'

And she said, 'You can see it from here.'

And I said, 'No, I can't. And also I need to know where there is a cash machine.'

And she pointed and said, 'There. That building. Says *Signal Point* on the top. There's a British Rail sign on the other end. The station's at the bottom of that. Patrick, if I've told you once, I've told you a thousand times. Don't pick things off the pavement and stick them in your mouth.'

And I looked and I could see a building with writing at the top but it was a long way away so it was hard to read, and I said, 'Do you mean the stripy building with the horizontal windows?'

And she said, 'That's the one.'

And I said, 'How do I get to that building?'

And she said, 'Gordon Bennett.' And then she said, 'Follow that bus,' and she pointed to a bus that was going past.

So I started to run. But buses go really fast and I had to make sure that Toby didn't fall out of my pocket. But I managed to keep running after the bus for a long way and I crossed 6 side roads before it turned down another street and I couldn't see it any more.

And then I stopped running because I was breathing really hard and my legs hurt. And I was in a street with lots of shops. And I remembered being in this street when I went shopping with Mother. And there were lots of people in the street doing their shopping, but I didn't want them to touch me, so I walked at the edge of the road. And I didn't like all the people being near me and all the noise because it was too much information in my head and it made it hard to think, like there was shouting in my head. So I put my hands over my ears and I groaned very quietly.

And then I noticed that I could still see the ⇌ sign that the lady had pointed at, so I kept on walking towards it.

And then I couldn't see the ⇌ sign any more. And I had forgotten to remember where it was, and this was frightening because I was lost and because I do not forget things. And normally I would make a map in my head and I would follow the map and I would be a little cross on the map that showed where I was, but there was too much interference in my head and this had made me confused. So I stood under the green and white canvas roof outside a greengrocer's shop where there were carrots and onions and parsnips and broccoli in boxes that had a plastic furry green carpet in them, and I made a plan.

I knew that the train station was somewhere near. And if something is nearby you can find it by moving in a spiral, walking clockwise and taking every right turn until you come back to a road you've already walked on, then taking the next left, then taking every right turn and so on, like this (but this is a hypothetical diagram, too, and not a map of Swindon)

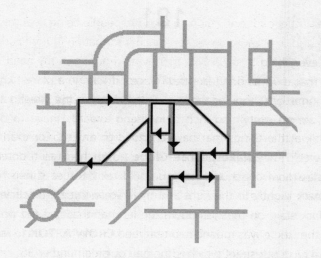

And that was how I found the train station, and I concentrated really hard on following the rules and making a map of the centre of the town in my head as I walked, and that way it was easier to ignore all the people and all the noise around me.

And then I went into the train station.

181

I see everything.

That is why I don't like new places. If I am in a place I know, like home, or school, or the bus, or the shop, or the street, I have seen almost everything in it beforehand and all I have to do is to look at the things that have changed or moved. For example, one week, the **Shakespeare's Globe** poster had fallen down in the classroom at school and you could tell because it had been put back slightly to the right and there were three little circles of Blu-Tack stain on the wall down the left-hand side of the poster. And the next day someone had graffitied **CROW APTOK** to lamppost 437 in our street which is the one outside number 35.

But most people are lazy. They never look at everything. They do what is called *glancing* which is the same word for bumping off something and carrying on in almost the same direction, e.g. when a snooker ball glances off another snooker ball. And the information in their head is really simple. For example, if they are in the countryside, it might be

1. I am standing in a field that is full of grass.
2. There are some cows in the fields
3. It is sunny with a few clouds.
4. There are some flowers in the grass.
5. There is a village in the distance.
6. There is a fence at the edge of the field and it has a gate in.

And then they would stop noticing anything because they would be thinking something else like, 'Oh, it is very beautiful here,' or, 'I'm worried that I might have left the gas cooker on,' or, 'I wonder if Julie has given birth yet.'[12]

But if I am standing in a field in the countryside I notice everything. For example, I remember standing in a field on Wednesday 15th June 1994 because Father and Mother and I were driving to Dover to get a ferry to France and we did what Father called *Taking the scenic route* which means going by little roads and stopping for lunch in a pub garden, and I had to stop to go for a wee, and I went into a field with cows in and after I'd had a wee I stopped and looked at the field and I noticed these things

1. There are 19 cows in the field, 15 of which are black and white and 4 of which are brown and white.

2. There is a village in the distance which has 31 visible houses and a church with a square tower and not a spire.

3. There are ridges in the field which means that in medieval times it was what is called a *ridge and furrow* field and people who lived in the village would have a ridge each to do farming on.

4. There is an old plastic bag from Asda in the hedge, and a squashed Coca-Cola can with a snail on, and a long piece of orange string.

5. The north-east corner of the field is highest and the south-

[12] This is really true because I asked Siobhan what people thought about when they looked at things, and this is what she said.

west corner is lowest (I had a compass because we were going on holiday and I wanted to know where Swindon was when we were in France) and the field is folded downwards slightly along the line between these two corners so that the north-west and south-east corners are slightly lower than they would be if the field was a flat inclined plane.

6. I can see three different types of grass and two colours of flowers in the grass.

7. The cows are mostly facing uphill.

And there were 31 more things in this list of things I noticed but Siobhan said I didn't need to write them all down. And it means that it is very tiring if I am in a new place because I see all these things, and if someone asked me afterwards what the cows looked like, I could ask which one, and I could do a drawing of them at home and say that a particular cow had patterns on it like this

And I realise that I told a lie in **Chapter 13** because I said, 'I cannot tell jokes', because I do know 3 jokes that I can tell and I

understand and one of them is about a cow, and Siobhan said I didn't have to go back and change what I wrote in **Chapter 13** because it doesn't matter because it is not a lie, just a *clarification*.

And this is the joke.

There are three men on a train. One of them is an economist and one of them is a logician and one of them is a mathematician. And they have just crossed the border into Scotland (I don't know why they are going to Scotland) and they see a brown cow standing in a field from the window of the train (and the cow is standing parallel to the train).

And the economist says, 'Look, the cows in Scotland are brown.'

And the logician says, 'No. There are cows in Scotland of which one, at least, is brown.'

And the mathematician says, 'No. There is at least one cow in Scotland, of which one side appears to be brown.'

And it is funny because economists are not real scientists, and because logicians think more clearly, but mathematicians are best.

And when I am in a new place, because I see everything, it is like when a computer is doing too many things at the same time and the central processor unit is blocked up and there isn't any space left to think about other things. And when I am in a new place and there are lots of people there it is even harder because people are not like cows and flowers and grass and they can talk to you and do things that you don't expect, so you have to notice everything that is in the place, and also you have to notice things that might happen as well. And sometimes, when I am in a new place and there are lots of people there it is like a computer crashing and I have to close my eyes and put my hands over my ears and groan, which is like pressing **CTRL + ALT + DEL** and shutting down programs and turning the computer off and rebooting so that I can remember what I am doing and where I am meant to be going.

And that is why I am good at chess and maths and logic, because most people are almost blind and they don't see most things and there is lots of spare capacity in their heads and it is filled with things which aren't connected and are silly, like, 'I'm worried that I might have left the gas cooker on.'

My train set had a little building that was two rooms with a corridor between them, and one was the ticket office where you bought the tickets, and one was a waiting room where you waited for the train. But the train station in Swindon wasn't like that. It was a tunnel and some stairs, and a shop and café and a waiting room like this

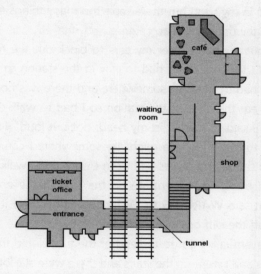

But this is not a very accurate map of the station because I was scared so I was not noticing things very well, and this is just what I remember so it is an *approximation*.

And it was like standing on a cliff in a really strong wind because it made me feel giddy and sick because there were lots of people walking into and out of the tunnel and it was really echoey and there was only one way to go and that was down the tunnel, and it smelled of toilets and cigarettes. So I stood against the wall and held onto the edge of a sign that said **Customers seeking access to car park please use assistance phone opposite, right of the ticket office** to make sure that I didn't fall over and go into a crouch on the ground. And I wanted to go home. But I was frightened of going home and I tried to make a plan of what I should do in my head but there were too many things to look at and too many things to hear.

So I put my hands over my ears to block out the noise and think. And I thought that I had to stay in the station to get on a train and I had to sit down somewhere and there was nowhere to sit down near the door of the station so I had to walk down the tunnel. So I said to myself, in my head, not out loud, 'I will walk down the tunnel and there might be somewhere I can sit down and then I can shut my eyes and I can think,' and I walked down the tunnel trying to concentrate on the sign at the end of the tunnel that said **WARNING CCTV in operation**. And it was like stepping off the cliff on to a tightrope.

And eventually I got to the end of the tunnel and there were some stairs and I went up the stairs and there were still lots of people and I groaned and there was a shop at the top of the stairs and a room with chairs in but there were too many people in the room with chairs in, so I walked past it. And there were signs saying **Great Western** and **cold beers and lagers** and **CAUTION WET FLOOR** and **Your 50p will keep a premature baby alive** for **1.8 seconds** and **transforming travel** and **Refreshingly Different** and **IT'S DELICIOUS IT'S CREAMY AND IT'S ONLY £1.30 HOT CHOC DELUXE** and **0870 777 7676** and **The Lemon Tree** and **No Smoking** and **FINE TEAS** and there were some little tables with chairs next to them and no one was sitting at one of the tables and it was in a corner and I sat down on one of the chairs next to it and I closed my eyes. And I put my hands in my pockets and Toby climbed into my hand and I gave him two pellets of rat food from my bag and I gripped the Swiss Army Knife in the other hand, and I groaned to cover up the noise because I had taken my hands off my ears, but not so loud that other people would hear me groaning and come and talk to me.

And then I tried to think about what I had to do, but I couldn't think because there were too many other things in my head, so I did a maths problem to make my head clearer.

And the maths problem that I did was called **Conway's Soldiers**. And in **Conway's Soldiers** you have a chess board that continues infinitely in all directions and every square below a horizontal line has a coloured tile on it like this

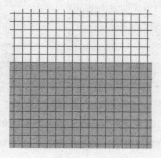

And you can move a coloured tile only if it can jump over a coloured tile horizontally or vertically (but not diagonally) into an empty square two squares away. And when you move a coloured tile in this way you have to remove the coloured tile that it jumped over, like this

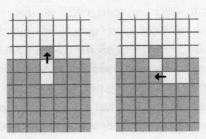

And you have to see how far you get the coloured tiles above the starting horizontal line, and you start by doing something like this

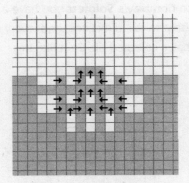

And then you do something like this

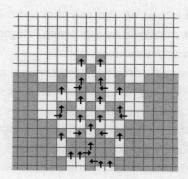

And I know what the answer is because however you move the coloured tiles you will never get a coloured tile more than 4 squares above the starting horizontal line, but it is a good maths problem to do in your head when you don't want to think about something else because you can make it as complicated as you need to fill your brain by making the board as big as you want and the moves as complicated as you want.

And I had got to

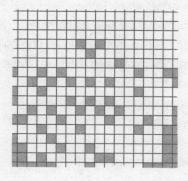

And then I looked up and saw that there was a policeman standing in front of me and he was saying, 'Anyone at home?' but I didn't know what that meant.

And then he said, 'Are you all right, young man?'

I looked at him and I thought for a bit so that I would answer the question correctly and I said, 'No.'

And he said, 'You're looking a bit worse for wear.'

He had a gold ring on one of his fingers and it had curly letters on it but I couldn't see what the letters were.

Then he said, 'The lady at the café says you've been here for 2½ hours and when she tried talking to you, you were in a complete trance.'

Then he said, 'What's your name?'

And I said, 'Christopher Boone.'

And he said, 'Where do you live?'

And I said, '36 Randolph Street' and I started feeling better because I like policemen and it was an easy question, and I wondered whether I should tell him that Father killed Wellington and whether he would arrest Father.

And he said, 'What are you doing here?'

And I said, 'I needed to sit down and be quiet and think.'

And he said, 'OK, let's keep it simple. What are you doing at the railway station?'

And I said, 'I'm going to see Mother.'

And he said, 'Mother?'

And I said, 'Yes, Mother.'

And he said, 'When's your train?'

And I said, 'I don't know. She lives in London. I don't know when there's a train to London.'

And he said, 'So, you don't live with your mother?'

And I said, 'No. But I'm going to.'

And then he sat down next to me and said, 'So, where does your mother live?'

And I said, 'In London.'

And he said, 'Yes, but where in London?'

And I said, '451c Chapter Road, London NW2 5NG.'

And he said, 'Jesus. What is that?'

And I looked down and I said, 'That's my pet rat, Toby,' because he was looking out of my pocket at the policeman.

And the policeman said, 'A pet rat?'

And I said, 'Yes, a pet rat. He's very clean and he hasn't got bubonic plague.'

And the policeman said, 'Well, that's reassuring.'

And I said, 'Yes.'

And he said, 'Have you got a ticket?'

And I said, 'No.'

And he said, 'Have you got any money to get a ticket?'

And I said, 'No.'

And he said, 'So, how precisely were you going to get to London, then?'

And then I didn't know what to say because I had Father's cashpoint card in my pocket and it was illegal to steal things, but he was a policeman so I had to tell the truth, so I said, 'I have a cashpoint card,' and I took it out of my pocket and I showed it to him. And this was a white lie.

But the policeman said, 'Is this your card?'

And then I thought he might arrest me, and I said, 'No, it's Father's.'

And he said, 'Father's?'

And I said, 'Yes, Father's.'

And he said, 'OK,' but he said it really slowly and he squeezed his nose between his thumb and his forefinger.

And I said, 'He told me the number,' which was another white lie.

And he said, 'Why don't you and I take a stroll to the cash-point machine, eh?'

And I said, 'You mustn't touch me.'

And he said, 'Why would I want to touch you?'

And I said, 'I don't know.'

And he said, 'Well, neither do I.'

And I said, 'Because I got a caution for hitting a policeman, but I didn't mean to hurt him and if I do it again I'll get into even bigger trouble.'

Then he looked at me and he said, 'You're serious, aren't you?'

And I said, 'Yes.'

And he said, 'You lead the way.'

And I said, 'Where?'

And he said, 'Back by the ticket office' and he pointed with his thumb.

And then we walked back through the tunnel, but it wasn't so frightening this time because there was a policeman with me.

And I put the cashpoint card into the machine like Father had let me do sometimes when we were shopping together and it said **ENTER YOUR PERSONAL NUMBER** and I typed in **3558** and pressed the **ENTER** button and the machine said **PLEASE ENTER AMOUNT** and there was a choice

← £10   £20 →

← £50   £100 →

Other Amount

(multiples of ten only) →

And I asked the policeman, 'How much does it cost to get a ticket for a train to London?'

And he said, 'About 20 quid.'

And I said, 'Is that pounds?'

And he said, 'Christ alive' and he laughed. But I didn't laugh because I don't like people laughing at me, even if they are policemen. And he stopped laughing, and he said, 'Yep. It's 20 pounds.'

So I pressed **£50** and five £10 notes came out of the machine, and a receipt, and I put the notes and the receipt and the card into my pocket.

And the policeman said, 'Well, I guess I shouldn't keep you chatting any longer.'

And I said, 'Where do I get a ticket for the train from?' because if you are lost and you need directions you can ask a policeman.

And he said, 'You are a prize specimen, aren't you?'

And I said, 'Where do I get a ticket for the train from?' because he hadn't answered my question.

And he said, 'In there,' and he pointed and there was a big room with a glass window on the other side of the train station door, and then he said, 'Now, are you sure you know what you're doing?'

And I said, 'Yes. I'm going to London to live with my mother.'

And he said, 'Has your mother got a telephone number?'

And I said, 'Yes.'

And he said, 'And can you tell me what it is?'

And I said, 'Yes. It's 0208 887 8907.'

And he said, 'And you'll ring her if you get into any trouble, OK?'

And I said, 'Yes' because I knew you could ring people from phone boxes if you had money, and I had money now.

And he said, 'Good.'

And I walked into the ticket office and I turned round and I could see that the policeman was still watching me so I felt safe. And there was a long desk at the other side of the big room and a window on the desk and there was a man standing in front of the window and there was a man behind the window, and I said to the man behind the window, 'I want to go to London.'

And the man in front of the window said, 'If you don't mind' and he turned round so that his back was towards me and the man behind the window gave him a little bit of paper to sign and he signed it and pushed it back under the window and the man behind the window gave him a ticket. And then the man in front of the window looked at me and he said, 'What the fuck are you looking at?' and then he walked away.

And he had dreadlocks, which is what some black people have, but he was white, and dreadlocks is when you never wash your hair and it looks like old rope. And he had red trousers with stars on. And I kept my hand on my Swiss Army Knife in case he touched me.

And then there was no one else in front of the window and I said to the man behind the window, 'I want to go to London,' and I hadn't been frightened when I was with the policeman but I turned round and I saw that he had gone now and I was scared again, so I tried to pretend I was playing a game on my computer and it was called **Train to London** and it was like **Myst** or **The Eleventh Hour**, and you had to solve lots of different problems to get to the next level, and I could turn it off at any time.

And the man said, 'Single or return?'

And I said, 'What does *single or return* mean?'

And he said, 'Do you want to go one way, or do you want to go and come back?'

And I said, 'I want to stay there when I get there.'

And he said, 'For how long?'

And I said, 'Until I go to university.'

And he said, 'Single, then,' and then he said, 'That'll be £17.'

And I gave him the fifty pounds and he gave me £30 back and he said, 'Don't you go throwing it away.'

And then he gave me a little yellow and orange ticket and £3 in coins and I put it all in my pocket with my knife. And I didn't like the ticket being half yellow but I had to keep it because it was my train ticket.

And then he said, 'If you could move away from the counter.'

And I said, 'When is the train to London?'

And he looked at his watch and said, 'Platform 1, five minutes.'

And I said, 'Where is Platform 1?'

And he pointed and said, 'Through the underpass and up the stairs. You'll see the signs.'

And *underpass* meant *tunnel* because I could see where he was pointing, so I went out of the ticket office, but it wasn't like a computer game at all because I was in the middle of it and it was like all the signs were shouting in my head and someone bumped into me as they walked past and I made a noise like a dog barking to scare them off.

And I pictured in my head a big red line across the floor which started at my feet and went through the tunnel and I started walking along the red line, saying 'Left, right, left, right, left, right,' because sometimes when I am frightened or angry it helps if I do something that has a rhythm to it, like music or drumming, which is something Siobhan taught me to do.

And I went up the stairs and I saw a sign saying, ← **Platform 1** and the ← was pointing at a glass door so I went through it, and someone bumped into me again with a suitcase and I made another noise like a dog barking, and they said, 'Watch where the hell you're going,' but I pretended that they were just one of the

Guarding Demons in **Train to London** and there was a train. And I saw a man with a newspaper and a bag of golf clubs go up to one of the doors of the train and press a big button next to it and the doors were electronic and they slid open and I liked that. And then the doors closed behind him.

And then I looked at my watch and 3 minutes had gone past since I was at the ticket office which meant that the train would be going in 2 minutes.

And then I went up to the door and I pressed the big button and the doors slid open and I stepped through the doors.

And I was on the train to London.

193

When I used to play with my train set I made a train timetable because I liked timetables. And I like timetables because I like to know when everything is going to happen.

And this was my timetable when I lived at home with Father and I thought that Mother was dead from a heart attack (this was the timetable for a Monday and also it is an *approximation*).

7.20 a.m.	Wake up	3.30 p.m.	Catch school bus home
7.25 a.m.	Clean teeth and wash face	3.49 p.m.	Get off school bus at home
7.30 a.m.	Give Toby food and water	3.50 p.m.	Have juice and snack
7.40 a.m.	Have breakfast	3.55 p.m.	Give Toby food and water
8.00 a.m.	Put school clothes on	4.00 p.m.	Take Toby out of his cage
8.05 a.m.	Pack school bag	4.18 p.m.	Put Toby into his cage
8.10 a.m.	Read book or watch video	4.20 p.m.	Watch television or a video
8.32 a.m.	Catch bus to school	5.00 p.m.	Read a book
8.43 a.m.	Go past tropical fish shop	6.00 p.m.	Have tea
8.51 a.m.	Arrive at school	6.30 p.m.	Watch television or a video
9.00 a.m.	School assembly	7.00 p.m.	Do maths practice
9.15 a.m.	First morning class	8.00 p.m.	Have a bath
10.30 a.m.	Break	8.15 p.m.	Get changed into pyjamas
10.50 a.m.	Art class with Mrs Peters[13]	8.20 p.m.	Play computer games
12.30 a.m.	Lunch	9.00 p.m.	Watch television or a video
1.00 p.m.	First afternoon class	9.20 p.m.	Have juice and a snack
2.15 p.m.	Second afternoon class	9.30 p.m.	Go to bed

[13] In the Art class we do Art, but in the First morning class and the First afternoon class and the Second afternoon class we do lots of different things like *Reading* and *Tests* and *Social Skills* and *Looking After Animals* and *What We Did At The Weekend* and *Writing* and *Maths* and *Stranger Danger* and *Money* and *Personal Hygiene*.

And at the weekend I make up my own timetable and I write it down on a piece of cardboard and I put it up on the wall. And it says things like **Feed Toby**, or **Do maths** or **Go to the shop to buy sweets**. And that is one of the other reasons why I don't like France because when people are on holiday they don't have a timetable and I had to get Mother and Father to tell me every morning exactly what we were going to do that day to make me feel better.

Because time is not like space. And when you put something down somewhere, like a protractor or a biscuit, you can have a map in your head to tell you where you have left it, but even if you don't have a map it will still be there because a map is a *representation* of things that actually exist so you can find the protractor or the biscuit again. And a timetable is a map of time, except that if you don't have a timetable time is not there like the landing and the garden and the route to school. Because time is only the relationship between the way different things change, like the earth going round the sun and atoms vibrating and clocks ticking and day and night and waking up and going to sleep, and it is like west or nor-nor-east which won't exist when the earth stops existing and falls into the sun because it is only a relationship between the North Pole and the South Pole and everywhere else, like Mogadishu and Sunderland and Canberra.

And it isn't a fixed relationship like the relationship between our house and Mrs Shears' house, or like the relationship between 7 and 865, but it depends on how fast you are going relative to a specific point. And if you go off in a space ship and you travel near the speed of light, you may come back and find that all your family is dead and you are still young and it will be the future but your clock will say that you have only been away for a few days or months.

And because nothing can travel faster than the speed of light this means that we can only know about a fraction of the things that go on in the universe, like this

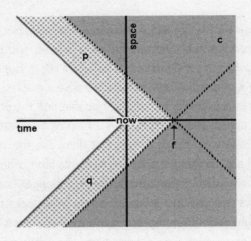

And this is a map of everything and everywhere, and the future is on the right and the past is on the left and the gradient of the line **c** is the speed of light, but we can't know about the things which happen in the shaded areas even though some of them have already happened, but when we get to **f** it will be possible to find out about things which happen in the lighter areas **p** and **q**.

And this means that time is a mystery, and not even a thing, and no one has ever solved the puzzle of what time is, exactly. And so, if you get lost in time it is like being lost in a desert, except that you can't see the desert because it is not a thing.

And this is why I like timetables because they make sure you don't get lost in time.

197

There were lots of people on the train, and I didn't like that, because I don't like lots of people I don't know and I hate it even more if I am stuck in a room with lots of people I don't know, and a train is like a room and you can't get out of it when it's moving. And it made me think of when I had to come home in the car from school one day because the bus had broken down and Mother came and picked me up and Mrs Peters asked Mother if she could take Jack and Polly home because their mothers couldn't come and pick them up, and Mother said yes. But I started screaming in the car because there were too many people in it and Jack and Polly weren't in my class and Jack bangs his head on things and makes a noise like an animal, and I tried to get out of the car, but it was still going along and I fell out onto the road and I had to have stitches in my head and they had to shave the hair off and it took 3 months for it to grow back to the way it was before.

So I stood very still in the train carriage and didn't move.

And then I heard someone say, 'Christopher.'

And I thought it would be someone I knew, like a teacher from school or one of the people who live in our street, but it wasn't. It was the policeman again. And he said, 'Caught you just in time' and he was breathing really loud and holding his knees.

And I didn't say anything.

And he said, 'We've got your father at the police station.'

And I thought he was going to say that they had arrested

Father for killing Wellington, but he didn't. He said, 'He's looking for you.'

And I said, 'I know.'

And he said, 'So, why are you going to London?'

And I said, 'Because I'm going to live with Mother.'

And he said, 'Well, I think your father might have something to say about that.'

And then I thought that he was going to take me back to Father and that was frightening because he was a policeman and policemen are meant to be good, so I started to run away, but he grabbed me and I screamed. And then he let go.

And he said, 'OK, let's not get over-excited here.' And then he said, 'I'm going to take you back to the police station and you and me and your dad can sit down and have a little chat about who's going where.'

And I said, 'I'm going to live with Mother, in London.'

And he said, 'Not just yet, you're not.'

And I said, 'Have you arrested Father?'

And he said, 'Arrested him? What for?'

And I said, 'He killed a dog. With a garden fork. The dog was called Wellington.'

And the policeman said, 'Did he now?'

And I said, 'Yes, he did.'

And he said, 'Well, we can talk about that as well.' And then he said, 'Right, young man, I think you've done enough adventuring for one day.'

And then he reached out to touch me again and I started to

scream again, and he said, 'Now listen, you little monkey. You can either do what I say, or I am going to have to make . . .'

And then the train jiggled and it began to move.

And then the policeman said, 'Shitting fuck.'

And then he looked at the ceiling of the train and he put his hands together in front of his mouth like people do when they are praying to God in heaven and he breathed really loudly into his hands and made a whistling noise, and then he stopped because the train jiggled again and he had to grab hold of one of the straps which was hanging from the ceiling.

And then he said, 'Don't move.'

And then he took out his walkie-talkie and pressed a button and said, 'Rob . . .? Yeh, it's Nigel. I'm stuck on the bloody train. Yeh. Don't even . . . Look. It stops at Didcot Parkway. So, if you can get someone to meet me with a car . . . Cheers. Tell his old man we've got him but it's going to take a while, OK? Great.'

And then he clicked his walkie-talkie off and he said, 'Let's get ourselves a seat,' and he pointed to two long seats nearby which faced each other, and he said, 'Park yourself. And no monkey business.'

And the people who were sitting on the seats got up and walked away because he was a policeman and we sat down facing one another.

And he said, 'You are a bloody handful, you are. Jeez.'

And I wondered whether the policeman would help me find 451c Chapter Road, London NW2 5NG.

And I looked out of the window and we were going past

factories and scrapyards full of old cars and there were 4 caravans in a muddy field with 2 dogs and some clothes hanging up to dry.

And outside the window was like a map, except that it was in 3 dimensions and it was life-size because it was the thing it was a map of. And there were so many things it made my head hurt, so I closed my eyes, but then I opened them again because it was like flying, but nearer to the ground, and I think flying is good. And then the countryside started and there were fields and cows and horses and a bridge and a farm and more houses and lots of little roads with cars on. And that made me think that there must be millions of miles of train track in the world and they all go past houses and roads and rivers and fields, and that made me think how many people must be in the world and they all have houses and roads to travel on and cars and pets and clothes and they all eat lunch and go to bed and have names and this made my head hurt, too, so I closed my eyes again and did counting and groaning.

And when I opened my eyes the policeman was reading a newspaper called The Sun, and on the front of the paper it said **£3m Anderson's Call Girl Shame** and it had a picture of a man and a picture of a lady in a bra underneath.

And then I did some maths practice in my head, solving quadratic equations using the formula

$$x = \frac{-b \pm \sqrt{(b^2 - 4ac)}}{2a}$$

And then I wanted to go for a wee, but I was on a train. And I didn't know how long it would take us to get to London and I felt a panic starting, and I started to tap a rhythm on the glass with my knuckles to help me wait and not think about wanting to go for a wee, and I looked at my watch and I waited for 17 minutes, but when I want to go for a wee I have to go really quickly which is why I like to be at home or at school and I always go for a wee before I get on the bus, which is why I leaked a bit and wet my trousers.

And then the policeman looked across at me and said, 'Oh, Christ, you've . . .' And then he put his newspaper down and said, 'For God's sake go to the bloody toilet, will you.'

And I said, 'But I'm on a train.'

And he said, 'They do have toilets on trains, you know.'

And I said, 'Where is the toilet on the train?'

And he pointed and said, 'Through those doors, there. But I'll be keeping an eye on you, understand?'

And I said, 'No,' because I knew what *keeping an eye on someone* meant but he couldn't look at me when I was in the toilet.

And he said, 'Just go to the bloody toilet.'

So I got up out of my seat and I closed my eyes so that my eyelids were just little slits so I couldn't see the other people on the train and I walked to the door, and when I got through the door there was another door on the right and it was half open and it said **TOILET** on it, so I went inside.

And it was horrible inside because there was poo on the seat of the toilet and it smelt of poo, like the toilet at school when Joseph has been for a poo on his own, because he plays with it.

And I didn't want to use the toilet because of the poo, which was the poo of people I didn't know and brown, but I had to because I really wanted to wee. So I closed my eyes and went for a wee and the train wobbled and lots went on the seat and on the floor, but I wiped my penis with toilet paper and flushed the toilet and then I tried to use the sink but the tap didn't work, so I put spit on my hands and wiped them with a paper tissue and put it into the toilet.

Then I went out of the toilet and I saw that opposite the toilet there were two shelves with cases and a rucksack on them and it made me think of the airing cupboard at home and how I climb in there sometimes and it makes me feel safe. So I climbed onto the middle shelf and I pulled one of the cases across like a door so that I was shut in, and it was dark and there was no one in there with me and I couldn't hear people talking so I felt much calmer and it was nice.

And I did some more quadratic equations like

$$0 = 437x^2 + 103x + 11$$

and

$$0 = 79x^2 + 43x + 2089$$

and I made some of the coefficients large so that they were hard to solve.

And then the train started to slow down and someone came and stood near the shelf and knocked on the door of the toilet, and it was the policeman and he said, 'Christopher . . .? Christopher . . .?' and then he opened the door of the toilet and said, 'Bloody hell' and he was really close so that I could see his walkie-talkie and his truncheon on his belt and I could smell his aftershave, but he didn't see me and I didn't say anything because I didn't want him to take me to Father.

And then he went away again, running.

And then the train stopped and I wondered if it was London, but I didn't move because I didn't want the policeman to find me.

And then a lady with a jumper that had bees and flowers made of wool on it came and took the rucksack off the shelf over my head and she said, 'You scared the living daylights out of me.'

But I didn't say anything.

And then she said, 'I think someone's out there on the platform looking for you.'

But I carried on not saying anything.

And she said, 'Well, it's your look-out,' and she went away.

And then three other people walked past and one of them was a black man in a long white dress and he put a big parcel on the shelf above my head but he didn't see me.

And then the train started going again.

199

People believe in God because the world is very complicated and they think it is very unlikely that anything as complicated as a flying squirrel or the human eye or a brain could happen by chance. But they should think logically and if they thought logically they would see that they can only ask this question because it has already happened and they exist. And there are billions of planets where there is no life, but there is no one on those planets with brains to notice. And it is like if everyone in the world was tossing coins eventually someone would get 5,698 heads in a row and they would think they were very special. But they wouldn't be because there would be millions of people who didn't get 5,698 heads.

And there is life on earth because of an accident. But it is a very special kind of accident. And for this accident to happen in this special way, there have to be 3 *Conditions*. And these are

1. Things have to make copies of themselves (this is called **Replication**)

2. They have to make small mistakes when they do this (this is called **Mutation**)

3. These mistakes have to be the same in their copies (this is called **Heritability**)

And these conditions are very rare, but they are possible, and they cause life. And it just happens. But it doesn't have to end up with rhinoceroses and human beings and whales. It could end up with anything.

And, for example, some people say how can an eye happen by accident? Because an eye has to evolve from something else very like an eye and it doesn't just happen because of a genetic mistake, and what is the use of half an eye? But half an eye is very useful because half an eye means that an animal can see half of an animal that wants to eat it and get out of the way, and it will eat the animal that only has a third of an eye or 49% of an eye instead because it hasn't got out of the way quick enough, and the animal that is eaten won't have babies because it is dead.

And people who believe in God think God has put human beings on the earth because they think human beings are the best animal, but human beings are just an animal and they will evolve into another animal, and that animal will be cleverer and it will put human beings into a zoo, like we put chimpanzees and gorillas into a zoo. Or human beings will all catch a disease and die out or they will make too much pollution and kill themselves, and then there will only be insects in the world and they will be the best animal.

211

Then I wondered whether I should have got off the train because it had just stopped at London, and I was scared because if the train went anywhere else it would be somewhere where I didn't know anybody.

And then somebody went to the toilet and then they came out again, but they didn't see me. And I could smell their poo, and it was different from the smell of the poo that I smelt in the toilet when I went in there.

And then I closed my eyes and did some more maths puzzles so I didn't think about where I was going.

And then the train stopped again, and I thought about getting off the shelf and going to get my bag and get off the train. But I didn't want to be found by the policeman and be taken to Father, so I stayed on the shelf and didn't move, and no one saw me this time.

And then I remembered that there was a map on the wall of one of the classrooms at school, and it was a map of England and Scotland and Wales and it showed you where all the towns were and I pictured it in my head with Swindon and London on, and it was like this in my head

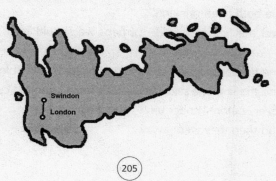

And I had been looking at my watch since the train had started at **12:59 p.m.** And the first stop had been at **1.16 p.m.** which was 17 minutes later. And it was now **1:39 p.m.** which was 23 minutes after the stop, which meant that we would be at the sea if the train didn't go in a big curve. But I didn't know if it went in a big curve.

And then there were another 4 stops and 4 people came and took bags away from the shelves and 2 people put bags on the shelves, but no one moved the big suitcase that was in front of me and only one person saw me and they said, 'You are fucking weird, mate' and that was a man in a suit. And 6 people went to the toilet but they didn't do poos that I could smell, which was good.

And then the train stopped and a lady with a yellow waterproof coat came and took the big suitcase away and she said, 'Have you touched this?'

And I said, 'Yes.'

And then she went away.

And then a man stood next to the shelf and said, 'Come and look at this, Barry. They've got, like, a train elf.'

And another man came and stood next to him and said, 'Well, we have both been drinking.'

And the first man said, 'Perhaps we should feed him some nuts.'

And the second man said, 'You're the one who's bloody nuts.'

And the first one said, 'Come on, shift it, you daft cunt. I need more beers before I sober up.'

And then they went away.

And then the train was really quiet and it didn't move again and I couldn't hear anyone. So I decided to get off the shelf and go and get my bag and see if the policeman was still sitting in his seat.

So I got off the shelf and I looked through the door, but the policeman wasn't there. And my bag had gone as well, which had Toby's food in it and my maths books and my clean pants and vest and shirt and the orange juice and the milk and the clementines and the custard creams and the baked beans.

And then I heard the sound of feet and I turned round and it was another policeman, not the one who was on the train before, and I could see him through the door, in the next carriage, and he was looking under the seats. And I decided that I didn't like policemen so much any more, so I got off the train.

And when I saw how big the room was that the train was in and I heard how noisy and echoey it was I had to kneel down on the ground for a bit because I thought I was going to fall over. And when I was kneeling on the ground I worked out which way to walk, and I decided to walk in the direction the train was going when it came into the station because if this was the last stop, that was the direction London was in.

So I stood up and I imagined that there was a big red line on the ground which ran parallel to the train to the gate at the far end and I walked along it and I said 'Left, right, left, right . . .' again, like before.

And when I got to the gate a man said to me, 'I think someone's looking for you, sonny.'

And I said, 'Who's looking for me?' because I thought it might be Mother and the policeman in Swindon had phoned her up with the phone number I told him.

But he said, 'A policeman.'

And I said, 'I know.'

And he said, 'Oh. Right.' And then he said, 'You wait here, then, and I'll go and tell them,' and he walked back down the side of the train.

So I carried on walking. And I could still feel the feeling like a balloon inside my chest and it hurt and I covered my ears with my hands and I went and stood against the wall of a little shop which said **Hotel and Theatre Reservations Tel: 0207 402 5164** in the middle of the big room and then I took my hands away from my ears and I groaned to block out the noise and I looked round the big room at all the signs to see if this was London. And the signs said

Sweet Pastries **Heathrow Airport Check-In Here** *Bagel Factory* **EAT** *excellence and taste* **YO!** sushi **Stationlink** Buses **W H Smith** MEZZANINE **Heathrow Express** Clinique First Class Lounge FULLERS easyCar.com *The Mad Bishop* and **Bear Public House** Fuller's London Pride Dixons **Our Price** Paddington Bear at Paddington Station **Tickets** Taxis ♦♦**Toilets** First Aid **Eastbourne Terrace** ▮▮ington **ton** Way Out **Praed Street The Lawn** Q Here Please Upper Crust Sainsbury's **Local** ⓘ **Information** GREAT WESTERN FIRST Ⓟ **Position** Closed **Closed** Position Closed Sock Shop Fast Ticket Point Ⓝ **Millie's Cookies**

Coffee FERGIE TO STAY AT MANCHESTER UNITED **Freshly Baked Cookies and Muffins** Cold Drinks **Penalty Fares** Warning **Savoury Pastries** Platforms 9-14 *Burger King* **Fresh Filled!** the reef° café bar **business travel** *special edition* TOP 75 ALBUMS Evening Standard

But after a few seconds they looked like this

Sweathr❉❉■ow○■Airpheck-*lagtory*EAenceandtaste ❎! suuSetHeesortCWHSmithEANEINStatnH✳ioe*adB*ho athrnieFirlassLoULLERnreHe*B*SeasyCar.com*TheMp*anard BebleFuler'sLonPr*ndo*idePaiesstrDzzixonsOur*is*PPurdEboi▤ ⏏ceicHousPatCngtoneaswatPoagtonTetsTa*elFac*⬧Toil eddistsFirs—❋✦ta⬥✳*Bu*ngfeFi5us✳✖HPDNLeTerrace▮ ▮▮ingtonW✝astaySt✦atio✎■nlinkOutC▦losed①& qed3iniBr1uowo[CliPraicxiskedPointDrS▦treetTheLy uawHea❖■rCrustMuflyB▥akl6dE①TonClose"⬥*excel le*toxpr*essnQinrePlek4shSaisesUp⬆←✦pensburiy'sLcidSoℎ kt①ickma**tion**REATM✚✚ASTERCookiesWESTEfinsCojRN 2FningSTanl⑥RsT℗P0all**nforositio**NCH✂⧣✳EnSTAYATS 3hopFast⊙⬥Positd①◗Penie✈❉sPloNla8⑨▮④⏪⬧tfoe9s WEf°cusCoffReosVeledPOSi⊗tnesskix①edcoreShoj⊛✄③ 5ALBialedMilliafébarbeeanCrKl'geing🕐F3illeFFTOUr❉mEGI Es9TEDFrese⏩□sanaltyFarrningSa❼vou*ryPa*stri14Bur zd!the𝕄▤●resit✳□rh▤▭aspecition TOP&UMSEvedard

because there were too many and my brain wasn't working

properly and this frightened me so I closed my eyes again and I counted slowly to 50 but without doing the cubes. And I stood there and I opened my Swiss Army Knife in my pocket to make me feel safe and I held on to it tight.

And then I made my hand into a little tube with my fingers and I opened my eyes and I looked through the tube so that I was only looking at one sign at a time and after a long time I saw a sign that said ⓘ **Information** and it was above a window on a little shop.

And a man came up to me and he was wearing a blue jacket and blue trousers and he had brown shoes and he was carrying a book in his hand and he said, 'You look lost.'

So I took out my Swiss Army Knife.

And he said, 'Whoa. Whoa. Whoa. Whoa. Whoa,' and held up both his hands with his fingers stretched out in a fan, like he wanted me to stretch my fingers out in a fan and touch his fingers because he wanted to say he loved me, but he did it with both hands, not one like Father and Mother, and I didn't know who he was.

And then he walked away backwards.

So I went to the shop that said ⓘ **Information** and I could feel my heart beating very hard and I could hear a noise like the sea in my ears. And when I got to the window I said, 'Is this London?' but there was no one behind the window.

And then someone sat behind the window and she was a lady and she was black and she had long fingernails which were painted pink and I said, 'Is this London?'

And she said, 'Sure is, honey.'

And I said, 'Is this London?'

And she said, 'Indeed it is.'

And I said, 'How do I get to 451c Chapter Road, London NW2 5NG?'

And she said, 'Where is that?'

And I said, 'It's 451c Chapter Road, London NW2 5NG. And sometimes you can write it *451c Chapter Road, Willesden, London NW2 5NG*.'

And the lady said to me, 'Take the tube to Willesden Junction, honey. Or Willesden Green. Got to be near there somewhere.'

And I said, 'What sort of tube?'

And she said, 'Are you for real?'

And I didn't say anything.

And she said, 'Over there. See that big staircase with the escalators? See the sign? Says *Underground*. Take the Bakerloo Line to Willesden Junction or the Jubilee to Willesden Green. You OK, honey?'

And I looked where she was pointing and there was a big staircase going down into the ground and there was a big sign over the top of it like this

And I thought *I can do this* because I was doing really well and I was in London and I would find my mother. And I had to think to myself *the people are like cows in a field*, and I just had to look in front of me all the time and make a red line along the floor in the picture of the big room in my head and follow it.

And I walked across the big room to the escalators. And I kept hold of my Swiss Army Knife in my pocket and I held onto Toby in my other pocket to make sure he didn't escape.

And *the escalators* was a staircase but it was moving and people stepped onto it and it carried them down and up and it made me laugh because I hadn't been on one before and it was like something in a science fiction film about the future. But I didn't want to use it so I went down the stairs instead.

And then I was in a smaller room underground and there were lots of people and there were pillars which had blue lights in the ground around the bottom of them and I liked these, but I didn't like the people, so I saw a photobooth like one I went into on 25th March 1994 to have my passport photo done, and I went into the photobooth because it was like a cupboard and it felt safer and I could look out through the curtain.

And I did detecting by watching and I saw that people were putting tickets into grey gates and walking through. And some of the people were buying tickets at big black machines on the wall.

And I watched 47 people do this and I memorised what to do. Then I imagined a red line on the floor and I walked over to the wall where there was a poster which was a list of places to go and it was alphabetical and I saw Willesden Green and it said £2:20 and then I went to one of the machines and there was a little screen which said **PRESS TICKET TYPE** and I pressed the button that most people had pressed which was **ADULT SINGLE** and **£2:20** and the screen said **INSERT £2:20** and I put 3 £1 coins into the slot and there was a clinking noise and the screen said **TAKE TICKET AND CHANGE** and there was a ticket in a little hole at the bottom of the machine, and a 50p coin and a 20p coin and a 10p coin and I put the coins in my pocket and I went up to one of the grey gates and I put my ticket into the slot and it sucked it in and it came out on the other side of the gate. And someone said, 'Get a move on,' and I made the noise like a dog barking and I walked forward and the gate opened this time and I took my ticket like other people did and I liked the grey gate because that was like something in a science fiction film about the future, too.

And then I had to work out which way to go, so I stood against a wall so people didn't touch me, and there was a sign for **Bakerloo Line** and **District and Circle Line** but not one for **Jubilee Line** like the lady had said, so I made a plan and it was to go to *Willesden Junction on the Bakerloo Line*.

And there was another sign for the Bakerloo Line and it was like this

← Bakerloo Line

platform **3** platform **4**

- **Harrow & Wealdstone** ⮀
- **Kenton**
- **South Kenton**
- **North Wembley**
- **Wembley Central**
- **Stonebridge Park**
- **Harlesden**
- **Willesden Junction** ⮀
- **Kensal Green**
- **Queens Park** ⮀
- **Kilburn Park**
- **Maida Vale**
- **Warwick Avenue**
- **Paddington** ⮀
- **Edgware Road**
- **Marylebone** ⮀
- **Baker Street**
- **Regent's Park**
- **Oxford Circus**
- **Piccadilly Circus**
- **Charing Cross** ⮀
- **Embankment**
- **Waterloo** ⮀
- **Lambeth North**
- **Elephant & Castle** ⮀

And I read all the words and I found **Willesden Junction** so I followed the arrow that said ← and I went through the left-hand tunnel and there was a fence down the middle of the tunnel and the people were walking straight ahead on the left and coming the other way on the right like on a road, so I walked along the left and the tunnel curved left and then there were more gates and a sign said **Bakerloo Line** and it pointed down an escalator, so I had to go down the escalators and I had to hold onto the rubber rail but that moved too so I didn't fall over and people were standing close to me and I wanted to hit them to make them go away but I didn't hit them because of the caution.

And then I was at the bottom of the escalators and I had to jump off and I tripped and bumped into someone and they said, 'Easy,' and there were two ways to go and one said **Northbound** and I went that way because **Willesden** was on the top half of the map and the top is always north on maps.

And then I was in another train station but it was tiny and it was in a tunnel and there was only one track and the walls were curved and they were covered in big adverts and they said **WAY OUT** and **London's Transport Museum** and **Take time out to regret your career choice** and **JAMAICA** and ⇌**British Rail** and ⊗**No Smoking** and **Be Moved** and **Be Moved** and **Be Moved** and **For Stations beyond Queen's Park take the first train and change at Queen's Park if necessary** and **Hammersmith and City Line** and **You're closer than my family ever gets**. And there were lots of people standing in the little station and it was underground so there weren't any windows and I didn't like that, so I found a seat which was a bench and I sat at the end of the bench.

And then lots of people started coming into the little station. And someone sat down on the other end of the bench and it was a lady who had a black briefcase and purple shoes and a brooch shaped like a parrot. And the people kept coming into the little station so that it was even more crowded than the big station. And then I couldn't see the walls any more and the back of someone's jacket touched my knee and I felt sick and I started groaning really loudly and the lady on the bench stood up and no one else sat down. And I felt like I felt like when I had flu and I had to stay in bed all day and all of me hurt and I couldn't walk or eat or go to sleep or do maths.

And then there was a sound like people fighting with swords and I could feel a strong wind and a roaring started and I closed my eyes and the roaring got louder and I groaned really loudly but I couldn't block it out of my ears and I thought the little station was going to collapse or there was a big fire somewhere and I was going to die. And then the roaring turned into a clattering and a squealing and it got slowly quieter and then it stopped and I kept my eyes closed because I felt safer not seeing what was happening. And then I could hear people moving again because it was quieter. And I opened my eyes. I couldn't see anything at first because there were too many people. And then I saw that they were getting onto a train that wasn't there before and it was the train which was the roaring. And there was sweat running down my face from under my hair and I was moaning, not groaning, but different, like a dog when it has hurt its paw and I heard the sound but I didn't realise it was me at first.

And then the train doors closed and the train started moving and it roared again but not as loud this time and 5 carriages went past and it went into the tunnel at the end of the little station and it was quiet again and the people were all walking into the tunnels that went out of the little station.

And I was shaking and I wanted to be back at home, and then I realised I couldn't be at home because Father was there and he told a lie and he killed Wellington which meant that it wasn't my home any more, my home was 451c Chapter Road, London NW2 5NG and it scared me, having a wrong thought like *I wish I was back at home again* because it meant my mind wasn't working properly.

And then more people came into the little station and it became fuller and then the roaring began again and I closed my eyes and I sweated and felt sick and I felt the feeling like a balloon inside my chest and it was so big I found it hard to breathe. And then the people went away on the train and the little station was empty again. And then it filled up with people and another train came with the same roaring. And it was exactly like having flu that time because I wanted it to stop, like you can just pull the plug of a computer out of the wall if it crashes, because I wanted to go to sleep so that I wouldn't have to think because the only thing I could think was how much it hurt because there was no room for anything else in my head, but I couldn't go to sleep and I just had to sit there and there was nothing to do except to wait and to hurt.

223

And this is another description because Siobhan said I should do descriptions and it is a description of the advert that was on the wall of the little train station opposite me, but I can't remember all of it because I thought I was going to die.

And the advert said

D r e a m holiday,
think Kuoni
in Malaysia

and behind the writing there was a big photograph of 2 orang-utans and they were swinging on branches and there were trees behind them but the leaves were blurred because the camera was focusing on the orang-utans and not the leaves and the orang-utans were moving.

And *orang-utan* comes from the Malaysian word **ōranghūtan** which means *man of the woods*.

And adverts are pictures or television programmes to make you buy things like cars or Snickers or use an Internet Service Provider. But this was an advert to make you go to Malaysia on a holiday. And Malaysia is in South-East Asia and it is made up of Peninsular Malaysia and Sabah and Sarawak and Labuan and the capital is Kuala Lumpur and the highest mountain is Mount Kinabalu which is 4,101 m high, but that wasn't on the advert.

And Siobhan says people go on holidays to see new things

and relax, but it wouldn't make me relaxed and you can see new things by looking at earth under a microscope or drawing the shape of the solid made when 3 circular rods of equal thickness intersect at right angles. And I think that there are so many things just in one house that it would take years to think about all of them properly. And, also, a thing is interesting because of thinking about it and not because of it being new. For example, Siobhan showed me that you can wet your finger and rub the edge of a thin glass and make a singing noise. And you can put different amounts of water in different glasses and they make different notes because they have what are called different *resonant frequencies*, and you can play a tune like **Three Blind Mice**. And lots of people have thin glasses in their houses and they don't know you can do this.

And the advert said

Malaysia, truly Asia.

Stimulated by the sights and smells, you realise that you have arrived in a land of contrasts. You seek out the traditional, the natural and the cosmopolitan. Your memories stretch from city days to nature reserves to lazy hours on the beach. Prices from £575 per person.

Call us on 01306 747000, see your travel agent or visit the world at www.kuoni.co.uk.

A world of difference.

And there were three other pictures, and they were very small, and they were a palace and a beach and a palace.

And this is what the orang-utans looked like

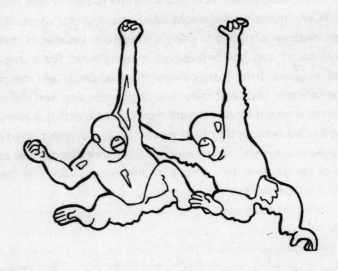

227

And I kept my eyes closed and I didn't look at my watch at all. And the trains coming in and out of the station were in a rhythm, like music or drumming. And it was like counting and saying 'Left, right, left, right, left, right . . .' which Siobhan taught me to do to make myself calm. And I was saying in my head, 'Train coming. Train stopped. Train going. Silence. Train coming. Train stopped. Train going . . .' as if the trains were only in my mind. And normally I don't imagine things that aren't happening because it is a lie and it makes me feel scared, but it was better than watching the trains coming in and out of the station because that made me feel even more scared.

And I didn't open my eyes and I didn't look at my watch. And it was like being in a dark room with the curtains closed so I couldn't see anything, like when you wake up at night, and the only sounds you hear are the sounds inside your head. And that made it better because it was like the little station wasn't there, outside my head, but I was in bed and I was safe.

And then the silences between the trains coming and going got longer and longer. And I could hear that there were fewer people in the little station when the train wasn't there, so I opened my eyes and I looked at my watch and it said 8:07 p.m. and I had been sitting on the bench for approximately 5 hours but it hadn't seemed like approximately 5 hours, except that my bottom hurt and I was hungry and thirsty.

And then I realised that Toby was missing because he was not in my pocket, and I didn't want him to be missing because we weren't in Father's house or Mother's house and there wasn't anyone to feed him in the little station and he would die and he might get run over by a train.

And then I looked up at the ceiling and I saw that there was a long black box which was a sign and it said,

```
1   Harrow & Wealdstone          2 min
3   Queens Park                   7 min
```

And then the bottom line scrolled up and disappeared and a different line line scrolled up into its place and the sign said

```
1   Harrow & Wealdstone          1 min
2   Willesden Junction           4 min
```

And then it changed again and it said

```
1   Harrow & Wealdstone
**  STAND BACK TRAIN APPROACHING  **
```

And then I heard the sound like swordfighting and the roaring of a train coming into the station and I worked out that there was a big computer somewhere and it knew where all the trains were and it sent messages to the black boxes in the little stations to say when the trains were coming, and that made me feel better because everything had an order and a plan.

And the train came into the little station and it stopped and 5 people got onto the train and another person ran into the little station and got on, and 7 people got off the train and then the doors closed automatically and the train went away. And when the next train came I wasn't so scared any more because the sign said `TRAIN APPROACHING` so I knew it was going to happen.

And then I decided that I would look for Toby because there were only 3 people in the little station. So I stood up and I looked up and down the little station and in the doorways that went into tunnels but I couldn't see him anywhere. And then I looked down into the black, lower-down bit where the rails were.

And then I saw two mice and they were black because they were covered in dirt. And I liked that because I like mice and rats. But they weren't Toby, so I carried on looking.

And then I saw Toby, and he was also in the lower-down bit where the rails were, and I knew he was Toby because he was white and he had a brown egg shape on his back. So I climbed down off the concrete. And he was eating a bit of rubbish that was an old sweet paper. And someone shouted, 'Jesus. What are you doing?'

And I bent down to catch Toby but he ran off. And I walked after him and I bent down again and I said, 'Toby . . . Toby . . . Toby' and I held out my hand so that he could smell my hand and smell that it was me.

And someone said, 'Get out of there, for fuck's sake,' and I looked up and it was a man who was wearing a green raincoat and he had black shoes and his socks were showing and they were grey with little diamond patterns on them.

And I said, 'Toby . . . Toby . . .' but he ran off again.

And the man with the diamond patterns on his socks tried to grab my shoulder, so I screamed. And then I heard the sound like swordfighting and Toby started running again, but this time he ran the other way, which was past my feet and I grabbed at him and I caught him by the tail.

And the man with the diamond patterns on his socks said, 'Oh Christ. Oh Christ.'

And then I heard the roaring and I lifted Toby up and grabbed him with both hands and he bit me on my thumb and there was blood coming out and I shouted and Toby tried to jump out of my hands.

And then the roaring got louder and I turned round and I saw the train coming out of the tunnel and I was going to be run over and killed so I tried to climb up onto the concrete but it was high and I was holding Toby in both my hands.

And then the man with the diamond patterns on his socks grabbed hold of me and pulled me and I screamed, but he kept pulling me and he pulled me up onto the concrete and we fell over and I carried on screaming because he had hurt my shoulder. And then the train came into the station and I stood up and I ran to the bench again and I put Toby into the pocket inside my jacket and he went very quiet and he didn't move.

And the man with the diamond patterns on his socks was standing next to me and he said, 'What the fuck do you think you were playing at?'

But I didn't say anything.

And he said, 'What were you doing?'

And the doors of the train opened and people got off and there was a lady standing behind the man with the diamond patterns on his socks and she was carrying a guitar case like Siobhan has.

And I said, 'I was finding Toby. He's my pet rat.'

And the man with the diamond patterns on his socks said, 'Fucking Nora.'

And the lady with the guitar case said, 'Is he OK?'

And the man with the diamond patterns on his socks said, 'Him? Thanks a fucking bundle. Jesus Christ. A pet rat. Oh shit. My train.' And then he ran to the train and he banged on the door which was closed and the train started to go away and he said, 'Fuck.'

And the lady said, 'Are you OK?' and she touched my arm so I screamed again.

And she said, 'OK. OK. OK.'

And there was a sticker on her guitar case and it said

And I was sitting on the ground and the woman knelt down on one knee and she said, 'Is there anything I can do to help you?'

And if she was a teacher at school I could have said, 'Where is 451c Chapter Road, Willesden, London NW2 5NG?' but she was a stranger, so I said, 'Stand further away' because I didn't like her being so close. And I said, 'I've got a Swiss Army Knife and it has a saw blade and it could cut someone's fingers off.'

And she said, 'OK, buddy. I'm going to take that as a no,' and she stood up and walked away.

And the man with the diamond patterns on his socks said, 'Mad as a fucking hatter. Jesus,' and he was pressing a handkerchief against his face and there was blood on the handkerchief.

And then another train came and the man with the diamond patterns on his socks and the lady with the guitar case got on and it went away again.

And then 8 more trains came and I decided that I would get onto a train and then I would work out what to do.

So I got on the next train.

And Toby tried to get out of my pocket so I took hold of him and I put him in my outside pocket and I held him with my hand.

And there were 11 people in the carriage and I didn't like being in a room with 11 people in a tunnel, so I concentrated on things in the carriage. And there were signs saying **There are 53,963 holiday cottages in Scandinavia and Germany** and **VITABIOTICS** and **3435** and **Penalty £10 if you fail to show a valid ticket for your entire journey** and **Discover Gold, Then Bronze** and **TVIC** and **EPBIC** and **suck my cock** and

⚠ **Obstructing the doors can be dangerous** and **BRV** and **Con. IC** and **TALK TO THE WORLD**.

And there was a pattern on the walls which was like this

And there was a pattern on the seats like this

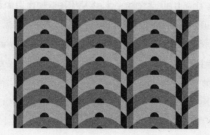

Then the train wobbled a lot and I had to hang onto a rail and we went into a tunnel and it was noisy and I closed my eyes and I could feel the blood pumping in the sides of my neck.

And then we came out of the tunnel and went into another little station and it was called **Warwick Avenue** and it said it in big letters on the wall and I liked that because you knew where you were.

And I timed the distance between stations all the way to

Willesden Junction and all the times between stations were multiples of 15 seconds like this

Paddington	0:00
Warwick Avenue	1:30
Maida Vale	3:15
Kilburn Park	5:00
Queen's Park	7:00
Kensal Green	10:30
Willesden Junction	11:45

And when the train stopped at **Willesden Junction** and the doors opened automatically I walked out of the train. And then the doors closed and the train went away. And everyone who got off the train walked up a staircase and over a bridge except me, and then there were only two people that I could see and one was a man and he was drunk and he had brown stains on his coat and his shoes were not a pair and he was singing but I couldn't hear what he was singing, and the other was an Indian man in a shop which was a little window in a wall.

And I didn't want to talk to either of them because I was tired and hungry and I had already talked to lots of strangers, which is dangerous, and the more you do something dangerous the more likely it is that something bad happens. But I didn't know how to get to 451c Chapter Road, London NW2 5NG so I had to ask somebody.

So I went up to the man in the little shop and I said, 'Where is 451c Chapter Road, London NW2 5NG?'

And he picked up a little book and handed it to me and said, 'Two ninety-five.'

And the book was called **LONDON AZ Street Atlas and Index Geographers A-Z Map Company** and I opened it up and it was lots of maps.

And the man in the little shop said, 'Are you going to buy it or not?'

And I said, 'I don't know.'

And he said, 'Well, you can get your dirty fingers off it if you don't mind,' and he took it back from me.

And I said, 'Where is 451c Chapter Road, London NW2 5NG?'

And he said, 'You can either buy the A to Z or you can hop it. I'm not a walking encyclopaedia.'

And I said, 'Is that the A to Z?' and I pointed at the book.

And he said, 'No, it's a sodding crocodile.'

And I said, 'Is that the A to Z?' because it wasn't a crocodile and I thought I had heard wrongly because of his accent.

And he said, 'Yes, it's the A to Z.'

And I said, 'Can I buy it?'

And he didn't say anything.

And I said, 'Can I buy it?'

And he said, 'Two pounds ninety-five, but you're giving me the money first. I'm not having you scarpering,' and then I realised that he meant £2.95 when he said *Two ninety-five*.

And I paid him £2.95 with my money and he gave me change just like in the shop at home and I went and sat down on the floor against the wall like the man with the dirty clothes but a long way away from him and I opened up the book.

And inside the front cover there was a big map of London with places on it like **Abbey Wood** and **Poplar** and **Acton** and **Stanmore**. And it said **KEY TO MAP PAGES**. And the map was covered with a grid and each square of the grid had two numbers on it. And **Willesden** was in the square which said **42** and **43**. And I worked out that the numbers were the numbers of the pages where you could see a bigger scale map of that square of London. And the whole book was a big map of London, but it had been chopped up so it could be made into a book, and I liked that.

But Willesden Junction wasn't on pages 42 and 43. And I found it on page 58 which was directly under page 42 on the **KEY TO MAP PAGES** and which joined up with page 42. And I looked round Willesden Junction in a spiral, like when I was looking for the train station in Swindon, but on the map with my finger.

And the man who had shoes that did not match stood in front of me and said, 'Big cheese. Oh yes. The Nurses. Never. Bloody liar. Total bloody liar.'

Then he went away.

And it took me a long time to find Chapter Road because it wasn't on page 58. It was back on page 42, and it was in square 5C.

And this was the shape of the roads between Willesden Junction and Chapter Road

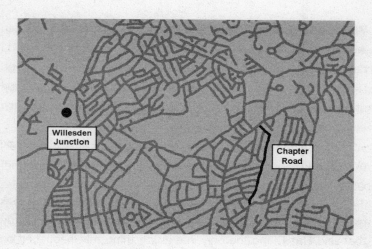

And this was my route

So I went up the staircase and over the bridge and I put my ticket in the little grey gate and went into the street and there was a bus and a big machine with a sign on it which said **English**

Welsh and Scottish Railways, but it was yellow, and I looked around and it was dark and there were lots of bright lights and I hadn't been outside for a long time and it made me feel sick. And I kept my eyelids very close together and I just looked at the shape of the roads and then I knew which roads were **Station Approach** and **Oak Lane** which were the roads I had to go along.

So I started walking, but Siobhan said I didn't have to describe everything that happened, I just have to describe the things that were interesting.

So I got to 451c Chapter Road, London NW2 5NG and it took me 27 minutes and there was no one in when I pressed the button that said **Flat C** and the only interesting thing that happened on the way was 8 men dressed up in Viking costumes with helmets with horns on and they were shouting, but they weren't real Vikings because the Vikings lived nearly 2,000 years ago, and also I had to go for another wee and I went in the alleyway down the side of a garage called **Burdett Motors** which was closed and I didn't like doing that but I didn't want to wet myself again, and there was nothing else interesting.

So I decided to wait and I hoped that Mother was not on holiday because that would mean she could be away for more than a whole week, but I tried not to think about this because I couldn't go back to Swindon.

So I sat down on the ground behind the dustbins in the little garden that was in front of 451c Chapter Road, London NW2 5NG and it was under a big bush. And a lady came into the garden and she was carrying a little box with a metal grille on one end and a handle on the top like you use to take a cat to the vet, but I couldn't see if there was a cat in it, and she had shoes with high heels and she didn't see me.

And then it started to rain and I got wet and I started shivering because I was cold.

And then it was 11:32 p.m. and I heard voices of people walking along the street.

And a voice said, 'I don't care whether you thought it was funny or not,' and it was a lady's voice.

And another voice said, 'Judy, look. I'm sorry, OK,' and it was a man's voice.

And the other voice, which was the lady's voice, said, 'Well, perhaps you should have thought about that before you made me look like a complete idiot.'

And the lady's voice was Mother's voice.

And Mother came into the garden and Mr Shears was with her, and the other voice was his.

So I stood up and I said, 'You weren't in, so I waited for you.'

And Mother said, 'Christopher.'

And Mr Shears said, 'What?'

And Mother put her arms around me and said, 'Christopher, Christopher, Christopher.'

And I pushed her away because she was grabbing me and I didn't like it, and I pushed really hard and I fell over.

And Mr Shears said, 'What the hell is going on?'

And Mother said, 'I'm so sorry. Christopher. I forgot.'

And I was lying on the ground and Mother held up her right

hand and spread her fingers out in a fan so that I could touch her fingers, but then I saw that Toby had escaped out of my pocket so I had to catch him.

And Mr Shears said, 'I suppose this means Ed's here.'

And there was a wall around the garden so Toby couldn't get out because he was stuck in the corner and he couldn't climb up the walls fast enough and I grabbed him and put him back in my pocket and I said, 'He's hungry. Have you got any food I can give him, and some water?'

And Mother said, 'Where's your father, Christopher?'

And I said, 'I think he's in Swindon.'

And Mr Shears said, 'Thank God for that.'

And Mother said, 'But how did you get here?'

And my teeth were clicking against each other because of the cold and I couldn't stop them, and I said, 'I came on the train. And it was really frightening. And I took Father's cashpoint card so I could get money out and a policeman helped me. But then he wanted to take me back to Father. And he was on the train with me. But then he wasn't.'

And Mother said, 'Christopher, you're soaking. Roger, don't just stand there.'

And then she said, 'Oh my God. Christopher. I didn't . . . I didn't think I'd ever . . . Why are you here on your own?'

And Mr Shears said, 'Are you going to come in or are you going to stay out here all night?'

And I said, 'I'm going to live with you because Father killed Wellington with a garden fork and I'm frightened of him.'

And Mr Shears said, 'Jumping Jack Christ.'

And Mother said, 'Roger, please. Come on, Christopher, let's go inside and get you dried off.'

So I stood up and I went inside the house and Mother said, 'You follow Roger,' and I followed Mr Shears up the stairs and there was a landing and a door which said Flat C and I was scared of going inside because I didn't know what was inside.

And Mother said, 'Go on, or you'll catch your death,' but I didn't know what *you'll catch your death* meant, and I went inside.

And then she said, 'I'll run you a bath,' and I walked round the flat to make a map of it in my head so I felt safer, and the flat was like this

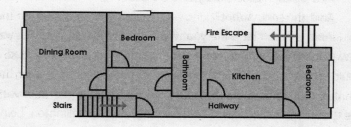

And then Mother made me take my clothes off and get into the bath and she said I could use her towel which was purple with green flowers on the end. And she gave Toby a saucer of water and some Bran Flakes and I let him run around the bathroom. And he did three little poos under the sink and I picked them up and flushed them down the toilet and then I got back into the bath again because it was warm and nice.

Then Mother came into the bathroom and she sat on the toilet and she said, 'Are you OK, Christopher?'

And I said, 'I'm very tired.'

And she said, 'I know, love.' And then she said, 'You're very brave.'

And I said, 'Yes.'

And she said, 'You never wrote to me.'

And I said, 'I know.'

And she said, 'Why didn't you write to me, Christopher? I wrote you all those letters. I kept thinking something dreadful had happened, or you'd moved away and I'd never find out where you were.'

And I said, 'Father said you were dead.'

And she said, 'What?'

And I said, 'He said you went into hospital because you had something wrong with your heart. And then you had a heart attack and died and he kept all the letters in a shirt box in the cupboard in his bedroom and I found them because I was looking for a book I was writing about Wellington being killed and he'd taken it away from me and hidden it in the shirt box.'

And then Mother said, 'Oh my God.'

And then she didn't say anything for a long while. And then she made a loud wailing noise like an animal on a nature programme on television.

And I didn't like her doing this because it was a loud noise, and I said, 'Why are you doing that?'

And she didn't say anything for a while, and then she said, 'Oh, Christopher, I'm so sorry.'

And I said, 'It's not your fault.'

And then she said, 'Bastard. The bastard.'

And then, after a while, she said, 'Christopher, let me hold your hand. Just for once. Just for me. Will you? I won't hold it hard,' and she held out her hand.

And I said, 'I don't like people holding my hand.'

And she took her hand back and she said, 'No. OK. That's OK.'

And then she said, 'Let's get you out of the bath and dried off, OK?'

And I got out of the bath and dried myself with the purple towel. But I didn't have any pyjamas so I put on a white T-shirt and a pair of yellow shorts which were Mother's, but I didn't mind because I was so tired. And while I was doing this Mother went into the kitchen and heated up some tomato soup because it was red.

And then I heard someone opening the door of the flat and there was a strange man's voice outside, so I locked the bathroom door. And there was an argument outside and a man said, 'I need to speak to him,' and Mother said, 'He's been through enough today already,' and the man said, 'I know. But I still need to speak to him.'

And Mother knocked on the door and said a policeman wanted to talk to me and I had to open the door. And she said she wouldn't let him take me away and she promised. So I picked Toby up and opened the door.

And there was a policeman outside the door and he said, 'Are you Christopher Boone?'

And I said I was.

And he said, 'Your father says you've run away. Is that right?'

And I said, 'Yes.'

And he said, 'Is this your mother?' and he pointed at Mother.

And I said, 'Yes.'

And he said, 'Why did you run away?'

And I said, 'Because Father killed Wellington who is a dog, and I was frightened of him.'

And he said, 'So I've been told.' And then he said, 'Do you want to go back to Swindon to your Father or do you want to stay here?'

And I said, 'I want to stay here.'

And he said, 'And how do you feel about that?'

And I said, 'I want to stay here.'

And the policeman said, 'Hang on. I'm asking your mother.'

And Mother said, 'He told Christopher I was dead.'

And the policeman said, 'OK. Let's . . . let's not get into an argument about who said what here. I just want to know whether . . .'

And Mother said, 'Of course he can stay.'

And then the policeman said, 'Well, I think that probably settles it as far as I'm concerned.'

And I said, 'Are you going to take me back to Swindon?'

And he said, 'No.'

And then I was happy because I could live with Mother.

And the policeman said, 'If your husband turns up and causes any trouble, just give us a ring. Otherwise, you're going to have to sort this out between yourselves.'

And then the policeman went away and I had my tomato soup and Mr Shears stacked up some boxes in the spare room so he could put a blow-up mattress on the floor for me to sleep on, and I went to sleep.

And then I woke up because there were people shouting in the flat and it was 2:31 a.m. And one of the people was Father and I was frightened. But there wasn't a lock on the door of the spare room.

And Father shouted, 'I'm talking to her whether you like it or not. And I am not going to be told what to do by you of all people.'

And Mother shouted, 'Roger. Don't. Just . . .'

And Mr Shears shouted, 'I'm not being spoken to like that in my own home.'

And Father shouted, 'I'll talk to you how I damn well like.'

And Mother shouted, 'You have no right to be here.'

And Father shouted, 'No right? No right? He's my fucking son, in case you've forgotten.'

And Mother shouted, 'What in God's name did you think you were playing at, saying those things to him?'

And Father shouted, 'What was I playing at? You were the one that bloody left.'

And Mother shouted, 'So you decided to just wipe me out of his life altogether?'

And Mr Shears shouted, 'Now let's all just calm down here, shall we?'

And Father shouted, 'Well, isn't that what you wanted?'

And Mother shouted, 'I wrote to him every week. Every week.'

And Father shouted, 'Wrote to him? What the fuck use is writing to him?'

And Mr Shears shouted, 'Whoa, whoa, whoa.'

And Father shouted, 'I cooked his meals. I cleaned his clothes. I looked after him every weekend. I looked after him when he was ill. I took him to the doctor. I worried myself sick every time he wandered off somewhere at night. I went to school every time he got into a fight. And you? What? You wrote him some fucking letters.'

And Mother shouted, 'So you thought it was OK to tell him his mother was dead?'

And Mr Shears shouted, 'Now is not the time.'

And Father shouted, 'You, butt out or I'll . . .'

And Mother shouted, 'Ed, for God's sake . . .'

And Father said, 'I'm going to see him. And if you try to stop me . . .'

And then Father came into my room. But I was holding my Swiss Army Knife with the saw blade out in case he grabbed me. And Mother came into the room as well, and she said, 'It's OK. Christopher. I won't let him do anything. You're all right.'

And Father bent down on his knees near the bed and he said, 'Christopher?'

But I didn't say anything.

And he said, 'Christopher, I'm really, really sorry. About every-thing. About Wellington. About the letters. About making you run away. I never meant . . . I promise I will never do anything like that again. Hey. Come on, kiddo.'

And then he held up his right hand and spread his fingers out in a fan so that I could touch his fingers, but I didn't because I was frightened.

And Father said, 'Shit. Christopher, please.'

And there were tears dripping off his face.

And no one said anything for a while.

And then Mother said, 'I think you should go now,' but she was talking to Father, not me.

And then the policeman came back because Mr Shears had rung the police station and he told Father to calm down and he took him out of the flat.

And Mother said, 'You go back to sleep now. Everything is going to be all right. I promise.'

And then I went back to sleep.

229

And when I was asleep I had one of my favourite dreams. Sometimes I have it during the day, but then it's a daydream. But I often have it at night as well.

And in the dream nearly everyone on the earth is dead, because they have caught a virus. But it's not like a normal virus. It's like a computer virus. And people catch it because of the meaning of something an infected person says and the meaning of what they do with their faces when they say it, which means that people can also get it from watching an infected person on television, which means that it spreads around the world really quickly.

And when people get the virus they just sit on the sofa and do nothing and they don't eat or drink and so they die. But sometimes I have different versions of the dream, like when you can see two versions of a film, the ordinary one and the *Director's Cut*, like **Blade Runner**. And in some versions of the dream the virus makes them crash their cars or walk into the sea and drown, or jump into rivers, and I think that this version is better because then there aren't bodies of dead people everywhere.

And eventually there is no one left in the world except people who don't look at other people's faces and who don't know what these pictures mean

and these people are all special people like me. And they like being on their own and I hardly ever see them because they are like Okapi in the jungle in the Congo which are a kind of antelope and very shy and rare.

And I can go anywhere in the world and I know that no one is going to talk to me or touch me or ask me a question. But if I don't want to go anywhere I don't have to, and I can stay at home and eat broccoli and oranges and liquorice laces all the time, or I can play computer games for a whole week, or I can just sit in the corner of the room and rub a pound coin backwards and forwards over the ripple shapes on the surface of the radiator. And I don't have to go to France.

And I go out of Father's house and I walk down the street, and it is very quiet even though it is the middle of the day and I can't hear any noise except birds singing and wind and sometimes buildings falling down in the distance, and if I stand very close to traffic lights I can hear a little click as the colours change.

And I go into other people's houses and play at being a detective and I can break the windows to get in because the people are dead and it doesn't matter. And I go into shops and take things I want, like pink biscuits or PJ's Raspberry and Mango Smoothie or computer games or books or videos.

And I take a ladder from Father's van and I climb up onto the roof, and when I get to the edge of a roof I put the ladder across the gap and I climb to the next roof, because in a dream you are allowed to do anything.

And then I find someone's car keys and I get into their car and

I drive, and it doesn't matter if I bump into things and I drive to the sea, and I park the car and I get out and there is rain pouring down. And I take an ice cream from a shop and eat it. And then I walk down to the beach. And the beach is covered in sand and big rocks and there is a lighthouse on a point but the light is not on because the lighthouse keeper is dead.

And I stand in the surf and it comes up and over my shoes. And I don't go swimming in case there are sharks. And I stand and look at the horizon and I take out my long metal ruler and I hold it up against the line between the sea and the sky and I demonstrate that the line is a curve and the earth is round. And the way the surf comes up and over my shoes and then goes down again is in a rhythm, like music or drumming.

And then I get some dry clothes from the house of a family who are dead. And I go home to Father's house, except it's not Father's house any more, it's mine. And I make myself some Gobi Aloo Sag with red food colouring in and some strawberry milkshake for a drink, and then I watch a video about the Solar System and I play some computer games and I go to bed.

And then the dream is finished and I am happy.

233

The next morning I had fried tomatoes for breakfast and a tin of green beans which Mother heated up in a saucepan.

In the middle of breakfast, Mr Shears said, 'OK. He can stay for a few days.'

And Mother said, 'He can stay as long as he needs to stay.'

And Mr Shears said, 'This flat is hardly big enough for two people, let alone three.'

And Mother said, 'He can understand what you're saying, you know.'

And Mr Shears said, 'What's he going to do? There's no school for him to go to. We've both got jobs. It's bloody ridiculous.'

And Mother said, 'Roger. That's enough.'

Then she made me some Red Zinger herbal tea with sugar in it but I didn't like it, and she said, 'You can stay for as long as you want to stay.'

And after Mr Shears had gone to work she made a telephone call to the office and took what is called *Compassionate Leave*, which is when someone in your family dies or is ill.

Then she said we had to go and buy some clothes for me to wear and some pyjamas and a toothbrush and a flannel. So we went out of the flat and we walked to the main road which was Hill Lane which was the A4088, and it was really crowded and we caught a No. 266 bus to Brent Cross Shopping Centre. Except there were too many people in John Lewis and I was frightened and I lay down on the floor next to the wristwatches and I screamed and Mother had to take me home in a taxi.

Then she had to go back to the shopping centre to buy me some clothes and some pyjamas and a toothbrush and a flannel, so I stayed in the spare room while she was gone because I didn't want to be in the same room as Mr Shears because I was frightened of him.

And when Mother got home she brought me a glass of strawberry milkshake and showed me my new pyjamas, and the pattern on them was 5-pointed blue stars on a purple background like this

And I said, 'I have to go back to Swindon.'

And Mother said, 'Christopher, you've only just got here.'

And I said, 'I have to go back because I have to sit my Maths A level.'

And Mother said, 'You're doing Maths A level?'

And I said. 'Yes. I'm taking it on Wednesday and Thursday and Friday next week.'

And Mother said, 'God.'

And I said, 'The Reverend Peters is going to be the invigilator.'

And Mother said, 'I mean, that's really good.'

And I said, 'I'm going to get an A grade. And that's why I have to go back to Swindon. Except I don't want to see Father. So I have to go to Swindon with you.'

Then Mother put her hands over her face and breathed out hard, and she said, 'I don't know whether that's going to be possible.'

And I said, 'But I have to go.'

And Mother said, 'Let's talk about this some other time, OK?'

And I said, 'OK. But I have to go to Swindon.'

And she said, 'Christopher, please.'

And I drank some of my milkshake.

And, later on, at 10:31 p.m., I went out onto the balcony to find out whether I could see any stars, but there weren't any because of all the clouds and what is called *Light Pollution* which is light from streetlights and car headlights and floodlights and lights in buildings reflecting off tiny particles in the atmosphere and getting in the way of light from the stars. So I went back inside.

But I couldn't sleep. And I got out of bed at 2:07 a.m. and I felt scared of Mr Shears so I went downstairs and out of the front door into Chapter Road. And there was no one in the street and it was quieter than it was during the day, even though you could hear traffic in the distance and sirens, so it made me feel calmer. And I walked down Chapter Road and looked at all the cars and the patterns the phone wires made against the orange clouds and the things that people had in their front gardens, like a gnome and a cooker and a tiny pond and a teddy bear.

247

Then I heard two people coming along the road, so I crouched down between the end of a skip and a Ford Transit van, and they were talking in a language that wasn't English, but they didn't see me. And there were two tiny brass cogs in the dirty water in the gutter by my feet, like cogs from a wind-up watch.

And I liked it between the skip and the Ford Transit van so I stayed there for a long time. And I looked out at the street. And the only colours you could see were orange and black and mixtures of orange and black. And you couldn't tell what colours the cars would be during the day.

And I wondered whether you could tessellate crosses, and I worked out that you could by imagining this picture in my head

And then I heard Mother's voice and she was shouting, 'Christopher . . .? Christopher . . .?' and she was running down the road, so I came out from between the skip and the Ford Transit van and she ran up to me and said, 'Jesus Christ,' and she stood in front of me and pointed her finger at my face and said, 'If you ever do that again, I swear to God, Christopher, I love you, but . . . I don't know what I'll do.'

So she made me promise never to leave the flat on my own because it was dangerous and because you couldn't trust people in London because they were strangers. And the next day she had to go to the shops again and she made me promise not to answer the door if anyone rang the bell. And when she came back she brought some food pellets for Toby and three **Star Trek** videos and I watched them in the living room until Mr Shears came home and then I went into the spare room again. And I wished that 451c Chapter Road, London NW2 5NG had a garden but it didn't.

And the day after that the office where Mother worked rang and told her she couldn't come back to work because they had got someone else to do her job for her, and she was really angry and she said that it was illegal and she was going to complain, but Mr Shears said, 'Don't be a bloody fool. It was a temporary job, for Christ's sake.'

And when Mother came into the spare room before I went to sleep I said, 'I have to go to Swindon to take my A level.'

And she said, 'Christopher, not now. I'm getting phone calls from your father threatening to take me to court. I'm getting it in the neck from Roger. It's not a good time.'

And I said, 'But I have to go because it's been arranged and the Reverend Peters is going to invigilate.'

And she said, 'Look. It's only an exam. I can ring the school. We can get it postponed. You can take it some other time.'

And I said, 'I can't take it another time. It's been arranged. And I've done lots of revision. And Mrs Gascoyne said we could use a room at school.'

And Mother said, 'Christopher, I am just about holding this together. But I am this close to losing it, all right? So just give me some . . .'

Then she stopped talking and she put her hand over her mouth and she stood up and went out of the room. And I started feeling a pain in my chest like I did on the underground because I thought I wasn't going to be able to go back to Swindon and take my A level.

And the next morning I looked out of the window in the dining room to count the cars in the street to see whether it was going to be a **Quite Good Day** or a **Good Day** or a **Super Good Day** or a **Black Day**, but it wasn't like being on the bus to school because you could look out of the window for as long as you wanted and see as many cars as you wanted and I looked out of the window for three hours and I saw 5 red cars in a row and 4 yellow cars in a row which meant it was both a **Good Day** and a **Black Day** so the system didn't work any more. But if I concentrated on counting the cars it stopped me thinking about my A level and the pain in my chest.

And in the afternoon Mother took me to Hampstead Heath in a taxi and we sat on the top of a hill and looked at the planes coming in to Heathrow airport in the distance. And I had a red ice lolly from an ice cream van. And Mother said she had rung Mrs Gascoyne and told her that I was going to take my Maths A level next year so I threw my red ice lolly away and I screamed for a long time and the pain in my chest hurt so much that it was hard to breathe and a man came up and asked if I was OK and Mother said, 'Well, what does it look like to you?' and he went away.

And then I was tired from screaming and Mother took me back to the flat in another taxi and the next morning was Saturday and she told Mr Shears to go out and get me some books about science and maths from the library, and they were called **100 Number Puzzles** and **The Origins of the Universe** and **Nuclear Power**, but they were for children and they were not very good so I didn't read them, and Mr Shears said, 'Well, it's nice to know my contribution is appreciated.'

And I hadn't eaten anything since I threw away the red ice lolly on Hampstead Heath so Mother made me a chart with stars on it like when I was very small and she filled a measuring jug with Complan and strawberry flavouring and I got a bronze star for drinking 200 ml and a silver star for drinking 400 ml and a gold star for drinking 600 ml.

And when Mother and Mr Shears argued I took the little radio from the kitchen and I went and sat in the spare room and I tuned it halfway between two stations so that all I could hear was white noise and I turned the volume up really loud and I held it against my ear and the sound filled my head and it hurt so that I couldn't feel any other sort of hurt, like the hurt in my chest, and I couldn't hear Mother and Mr Shears arguing and I couldn't think about not doing my A level or the fact that there wasn't a garden at 451c Chapter Road, London NW2 5NG or the fact that I couldn't see the stars.

And then it was Monday. And it was very late at night and Mr Shears came into my room and woke me up and he had been drinking beer because he smelled like Father did when he had been drinking beer with Rhodri. And he said, 'You think you're so fucking clever, don't you? Don't you ever, ever think about other people for one second, eh? Well, I bet you're really pleased with yourself now, aren't you?'

And then Mother came in and pulled him out of the room and said, 'Christopher, I'm sorry. I'm really, really sorry.'

The next morning, after Mr Shears had gone to work, Mother packed lots of her clothes into two suitcases and told me to come downstairs and bring Toby and get into the car. And she put the suitcases into the boot and we drove off. But it was Mr Shears' car and I said, 'Are you stealing the car?'

And she said, 'I'm just borrowing it.'

And I said, 'Where are we going?'

And she said, 'We're going home.'

And I said, 'Do you mean home in Swindon?'

And she said, 'Yes.'

And I said, 'Is Father going to be there?'

And she said, 'Please, Christopher. Don't give me any hassle right now, OK?'

And I said, 'I don't want to be with Father.'

And she said, 'Just . . . Just . . . It's going to be all right, Christopher, OK? It's going to be all right.'

And I said, 'Are we going back to Swindon so I can do my Maths A level?'

And Mother said, 'What?'

And I said, 'I'm meant to be doing my Maths A level tomorrow.'

And Mother spoke very slowly and she said, 'We are going back to Swindon because if we stay in London any longer . . . someone was going to get hurt. And I don't necessarily mean you.'

And I said, 'What do you mean?'

And she said, 'Now I need you to be quiet for a while.'

And I said, 'How long do you want me to be quiet for?'

And she said, 'Jesus.' And then she said, 'Half an hour, Christopher. I need you to be quiet for half an hour.'

And we drove all the way to Swindon and it took 3 hours 12 minutes and we had to stop for petrol and Mother bought me a Milky Bar but I didn't eat it. And we got caught in a long traffic jam which was caused by people slowing down to look at an accident on the other carriageway. And I tried to work out a formula to determine whether a traffic jam would be caused just by people slowing down and how this was influenced by a) the density of traffic, and b) the speed of the traffic, and c) how quickly drivers braked when they saw the brake lights of the car in front coming on. But I was too tired because I hadn't slept the night before because I was thinking about not being able to do my Maths A level. So I fell asleep.

And when we got to Swindon Mother had keys to the house and we went in and she said, 'Hello?' but there was no one there because it was 1:23 p.m. And I was frightened but Mother said I would be safe, so I went up to my room and closed the door. I took Toby out of my pocket and I let him run around and I played **Minesweeper** and I did the **Expert Version** in 174 seconds, which was 75 seconds longer than my best time.

And then it was 6:35 p.m. and I heard Father come home in his van and I moved the bed up against the door so he couldn't get in and he came into the house and he and Mother shouted at each other.

And Father shouted, 'How the fuck did you get in here?'

And Mother shouted, 'This is my house, too, in case you've forgotten.'

And Father shouted, 'Is your fucking fancy man here, as well?'

And then I picked up the bongo drums that Uncle Terry had bought me and I knelt down in the corner of the room and I pressed my head into the join between the two walls and I banged the drums and I groaned and I carried on doing this for an hour and then Mother came into the room and said Father had gone. And she said Father had gone to stay with Rhodri for a while and we would get a place to live of our own in the next few weeks.

Then I went into the garden and I found Toby's cage behind the shed and I brought it inside and I cleaned it and put Toby back in it.

And I asked Mother if I could do my Maths A level the next day.

And she said, 'I'm sorry, Christopher.'

And I said, 'Can I do my Maths A level?'

And she said, 'You're not listening to me, are you, Christopher?'

And I said, 'I'm listening to you.'

And Mother said, 'I told you. I rang your headmistress. I told her you were in London. I told her you'd do it next year.'

And I said, 'But I'm here now and I can take it.'

And Mother said, 'I'm sorry, Christopher. I was trying to do things properly. I was trying not to mess things up.'

And my chest began hurting again and I folded my arms and I rocked backwards and forwards and groaned.

And Mother said, 'I didn't know we'd be coming back.'

But I carried on groaning and rocking backwards and forwards.

And Mother said, 'Come on. This isn't going to solve anything.'

Then she asked if I wanted to watch one of my **Blue Planet** videos, about life under the Arctic ice or the migration of humpback whales, but I didn't say anything because I knew I wasn't going to be able to do my Maths A level and it was like pressing your thumbnail against a radiator when it's really hot and the pain starts and it makes you want to cry and the pain keeps hurting even when you take your thumb away from the radiator.

Then Mother made me some carrots and broccoli and ketchup, but I didn't eat them.

And I didn't sleep that night either.

The next day Mother drove me to school in Mr Shears' car because we missed the bus. And when we were getting into the car, Mrs Shears came across the road and said to Mother, 'You've got a fucking nerve.'

And Mother said, 'Get into the car, Christopher.'

But I couldn't get into the car because the door was locked.

And Mrs Shears said, 'So, has he finally dumped you, too?'

Then Mother opened her door and got into the car and unlocked my door and I got in and we drove away.

And when we got to school Siobhan said, 'So you're Christopher's mother.' And Siobhan said that she was glad to see me again and she asked if I was OK and I said I was tired. And Mother explained that I was upset because I couldn't do my Maths A level so I hadn't been eating properly or sleeping properly.

And then Mother went away and I drew a picture of a bus using perspective so that I didn't think about the pain in my chest and it looked like this

And after lunch Siobhan said that she had spoken to Mrs Gascoyne and she still had my A level papers in 3 sealed envelopes in her desk.

So I asked if I could still do my A level.

And Siobhan said, 'I think so. We're going to ring the Reverend Peters this afternoon to make sure he can still come in and be your invigilator. And Mrs Gascoyne is going to write a letter to the examination board to say that you're going to take the exam after all. And hopefully they'll say that that's OK. But we can't know that for sure.' Then she stopped talking for a few seconds. 'I thought I should tell you now. So you could think about it.'

And I said, 'So I could think about what?'

And she said, 'Is this what you want to do, Christopher?'

And I thought about the question and I wasn't sure what the answer was because I wanted to do my Maths A level but I was very tired and when I tried to think about Maths my brain didn't work properly and when I tried to remember certain facts, like the logarithmic formula for the approximate number of prime numbers not greater than (x), I couldn't remember them and this made me frightened.

And Siobhan said, 'You don't have to do it, Christopher. If you say you don't want to do it no one is going to be angry with you. And it won't be wrong or illegal or stupid. It will just be what you want and that will be fine.'

And I said, 'I want to do it' because I don't like it when I put things in my timetable and I have to take them out again, because when I do that it makes me feel sick.

And Siobhan said, 'OK.'

And she rang the Reverend Peters and he came into school at 3.27 p.m. and he said, 'So, young man, are we ready to roll?'

And I did **Paper 1** of my Maths A level sitting in the Art Room. And Reverend Peters was the invigilator and he sat at a desk while I did the exam and he read a book called **The Cost of Discipleship** by Dietrich Bonhoeffer and ate a sandwich. And in the middle of the exam he went and smoked a cigarette outside the window, but he watched me through the window in case I cheated.

And when I opened the paper and read through it I couldn't think how to answer any of the questions and also I couldn't breathe properly. And I wanted to hit somebody or stab them with my Swiss Army Knife, but there wasn't anyone to hit or stab with my Swiss Army Knife except the Reverend Peters and he was very tall and if I hit him or stabbed him with my Swiss Army Knife he wouldn't be my invigilator for the rest of the exam. So I took deep breaths like Siobhan said I should do when I want to hit someone in school and I counted fifty breaths and did cubes of the cardinal numbers as I counted, like this

1, **8**, **27**, **64**, **125**, **216**, **343**, **512**, **729**, **1,000**, **1,331**, **1,728**, **2,197**, **2,744**, **3,375**, **4,096**, **4,913** . . . etc.

And that made me feel a little calmer. But the exam was 2 hours long and twenty minutes had already gone so I had to work really fast and I didn't have time to check my answers properly.

And that night, just after I got home, Father came back to the house and I screamed but Mother said she wouldn't let anything bad happen to me and I went into the garden and lay down and looked at the stars in the sky and made myself negligible. And when Father came out of the house he looked at me for a long time and then he punched the fence and made a hole in it and went away.

And I slept a little bit that night because I was doing my Maths A level. And I had some spinach soup for supper.

And the next day I did **Paper 2** and the Reverend Peters read **The Cost of Discipleship** by Dietrich Bonhoeffer, but this time he didn't smoke a cigarette and Siobhan made me go into the toilets before the exam and sit on my own and do breathing and counting.

And I was playing **The Eleventh Hour** on my computer that evening when a taxi stopped outside the house. Mr Shears was in the taxi and he got out of the taxi and threw a big cardboard box of things belonging to Mother onto the lawn. And they were a hairdryer and some knickers and some L'Oreal shampoo and a box of muesli and two books, **DIANA Her True Story** by Andrew Morton and **Rivals** by Jilly Cooper, and a photograph of me in a silver frame. And the glass in the photograph frame broke when it fell onto the grass.

Then he got some keys out of his pocket and got into his car and drove away and Mother ran out of the house and she ran into the street and shouted, 'Don't fucking bother coming back, either!' And she threw the box of muesli and it hit the boot of his car as he drove away and Mrs Shears was looking out of her window when Mother did this.

The next day I did **Paper 3** and the Reverend Peters read the Daily Mail and smoked three cigarettes.

And this was my favourite question

Prove the following result:

"A triangle with sides that can be written in the form $n^2 + 1$, $n^2 - 1$ and $2n$ (where $n > 1$) is right-angled."

Show, by means of a counter example, that the converse is false.

And I was going to write out how I answered the question except Siobhan said it wasn't very interesting, but I said it was. And she said people wouldn't want to read the answers to a maths question in a book, and she said I could put the answer in an *Appendix* which is an extra chapter at the end of a book which people can read if they want to. And that is what I have done.

And then my chest didn't hurt so much and it was easier to breathe. But I still felt sick because I didn't know if I'd done well in the exam and because I didn't know if the examination board would allow my exam paper to be considered after Mrs Gascoyne had told them I wasn't going to take it.

And it's best if you know a good thing is going to happen, like an eclipse or getting a microscope for Christmas. And it's bad if you know a bad thing is going to happen, like having a filling or going to France. But I think it is worst if you don't know whether it is a good thing or a bad thing which is going to happen.

And Father came round to the house that night and I was

sitting on the sofa watching *University Challenge* and just answering the science questions. And he stood in the doorway of the living room and he said, 'Don't scream, OK, Christopher. I'm not going to hurt you.'

And Mother was standing behind him so I didn't scream.

Then he came a bit closer to me and he crouched down like you do with dogs to show that you are not an Aggressor and he said, 'I wanted to ask you how the exam went.'

But I didn't say anything.

And Mother said, 'Tell him, Christopher.'

But I still didn't say anything.

And Mother said, 'Please, Christopher.'

So I said, 'I don't know if I got all the questions right because I was really tired and I hadn't eaten any food so I couldn't think properly.'

And then Father nodded and he didn't say anything for a short while. Then he said, 'Thank you.'

And I said, 'What for?'

And he said, 'Just . . . thank you.' Then he said, 'I'm very proud of you, Christopher. Very proud. I'm sure you did really well.'

And then he went away and I watched the rest of *University Challenge*.

And the next week Father told Mother she had to move out of the house, but she couldn't because she didn't have any money to pay rent for a flat. And I asked if Father would be arrested and go to prison for killing Wellington because we could live in the house if he was in prison. But Mother said the police would only arrest Father if Mrs Shears did what is called *pressing charges*, which is telling the police you want them to arrest someone for a crime, because the police don't arrest people for little crimes unless you ask them and Mother said that killing a dog was only a little crime.

But then everything was OK because Mother got a job on the till in a garden centre and the doctor gave her pills to take every morning to stop her feeling sad, except that sometimes they made her dizzy and she fell over if she stood up too fast. So we moved into a room in a big house that was made of red bricks. And the bed was in the same room as the kitchen and I didn't like it because it was small and the corridor was painted brown and there was a toilet and a bathroom that other people used and Mother had to clean it before I used it or I wouldn't use it and sometimes I wet myself because other people were in the bathroom. And the corridor outside the room smelled like gravy and the bleach they use to clean the toilets at school. And inside the room it smelled like socks and pine air freshener.

And I didn't like waiting to find out about my Maths A level. And whenever I thought about the future I couldn't see anything clearly in my head and that made a panic start. So Siobhan said I shouldn't think about the future. She said, 'Just think about today. Think about things that have happened. Especially about good things that have happened.'

And one of the good things was that Mother bought me a wooden puzzle which looked like this

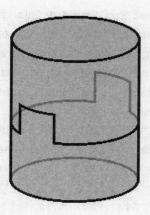

And you had to detach the top part of the puzzle from the bottom part, and it was really difficult.

And another good thing was that I helped Mother paint her room **White With A Hint Of Wheat**, except I got paint in my hair and she wanted to wash it out by rubbing shampoo on my head when I was in the bath, but I wouldn't let her, so there was paint in my hair for 5 days and then I cut it out with a pair of scissors.

But there were more bad things than good things.

And one of them was that Mother didn't get back from work till 5:30 p.m. so I had to go to Father's house between 3:49 p.m. and 5:30 p.m. because I wasn't allowed to be on my own and Mother said I didn't have a choice so I pushed the bed against the door in case Father tried to come in. And sometimes he tried to talk to me through the door, but I didn't answer him. And sometimes I heard him sitting on the floor outside the door quietly for a long time.

And another bad thing was that Toby died because he was 2 years and 7 months old which is very old for a rat, and I said I wanted to bury him, but Mother didn't have a garden, so I buried him in a big plastic pot of earth like a pot you put a plant in. And I said I wanted another rat but Mother said I couldn't have one because the room was too small.

And I solved the puzzle because I worked out that there were two bolts inside the puzzle and they were tunnels with metal rods in like this

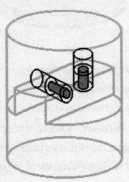

And you had to hold the puzzle so that both rods slid to the end of their tunnels and they weren't crossing the intersection between the two pieces of the puzzle and then you could pull them apart.

And Mother picked me up from Father's house one day after she had finished work and Father said, 'Christopher, can I have a talk with you?'

And I said, 'No.'

And Mother said, 'It's OK. I'll be here.'

And I said, 'I don't want to talk to Father.'

And Father said, 'I'll do you a deal.' And he was holding the kitchen timer which is a big plastic tomato sliced through the middle and he twisted it and it started ticking. And he said, 'Five minutes, OK? That's all. Then you can go.'

So I sat on the sofa and he sat on the armchair and Mother was in the hallway and Father said, 'Christopher, look . . . Things can't go on like this. I don't know about you, but this . . . this just hurts too much. You being in the house but refusing to talk to me . . . You have to learn to trust me . . . And I don't care how long it takes . . . If it's a minute one day and two minutes the next and three minutes the next and it takes years I don't care. Because this is important. This is more important than anything else.'

And then he tore a little strip of skin away from the side of the thumbnail on his left hand.

And then he said, 'Let's call it . . . let's call it a project. A project we have to do together. You have to spend more time with me. And I . . . I have to show you that you can trust me. And it will be difficult at first because . . . because it's a difficult project. But it will get better. I promise.'

Then he rubbed the sides of his forehead with his fingertips, and he said, 'You don't have to say anything, not right now. You just have to think about it. And, um . . . I've got you a present. To show you that I really mean what I say. And to say sorry. And because . . . well, you'll see what I mean.'

Then he got out of the armchair and he walked over to the

kitchen door and opened it and there was a big cardboard box on the floor and there was a blanket in it and he bent down and put his hands inside the box and he took a little sandy-coloured dog out.

Then he came back through and gave me the dog. And he said, 'He's two months old. And he's a Golden Retriever.'

And the dog sat in my lap and I stroked it.

And no one said anything for a while.

Then Father said, 'Christopher. I would never, ever do anything to hurt you.'

Then no one said anything.

Then Mother came into the room and said, 'You won't be able to take him away with you, I'm afraid. The bedsit's too small. But your Father's going to look after him here. And you can come and take him out for walks whenever you want.'

And I said, 'Does he have a name?'

And Father said, 'No. You can decide what to call him.'

And the dog chewed my finger.

And then it was 5 minutes and the tomato alarm went. So Mother and I drove back to her room.

And the next week there was a lightning storm and the lightning hit a big tree in the park near Father's house and knocked it down and men came and cut the branches up with chainsaws and carried the logs away on a lorry, and all that was left was a big black pointed stump made of carbonised wood.

And I got the results of my Maths A level and I got an A grade which is the best result and it made me feel like this

And I called the dog Sandy. And Father bought him a collar and a lead and I was allowed to take him for walks to the shop and back. And I played with him with a rubber bone.

And Mother got flu and I had to spend three days with Father and stay in his house. But it was OK because Sandy slept on my bed so he would bark if anyone came into the room during the night. And Father made a vegetable patch in the garden and I helped him. And we planted carrots and peas and spinach and I'm going to pick them and eat them when they're ready.

And I went to a bookshop with Mother and I bought a book called ***Further Maths for A Level*** and Father told Mrs Gascoyne that I was going to take A level Further Maths next year and she said, 'OK.'

And I am going to pass it and get an A grade. And in two years' time I am going to take A level Physics and get an A grade.

And then, when I've done that, I am going to go to university in another town. And it doesn't have to be in London because I don't like London and there are universities in lots of places and not all of them are in big cities. And I can live in a flat with a garden and a proper toilet. And I can take Sandy and my books and my computer.

And then I will get a First Class Honours Degree and I will become a scientist.

And I know I can do this because I went to London on my own, and because I solved the mystery of Who Killed Wellington? and I found my mother and I was brave and I wrote a book and that means I can do anything.

Appendix

Question

Prove the following result:

"A triangle with sides that can be written in the form $n^2 + 1$, $n^2 - 1$ and $2n$ (where $n > 1$) is right–angled."

Show, by means of a counter example, that the converse is false.

Answer

First we must determine which is the longest side of a triangle with sides that can be written in the form $n^2 + 1$, $n^2 - 1$ and $2n$ (where $n > 1$)

$$n^2 + 1 - 2n = (n - 1)^2$$

and if $n > 1$ then $(n - 1)^2 > 0$

therefore $n^2 + 1 - 2n > 0$

therefore $n^2 + 1 > 2n$

similarly $(n^2 + 1) - (n^2 - 1) = 2$

therefore $n^2 + 1 > n^2 - 1$

This means that $n^2 + 1$ is the longest side of a triangle with sides that can be written in the form $n^2 + 1$, $n^2 - 1$ and $2n$ (where $n > 1$).

This can also be shown by means of the following graph (but this doesn't prove anything):

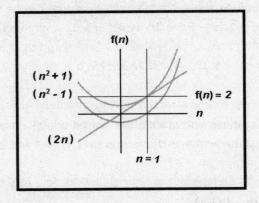

According to Pythagoras' theorem, if the sum of the squares of the two shorter sides equals the square of the hypotenuse then the triangle is right-angled. Therefore to prove that the triangle is right-angled we need to show that this is the case.

The sum of the squares of the shorter two sides is $(n^2 - 1)^2 + (2n)^2$

$(n^2 - 1)^2 + (2n)^2 = n^4 - 2n^2 + 1 + 4n^2 = \underline{n^4 + 2n^2 + 1}$

The square of the hypotenuse is $(n^2 + 1)^2$

$(n^2 + 1)^2 = \underline{n^4 + 2n^2 + 1}$

Therefore the sum of the squares of the shorter two sides is equal to the square of the hypotenuse and the triangle is right-angled.

And the converse of "A triangle with sides that can be written in the form $n^2 + 1$, $n^2 - 1$ and $2n$ (where $n > 1$) is right-angled" is "A triangle that is right-angled has sides whose lengths can be written in the form $n^2 + 1$, $n^2 - 1$ and $2n$ (where $n > 1$)".

And a counter example means finding a triangle which is right-angled but whose sides cannot be written in the form $n^2 + 1$, $n^2 - 1$ and $2n$ (where $n > 1$).

So, let the hypotenuse of the right-angled triangle **ABC** be **AB**

and let **AB = 65**

and let **BC = 60**.

Then $CA = \sqrt{(AB^2 - BC^2)}$

$\qquad = \sqrt{(65^2 - 60^2)} = \sqrt{(4225 - 3600)} = \sqrt{625} = 25$.

Let $AB = n^2 + 1 = 65$

then $n = \sqrt{(65 - 1)} = \sqrt{64} = 8$

therefore $(n^2 - 1) = 64 - 1 = 63 \neq BC = 60 \neq CA = 25$

and $2n = 16 \neq BC = 60 \neq CA = 25$.

Therefore the triangle **ABC** is right-angled but it does not have sides which can be written in the form $n^2 + 1$, $n^2 - 1$ and $2n$ (where $n > 1$). **QED**

www.vintage-books.co.uk

Supporters and Sponsors

World Book Night is supported by the generosity of among others:

BML

Clays

The CPI Group

Forest Stewardship Council

Hachette

Holmen Paper

Kodak

Nielsen Bookscan

NPA

Penguin Books

Pentagram Design

Proper Productions

Quo Vadis

Stora Enso

TBS

World Book Night's partners include:

BBC Two

The Booksellers Association of England and Ireland

The Publishers Association

The Reading Agency

We would like to thank them all for their unflagging support.

If you want to find your local bookshop or library, go to **www.worldbooknight.org**

'Mark Haddon's portrayal of an emotionally
dissociated mind is a SUPERB ACHIEVEMENT...
Wise and bleakly funny...'
IAN McEWAN

'A REMARKABLE book...An impressive
achievement and a rewarding read'
TIME OUT

The Curious Incident of the Dog in the Night-Time is a murder mystery novel
like no other. The detective, and narrator, is Christopher Boone. Christopher is
fifteen and has Asperger's Syndrome. He knows a very great deal about maths
and very little about human beings. He loves lists, patterns and the truth.
He hates the colours yellow and brown and being touched. He has never
gone further than the end of the road on his own, but when he finds a
neighbour's dog murdered he sets out on a terrifying journey which
will turn his whole world upside down.

'EXCEPTIONAL by any standards...'
SUNDAY TELEGRAPH

'Superbly realised...
A funny as well as a sad book...
BRILLIANT'
GUARDIAN